HAYES BROTHERS SERIES BOOK THREE

TOO sweet

I. A. DICE

The artwork for the Hayes Brothers series, has been sketched by an amazing artist - Danny O'Connor DOC Art. He captured every FMC in the series perfectly and I absolutely love every piece he kindly created to bring the girls to live.

You can follow his work here:

Facebook: Danny O'Connor (DOC)

Instagram: @artbydoc

Website: www.docart.bigcartel.com

Editor: Dave Holwill

TOO
sweet

One

Nico

FUCKING COLLEGE KIDS...

Cars line the curbs on both sides of the street: everything from flashy Ferraris, all-out American muscle to a baby-pink Fiat and even a yellow school bus some senseless moron parked at the bottom of the driveway, blocking the way.

Kids swarm the street, booze in hands, not enough clothes on their backs, and way too loud.

More are coming, flocking, fucking crowds of them.

Half the college football team strut up the driveway in purple jerseys, cockier than cocky, their arms around young babes in bikinis or miniskirts. It's sixty-five degrees outside, but cool evening air doesn't stop them from flaunting their lean bodies.

I rock back and forth in the driver's seat, looking through a narrow gap between the mass of bodies for any free space on my driveway.

There's none.

It's packed.

Twenty-odd cars are parked all over the place as if the valet for the evening parked them wearing a blindfold.

I inhale a deep breath, shift into reverse, and whirl around the kids, trying not to run anyone over, even though I really want to when a drunk prick steps into the middle of the street, his hands outstretched.

I have no choice but to stop.

Why did I agree to this again?

Instead of honking, I rev the engine. The deafening roar of the V8 startles a few babes, who break into infantile giggles, twirling their long, platinum locks around their fingers. Two even wink in my direction.

Don't fucking bother.

"Shit! Get off the road, you idiot." Someone yanks the kid off my spoiler. "You know who this is?" he says, his hushed voice still audible through my open windows. "Don't piss him off, dude."

At least they know.

Of course they fucking know.

Everyone knows whose garden they're raiding tonight.

They step aside, and I release the brake, reversing further down the street. Anger warms my chest until I'm talking myself out of reaching into the glove box for a pack of smokes. I quit four weeks ago—the seventeenth attempt during the last three years—but I ponder lighting one up twenty times a day.

Five minutes later, after leaving my shiny toy way too far from my house, I'm back on the driveway. It cleared a bit.

Not of cars, though.

Fewer kids linger out the front, most in the garden by now,

where a new-age techno beat pumps through a dozen tall speakers, making my bones shake. It took my brothers and the DJ the entire afternoon to connect the sound system.

I jog up the concrete steps to the main door but halt halfway there, catching movement in my peripheral vision... a porn clip in the making. One of the football jocks rams his dick into a drunk brunette who's spread-eagled on the hood of my brother's Mustang. Boobs, barely covered by a skimpy bikini bra, threaten to bounce out every time the obnoxious asshole rams into her like a machine gun.

He'll have a goddamn coronary if he keeps up that pace much longer.

I should tell them to get the hell out of there before they dent Cody's car, but if I say a word, he will, too. And that will count as an excuse to make him bleed.

I'm on a tight schedule. No time to throw punches this evening. My fuse has been way too short since I quit smoking. It's never long, but it's been almost nonexistent lately.

Better not to get involved.

If Cody didn't want his car serving as a fuck-bench for the night, he should've parked in the garage. Although, he probably pulled the short straw with Colt and Conor, who form two-thirds of the Holy Trinity: identical triplets.

The garage has five spaces, but I own three cars, so one of my brothers parks under the clouds. They don't complain. They can't. I let them move in with me the summer after they graduated high school, so they could spread their wings like teenagers should, away from our overprotective mother's watchful eyes.

That was two years ago. They're *twenty* now, and that sure makes me feel old. I still remember the day they were born.

They're turning twenty-one in a few months, but Mom still treats them like they're five at most. Maybe because they came as a surprise nine years after my parents decided four sons were enough kids to have.

Or maybe because they're wild.

I insert the key into the lock and take a deep breath to cool my jets before I turn it, rather proud I didn't smoke.

Stick to the plan.

Fifteen minutes. In and out. Shower, change of clothes, then out again, away from the mayhem till it passes, and my garden will be mine again by tomorrow.

I push the door open, and I'm fuming again.

Last year, after the triplets threw their first Spring Break Inauguration party, I remodeled the ground floor. Not by choice. The damage their idiot friends caused forced my hand, so this year, I set hard rules.

The main one: don't let anyone inside the house.

Looks like that's too much to ask for because the door to the guest bathroom down the corridor stands wide open. Conor is there, leaning against the frame. A puzzled expression taints his features, and he's cluelessly scratching his chin.

Colt's taking two steps at a time, almost flying down the stairs with a travel-sized bottle of mouthwash, toothpaste, and a toothbrush in hands.

And then, I hear it... someone's puking.

"What the fuck is going on?" I boom, halting Colt at the bottom step. "Why are you here?"

He shifts his weight from one foot to the other, an *argh, fuck* look crossing his face. "Sorry, bro," he says, but there's nothing apologetic about that *sorry.* "There's been a small incident, and Mia—"

"You brought a drunk chick in here to puke?!" I toss the keys into a decorative bowl on the side table by the staircase. "This is the last party you're hosting in my house. Get her the fuck out of here before I do."

He lunges forward, clamping his jaw as he drops everything he held to the floor to free his hands. He grips a fistful of my shirt, shoving me toward the living room, his eyes narrowed, chest heaving. "She's not drunk. She's *scared*, so you better shut up and let us handle it."

I glance at where he holds me, wrinkling the fabric. That's the first time he dared to get in my face. I can't decide if I'm proud he's got the balls to threaten me or if I'm pissed off he's got the nerve to touch me.

I think, most of all, I'm confused. "Scared? She's puking because she's *scared*?"

Colt nods, opening his fist before stepping away, his back arrow straight. "Just give us a few minutes to calm her down, alright?"

How scared does a girl need to be to throw up?

A few scenarios fill my mind. The anger stirring within me like a thunderstorm morphs into a full-blown tornado.

Maybe someone died: drowned in my pool, and the cops are on their way, led by my eldest brother, Shawn.

"What the hell happened? I swear, if you tell me someone died, you'll be packing your shit in five minutes."

"Died?" Colt's eyebrows shoot up, and he snorts a derisive laugh. "Drama Queen much? No one died."

"Then *what* got this puking chick scared?"

"Brandon forced her into his lap. She elbowed his face and broke his nose. Just get on with whatever you came here for. We'll calm her down and get her out of here."

I imagine a tall, overweight woman with a black belt in karate because there's no way any other woman could take on Brandon Price. He's a quarterback. Built like a true quarterback, too.

Relieved as I am that no one's leaving the party in a body bag, I can't draw a link between Brandon's broken nose and the girl's fear. She should be proud.

Colt's gone before I ask any supporting questions, and I realize that I don't give a fuck. My focus is on leaving the house as fast as possible without looking out the windows to assess the mayhem in my garden.

So that's what I do. My phone rings when I'm halfway up the stairs. I slide my thumb across the screen, pressing it to my ear. "I need fifteen minutes, Theo."

"Hurry up," he yells, excited like a kid on Christmas Eve. "We're on our way."

Since Theo married Thalia, Logan knocked up Cassidy, and Shawn adopted Josh, we rarely catch up. Now that we finally planned a night away from the usual bullshit, I'm buzzing at the thought of spending the evening with my brothers.

It's been too long.

I climb another flight of stairs to my bedroom. It spans the whole second floor of the six-bedroom house: my private bachelor pad with the largest bed money can buy, a showcase shower, and a stand-alone bathtub.

This space used to be a recording studio for some up-and-coming-never-made-it pop star, so it's soundproof. I hardly take advantage of that fact because I don't bring women home often but considering all the chicks my brothers fuck in their rooms one floor down, a soundproof bedroom is a blessing.

I hit the shower, then squeeze into a gray, long-sleeved t-shirt, pairing it with black jeans. A silver watch, bracelets, cologne, sneakers, then an AirPod in my left ear, my Spotify playlist soothing my mind on low volume.

My job—my *life*—is overly demanding. My thoughts rush at a hundred miles an hour, never stopping. Music is the only thing keeping me relatively sane. The only thing that keeps me grounded. Without it, I would've ended up in the looney bin years ago.

I force my hair into submission, raking my hand through it on my way downstairs. The second I exit the comfort of my soundproof bedroom, my temper flares, flashing bright red inside my head.

Someone's playing my piano.

The two hundred grand Model C Steinway in the living room. The piano my mother bought, hoping I'd keep playing after I moved out of the family home ten years ago. She has seven sons, but to this day, she claims only I inherited her musical talent. The story has it I crawled onto her lap before I could walk, watching her fingers glide across the keyboard.

I call bullshit. It's a tale my mother made up as a means of encouragement so I'd sit through those torturous lessons. I love the sound of a piano, but I hated playing, and when the time came to get my own house, I stopped.

Deep breaths, man. Calm down.

Yeah, as if that'll work. Anger dances in my gut, stewing like a wasp trapped in a matchbox.

My mother and the older gentleman who tunes it once a year are the only two people allowed to touch my piano.

Normally, I'd unplug the sound system, scream my head off at the triplets and kick every kid out of the garden, but before I reach the stairs that'll take me to the ground floor, the anger bubbling in my veins fades, leaving no trace.

A piano does that to me. It quietens my mind to the point

where I don't need an earphone, and *this* song could drag me out of the darkest place.

The melody flowing from downstairs overwhelms the new-age electro beat blasting in the garden, and "Fantasy" by Black Atlass playing in my ear.

Whoever is there, touching my fucking piano, is talented. Each note wraps itself around my tortured mind, soothing my frayed nerves. Whoever is there plays better than my mother, and I never thought that anyone, save for the author, could play this song better.

Ten seconds later, I'm in the living room doorway, the AirPod in my hand. Cody sits at the foot of the corner sofa, toying with his cell phone, wearing nothing but yellow shorts, his chest bare. Dark sunglasses are pushed on top of his head, digging into the man bun Colt and Conor mock daily. He tucks the phone away when he sees me resting against the doorframe, my attention centered on the girl playing John Lennon's "Imagine" of all songs.

"Hey, bro," he whispers, crossing the room. "Sorry about this. Mia needed to calm down. Piano does the trick."

Mia. The puking chick. Not a six-foot-tall karate champion. Far from it. She's petite, her face hidden behind a curtain of dirty-blonde waves cascading down her waist.

Normally, that'd be my interest down the drain, but I can't tear my eyes off her fingers gently skimming the keys, transitioning from one note to the next with effortless precision.

A surge of liquid heat flooding my system eases the ever-present tension seizing my bunched muscles. It's almost fucking unnatural not to feel my ribs cinched around my lungs, not to hold my fists clenched, not to lock my jaw and grind my teeth.

My body gives into the calm melody, switching off the

9

high-alert mode I'm always in, and I pull down a deep breath, filling my lungs with ease for a change.

"*She* broke Brandon's nose?" I mimick Cody's hushed tone.

I don't want to talk. I don't want to disturb her, but I hope she'll turn around. She doesn't.

She doesn't acknowledge me in any way, as if she hadn't heard me... as if she's alone with the piano.

"Yeah," is all Cody says.

So helpful.

By the look of her, she's five-foot-nothing and less than a hundred pounds, making the nose-breaking incident hard to comprehend. Snapping a bone requires strength. I'd know.

"How did she manage that?"

A proud smirk crosses Cody's face as he turns to Mia, a warm glow in his eyes. The bitter stench of beer wafting in the air tells me he's had a few, but he's sober enough not to swoon. And yet, here he is, dangerously close to looking like a love-sick puppy. "We're teaching her some self-defense moves. She's getting good."

Good? Great, if you ask me. Taking on Brandon Price is an accomplishment. Especially for a pocket-sized girl like Mia. Bragging rights earned until the end of college and every reunion going forward.

"Where's Colt and Conor?" I ask, watching Mia's hands flit down the keyboard. She wears at least a dozen gold rings, some low where they're supposed to be, others higher, above the middle joint.

"They're kicking Brandon out."

As the song nears the end, I wait for Mia to turn around, but she morphs the melody into another: "Can't Help Falling in Love" by Elvis Presley. A nagging curiosity burns me up from the inside out, leaving a smoke of question marks behind.

Who is she?

A pastel pink skirt she wears, sprawled over the stool, falls to her knees, and the white of her blouse peeks between her thick, wavy hair. I glance at the cream rug where she rests her feet, dressed in pink heels with little bows at the back.

Seriously, *who* is she?

She's at a Spring Break party. Ninety percent of girls in attendance wear bikinis, and she's dressed in pink.

Fucking *pink*.

"What did Brandon do to scare her?"

"He's got a thing for Mia. She keeps shooting him down, so he's growing impatient. He forced her onto his lap, and she elbowed his face."

"Colt told me that much." My voice is almost a whisper. "I'm asking what got her scared enough to throw up."

"She always pukes when she's scared." He shrugs like it's not a big deal. "She doesn't do well with confrontation." He looks at her, his voice back to normal level when he says, "I'll get you a drink, okay? We should head out soon, Bug. Will you be okay to go back on stage?"

She must be one of the dancers hired for the party. It'd explain her pink skirt.

Cody grabs a bottle of wine from the drinks cabinet, pours half a glass, and tops it up with Sprite.

White wine spritzer at a Spring Break party?

Beer in red solo cups is what college kids got me used to. Mia might've soothed my agitation with music, but it's back twice as strong. I can't make a single assumption about her.

It's unsettling... the not knowing.

Curiosity sprouts inside me like a magic bean, growing

fast until I think I'll crawl out of my fucking skin if I don't see her face.

Turn around, Mia.

"Last one," she utters quietly, the words like both a plea and a promise.

"Yesterday" by The Beatles reverberates through the living room. My skin breaks out in goosebumps as pleasant shivers slide down the length of my spine. She's too young to convey the emotions as if she's McCartney himself.

The melody is overcome when someone calls my cell. Mia doesn't startle, doesn't flinch, and doesn't stop playing at the interruption. Nothing calms my fucked-up mind like piano music, and that's probably why I remain rooted to the spot instead of taking the call out in the hallway.

"Rise and shine!" Theo booms. "You ready yet?"

No. I need to see this girl before I leave. "Five minutes."

"Hurry up, bro. We don't have all night! Logan's got a two am curfew, so move your ass. We're waiting outside."

I cut the call, watching Cody cross the room with purpose, shoulders tense, eyes not veering from Mia. The newly acquired muscles on his back flex when he pumps his fists. It's a nervous gesture. I know because I do the same fucking thing when I'm trying to compose myself.

He stops on Mia's right, a step behind the stool: an oversized shadow ready to protect her. The melody fades. The room falls silent save for the techno beat blaring outside, and Mia slowly rises to her feet.

Too bad Cody's blocking my line of sight.

Move, Cody.

I don't know why I want to see her, but I do. I want to see the face behind the talent. The face responsible for Brandon's humiliation. The face of a girl who wears heels with bows and pukes when she's scared.

"Is Brandon still here?" she asks.

Cody wraps his arm around her, and the single click of her heel on the tiled floor tells me he pulled her closer.

That's interesting.

My brothers don't usually date, but his hold on Mia clearly shows she's more than just another fuck. It's in his stance—the protectiveness.

"Conor and Colt are trying to get rid of him. Don't worry, even if he stays, I won't let him anywhere near you, Bug." He dips his head, and though I only see his back, I know he stamped a kiss on her hair. "Are you sure you're okay?"

Move, Cody. Show me your girl.

As if he hears my screaming mind, he lets go of Mia to fetch the wine, and finally, *finally*, I see her.

She looks like a senior... in fucking high school. Her white off-shoulder blouse is tucked into that layered tulle skirt sitting two inches over her knees.

It's modest. It's girly. It reminds me of candy floss, but somehow, it's inappropriate because my mind runs wild, imagining everything she's not showing.

She stands thirty feet away, yet her large eyes are so green the color is unmistakable. Skin like honey, small nose slightly upturned at the end, and those lips... natural, I can tell. Heart-shaped, bee-stung, so full it borders on ridiculous.

No fillers.

No makeup, either. Nothing. No lipstick, lip gloss, eyeshadow, or other stuff women use.

A soft glow of pink brightens her cheeks when she looks past Cody. She toys with her rings, tugging and twisting when

13

our eyes lock. I have the urge to say *boo* just to watch her flinch. She looks afraid of her own shadow but holds my gaze despite her cheeks growing hotter. It's cute. I'm sure she'd rather let the ground swallow her whole.

"Hi." A hint, barely a suggestion of a smile pulls at the corners of her pouty mouth before she bites her cheek to keep it in check. "Thank you for letting me finish."

Words somehow fail me for the first time ever. I don't know what to say... *You're welcome? No problem?*

Nothing sounds right.

"You're gorgeous," comes out instead. I smirk internally when her lips part into an inaudible *oh.*

Cody's head snaps to me, a hard edge to his narrowed eyes. Yeah, I might've crossed a line, but fuck if that's not true.

Mia shakes off the initial shock, using both hands as she tucks dirty-blonde strands behind her ears. "Um, thank you."

"Don't thank me."

She blushes harder, tugging her bracelets, and shifts her attention to Cody when he catches her hand, interlocking their fingers.

"You ready? Six is probably growing impatient." He waits for Mia to nod. "Good. Say *bye.*"

"Bye," she mouths, following it with an awkward wave.

Cody leads her out of the room, sending me a warning glare full of threats as if he's afraid I'll drag Mia upstairs to fuck the shyness out of her system.

He should know better.

I don't waste time with college girls. Pretty and tight as they are, they're too young and too clingy.

Two

Nico

IT'S HALF PAST TWO IN THE MORNING when I come back home a bit drunk and oddly at ease after spending six hours with my brothers.

The party's still rampant in the garden, although not as loud. Most kids are gone or sleeping wherever there's space. I scan the crowd out the living room window, doing my best not to burst into flames at the mayhem in the garden.

Broken furniture, a table at the bottom of the pool, confetti littering the lawn, and an upside-down rent-a-john.

The triplets jump to the beat, surrounded by a wreath of young, sexy bodies. They turned down the music, but the windows in the living room still shake when "Touch It" by Busta Rhymes blares from the tall speakers. They're lucky my room's soundproof, or I'd cut the power and kick out anyone who can still walk. It's almost three in the morning, anyway.

They should be in beds by now.

I leave the car keys on the coffee table, double-check the front door's locked, grab a bottle of water from the refrigerator, and climb the stairs. A faint streak of light marks the marble tiles in the otherwise dark house, coming from a crack in the guest bedroom door.

Before I form a coherent thought and start fuming that the triplets let someone stay the night, I enter the room, stopping dead in my tracks the second I glance at the bed.

Instead of a drunk guy or a couple in the act, a pretty little blonde lies on her side, facing the door, wavy hair framing her calm face. Her eyes are closed, her cheek pressed into a pillow she flipped vertically and used for cuddling.

She looks even smaller on the California-King-sized bed, her tiny body curled under the white sheets in an almost fetal position. The soft, orange glow of the night lamp bathes her skin, and long eyelashes cast shadows on her cheeks. I guess she was reading in bed because a worn copy of some book lays on the floor as if she dropped it when she fell asleep.

Why is she in the guest bedroom instead of Cody's room across the hall? Either he's ashamed of the mess he made there since the maid came round yesterday, or Mia's too shy to sleep beside him.

Neither sounds right...

Maybe she's afraid of snakes. Logan's python came to live with me when Cassidy moved in with him, but the huge vivarium didn't work in the living room, so Cody happily relocated it, and the fifteen-foot monster, to his bedroom.

I lose interest in pondering the question when Mia stirs, nuzzling her nose deeper into the pillow.

I stand perfectly still. If she wakes up, I'm fucked.

Thankfully, she doesn't.

I should leave. I read somewhere that the brain keeps a watch during sleep. It'll be better if I'm not here if it detects my presence and wakes her up.

I flick off the night lamp, setting her book—"Alice in Wonderland" by Lewis Caroll—on the side table.

Ten seconds later, I'm out the door, leaving it cracked open like it was before I barged in like I own the place.

I do, but that's beside the point.

Three steps away from the bedroom, I freeze again. My breath stalls as a loud gasp pierces the silent air; followed quickly by the ruffling of bedsheets, a quiet whimper, and frantic tapping of what I think is Mia's hand against the bedside table before the night lamp flickers back on.

Music from the garden fills the house. Different music plays in my left ear, but my senses are suddenly so agile I hear every deep breath she takes before the sheets ruffle again, and the room falls silent.

Shit. That was close.

With a deep breath of my own, I take light, silent steps to the second floor. The sweet scent of artificial smoke from the club and the nauseating perfumes of the brunette who hung on my arm whenever I went to the bar lingers on my clothes and hair.

No way I'll fall asleep smelling like cheap perfumes.

I strip, throw everything in the hamper, and step into the showcase shower. Hot water hits my back, relaxing my bunched muscles and steaming the glass. I rest my arm on the tiles, hanging my head low.

Instead of the tall, slim sex bomb with sleek, liquid chocolate hair I met at the club tonight, my thoughts loop around my brother's little girl.

My guards are lowered in the comfort of my house, but when Mia's lips flash before my eyes and my dick turns hard in no seconds flat, I'm beyond confused.

What the hell?

She's blonde. I don't care much for blondes.

She's in college. I don't deal with college chicks since I graduated college myself.

She's short, shy, dainty... not my type, but here I am, sporting a raging hard-on.

That's bad.

Very fucking bad.

Inappropriate.

I can't think about her that way. She's Cody's. Out of my reach and—should be—off my radar.

My dick disagrees, twitching when more arousing images flicker on the edge of my consciousness: flushed cheeks, big, green irises, the inch of collarbone peeking above her blouse...

I fight my instincts for a few moments before I give in and grip the base of my cock, pumping up and down, every tight stroke painfully slow while I picture Mia lying on the piano stool, long hair cascading to the floor.

I pump faster, imagining her pink heels with little bows resting on my back, my face between her thighs, under her pink tulle skirt. I almost hear her moan in that soft voice, feel her skillful fingers tugging on my hair while she squirms on my lips until she cries out my name as she comes, satisfied and trembling.

"Fuck," I groan, shuddering with release and shooting my load on the tiles, the orgasm so intense my knees buckle.

That's not good.

Not good at all.

***

The house is quiet when I descend the stairs around ten in the morning, ready for a workout. It didn't slip my attention that the guest bedroom Mia occupied last night stood open, the room empty.

"Good morning," Cody says, switching on the coffee maker. "What time did you get back?"

"Where's your girl?" I counter, resting against the island. "I saw you put her in the guest bedroom last night."

The only reason I say *your girl* is to check if he'll correct me. It doesn't seem likely, considering the love-sick puppy look is back. It's odd. Mia's not the triplets' usual type. I've seen the girls they bring home. They're nothing like Mia. They're confident and chatty.

"I took her home an hour ago. I should've checked with you if she could stay the night, but it—"

Conor interrupts his monologue, entering the room, and rubbing sleep from his eyes, his curly hair a disgraceful mess. I use Cody's sudden inability to finish a sentence to dismiss his upcoming apology with a wave of my hand.

"I don't mind. I am curious, though. Why the guest bedroom? And why haven't you told me about her?"

"Mia's not mine, Nico," he admits slowly, each word calculated. "You could say I'm working on it."

Conor spins in place. A snort of amazed horror sputters past his lips, the half-drunken bliss that twisted his features a second ago now gone. "You're *what?* You think you can go after Mia without checking with Colt and me first?"

I fold my arms over my chest, one eyebrow raised. He's as territorial about Mia as Cody, and by the sound of things, Colt might be the same.

It's not like they give a fuck about anyone other than family, which is reasonable, I guess. They don't have long until graduation. Once college is over, they'll enter the mediocre joys of adult life, so they're using and abusing the last years of freedom: partying and getting their dicks wet five times a week.

"I wanted to run it by you, but shit got out of hand fast last night. First Brandon, and—" He stops, sucking in a harsh breath like he needs a moment to think through his next words. "And then Spencer swooped in like a fucking Knight in shining armor... I couldn't sit back and watch him hit on her, so I asked her to be my plus one for Mom's Charity Ball next month."

Shit, the Ball. I should tell my assistant, Jasmine, to save the date before she makes plans with her girlfriend, forcing me to invite a random woman. There's still time—five weeks— but Jas plans her life months in advance.

"You *what?!*" Conor heaves again, blowing his curls away from his forehead. "You can't do that!"

Cody steps from one foot to another, suddenly defensive. "Why? No dibs on chicks, remember?"

The last of the Holy Trinity joins our gathering. The one who's most like me, so this is about to get interesting. Instead of hitting my home gym in the basement, I get comfortable on the tall barstool, sipping coffee and watching my nine-years-younger brothers pick up their figurative swords.

"Guess who made a move on our girl last night," Conor growls at Colt, who immediately zeroes in on me, nostrils flared, murder on his mind. *Wrong address, bro.* "Not him!"

Conor rolls his eyes. "Cody!"

All hell breaks loose.

I watch, confused, amused, and proud that they're showing some emotion.

"What the hell changed, Cody?" Colt demands, voice thick with barely controlled annoyance.

Cody spreads his hands as if to say *shit happens*, flaring Colt's temper more, evident by the pinched whiteness of his lips. For the next five minutes, Cody's getting schooled, threatened, and growled at.

They'd behead him if they had the swords.

"Don't you think you're overreacting?" I cut in, feeling a little sorry for Cody. Mia's a looker. No wonder he's into her. "Who is this chick to get all of you so bent out of shape?"

"She's our lil' sis," Conor says, his hands balled into tight fists at his sides. "Shut up. This doesn't concern you."

Lil' sis? They bugged Mom for a sister since they turned three. She almost gave in. *Almost.* Thankfully, the thought of having an eighth boy or, God forbid, another set of triplets was too big a risk.

It's a blessing we don't have a sister. She'd hate our guts when we'd start scrutinizing her boyfriends and weeding out those who couldn't meet our expectations.

Mom dreamed of a daughter for years, hence seven sons. After the triplets were born, she settled for getting daughters-in-law instead.

So far, she's shit out of luck, though.

Shawn married a guy, and Logan's wife-to-be spent her last three months of pregnancy on bed rest. Now that Noah's here, Cassidy's too busy fussing over him to get mani-pedis with Mom.

She gets along with Theo's wife, Thalia, much better now

than she used to, but I'm willing to bet a lot of money it's not a bond she dreamed of.

"Cody... Jesus!" Conor huffs, biting into an apple, then talking around the big chunk. "Unless you're absolutely sure you want to commit, don't you fucking dare mess Mia about."

"I'm sure, alright? Believe me. I'm dead *serious.*" He eyes the two of them, a silent declaration in his look.

I can do the same with every one of my brothers, but the triplets have their own wavelength. Whenever they trade those loaded looks, I've no idea what's going on.

"Give him a break," I say. "She's cute. What harm will a bit of fun do?"

Wrong thing to say...

"Fun?" Colt grinds out. "Mia's not made for *fun*, Nico."

"And I'm not looking for *fun*," Cody chips in, setting his cup in the sink. "Instead of wasting your breath telling me shit I already know, we should start clearing the garden."

Two minutes later, I'm alone. Who knew my brothers would grow up to be so chivalrous?

Three

Mia

THE BELL CHIMES when I push the door open. I'm early. My appointment's still fifteen minutes away, but I don't want to loiter in the street.

A distinct smell of green soap hangs in the air, and the black-painted walls are covered in chalk drawings and mirrors. My heels click against the dark, hardwood floor as I take a few steps further inside.

A tall, blonde woman in black rims stands behind the counter, tapping the screen of her iPad with a stylus. She peers up, blue eyes sparkling with amusement as she gives me a slow once-over. "Do you have an appointment?"

I come closer, clutching my small bag in both hands. "Yes. I'm booked in at six o'clock."

She checks me out again, tapping the screen. "Toby!" she yells over her shoulder. "Your six o'clock is here!"

A vintage room divider separates the entryway from the rest of the studio, blocking the view, but footsteps reach my ears seconds before the artist approaches. His arms and neck are covered in mismatched colorful pictures that somehow work great together.

"Hey, Mia," he says, wearing a subtle smirk.

I narrow my eyes, racking my brain for clues. He looks familiar, but it takes me a moment to place him. He's the first—and only—guy my sister cried over when he snuck out of our house last year and never called.

Aisha nearly always cuts them loose after one night, but it was a different story with Toby. They spent two weeks traveling Mexico together after they met in a club and randomly decided to take a road trip. All was well until they came back, and Toby left Aisha's bed before she woke up.

"Hi, I didn't realize you're a tattoo artist. Sorry I'm early."

"Nah, it's alright." He takes the iPad and runs his eyes over the screen. "Right, it says here you're supplying the design. Come on, you can tell me what we're doing."

I follow him behind the room divider, further into the large space filled with big mirrors and white chairs like those you find at a gynecologist's but with more moving parts.

A young guy lies back in one, utterly relaxed, while the artist inks his pecs. His eyes land on my face for a moment but don't stay there long before they drop to my boobs. Not that he can see much. Every inch of my cleavage is inside my dress.

Toby directs me to the left, where a glass coffee table is tucked between two leather couches.

"You want a coffee?" he asks. "Latte?"

"Yes, please."

"Yo, Knox!" he yells toward the back, where a guy I've seen

at college mops the floor. "Black coffee and a latte."

"Coming right up, boss."

I pull out a folded piece of paper, handing it over to Toby. It's a simple tattoo, the letter Q with the symbol for Spades from a pack of cards underneath. "This is what I want."

He glances at the page, scratching his chin, his eyes flicking between me and the design. "Alright... how about you tell me the story behind this ink."

"It's Queen of Spades," I explain like it's not obvious. "I play Bridge. Spades is the strongest suit, and people I play with took to calling me the Queen of Spades."

"Bridge?" Toby cocks an eyebrow, fighting a smile. "You want this because of a card game?"

"Yes. Is something wrong with that?"

Knox approaches, balancing two cups and a sugar bowl on a small tray. He carefully places the latte in front of me then does the same with Toby's black coffee.

"I bet you don't know the street meaning of this." Toby rests his elbows on his knees, putting one sugar in his cup. "If it's tattooed on a white girl, it means she's got a sexual preference for black men."

"Oh," I mouth. There goes my tattoo idea. My stomach sinks, and pulse hammers faster. Why didn't I check this online? It'd take one Google search. "I didn't know that."

The overdoor bell chimes, and heavy footsteps thump into the room.

"I don't care what you put on your skin. You just don't strike me as someone who'd advertise things like that on her body."

I shake my head again, covering the froth in my latte with two spoons of sugar. Weekly Bridge sessions became a part of my life last year. Thanks to the people I play with, my life has become fuller. Easier.

"Mia?"

A familiar voice reaches my ears, and I flinch, startled by his presence. Too bad I'm holding coffee. My hand twitches and half of the cup spills over my legs.

"Shit," Toby huffs, reaching to the closest station for a roll of paper towels. "Knox, get the first aid kit."

"That's not necessary." I set the cup aside, my cheeks burning hotter than my thigh. "It's just a surface burn." I pat dry my dress, chancing a glance over my shoulder. Nico stands a few feet away in a pair of navy trousers and a white t-shirt, holding a box with takeout food in his hand. "Hi."

"Hi," he echoes.

It's such a short, sweet word, yet it doesn't sound pleasant on his lips. More like a fired bullet.

"Skittish much?" he asks.

Not usually, but his presence turns me into a ball of nerves. "Sorry, I was miles away."

He sits beside me, the rich scent of his cologne pungent in the air, targeting my nose and doing weird things to my belly. He hands the box to Toby and his hand jerks toward my skirt like he wants to lift it higher.

I flinch again, unable to stop myself, and scoot as far as the two-seater sofa allows. Hayes brothers come in varying degrees of funny, caring, and confident with a sprinkle of arrogance, but something about Nico has a contradictory effect on my mind and body.

The powerful aura surrounding him makes me want to stand to attention, shouting *sir, yes, sir*, but at the same time, I imagine crawling onto his lap and hiding my face in the crook of his tattooed neck.

"Are you done?" The coldness in his voice balances just above freezing, tinged with husky anger that sends chills down my spine. "I want to check how bad it is."

On instinct, I angle my body the other way.

As if that'll save me...

Despite the fight or flight response urging me to flee, my insides turn hot when *you're gorgeous* resonates through my head. I've recalled those words too many times. I've recalled his broad shoulders, dark hair, and low, rough voice even more.

"Thank you," I say, clasping my damp skirt to make sure he can't yank it up and check the burn on my thigh, but at the same time, I defy my instincts, meeting his searing gaze. "It's not that bad."

He studies me for a moment like he's trying to read my mind, his features pinched, a muscle feathering his jaw. "Fine. What are you getting done?"

Toby interjects with a short, awkward laugh. "Nothing now, right?"

I'm about to agree when an idea pops into my head. It's not what I wanted, but it's close enough and still marks the time I spend playing Bridge. "Is there anything wrong with Queen of Hearts?"

"No, that's cool. You want that?"

"Yes." I touch the outer side of my wrist. "Here."

"Queen of Hearts?" Nico asks, summoning my attention just as Knox approaches with another black coffee for him. "The card suit?"

"Yeah, she plays Bridge," Toby answers for me, pushing his food aside. "Didn't you say over the phone that you need to head back to the office?"

"Plans change," Nico clips, pinning Toby with a pointed

stare. "I'm done for the day."

"Why didn't you grab something to eat?"

"I ate."

Toby cocks an eyebrow but loses the stare battle and shrugs, looking back at me. "You got any tattoos? Do you know how this will go?"

"I've got a few. I'm aware of the process."

"Okay, let's get this done. It won't take long." He gets up, gesturing for me to follow. "You want black or red ink?"

I sit on the white torture chair, glancing away from the mirror. "Red, please."

"How are you with pain? Should I fetch the anesthetic?"

"No, don't worry. I won't cry."

He smirks, hauling a small stool closer, then positions my wrist on the arm support. "How's your sister?"

"She's okay. Partying like always."

"I haven't seen her in a while."

"She lived in London for a few months but didn't like it and moved back two weeks ago. She's organizing a girls' night out tonight. You'll find her in *Q* if you missed her."

"What a *coincidence*." He glances at Nico, clearly amused. "That's where we're going tonight. You need to meet her, man. I don't know another girl who can party like Aisha."

"I know her. She's not my favorite person."

The first sharp prickle of the needle assaults my nerve endings, but I'm too busy with my thoughts to feel pain, however mild. My sister is a nymphomaniac. Self-proclaimed, but I bet the doctors would agree.

The mere thought of Nico knowing her turns my stomach. Has he snuck out of our house after making her scream in the bedroom adjacent to mine?

He makes my heart race for two different reasons, and I'm not sure which is stronger: lust or unease.

I wince, what Toby misinterprets for pain.

"Five minutes, and I'm done," he assures.

"Cody asked you last week if you're okay to go back on stage," Nico says, the sharpness of his voice softening with every word. "Are you a dancer?"

"Um, no. I sometimes work with the DJ who played at the party. Your brothers like the covers we record, so they asked me to sing a few songs."

He falls silent, staring into my eyes with the intensity of a diving hawk. "Piano, vocals... What else?"

"Piano is my passion. Singing is just for fun." With my free hand, I find the corner of my dress, twisting the fabric between my fingers. "I write songs, and thanks to Six, I meet people from the industry."

"Do you have time later? I want to show you something."

God, how can an invitation sound like a threat?

The thought of being alone with him makes me feverish, stressed, and snug at the same time. Whenever he looks at me, my legs want to run, while my ovaries would prefer to crawl out of my body and stroke him.

"Sorry, but I have plans."

"Next time," he replies, glancing at my wrist, and for once, I read him with ease when his eyes widen a little. "You good?"

"She's fine," Toby supplies, positioning a small towel under my wrist to catch the excess blood. "You know the anesthetic's not an injection, right? It's a cream, Mia. Next time, ask for it instead of taking pain meds before your appointment," he chuckles.

Pain meds are not the reason I'm bleeding so much from a tiny tattoo, but considering four artists turned me down in the past when I explained I might bleed excessively, I don't correct Toby.

Three minutes later, he's done. He disinfects the new ink, then covers it with aftercare cream. It's perfect. Small, but not too small, the letter and heart symmetrical, even though he didn't use a stencil.

"Thank you. And thank you for explaining the meaning of the other one." I grab gauze from my bag, make a quick dressing, and hold my hand vertically to discourage bleeding.

"Yeah, no worries. Take care, Mia. Don't wear bracelets until it's healed."

My eyes cut to Nico, another awkward wave on the go before I can stop myself. "Bye."

"I'm going, too. I'll walk you out."

"Where are you going?" Toby frowns, opening the takeout box. "You just fucking got here. Sit down."

Nico doesn't explain, just pats Toby's shoulder, then grabs his keys from the coffee table while I move to pay for the tattoo.

"Where's your car?" He looks up and down the street once we leave the studio.

"I can't drive." A glint of surprise flickers across his face and I realize it sounds like I'm too young to drive. "I mean, I'm a terrible driver. Five minutes into my first lesson, I crashed the instructor's car. I never took the wheel again."

The lights on a green Mercedes parked by the curb flash twice. "Get in. I'll take you wherever you need to be."

"It's nice of you to offer, but I'll take a cab."

His features pinch, annihilating the softness that was there a second ago. "I won't hurt you, Mia. You know that, right?"

I'm not a great judge of character, but I'm not paranoid enough to think my friend's brother—the mayor's son and grandson to the loveliest eighty-year-old woman I ever met—could hurt me.

"Yes."

"Then get in."

I shake my head again. "The cab is fine, thank you." I rock on my heels, and when he doesn't reply, I add *bye* before my heels click-clack against the pavement as I walk away, calming down with each step away from Nico.

"I'll see you in *Q*," he says behind me.

"You won't."

I'm not invited to hang out with my sister. The difference in age, worldview, style, and character has been taking a toll on us for years.

"Bye," I say again before sliding into the backseat of a cab.

Four

Mia

THE HOUSE IS QUIET AS ALWAYS. Aisha's out, although this week, instead of picking another man at the club, she's having dinner with the one she picked last week during her girls' night out in Q—Toby, the tattoo artist. It looks like they're giving it a second chance.

I don't think she ever went out on a proper date before tonight. She ran between the bathroom and her bedroom for two hours, getting ready, and kept knocking on my door, showing off skimpy dress after skimpy dress before she settled for a baby-pink wrap number.

It's something I'd wear if the cleavage wasn't so deep.

A cab waits for me on the driveway; the driver, Arthur, is one of the few I trust enough not to clutch the pepper spray tucked in my bag. He's an older man, probably in his late fifties, always entertaining me with a chat.

"You look pretty tonight, Mia," he says when I take the back seat, readjusting my green polka-dot dress. "I think my daughter has that same dress, just blue."

Oh, that makes me feel *great*... His daughter is eleven.

Maybe I should make a rule not to buy clothes in the kiddie section, no matter how much I love them. It's not like I purposely shop there, but a pretty sweater or a dress catches my eye every now and then, and I can't resist. My compact size means I fit into teenage clothes just fine, and sometimes the dresses are too pretty to pass.

"Where are we going?" he asks, making a three-point turn on the gravel.

"*Rave*, please."

"That club? I'd never guess you're twenty-one."

I'm not. Most people in those clubs aren't twenty-one. Aisha got me my first fake ID two years ago during a short-lived phase of inviting me out with her friends. Short-lived because I wasn't much fun sitting in the booth, sipping lemonade, and ignoring her friends' digs.

Arthur turns left onto the road, starting his catch-up monologue. He usually brings me home from lousy dates, so I'm well-informed about his life.

Newport Beach is big enough that you don't know everyone but small enough that getting from point A to B doesn't take long. Ten minutes later, after telling me his son joined the military, Arthur parks the cab outside the club.

"Call me when you're ready to go home. I'm working till two in the morning."

"Thank you, I'll call if I need a ride." I pay the fare, exiting the car before he tries to give me the few dollars' change.

It's only ten o'clock, but it's the last weekend of Spring Break, so *Rave* is packed. Just to be safe, I glance around, scanning the crowd of partygoers inside, searching for the football jocks. They travel in packs, so if one's here, the rest lurk nearby.

I'm avoiding Brandon, expecting him to retaliate in some elaborate, twisted way for breaking his nose

It's not like I punched him out of the blue that night.

I sat on a large outdoor sofa in Nico's garden, looking through the list of songs Six sent, checking what I'd be singing next. I failed to notice the pompous quarterback heading my way until he dropped into the seat beside me.

I got up immediately but didn't take one step before I fell straight into his lap...

"Can you feel that?" Brandon hisses in my ear, moving his hips up, his erection butting against my thigh. "That's what you do to me. You need to take care of that, kitten. I've been imagining you naked since my New Year's Eve party." He grabs my thighs when I try to move. "Not so fast. Fuck... you smell good."

"You have until I count to three to let go."

He laughs, the sound low, throaty. "And if I don't?" His teeth graze my earlobe.

"One."

Another short laugh, louder, and he jerks his hips higher. "I bet you're tight. So fucking wet. I'll make you scream, shake, and beg for more, kitten. Just say yes."

"Two."

His fingers dig into my skin. "Fuck, kitten... stop teasing." Another loaded growl leaves his lips.

"Three."

One precise elbow throw and a dash inside Nico's house

later, I puked in the downstairs toilet.

What else is new?

Thankfully neither Brandon nor his friends are here, which is good, but I can't see the triplets, either, and that's not good. Colt texted me an hour ago, saying I should come over. With zero better plans, I took him up on the offer, but it looks like I arrived too late.

The triplets became part of my life when they saved my ass one night in *Q* last year. They've kept an eye on me since. I don't know how I managed without them. The way we *clicked* is bizarre, but I couldn't have hoped for better friends.

It's a shame we didn't get there sooner.

Although, given my history, maybe that's for the best. The triplets were always in the spotlight. Three identical brothers, their mother a former Miss California title winner, their father a mayor... Yes, the triplets were *always* the heart of any gathering. We've attended the same schools for fifteen years. I'm a year younger, and as an outcast, I was invisible to anyone not trying to make my life miserable.

Avoiding eye contact with everyone inside *Rave*, I squeeze past the line at the bar and round the corner, heading for the staircase to the VIP section where I might find the triplets.

Once there, I scan the booths, two lines creasing my forehead. Where are they? I spin on my heel and almost jump out of my skin when a warm hand grips my upper arm, halting me in place.

His touch sends an electric impulse rushing through my bloodstream. Goosebumps dot my skin, forcing the hairs on my neck to rise. If not for my body's reaction, I'd be clutching my bag, getting ready to unleash the pepper spray, but my suddenly weak knees hint who's behind me.

I turn around again, my heart triphammering, hot flushes running down my spine. Nico stands a foot away, gouging his long fingers into my flesh hard enough to leave bruises. The ruthlessness he emanates isn't aimed at me. It's just a part of his disturbing charm that renders me speechless.

I'm not good with confrontation.

"What the hell are you doing here alone?" he clips, yanking his earphone out of his ear.

Maybe a bit of his attitude is aimed at me after all. He towers above me, a tall, broad-chested wall of muscles. Olive veins snake up his hands and forearms, covered here and there by black ink. The tattoos on his impressive biceps dance with every move he makes.

"Does Cody know you're here?"

I swallow around the tightness of my throat as my stomach churns, nausea kicking up the gears as Nico digs his fingers harder into my skin.

"Let me go," I say, steadying my breathing.

He won't hurt me.

He said so.

He's just a big brute.

He probably doesn't realize how hard he's holding me.

"I asked you a question, Mia." My name rolls off his tongue, erotic and possessive.

Fear and desire mix in my head, but even the heat flaring at the backs of my thighs doesn't ease the mild panic burning through my veins. "They don't know I'm here. You have until I count to three to let me go, Nico. It hurts."

His brows furrow in confusion as he glances down to where his hold loosens slowly before he lets go, raking his hand through his jet-black hair. "Why are you here, kid?"

I'm torn between running away with my tail tucked between my legs and rising on my toes to kiss him.

I'm not sure I can reach, though.

He's too tall, and I'm too chicken. I wouldn't get far if I ran, so I stand still, nailed to the spot. His cologne, a combination of bergamot, cedar, and a spicy note, overpowers every other smell here.

"I'm not a kid," I mutter, my cheeks growing hotter. "Colt sent me a text earlier saying they're here and to join them. Have you seen them?"

"They left half an hour ago."

I pull my phone out, inhaling deeply as if it'll help me get a hold of myself. Not likely. My hands shake, my pulse soars, and I can't focus on the text message.

It takes three tries before the words make sense.

Me: You said Rave. *You're not here. Where are you?*

Colt: Sorry, Nico's there with friends. We evacuated to Q. *I'll wait for you outside.*

He could've texted me sooner. Then again, I should've told him I'm coming instead of just arriving.

"They moved to *Q*," I say, and Nico inches closer.

I wish he wouldn't. He's too close. So close I can make out gold specks in his almost black irises. So close that I'm enveloped by the heat radiating from the bulk of his body.

There's a forest tattooed on his forearm. Tall, dark trees, a wolf, small birds, and mountains in the background. A stormy sky with lightning stretches up his elbow. The trees are burning. Smoke swirls higher, above the sky. There's more there—a bird, I think, but it's hidden under his sleeve.

Burning curiosity conquers embarrassment, pushing me to roll up the sleeve, and uncover a raven in flight. An unhealthy thrill zips through my nerve endings when Nico covers my hand with his, pressing it harder against his warm skin.

"I-I'm sorry. It's beautiful... the bird."

He clenches his jaw, flinching his hand from mine and shoving both of his into his pockets. "Why are you here alone? Where are your friends?"

I want him to touch me again. Take my hand or cuff my wrist... even if it'll hurt a little.

I don't know what to do with myself as we stand here, too close but not close enough, so I start twisting my rings. "I told you. They're in _Q_. Colt said they're here. He didn't text me when they changed club, and I didn't text him to say I was coming, so it's my fault."

A ghost of a smile lifts his mouth. "Come on." He nudges his chin toward the staircase. "I'll take you to them."

"No, that's okay. I know the way."

"I'm sure you do, but I'm not letting you out of my sight until you're safe with my brothers, Mia. I can't force you to get in my car, but I will walk you to _Q_. Don't argue."

Seeing as he won't back down, we start walking. I carefully lead the way like I'm taking my first steps, feeling self-conscious while he trails behind me, watching... judging.

"_Q_ is just around the corner," I say once we're outside, hoping he'll reconsider. "I can manage on my own."

He shakes his head, making the black, messy hair bounce along his forehead. "You shouldn't have to manage on your own, kid." He falls into step, urging me to do the same. "Where did you learn to play the piano?"

Keeping up with his long legs proves a struggle. He's six-foot-three while I'm a whole foot shorter, and that's only because I'm wearing three-inch heels. I fall back a few steps— a blessing in disguise. It's easier being around him when he's not crowding my personal space.

At the same time, I hate the distance.

It's silly how I react to him as if he's a powerful magnet spinning me like a compass needle. It's not his looks that leave me breathless, even though he's a sight to behold.

It's his stance. The ruthless confidence. How he walks, talks, and smells like a divine mixture of masculinity, pheromones, and sex. At least that's how I imagine sex smells.

"My grandfather was a piano teacher."

Nico glances over his shoulder, stopping when he spots me a fair distance behind. "You need two steps for one of mine, don't you?"

"Sorry, I wasn't graced with height. Or speed."

He chuckles, the sound thick, reminding me of tar on a hot summer day, his chest moving up and down. His whole face lights up. The harsh features soften, eyes sparkle, and he looks unnaturally carefree for a second.

He's beautiful.

It's not something he'd want to hear. Hot, handsome—yes, but beautiful? No. He wouldn't want to hear that. He is, though. Beautiful and not half as scary when he smiles.

I know more about Nico than I'd care to admit aloud. Since we met two weeks ago, I've paid more attention to what his grandmother, Rita, says about *him* in particular when we play Bridge. Her grandsons are her favorite topic.

"You may have pulled a short straw there but you got a long one in talent. Why do you play old songs?"

He likes old songs. Aerosmith is his favorite band. Or used to be when he was younger. Rita doesn't know much about what he enjoys now.

"I don't always. You only heard me play when I had to clear my head. Classics work best. I like all kinds of music. New-age computer-generated music's great for a party, but not what I listen to when I'm alone."

He stops, putting one of the earphones dangling from the collar of his t-shirt in his ear before he hands me his phone. "So what's your alone music? Show me."

The distance between us is less than a foot. The heady scent of his cologne assaults my nose, his chest in my face. Literally.

Even in three-inch heels, I'm eye level with his pecs. I hold the phone, unsure what to play. I like intimate music. Slow, emotional, a little dark. Not necessarily old, just full of emotion. Inhaling a deep breath, I pull up one of my playlists on Spotify.

"Left Alone" by Allan Rayman fills his ears a moment later. The song is heavy, the lyrics full of meaning. I know every word. Watching Nico listen to Allan's raspy voice and slow melody, I realize the lyrics fit him perfectly.

A lone wolf.

It's unnerving how he never looks away from me, but I'm at ease despite the intimate atmosphere. I avert my gaze first, watching him save my playlist to favorites.

"Give me your phone." He tugs the cord until the earphone pops out. "Your playlist for mine."

"Oh, okay. That's fair." I open my bag, and the pepper spray peeks out of its small confinement.

Nico grabs the can, inspecting the label and expiry date. "Why do you have this, Mia?"

He uses my name a lot. It's intimate... like we're in bed in

44

the heat of the moment, and he's trying to draw my attention.

"Better safe than sorry."

"I don't like repeating myself, kid. Most people don't buy pepper spray unless they feel threatened, so I'll ask *again*. Why do you think you need to have this on you?"

"No reason."

He's silent for a whole minute, grinding his teeth before he exhales in a sharp gush. "You're a lousy liar. This..." He shoves the can back in my purse, "...is shit. If you need it, get something with a better range."

That's what Cody told me when I showed it to him a week after the incident that forced me to buy it.

One evening. One date. A scarred psyche forever.

The triplets were there the night Asher Woodward spiked my drink and dragged me out of the club. They never acknowledged my existence before but came looking for me when I disappeared from the booth opposite theirs. They found me just in time. Twenty seconds later and Asher would've gotten what he wanted.

Once Cody pulled him away, I puked all over Colt's shoes. He still finds it funny. Unfortunately, it wasn't the only time the triplets saw me throw up. During the past year, they held my hair at least half a dozen times.

"Cody said the same thing. He wanted Shawn to get me a taser, but I don't think I'd have the guts to use it."

Shawn is Nico's oldest brother and Deputy Chief of police in Newport Beach. There's also Theo, who designs games, and Logan, who took over the largest construction company in The OC once Grandad Hayes retired.

"A taser?" Nico seethes. "And you think I'll believe you don't have a reason for that can in your bag? Why do you need it?"

"I don't. Cody's overreacting." I nip the topic in the bud by handing him my phone, so he can save his playlist in my Spotify library.

A moment later, we're walking again, the atmosphere no longer casual. I don't like the sudden silence or his obvious exasperation. I guess he saw right through my lie.

The entrance to *Q* comes into view when we round the corner. Colt casually leans against the wall, phone in one hand and a cigarette in the other. He lifts his head, probably hearing my heels clicking. The triplets are alike, but they're different from Nico. Shorter by about three inches, skinnier—maybe because of their age, and lighter in complexion.

"I found her in *Rave*," Nico says.

"And you thought you'll escort her? Thanks. I'll take it from here."

Instead of retreating, Nico balls his hands into tight fists. "Where's Cody?"

"Inside," Colt huffs, raking his fingers through his dark curls, styled to the front and shorter on the sides. "He's getting you a drink, Mia. I hope you're wearing comfortable shoes because he wants to dance. I doubt he'll let you rest tonight."

Good.

It's been a while since we went out together. All three of them are great dancers. Colt has the best moves, Conor makes me dizzy when he twirls me around too fast, and Cody takes the longest to run out of steam.

"That's exactly what I need tonight. I'll go find him." I turn to Nico with one more wave. It looks childish... no wonder he calls me a kid. I should stop doing that. "Thank you."

"Don't let her go in alone." He glares past me at his brother. "Either you go with her, or I will."

"I've got her, Nico."

They stare each other down like it's a game, and the first to avert his gaze loses.

Colt does.

Of course it's Colt. Nico doesn't back down.

His eyes are on me next, the intensity of his gaze heating my cheeks. "Be good, Mia," he says, drawing out my name in a way that makes me wet with need.

Lord, I think he could talk me to an orgasm.

Five

Nico

THE SOUND OF THE PIANO GREETS ME when I enter my house after a long day at work. It's been over two weeks since someone touched that thing. And just like last time, the noise in my head fades into the background.

I don't have to walk into the living room to know Mia's there, playing "Painting Greys" by Emmit Fenn—one of the songs from my playlist.

I didn't expect her to listen.

Leaving the keys on the side table, I cross the hallway far too eagerly. She looks obscenely cute in a pink pinafore dress and a long-sleeved top. No heels today, just snow-white sneakers. I make a mental note to ask Cody if his girl always looks like a little marshmallow.

Wrong visual. Marshmallows are food. Food is meant to be eaten, and fuck if eating Mia hasn't crossed my mind a million times already.

"Hi," she says without glancing backward. "Do you mind?"

I'm not sure how she knows it's me. Whether she distinguishes my step from the triplets or if she smells my cologne.

"Not at all. Have at it."

I pull my AirPod out and take a seat on the armrest of the couch, watching her play. She tilts her head, grazing her cheek over her shoulder. I don't think it's a nervous gesture. More like she's seeking comfort. "Your brothers are getting ready, and I couldn't help myself. I love this piano."

It takes me by surprise, but there's no denying it—I love when she plays this piano. She's ridiculously talented. Even my mother can't elicit such emotion from a simple melody. Each note Mia plays burrows its way under my skin.

"You can play here whenever you want."

She slowly turns on the stool when the song ends, her fingers partly hidden under the long sleeves. Eyes green like freshly mowed grass stare into mine, forcing my heart's rhythm into a higher gear.

I wonder if that's what cartoonists imply when drawing characters' hearts stretching a foot away from the body, stretching the skin to breaking point with each beat.

Every man has a type.

Blondes, brunettes, tall, short. After all, beauty is subjective. Just because I find a woman attractive doesn't mean other men do. Take my brothers and me. Theo's wife, Thalia, is my type by default—a tall, sharp-tongued, confident brunette, yet she doesn't strike the right chord for me. Theo, on the other hand, looks at her like she's a goddess incarnated.

I'm drawn to women with protruding cheekbones, long, dark hair, and wasp waists. The sophisticated divas who seductively sway their hips, holding their heads up high. Those who ooze sexuality and confidence. Those who seduce a man with one look. They can bait, hook and haul my ass to their table with a lick of a tongue across blood-red lips.

Mia's not that type, but she is gorgeous. Cuter than fucking cute. A total opposite of what I usually go for with that pretty, round face of hers and tiny curvy body.

I've always been a sucker for pretty, shiny things...

Mia's exactly that. Pretty and shiny like the colorful, butterfly-shaped brooch pinned to her blouse.

"Don't say that. I might abuse the privilege."

"No one save for my mother touches this thing. It could use the attention. Play whenever you're around."

However often that may be.

I want her here; but I really don't fucking want her here because I don't understand my fascination with this girl. I'm way out of my depth. I should divert my needs to someone else *pronto*. Newport is full of willing women.

Too bad not one piqued my interest lately enough to buy her a drink, let alone fuck her. They're all lacking in one way or another. Too much cleavage, too much makeup, skirts too short, boobs too fake, voice too high.

"Thank you," Mia says. "I've got a Yamaha at home, but it's not as good as this. My dad bought the first piano he saw when Grandad started giving me lessons. I've been meaning to change it, but..." She flashes me another one of those shy, barely-there smiles. "Sentimental value."

I cross the room to make a drink. Mia's sweet perfume hangs in the air here, targeting my nose as I move. "You want wine?" I ask, reaching for a crystal glass. She shakes her head, toying with her bracelets. "My mother has a 1904 Steinway in her living room. That's what I wanted to show you after you had your tattoo done. I knew you'd appreciate it."

"I'm sure I will. Monica asked if I could play at the Ball. She said she always brings that piano to the venue."

Monica? "How do you know my mother?"

"I've been helping a little with the Charity events she organizes." She tugs her sleeves until her hands are almost completely covered, then picks at a loose thread.

She's nervous around me.

I don't like that. I want her at ease. Comfortable.

Cody's words pop into my mind.

"Mia needed to calm down. Piano does the trick."

"Play something for me."

Scarlet paints her cheeks as if someone pressed a button on her neck that sends blood to her face.

Fuck...

Why is that so satisfying?

She turns around, her fingers back on the keys. My body erupts into a fit of hot and cold sweats when "Dream On" by Aerosmith fills the room. I could listen to this song for hours on end, never growing bored.

How the hell does she know it's my favorite?

The melody seems softer, a little slower, and... she opens her mouth to *sing*. She's a gentler version of Dolly Parton; her voice soft, laced with a raspy undertone you can't hear when she speaks but overpowers you once she hits the higher registers.

The urge to join her hits me like a freight train.

I grip the armrest, gouging my fingers into the leather, anchoring myself in place. I've not touched the piano in ten years, but I want to sit beside Mia and play.

No.

I want to sit *behind* her... my legs boxing her thighs, my arm across her middle, one hand on the keys, her back flush against my chest. The sweet smell of her perfume. The warmth of her body...

What the fuck is it about her?

Her blonde locks swinging from left to right in a ponytail as she plays are all I see; the lyrics pouring from her pouty mouth are all I hear. I'm in a daze until the melody ceases too soon.

"I believe that's your favorite song," she says, turning around.

"How did you know?"

"I know a lot about you. You're a stockbroker. A very good one. Your birthday's next week. You don't like birthday cake and eat apple pie with raisins instead. You like spaghetti, warm chocolate brownies, sky diving, and the color green."

I cock a questioning eyebrow but don't stop her. This isn't the kind of information my mother would share if she played cupid—which she does often lately—so I know Mia's not getting it from her.

"When you were four, Theo broke your foot with an iron. You've got a birthmark on your right shoulder in the shape of a bunny. Your favorite movie growing up was *Oscar* with Stallone, but your mom didn't let you watch it. Not that it stopped you... you watched it *elsewhere*." She bites down a smile. "Should I keep going?"

The corner of my lips turns up against better judgment. It's hard not to smile when she's around, a little ray of sunshine. "Those Bridge sessions... you play with my grandmother, don't you? Am I the only one she talks about, or just the only one you pay attention to?"

Someone pushes that cheek-reddening button again.

"I can tell you something about all your brothers. When he was five, Shawn thought forcing Logan into the tumble dryer would be funny. He only went in halfway but braced his elbows inside. It took your mom an hour to get him out."

"I don't remember that, but I heard about it. Why do you play with my grandparents? They're eighty."

"Which part surprises you? That I know how to play Bridge or that I play with people four times my age?"

Both. Bridge is not an easy game. I tried wrapping my head around the rules more than once. I gave up quickly, even though numbers are my forte.

"I like spending time with them," she continues. "I like when Rita talks about the seven of you with so much love in her voice, and I like their stories about life in the fifties."

She's a college girl. Far from those my brothers got me used to, though. Other than a handful of smart, normal girls, they mostly bring home poster kids for *stereotype*. Those who care more about their appearance and getting attention from boys than anything else.

It's fine, I guess. They're young. That's what youth is about—*fun*, but those types of girls only appeal to boys. They may be admired while at school, but once those years are over, boys become men. They want more than short skirts, immaculate makeup, and mind-blowing blowjobs.

"How did you join their group?"

"Well, Kenneth, who plays with them, is my neighbor. I help him with small chores, so we're pretty close. When their fourth, Patti, fell ill last year, he asked if I could play with him and your grandparents just that once." A sad grimace twists her lips. "Patti passed away a few days later. I've played every week since."

"It's unfair you know all about me, and I know nothing about you."

She crosses her ankles, pulling her shoulders back. "I'm not interesting."

"I very much doubt that." Footsteps thump on the stairs, halting our conversation. I can't help the hot ball of irritability swelling behind my ribs that our alone time was cut short. "Where are you heading tonight?"

"We're still arguing about that."

"We're *not* arguing, Bug." Cody arrives in a black tee and fitted jeans, his hair tied back in a low bun. "You're just too stubborn." He rests his fists on the stool, framing her thighs, and pecks the crown of her head. "Indulge me, okay?"

Mia starts the nervous ritual again, toying with her rings when Cody straightens up, lifting his chin at me in greeting.

"You promised we'll go to the arcades," she says. "You promised to show me how you cheat the claw machine."

"I will, but first, you should practice. When I'm happy you can keep yourself safe, I'll buy you ten damn teddies, alright?"

She rises to her feet, stepping away from the piano. "If I can break free, we're going to the arcades. Go on. Grab me."

She's adorable.

Five-foot-nothing acting tough. It's like watching a Yorkie pick a fight with a German Shepherd.

"Drop your hands," Cody says, taking a firm stance behind Mia, the tension in his posture clearly visible.

Once she complies, he wraps himself around her ribs, clamping her arms against her body. It takes Mia two seconds to assess her position before she glances at me, taking Cody's hand and bending his index finger all the way back. A pained grimace taints his features, and his hold loosens, allowing her to spin around and step on his foot.

"Now imagine I'm in heels, which I always wear on dates," she tuts, beaming a smile full of mischief. "I think I'm free."

Cody drapes his arm around her back, his fingers splayed across the middle, forcing Mia closer. "Because we already practiced this. There's a ton more I want to teach you. We'll go to the arcades tonight, but don't think this is over."

"You should box her in better," I say. I don't want them to leave. Although, that's not the main reason I opened my mouth. Cody's about ready to kiss her, and no way in hell can I calmly watch. "She knows how to break free when she can use her arms and legs. What happens if she can't?"

"I broke Brandon's nose!" she whines, stepping away from Cody. "I can take care of myself well enough."

You shouldn't. You should be cared for.

"You broke his nose because he didn't expect you to break free. Brandon thinks a lot of himself, Mia. Anyone attacking you will know how to limit your moves effectively. Brandon forced you into his lap, right?"

"His mistake. There's always a soft spot available no matter how a man grabs me."

No, there's not. Not an obvious one, at least.

"Stop her moving her arms and legs, then show her how to break free," I tell Cody.

"We're not practicing sick, getting-tied-up scenarios. That's way too extreme. Basic self-defense will be enough to deal with Brandon if he tries his luck again."

You should fucking deal with him.

Colt and Conor join us, both dressed to head out. They

greet me before plopping down on the couch, silent observers. "I didn't say you should tie her up. Just limit her moves."

Cody studies me, then glances at Colt and Conor like he's searching for backup. Or maybe a second opinion. I can't tell. "I don't know how to immobilize her like that," he admits. "How do I do this?"

I try explaining how he has to grab Mia, but he fails miserably. Either he's worried he'll scare her, afraid he'll hurt her, or he can't follow instructions because Mia frees her elbow every time. He's not putting enough strength into the hold.

"Can I try?" I ask. He grinds his teeth but bobs his head once, eyes shooting daggers my way. I don't give him time to think this through, looking at Mia. "You won't be able to move once I grab you, so you need to trust I won't hurt you."

That might be a challenge... I don't think she trusts me. She's as skittish as a baby deer, flinching whenever I get close.

Intimidating—that's everyone's one-word description of me. Thalia and Cass admitted I put them on edge like a snarling dog with rabies. Nothing new there. Most people straighten their backs in my presence, but it drives me up the wall to see it from Mia.

All my life, I pursued women who made me feel like I was licking honey off a freshly sharpened knife edge. Mia's not even blunt-side sharp. She's soft. Fragile, as if assembled from delicate soap bubbles.

I've no idea how to handle that. I'm a bull in a fucking China shop around her.

The triplets silently watch the unfolding scene. With each passing second, I drown them out until I don't see them anymore. It's just the boorish me and the gentle *her*. She swallows hard, taking a few small, hasty steps down the couch.

Once she's within reach, I cuff her wrist, cursing internally when she flinches at the urgency of my touch.

Possessive. *That's* how I feel when she's in my personal space. A dog with a bone.

I tug her hand, forcing her to nestle that perfect ass in the space between my legs. I've never been this self-conscious, never wondered if I gripped, yanked, or squeezed a woman too hard... now I'm hyperaware of what I'm doing, and I think my hold on Mia's wrist might be too tight.

I'm also hyperaware this was a bad idea.

The hairs on my neck rise. Blood in my veins flows like cherry slurpy. My pulse accelerates the second she curves into my arms, fitting perfectly. The honeysuckle smell of her perfume or body lotion is nothing short of intoxicating. I'm glad I chose a long-sleeve tee today, or how she makes me feel would be clearly visible to my brothers.

Fuck... even I didn't realize how powerful this pull between us is. Now that she's close, my whole body hums with a feverish, impatient, get-it-done-now kind of energy.

I take her hands, wrapping our arms around her docile frame like a straitjacket. My legs box hers in, squeezing them together with my ankles crossed over her feet. Her breathing hiccups. Mine catches in my throat before I shakily push it past my lips, resting my chin on top of her head where she can't headbutt my nose.

And she fucking *melts* against me.

Jesus...

What am I going to do with you, baby?

My lungs decompress, squeezed by an invisible iron clamp when her heart picks up rhythm under my fingertips, matching the frantic beat of mine.

"You're panicking," I say, my voice steady even though my stomach twists like a wrung-out towel.

"Calm down, Bug, you're fine," Cody adds, reminding me of his existence. "He won't hurt you."

Protectiveness goes *bang* inside me, swelling, growing, and spreading through my structure. No way in hell I'll ever hurt her. She knows I won't.

At least, I hope she does.

"You need to stay calm, Mia," I continue. "Fear will choke you. You won't break free if you're not thinking clearly. Take a deep breath for me."

She does, slowly filling her lungs. I breathe with her until we both calm the fuck down.

"Good. You're fine. I'll let you go if you ask."

"Let me go."

I do. Immediately. Scaring her is the last thing on my list. My legs open, and arms rise, but she doesn't budge.

"Okay. I just had to check," she says. "You can continue."

And I do. *Immediately.* Hungry for that peaceful trance-like state when she's safely tucked against me.

Seconds later I've got her immobilized, my chin on her shoulder this time, so she doesn't crush my windpipe with the back of her head. "Now, think." I tighten my hold around her fingers. "You can't move your arms or legs. You can't shove me away. What can you do?"

"Um..." She considers her position, trying to wriggle free like she did with Cody, but it's useless.

Now that she's flush against me, I feel her with every fiber in me. I'm not letting her go until I absolutely have to.

"I can hit you with the side of my head."

"No. Don't ever try that. It could work, but you'll black out

60

if you hit your temple against the wrong spot."

Instinctively my thumb grazes hers in an odd, mechanical reflex. I shouldn't do that.

Where is this urge to soothe her coming from?

I've always been grossly overprotective, but it manifested in unhealthy jealousy, rage fits, and fist-throwing at anyone who said one wrong word to my ex. I never soothed Kaya unless she was bawling her eyes out. Even then, I didn't do a good job because I was more annoyed than concerned.

Not now. The need to keep Mia calm fastens itself around my throat so tightly I'll choke if she's not at ease.

"Accept that you can't hit me," I continue. "You have to be more creative."

It takes a moment, but she tilts her head, accidentally brushing those full, soft lips against my jaw. "I can bite you."

"Good girl." I inhale a subtle deep breath, shepherding the desire rekindling in my gut. "Bite hard enough, and the guy will let go. It's a reflex. Hands go where it hurts. Once you can use your hands, you know what to do, right?"

She nods, and very reluctantly, I *let. Her. Go.*

"Fine," she tells Cody, back on her feet. "We can practice tonight but promise you'll take me to the arcades this week."

"You know any more moves like that?" Colt asks me, creases lining his forehead. "Anything we can teach her?"

Unfortunately, I do. I learned how to restrain a woman when I dated Kaya. She was an alcoholic. Out of control. Whenever she got hammered, she either threw anything within reach at me or tried to hurt herself. "Yeah. I know a few things."

We go over two more scenarios. After a couple of attempts to explain how Cody should do it, he waves me off and leaves me in charge.

Fine by me.

I have Mia pinned against the wall half a minute later, her wrists locked in my hand, legs boxed by one of mine. I tell her—*calmly*—what her next move should be while I scream inside my head, schooling myself not to do something stupid.

There are more things she should learn, more things I could show her, but she'd have to lie down, and if I cover her body with mine, there'll be no rationalizing.

Instead of turning my brother against me, I call it a night.

Mia
First day at kindergarten

"*COOTIES!*" *Jake yells, pointing his finger at me. "She's got cooties! Stay away!"*

All the other children squeal and stumble back, leaving me alone in the middle of the room.

"I don't have cooties!" I say, my voice squeaky.

"You do! You've got cooties! Don't touch me!"

"I don't have cooties!" I cry again and take a step forward. Tears pool in my eyes when all the other children start running away every time I step toward them.

I don't want to be here. I miss Daddy and my sister.

The children are mean, and Mrs. Jeffrey smells like onions.

"Don't let her touch any toys!" Jake commands again. "She's got cooties! If you touch her, you'll have it too!"

He runs around, scooting toys off the floor and throwing them in one corner. All the other children follow his lead until all the toys are out

of my reach.

"Now, now, Jake, that's not nice, is it?" Mrs. Jeffrey asks, lifting her head from a stack of papers on her desk. "Play nice. All of you." She looks back down, and Jake whispers to the other kids, pointing his finger at me and laughing while I stand there, alone, sad, and crying.

Six

Mia

I LEAVE THE CLASSROOM, avoiding eye contact with other students like I did in elementary, middle, and high school. I no longer have a reason to hide, but it's a habit I can't get rid of. After years of bullying, staying out of everyone's way is second nature. I'm a master of avoidance.

Students from all over the country study here, but a big chunk moved from the same private high school in Newport. Thankfully, Jake Grey's influential father shipped him off to Brown. With the instigator of the bullying I endured for years gone, the harassment almost ceased in college.

His friends still find it entertaining to call me names sometimes, though it doesn't happen often, and no one pushed me, tripped me, or slingshot a spitball at me since graduation.

Makes for a nice change.

I've been fairly undisturbed for six months, minding my

own business. Students hardly noticed my existence... until the Spring Break party. Now, the spotlight's back on my face. Although in a different way than I'm used to.

People pass me by, looking me over with approving smiles instead of distasteful scowls. A few even say *hey, Mia,* as I rush down the corridor leading to the courtyard.

Looks like manhandling and humiliating the football captain works wonders on social status...

It helps that Brandon's a jerk. Most want him to fall from the pedestal he put himself on. I may have wobbled the foundations a bit.

Still, I expected rude comments or the occasional pushing and shoving from his friends while Brandon took time off school to heal his nose, but no. Everyone is eerily nice, which is why I'm looking over my shoulder again.

Past experience has taught me that my peers only act nice if they're planning something I won't like.

A familiar silhouette catches my attention while I wait for the triplets, resting against a low pillar surrounding the half-moon concrete steps outside the main building.

Brandon and two guys from the football team exit the building, a pompous aura enveloping them like a green, foul cloud. His eyes lock with mine, and a flicker of anger shadows his entitled face before his lips twist into a sly smirk.

Damn it... I'm in so much trouble.

There's nowhere to run. Nowhere to hide. I'm trapped, even out here in the open.

His nose might be healed, but his ego remains bruised. Knowing Brandon, I might need a bunker to survive his wrath.

"Well, well, well," he snarls, prancing closer. "If it isn't my feisty kitten." He halts his minions with a flick of his wrist, then combs back his ash-blonde hair.

My pulse skyrockets faster than I can think.

Faster than I can *blink*.

I step away, not daring to turn my back on him: an animal on the prowl. A lion stalking an antelope.

An antelope that embarrassed him in front of his friends.

"I'm sorry," I say, the first signs of nausea rolling in the pit of my stomach. I'm an utter wuss, taking a step back for each one he takes forward. Five steps later, my back hits the cold wall of the building. "I warned you not to touch me."

"Yes, you did," he coos, crowding my space, his stormy gaze roving my frame. What a waste of beautiful eyes—cold, grayish blue—on someone with such an ugly soul. I'll give it to you," he purrs, bracing one hand against the brickwork. "You're a handful." He bends lower, looking me over with a cunning smirk as his other hand rises to touch me. "But that's why I've got two hands, kitten."

So, *so* original. He's a walking cliché, but his menacing tone starts a tremble in my knees. I wouldn't put it past Brandon to get even by breaking *my* nose. A quake of fear stirs in my mind at the thought.

He won't hurt you. Not here with so many witnesses.

I jerk my head to the side, my cheek brushing the bricks, and his fingers grasp thin air.

I wish I was made of tougher material. I wish I didn't feel overwhelmed whenever I'm even an inch outside my comfort zone. The self-defense classes help, but courage is harder to muster against Brandon instead of the triplets. Even facing Nico isn't half as unnerving. Despite his intimidating appearance, I *know* he won't do anything I don't want.

I can't say the same for Brandon.

"Why so jumpy, kitten?" he smirks, brushing a few locks behind my ear, his touch gentle for a second before he grabs my jaw, turning my head. "I've missed every Spring Break party because of you. You owe me two weeks. Two fucking weeks of getting my dick wet. You'll pay it back. Fourteen nights in my bed. *Willingly.*"

And to think I considered asking the jerk to punch my V card a few months ago.

He'd do it. Gladly.

There isn't a girl he'd say *no* to, and with his experience, it seemed as good an idea as any.

Thankfully, I never asked, but I confided in Callie—Colt's girlfriend at the time. She seemed nice, and we hung out a lot. I wouldn't have told her if I knew they'd break it off less than a month later. Once she was through with Colt, she blabbed to anyone who'd listen: my humiliating punishment for trusting someone other than the triplets.

Brandon's been trying to pop my cherry ever since.

The roar of a loud engine steals his attention. He casts a glance over his shoulder, teeth gnashing.

"You have until I count to three to let me go," I whisper, summoning tiny bits of courage lying dormant within me.

His hold loosens, but instead of letting me go, he inches closer, his lips brushing my ear as he speaks quietly. "I want that first, kitten. I'll make you come so fucking hard you'll beg for more. Say *yes*."

"One," I utter, my eyes jumping from Brandon's face to his chest, then the ground. "You know I'll hurt you. Let me go."

A self-indulgent smirk tells me he'd like to see me try. He looks around again, his hand still gripping my jaw, the hold turning featherlight when he spots Cody crossing the courtyard.

"Two."

"This isn't over, kitten." He dips his head, licking my ear. "You'll break. *I* will break you. Mark my words. Give up while you can." He leans in even closer, his nose almost touching my cheek. He grips my waist, fists my dress, and inhales deeply. "Fuck... I might keep you longer once you're mine. You have until next week to decide." He pushes away from the wall, not waiting for anything else, and motions his buddies to follow.

I can't move a muscle, glued to the spot, flush against the wall, my breathing irregular as dry heaves loom nearby.

Dropping my bag, I fall to my knees, searching for mouthwash. The peppermint scent helps control nausea and saved me from puking more times than I can count.

My hands shake. My eyes fill with tears, the scene embarrassing at best. The gazes of many onlookers burn holes in my skull, but I don't dare check how many students have stopped to watch the free entertainment.

"Shit, what did Brandon say?" Cody crouches beside me, unscrewing the mouthwash. "There you go, Bug. Breathe."

I inhale deeply, holding the back of my hand firmly against my lips. "He's annoyed about his nose."

"Yeah, I figured that much," he mumbles, gently stroking my back. "Come on, I'll take you home."

Three more sniffs and I tuck the bottle back in my bag.

The first person I see when Cody hauls me to my feet is Blair—Brandon's self-proclaimed girlfriend. She must've seen him invade my personal space and her jealousy is on display, foretelling trouble. She silently simmers thirty feet away, glaring at me like she imagines ripping the hairs from my skull one by one.

Cody drapes his arm over my shoulders, but the protective

gesture doesn't faze Blair. She stilettoes toward us, wearing a fake smile with a matching hard edge in her light brown eyes.

"You have a death wish, bitch?" She kicks the drama up a notch, hurling the contents of her takeaway cup in my face. "Whoops," she chirps, beaming when the caramel latte drips from my eyelashes, down my chin, and the front of my knitted dress. "I must've tripped."

"What the fuck!" Cody booms, taking a threatening step forward. "Are you out of your fucking mind?!"

The only upside is that the coffee wasn't hot enough to burn. I'm on the verge of projectile-vomiting again when I hear Blair's friends laughing, and in the distance, Brandon throws his head back, cackling like a demented hyena.

I've lived through fifteen years of this. You'd think I'd be used to it by now, but the shame doesn't lessen with time. It's even more humiliating the older I am because *this* is juvenile. It shouldn't be happening in college. I really hoped it wouldn't. We're adults for crying out loud!

Too bad not everyone got the memo.

"Get the fuck out of here, Blair, or I swear I'll—"

"What?" She licks her lips, taking a second to look him over, her gaze lingering on his broad, muscular chest. "You're all talk," she adds, then her ponytail whips Cody's face as she walks away with a triumphant smile, her head high, eyes on the green Mercedes parked where it shouldn't.

Cars have no access to the courtyard, but just as Blair didn't get the adult memo, Nico didn't get the not-allowed memo.

I doubt he understands the meaning of the phrase.

He stands by his sporty car with Conor and Colt, Wayfarers pushed up the bridge of his nose.

I'm back in the hot seat. Ruled by him. Consumed by the

pull whizzing between us. Mint won't help me this time. It was bad enough being laughed at by half the students, but knowing Nico witnessed the adolescent drama is too much for my spineless self.

A tight pinch of pain squeezes my stomach when I turn on my heel, keeping a steady pace up the concrete steps.

Once inside, I sprint to the nearest restroom and slam the door with a bang. I burst into the first cubicle, hugging the toilet at the last moment.

Today's breakfast, lunch, and two cups of coffee make a reappearance. My eyes water. Bitter bile burns my throat. Cold sweat coats my back as I heave, gasp, and shake, ejecting wave after wave of partly digested food.

This is why I always have mouthwash in my bag—to keep the puking incidents to a minimum. They started in middle school when Blair stole my clothes while I showered after gym class, right before lunch break, during which the football team had an emergency meeting ahead of their homecoming game.

Before the teacher came to my rescue, I sat on the floor, my arms and legs covering as much flesh as they could while the boys hollered, throwing cups of cold water at me so I'd flinch and accidentally flash them.

I've not taken a shower at school since.

Once my stomach's empty, I lean on the cubicle door, breathing in through my mouth and out through my nose. I'm not surprised when the door opens again. Heavy footsteps reverberate through the space, the walk easily recognizable.

"You good, Mia?" Cody stops by the cubicle, his shoes peeking under the door.

"Yes. Same old, same old." I force out a pathetic chuckle, wincing at the vile taste of vomit greasing my tongue.

With the mouthwash still in hand, I gather myself off the ground and leave the stall to rinse my mouth.

"You gonna tell me what Brandon really said?"

"Nothing new." I spit green liquid in the sink. "He wants me in his bed, same as always."

"I wish he'd back off," he sighs, massaging his temples.

"He's unhappy about missing the parties."

I pull a toothbrush from my bag and brush my teeth twice before we leave the building. The courtyard cleared during the last ten minutes. It's just me, the triplets, and Nico left.

He's still casually leaning against the hood of his car, Wayfarers now resting on the top of his head.

He slowly takes me in, bit by bit, the intensity of his gaze heating my cheeks.

I've been around him a few times, but I can't get over his masculine energy: all testosterone, threat, and sex.

"I'll drop Mia home and meet you at the dealership in an hour," Cody says, but Nico's silent, incisive attention remains on me.

"You go," I say, picking my nails. "I'm going shopping."

Cody frowns, wrapping an arm around my middle.

I shouldn't have agreed to be his plus one for the Charity Ball. The triplets and I are like family. We're physical. We hug. Colt spends most lunch breaks sleeping with his head in my lap, and Conor has me sitting in his when we share a box of ice cream. It's purely platonic, but Cody... something's changed lately. He kisses my head, holds my hand, and touches me more than his brothers.

"You're in no state to go shopping. You need a shower, Mia. I'll take you home."

"Oh..." I glance at the brown stains on my dress, pressing

the damp fabric. "I forgot about that. At least I smell nice."

The triplets chuckle, shaking their heads, but Nico's not amused. I thought we were past the glaring. Still, even the icy stare of his dark, almost black irises fuels my burning ache.

As a little girl, I watched too many fairy tales, dreaming up my perfect man early into my teenage years.

A true gentleman.

Tall.

Handsome with a great sense of humor.

Smart. Polite.

Nico's a long way off that. Half the time, I don't think I'm even comfortable around him. He rarely smiles, and there's always that irritated spike to his voice.

I crushed on a few boys before. I've been on a dozen dates this past year, but I've never been attracted to anyone like this. Not one man who crossed my path thus far awoke the will to surrender my mind *and* body... until him.

Just my luck he doesn't like college girls or blondes.

"Why did Blair spill coffee on you?" he asks. His clipped tone knots my stomach.

I don't understand him. He's a kaleidoscope of ruthless, crude, and arrogant ninety-nine percent of the time, but when we sat in his living room, he seemed at ease. I thought I broke through his tough exterior. I mean, he *smiled*. It's probably sad that making him smile was the highlight of my day, but it was.

"She's in love with Brandon," I explain, pinching the hem of my dress. Maybe I should wring the coffee out... "He got too close to me."

"So Brandon's in love with you?"

Colt scoffs, scratching his chin. "Brandon's only in love with himself. He wants Mia in his bed, and he's frustrated she doesn't want to be there."

"He can't stomach that she keeps shooting him down so he tries all sorts of stupid things to fuck her," Cody adds, making me cringe.

If my age and hair color wasn't a good enough reason for Nico to steer clear, the undeniable drama sure is.

Seven

Nico

FREQUENCY ILLUSION.

It's a thing. I googled the phenomenon because it bothered me that suddenly Mia appears wherever I go.

Even though Newport Beach isn't big, I hadn't seen her *once* before the Spring Break party, but since then, I've already seen her a dozen times.

She's everywhere. Rushing down the street with a cup of coffee in hand; collecting takeout from a restaurant I'm getting food from; in the café by Toby's studio; on the back seat of a cab when I stop at the lights.

Turns out, I'm not going mad, and it's not a freak coincidence. It's just how our brain works. Once we've noticed something the first time, we see it more often, leading us to believe it's a high-frequency occurrence.

It's not. I notice Mia because I met her. I probably saw her a hundred times before but never noticed because my brain wasn't looking.

Now it's on the lookout non-stop. I see her... and whenever I do, I drive myself crazier because I don't fucking want to see her. I don't want to think about her.

She's a college chick. A *teen*.

Blonde.

Shy.

Dainty.

Granted: pretty with great taste in music, clever, and unreasonably adorable, which isn't something I ever found attractive, but here we are.

Despite seeing her almost every day, I don't engage unless I bump into her somewhere where there's no choice, like *Rave*. Although that's not the best example considering I shot out of my seat the second I spotted her in the crowd, leaving my friends with deep lines creasing their foreheads.

But... I don't stop the car when I see her out in the street, even though I really, *really* want to.

That's got to count for something.

Her playlist plays in my car, office, and ear non-stop, fueling my intense craving for the pretty little blonde.

My brothers don't help, unknowingly reminding me I'm an asshole. Whenever Colt or Conor ask Cody how he's doing with Mia, I hate myself more. The fact he made zero progress doesn't help. I hope the obsessive thoughts will cease once she's officially his, but he's not moving forward.

"She's like a doe, Nico. I'll scare her off if I make one false move. I need to tread lightly."

She'll never be his with that attitude. Mia's shy, awkward, and gullible, which is why she needs a man who'll take control.

Cody tiptoes too much. He's overly careful like he's dealing with a mythical creature that'll disappear in a puff of smoke. He needs a few lessons, but I can't find the words when I try giving him pointers.

That's a lie.

I can find the words just fine, but I don't want to because I'm a selfish bastard, and I don't want to help him.

It's finally Friday today. Last day of the week. I deserve a prize considering I've successfully talked myself out of finishing work early to drive to college under some idiotic pretext to get a glimpse of Mia.

Fucking ridiculous.

I'm only hooked because I can't have her.

Yeah, that's it. She's out of my reach. Unavailable. Claimed by my brother, and I don't do well when I'm not allowed.

Never touch your brother's girl is one of the top rules among the Hayes. Mia's not technically Cody's, but I'll be damned if I'm the reason he doesn't get the girl he wants.

No dibs on chicks is in the rules, too, but it only applies if we met her at the same time.

We didn't.

He was first.

The last time I saw Mia was Monday when she got a mouthful and dress-full of coffee from my client's daughter outside college. I thought shit like that only went down in high school. It did when I was a teenager.

Looks like a lot has changed since then.

I don't need drama. My life's already overwhelming, fast-paced, and challenging. I hardly ever stop working. If I'm not at the office, I deal with emergencies, manage *Q,* the Country Club, my restaurant, and four cocktail bars. I solve issues with vendors and contractors. I deal with employees, clients, and partners. On top of that, I have six brothers, three of which live in my house. They all need me, be it for help, advice, or a chat.

And then there's my mother.

After Logan got Cassidy pregnant, she changed her tune from '*I don't want any women stealing my sons*' to '*all my sons should make many, many babies so I can spoil them rotten.*' I'm dodging her cupid alter ego at every turn.

It's exhausting. I'm running on fumes and desperately need a vacation before my brain melts, but I don't trust anyone enough to leave them in charge while I switch my phone off for a week or so. What's the point in taking time off if I can't relax?

I've got enough on my plate, but fuck... seeing Mia sprint inside the building, her pretty face a gnarly shade of pale green, made me feel about as calm and comfortable as a father waiting for his teenage daughter on prom night. If Cody hadn't followed her inside, I'd have been there, holding her hair while she puked.

Later that day, I almost called Blair's father to tell him he should take his business elsewhere or teach his daughter not to be such a bitch, but I talked myself out of it. Whatever the deal between Mia and Blair, it's not my fucking problem.

My assistant, Jasmine, enters my office around five in the afternoon to give me an end-of-the-week run-down. I'm thankful for the distraction. I can't focus on anything other than Mia lately.

The attraction grew so swiftly that I missed when it became an idiotic obsession. Erotic fantasies turned more vivid since the self-defense class instructor Nico Hayes taught in his living room last week. I can't stop recalling how perfectly her sweet-smelling body molded into me.

She's Cody's! I school myself, not for the first time. Not even the hundredth.

If anyone asks how fucked I am on a scale of one to ten, with one being not at all and ten being incredibly fucked, I'm around forty-seven.

This is wrong. The thoughts that plague me, the inappropriate dreams that have me slamming my phone to snooze the alarm and spend a little longer watching Mia writhe beneath me as I drive into her.

The cold, harsh truth is that I'd break her five different ways if she let me close.

It's time to get off my ass and find a distraction.

***

"What's going through that head of yours?" Logan asks, snapping me out of my thoughts and back to reality. Back into my house, packed with family and friends.

It's my birthday today. The last hurrah. Three hundred and sixty-five days from now, I'll no longer be twenty-something. I'll be *thirty*.

As soon as I stepped through the threshold, after ten hours at the office, everyone yelled *surprise* as if all their cars in the driveway didn't tip me off.

Out of all my brothers, only Shawn isn't here yet with his husband, Jack, and their son, Josh, but they're not why my eyes are drawn toward the door every few seconds. I'm waiting for a particular blonde to get here already so I can get my fix of her pretty face. The triplets organized this party behind my back. I assume she's been invited.

"Long day," I lie, taking a Corona out of the fridge. "How's

Cassidy doing? She still want to cut your dick off?"

He chuckles, shaking his head. "Nah, she's better now. I think she's starting to forget. Give it another couple of months, and she'll let me knock her up again."

"Don't rush her, Logan. She's been on bed rest for three months and in labor for three fucking days."

I spent those three days in the waiting room at the hospital, working on my laptop from the comfort of a blue plastic chair. I was there, serving as Logan's punching bag, errand boy, and verbal abuse outlet while Cass was in agony for sixty-nine hours, bringing my godson into the world. There were problems with dilation, Noah's position, and a bunch of other things I didn't want to hear but can never *un*hear.

"At least wait until Noah's crawling and eating something other than her boobs."

"Don't," Logan clips, his tone artificially stern. He's thirty-one, but you wouldn't guess it with how the mention of boobs has him biting back a smile. He slaps my shoulder, squeezing hard. "Don't talk about her boobs."

"Did I hear boobs?" Theo enters the kitchen with a beer in hand and a high-alert look on his face. The Hayes stop maturing around college graduation. Then we just grow old. "Whose boobs are we talking about?"

"Mine." Logan proudly points at himself, then chugs half his beer.

"Yeah, I think they're Noah's for the time being, bro." I pat his back. "If you want another kid soon, those boobs won't be yours for a long time."

"God, you're such *men*." Thalia rolls her eyes, joining us with Noah cocooned in her arms. "Take him, will you?" she pleads, elbowing Theo's ribs. "I need to pee really, *really* badly, and

83

Cass is talking with your mom."

"Yeah, sure." He sets his beer aside, scooting little Noah into his arms, cradling the nine-week-old boy to his chest with surprising ease. "I guess I should practice, right?"

Logan and I exchange a dumbfounded glance before we stare at Thalia.

"You're pregnant?"

She whacks the back of Theo's head. "You can't keep your mouth shut to save your life," she huffs, elbowing him again for good measure. "We were supposed to wait!"

"Wait for what?" I ask. "Why is this family suddenly keeping secrets? First, Logan with Cass, now you with the pregnancy. What's that about?"

"It's your birthday, Nico. We didn't want to steal the spotlight. We've been trying since Theo got jealous that Logan beat us to the punch. It was a bit of a shock when we finally saw two pink lines yesterday."

"Spotlight?" I scoff, pulling her into my arms. "You're weird, you know that? Congratulations. Dibs on godfather."

"No fucking way!" Logan booms, shoving me aside and pulling Thalia into a tight hug. He doesn't pass up the opportunity to glare at me over the mass of her curls. "You're Noah's godfather; Theo's godfather to Josh. My turn." He pats Theo's back, grinning from ear to ear. "Don't you dare have a daughter first. That privilege is mine."

"As evident by your son in my arms," Theo coos, running his finger down Noah's cheek. "He looks like his mommy."

No, he doesn't. He's Logan's miniature carbon copy, but Theo's been winding him up since the kid was born.

Logan wraps his arm around Thalia, courageous because he knows Theo won't punch him while holding the kid. "See, baby? He looks just like you."

"*Men*," she mutters again, beaming from ear to ear, then rushes out of the room, suddenly remembering she had to pee.

The news about baby Hayes number three travels around the house like a zap of lightning. Within minutes, Mom's tearful, hugging Theo and rubbing Thalia's still-flat tummy.

They're engulfed by whispered congratulations, so I leave them to enjoy their moment and entertain the crowd for a while, taking a minute here and two there to answer calls. Work never stops.

Another hour passes, and still no sign of Mia.

"Where's your girl?" I ask Cody, finding him in the hallway. The line sounded much more casual in my head.

"She won't make it. Her dad flew in with a surprise visit earlier today. They're having dinner."

I guess Aisha's not as close with her father as Mia since she's here—hanging on Toby's arm—celebrating my birthday. Fuck knows why. I don't even like the girl.

"She won't eat dinner all evening," I say. My back straightens while my body and mind rebel against the words piling on the tip of my tongue. Grinding my teeth, I force the next sentences out because they'll benefit *me*. "If you want her, make an effort. Call her. Pick her up. Spend time with her."

Cody smirks, chugging from his beer bottle. "No way she'll ditch her dad. He only flew in for one day. Until he leaves tomorrow, she's unavailable."

"Daddy's girl?"

"Big time," he chuckles. "And he's not my biggest fan, so I'm shit out of luck tonight."

"Why? What did you do?"

"Mia invited us to dinner so we could meet the guy before

the season started," Conor supplies, stopping beside us. "And Cody here, the genius..." He pats his head, "...had one too many drinks and told Jimmy his pit crew sucks. Jimmy's the—"

"I know who he is," I cut in, the muscles on my back petrifying. My unwanted crush on Mia suddenly becomes even more disturbing. The pit crew reference is enough to know who her father is. "He's a friend of mine."

We met a few years ago at the Country Club. He's the reason the triplets and I got into F1. I manage his money, and whenever he's back in Newport, we play golf.

And now I want to fuck his daughter...

Eight

Nico

SATURDAY.

Five.

Holy shit.

It feels like I'm counting down to something. An event of epic proportions. A paradigm shift of sorts, but the truth is I'm counting *up*.

Up from the last time I saw Mia.

Five days.

In desperate need of a distraction, I send a quick text to the Hayes group chat.

Me: Who's free tonight?

Shawn: Birthday afterparty? I wish, but Jack is flying to Chicago in an hour, and Josh has green goo pouring out of his nose.

Theo: Too much information, Shawn. And not tonight, Nico. Thalia's been sick all afternoon. I think she threw up half her insides. Morning sickness my ass. It's not just mornings!

Shawn: Too much information, Theo.

Me: You all should be glad people don't need a license to have kids.

In all fairness, Shawn and Logan are great dads, and I know Theo will be, too, but life would be boring if we stopped riling each other up at every turn.

The license thing, though... it's fucked up if you think about it. You need a license to drive a car, but you don't need one to raise a human being?

Someone should introduce that.

Logan: You sure wouldn't pass the test, bro.

See? Fun.

Cody: We're in Vegas.

Logan: Cass is out. I'm holding down the fort. No green goo or puke here. We're due code brown soon, though. You're welcome to stop by. I'll teach you how to change a diaper.

And underneath his text, a picture of him and little Noah in matching jerseys. Soon enough, they'll be wearing matching caps, I'm sure.

Conor: Dude! I'm eating! Stop with the disgusting bodily fluids.

Logan: You're always eating!

Cody: You need us, Nico? We can face-time.

Conor stuffing his face with whatever he's in the mood for, mumbling every sentence, Colt with his piss-poor moody attitude, and the one I'm trying *not* to stab in the back.

Not what I need right now.

Me: No. I'll call Toby and Adrian.

Less than an hour later, the three of us enter *Tortugo* per Toby's request. Adrian's always game, and while I should be dealing with the power outage that happened earlier in *Q*, I left it to the general manager. Something I should do more often, considering it's his job.

Too bad he's cluelessly running every tiny detail by me at all hours. I should hire a professional to find the reason for the outage, but I let myself off the hook so I can screw my head back in place.

Pun intended.

We stop at the bar, ordering beers, ready to get a few down our throats before we hit the club. I'm on the hunt, glancing around the room, searching for the perfect woman to take home tonight. Instead of a sharp-featured brunette, I spot a blonde I know all too well.

"Am I paranoid or..." Aisha says, amusement lacing her voice as she stops before us, "...are you *stalking* me, Toby?" She grins, their weird, flirtatious tug-of-war about to begin—again.

Toby and Aisha had a thing last year when they spent two weeks traveling all over Mexico. Things were going well till he cut her loose when they got home. He'd never admit it out loud, but he got scared. We've been friends for years. I know how he thinks. He was falling in love too fast, so he dumped her.

"You'd like that, wouldn't you?" Toby muses, cuffing Aisha's wrist to pull her closer. "I read your books, *baby girl*. I know what you like."

I tune them out.

Aisha has an undeniable ability to drive me up the wall with her presence alone. I don't know what it is about her. She can be a bit ostentatious but overall she's a good kid; yet my blood boils whenever she's around.

Before she hooked up with Toby, she tried it on with me. I shot her down and she decided we should be friends. Apparently, I was the first guy who said *no* to her, and she took that as a great basis for friendship.

She's been getting on my nerves ever since.

Most people aren't comfortable around me. I've got a tight circle of friends who know there's no reason to hold themselves wound up tight in my presence, but everyone else is always wary. Some are downright scared.

Not Aisha. She finds annoying me entirely too entertaining, and now that she's dancing back and forth with Toby again, I see her more often than I'd like.

I take a long, hard look around the bar, scanning many women and waiting until something *clicks* inside my head.

It does. Louder than a fired gun.

I look again, double-checking my eyes aren't playing tricks on me.

Fuck.

I squeeze the back of my neck, my entire body flooding with blazing heat. Huffing an exasperated puff of air down my nose, I glance at the ceiling, muttering profanities until the dictionary of filthy words runs dry.

She's here.

She's fucking *here*, of all places.

She stands twenty feet away on her toes, despite wearing heels. That's how tiny she is. Even in heels, she'd fit under my arm without an issue. The baby-blue dress she wears is an inch below the knee, flared from the waist down. Her blonde hair is in two braids hanging down her front to her waist.

The bartender slides a wine glass her way, and she turns around, those emerald greens of hers laser-focused on one of the tables. She's a far cry from what I got myself used to. Oddly refreshing with the aura of goodness humming around her. I never noticed girls like Mia, but she stole my attention with piano, and there was no overlooking her after that.

I move away from the bar on autopilot, following in her footsteps. The honeysuckle scent lingers like an invisible trail leading to treasure. I catch her wrist before she approaches whichever table she's heading to. The touch of her skin sends a shot of endorphins through my system, but it's not enough to ease my flaring temper.

"What the fuck are you doing here, Mia?"

The triplets are in Vegas, and the thought of her not being looked after makes my skin crawl. There are far too many sleazy assholes roaming Newport Beach for a girl like Mia to be out without a bodyguard.

"Why are you shouting at me?" She gawks at my hand holding her wrist. Her eyes narrow, and the self-defense skills my brothers taught her resurface. She glances at my throat, then quickly checks the position of my legs.

She's afraid. She flinched *again* when I touched her.

How the hell am I supposed to deal with her when she's so skittish? I want to wrap her in my arms, curve her into my chest, and hold her until she calms down, but it'd probably have the opposite effect.

She's pocket-sized, but she broke Brandon's nose, and I think she could cause me some damage, too. Explaining to Cody why his little girl felt the urge to take me down would be problematic, so I drop her hand, taking half a step back. I pump my fists, reining in the turmoil of my emotions.

It doesn't work.

My pulse soars again, whooshing in my ears when I notice fading, yellowy-green bruises dotting Mia's arms.

Both arms.

Upper, lower, wrists... dozens of bruises, most the size of a silver dollar, others bigger, some smaller.

I grab her again, yanking her closer to gently trace the pad of my thumb over the marks. "Who the fuck did that to you?"

She doesn't reply, just stares at me blankly with those unbelievable eyes like she hasn't heard what I said or doesn't know how to respond.

I want to grip her shoulders and shake words out of her. Fury bubbles in my veins, throbbing in my temples, but I grit my teeth, swapping anger for fake calm. "Mia, who did this? I need a name. Now."

"It's nothi—"

"Don't brush me off. *Who* did this?"

She squirms, her cheeks scarlet as she tries to tug her hand free, shuddering softly and angling her head back to look into my eyes. "Um... it was you."

Three words. Just three small words, but their meaning hits like a lightning bolt.

"Me?" I let her go, stumbling back a whole step this time. Confusion wins the battle against rage, still sizzling at the back of my mind. "What? I never hurt you. I never fucking touched you, Mia."

Not like this.

"Yes, you did. You grabbed me at *Rave*." She points to four bruises around her upper arm, making my stomach bottom out. "And you held me when you taught me self-defense." She touches the bruises around her lower arms and wrists.

"Fuck..." I can barely swallow around the lump in my throat as I curl my fingers under her chin. "I'm sorry. I didn't realize I gripped you so hard." I remember thinking my hold on her was tight, but not *that* tight.

"It's okay." She flashes me a smile, playing this down. It does nothing to loosen the chain coiled around my chest. "Really, it's fine. I've got—"

"It's *not* fine." This is as far from fine as it gets. "Why didn't you tell me I was holding you too hard? You should've said something."

"It's okay." She steps closer to place her small hand on my bicep. The warmth of her palm radiates all over me, and my heart rate slows on cue. "Please don't make a big deal out of it. I've got VWD. I bruise easily."

"VWD?"

"Von Willebrand Disease. My blood doesn't clot properly. I bleed excessively and bruise like a peach." She gently brushes her fingertips higher, then back down, trying to soothe me. "I'm fine. It doesn't hurt if that's what you're wondering. I'm tougher than I look, Nico."

I push a calming breath down my nose, but it doesn't work. I've never hurt a woman. Not even Kaya when she threw a kitchen knife at me, missing my head by not many inches.

And Mia's tiny, delicate: fucking fragile. My insides knot so hard it'll take days before the tension eases.

The clotting disorder explains why she soaked through the gauze before we left the tattoo studio. "You shouldn't be getting tattoos, right?"

She nods, her cheeks pinking up. "Not really, but I'm only type two, so not that bad. I take necessary precautions. All my tattoos are tiny, and I've never had issues."

"Ah, there you are." Aisha stops beside us, cutting in before I can apologize again. "I need to take a rain check, sis. I'll make it up to you, I promise." She pulls a peacock feather out of her bag, handing it over to Mia, then shoves her hand back in to retrieve a small, white box tied with a pink ribbon. "Happy birthday."

A sad, defeated grimace crosses Mia's face before it morphs into an unconvincing smile. "Thank you. Have fun."

"Oh, I will." Aisha leans in and pecks her cheek, then turns to me. "Come on, baby boy. We're going to *Q*." She doesn't wait for a reply. She just walks away with a seductive sway of her hips designed to entice Toby, who watches her every move.

I imagine wringing her slim, long neck. She knows how much *baby boy* riles me up, and she hardly passes the chance to throw that in my face.

"She's ditching you on your birthday?" I ask Mia.

"No, of course not." She pinches the feather between her fingers. "My birthday was yesterday, but she was busy celebrating yours."

We share a birthday? That makes her *exactly* ten years younger than me... too young.

"What's the feather about?" I ask, pushing that thought away.

"It's... it was a silly, childish tradition. It stopped working a long time ago."

"Keep going. I want to know."

She tucks it in her bag, sliding the zipper left and right. "I found it at the Zoo when I was ten. Aisha's six years older than me and a much different person. She never liked spending time together unless she could get something out of it.

"I didn't see her much once she started high school, so we made a deal. Whoever had the feather could ask the other for anything. You didn't have to agree, but if you did, you had to go through with it."

She takes a small sip of her spritzer, moistening those heart-shaped, bee-stung lips I can barely stop myself from kissing.

"What did you wish for?"

"Time. I wanted to watch a movie with her, go shopping, or have her braid my hair. She wanted money or that I'd cover for her whenever she stayed out partying late. She held onto the feather for weeks but never backed out of a wish. It changed when she started college... I can't remember the last time she didn't back out." She takes a deep breath, shrugging softly like it's not a big deal, but her eyes tell a different story. She's disappointed. "You should join them before they leave without you." She points to where Toby and Adrian shoot me impatient stares. "Goodnight, Nico."

She spins on her heel, not letting me get a word in, and walks toward the bar.

I can't fucking move watching her hips, hidden under the flared skirt, sway from left to right; the bows on the back of her heels; the one-inch-wide strip of lacy fabric running from her neck and disappearing under the skirt.

How can she show so little yet be so sexy?

She hands her wine back to the bartender, and as she turns to leave, a cocky-looking prick wraps his arms around her middle, pulls her back, and whispers something in her ear.

And that's enough to flare my temper.

She spins back to face him, his hand gliding down her spine and stopping on the small of her back as he towers above her. I know that kid. Justin Montgomery. He's the triplets' friend from college. A football player, I think. Loud, pompous, and spoiled by his rich mommy: a small-screen actress.

I watch them talk. I'm facing Mia's back, so I can't see her face when Justin laughs, shaking his head at whatever she said. My temper flares more when he spreads his fingers over her back, pressing her closer to his chest.

She's not his to touch, but she's not reacting.

Not pushing the asshole away.

He dips his head, grazing his lips along the crook of her neck, and moves his free hand to her butt, squeezing hard.

That's when she braces against him. The gesture lacks resolve like she doesn't really want him to let go, and I'm hit with a bad case of deja-vu.

I've seen this before.

Too many times.

Flashbacks flood my mind, summoning endless nights when I saw Kaya out on the dancefloor, letting some random douchebag grope her while I sat in the booth, watching her piss-poor attempts at breaking free.

She didn't want to break free, though. She just made it look like she wasn't letting the man touch what was mine.

I wish I'd known she did it on purpose.

She wanted me to burst into flames, fly down the stairs, and beat the hell out of the guy who did nothing more than put his hand up the skirt of a girl who *let* him. I wish I saw through the '*I'm so sorry, baby. I tried to stop him, but I was so scared!*' bullshit.

Not a weekend went by without a brawl. Not one without shit hitting the fan. Kaya loved my temper. She loved my jealousy and fueled the fire with bucketloads of gasoline.

Seeing me throw my fists was the biggest turn-on for her. Whenever I made someone bleed, she dragged me out of the club to suck my dick or ride me in the back seat of my car.

She trained me like a puppy—instant reward.

The overprotective, possessive side of my personality didn't help me see reason. I was blind to the obvious for seven long months, losing my goddamn mind whenever anyone touched even one inch of her body... whenever she looked at me with those beautiful, theatrically scared eyes.

It wasn't until I caught her cheating that I saw our relationship in a different light and Kaya for who she really was. A manipulative, vile drama starter. An attention seeker. A leech sucking out my energy.

Once the unexplainable spell she had me under dispersed, I swore I'd never let another woman get me under her thumb like that. I'd never get involved with another drama queen.

And here I am, watching Mia turn around, away from Justin. Her big, round eyes scan the room before they cut to me, helplessness painted across her pretty face.

She's just like Kaya. A damsel in imaginary distress.

She *let* Justin touch her. She didn't do anything to stop the asshole groping her, and now she shoots me the look. The *please help me* look Kaya sent my way every weekend.

Fuck my life.

No matter how appealing the idea, I can't leave her to fend

for herself. My brother is into that girl. Not for long because I'm not keeping this to myself. I'll tell him she's not worth the hassle, but for now, I can't walk away.

The triplets consider her their little sister.

They're protective of her.

Probably because she gives off that deer-in-the-headlights vibe... she has them wrapped around her finger.

My temper goes from zero to prison when Justin cuffs Mia's wrist, not letting her leave.

I cross the room and nail his face before he sees me coming. Next thing I know, he's on the ground, clutching his bleeding lip. Another flashback hits me, fueling my anger to the point I could crack open Justin's skull like an egg. The faces of all the guys I put in a similar predicament flicker on the backs of my eyelids. So many unnecessary fights.

"What the fuck?!" Justin booms, poking my chest once he hauls himself up. "What's your problem, Nico?"

"Beat it, kid. She's not yours."

"How do you know? Maybe she *is*."

Like hell.

"I told you I'm not interested, Justin," Mia says, quivering like a two-day-old puppy whisked from the litter, her cheeks white for a change.

She's a better actress than Kaya, I'll give her that. Her unease rings genuine, but I'm not falling for that. It's a fucking play. She's in character. Acting the same way Kaya did.

Justin turns to her, but I grab his collar and shove him against the bar. "I said *beat it* before I lose my patience."

From the corner of my eye, I see Mia, pale like a ghost, sink to her knees and rummage through her bag. She pulls out a travel-size bottle of mouthwash and unscrews the cap with trembling hands, inhaling the minty scent.

"Out," I clip, pushing Justin toward the door.

He readjusts his t-shirt, shooting me a dirty look. Not as dirty as the one he shoots Mia, though.

I crouch before her, reaching for her shoulders to haul her up, but she jerks away so suddenly that she spills half the mouthwash down her dress.

"Don't make a fucking scene. You let him touch you. Don't act distraught now." I reach for her again, and she falls back on her ass, scrambling away, those big eyes searching for a way out. It only pisses me off more. "Get up. I'm taking you home."

"No, no, I-I—" She pauses, inhaling at what's left of the mouthwash.

She glances past me. I look around, too, remembering Aisha's here. She should be the one to escort Mia home, but a quick scan of the bar tells me she's gone.

So are Toby and Adrian.

I pinch the bridge of my nose. Great. Just fucking great. Looks like I have no choice but to deal with the little diva.

Nine

Mia

ONE EVENING. That's all I asked of Aisha. One evening together to catch up. I thought she'd endure a few hours since it was my birthday yesterday.

Unfortunately, I was born the same day as Aisha's new boyfriend's friend. Not even the peacock feather can grant me time with my sister anymore. I know it's childish, but it represented something important when we were younger.

Not now. If not for Dad making her promise she won't move out till I graduate, she'd be long gone. And she probably wouldn't keep in touch.

I'm surprised she hadn't stayed in London with Mom since it was the only place Dad couldn't forbid her from moving to.

"Not good?" the bartender asks when I place my almost untouched drink on the bar. "What's wrong with it?"

"Oh, no. Nothing, I'm just leaving."

He offers me a curt nod, snatching the spritzer off the counter. Before I take five steps, someone wraps their hand around my middle, pulling me back.

"Not so fast, Mia," Justin purrs in my ear, grinning when I spin to face him. "I'll get you a drink."

"No, thank you. I'm leaving."

"Come on, one drink, sweetheart. Let me take you back to my place tonight. You won't regret it, I promise." He spreads his fingers over the small of my back, making me shudder.

"Let me go, Justin. The answer is *no*, and you have—"

"Until you count to three, right?" He dips his head, speaking into the crook of my neck. "I won't be such a fucking ass about this as Brandon."

My heart thumps faster, jinxing my ability to focus and assess our position. "One," I mutter, though I can't concentrate enough to plan how I'll break free. His hold isn't strong, but he's angled his body away like he knows my best shot is his groin. "I'm not interested, Justin."

"Don't make such a big deal out of this. It's just sex. An hour with me, and Brandon will stop plotting how to get you in bed. He's getting creative, you know?" He drags his free hand down the line of my waist. "You won't enjoy what he has in store for you next."

"What does that mean? What's he planning?"

"I wish I could tell you, but I like my teeth too much. Believe me, I'm trying to do you a solid here."

"Two," I say, shuddering at the thought of Brandon's creativity. "You'd be doing me a solid if you convinced Brandon I'm not worth the hassle."

He chuckles softly. "What's the fun in that? I'd much rather have you so I can rub it in his face that you chose me. He'll break you, Mia. It's just a matter of time. You're not escaping this." He grips my butt, squeezing hard. A ball of nausea sinks into my stomach.

"Three." I brace against his chest, my hands weak, mind in tumult.

I'm more concerned about Brandon's newest idea than Justin. He won't hurt me. He's actually the only decent guy among Brandon's friends.

Point invalidated by his hands groping my ass, but still... there are worse guys in Brandon's shadow.

"We're in public," I remind him. "You won't get away with touching me against my will here."

His hold loosens before I even try to shove him back. He's not stupid enough to manhandle me while dozens of people watch—bartender and security guard included.

I spin on my heel, aiming for the door, my heart falling to my knees. More guys from the football team lurk by the window, their amused eyes following my every move. I don't want to check if any of them have a similarly noble idea of using me to *stick it in Brandon's face.*

Maybe Aisha could wait with me for a cab...

But instead of her, my eyes find Nico, still where I left him, a look of mulish bad temper carved into his face.

I thought he left, but no... he saw the whole thing.

Of course he did. Just my luck.

Justin grabs my wrist, yanking me back. "I'd never fuck you without permission," he growls. "I'm not a rapist, sweetheart. I'm simply giving you an alterna—"

His words die a sad death when a clenched fist connects with his cheekbone, swishing less than an inch from my face. A kind of disturbing, nonchalant violence buzzes in the air like spent gunpowder, and my stomach somersaults back, nausea in the highest gear.

"What the fuck?!" Justin cries, holding his bleeding lip. "What's your problem, Nico?"

"Beat it, kid. She's not yours."

"How do you know? Maybe she is!"

Nico moves his searing gaze to me, and I shake my head, my vocal cords tangled together. All color drains from my face. Body-wide shudders don't help me focus enough to get words out. I've never been more afraid of a person in my life. Not even Asher scared me as much as Nico does right now, glaring at me like some prophet about to invoke the wrath of God.

"I told you I'm not interested, Justin," I stutter, swallowing back the bile coating my throat.

I drop my bag on the ground and sink, digging in there until my fingers come across my mouthwash. The peppermint smell doesn't stop my hands trembling or my heart racing, but five deep breaths settle my stomach enough that I won't puke my guts in the middle of the bar.

Just when I think I have a hold on myself, Nico crouches before me, all fire, brimstone, and death. I jerk back, startled by the sinister edge in his almost black eyes.

"Don't make a fucking scene," he clips, every razor-sharp word punctuated with pure disdain. "You let him touch you. Don't pretend you're distraught now." He reaches for me again, but I'm so taken aback by his tone that I fall flat on my butt. "Get up. I'm taking you home."

"No, no, I-I—" I pause, closing my eyes briefly.

You let him touch you.

I didn't, I... I just... ugh, my head is spinning, and the thunder of my pulse gets in the way of my concentration.

I *didn't* let Justin touch me. It's just that flashbacks of the night I was almost raped seize my mind whenever someone grabs me unexpectedly.

I kicked and screamed as much as my mellow, drugged body allowed when Asher spiked my drink. I fought him, using the little strength I had, but the effect was different than I hoped. Instead of letting go, he slapped his hand over my mouth to keep me quiet.

My mind blanked.

I couldn't form one coherent thought. I couldn't break free or make a sound. That night, I learned I have a better chance of getting out of trouble if I remain calm and plan my moves.

That's why I gave Brandon to the count of three before I sent my elbow flying. That's why Justin got the same. It's not time for them to grope me. It's time for *me* to find courage, assess my position, and believe that I *can* break free.

"I said *get up*, Mia. Now," Nico says, his words sharp enough to cut glass. "*Up.*"

I do as told, gathering myself off the ground as I tuck the mouthwash back into my purse. "I know my way home."

"I bet," he snaps, towering above me. "I won't let you take a cab alone, so get moving. I don't have all night, kid."

The anger radiating off him finds its way into me, latching onto my nerve endings and igniting my mind with an unexpected burst of courage. Words I'd never normally even think roll off my tongue without hesitation.

"I'm not a kid, and you're not going with me. Join your friends. I can take care of myself." I walk around him, heading for the door, but he doesn't let me get away.

He grips my arm, making me shudder for two unrelated reasons. One: I'm no longer comfortable around him, and two:

an unhealthy thrill sweeps me from head to toe, contradicting the first thought. He's riled up, ticking like a bomb, but in all his brute glowering annoyance, he's *gentle.*

"I'm not asking for permission, Mia. I'm taking you home." He ushers me outside, taking no care to make sure I keep up with his long legs. He basically drags me, but his touch is still nowhere near bruising point.

"That's very thoughtful." I snatch my hand free and open the door to the closest cab. "I'll be okay on my own. I've done this before. Whatever your problem is, go stew somewhere else. I don't need your attitude."

Before I can theatrically slam the door shut, he's there, holding it open, getting in, and forcing me to scoot over. "The address?"

"I said—"

"I know what you fucking said! Believe me, the last thing I want to do tonight is babysit a juvenile drama queen, but Cody wouldn't be happy to know I left you alone, so be a doll and don't fucking argue." He pulls his phone out, his thumbs tapping against the screen. Half a minute later, he pats the driver's shoulder. "Number nine Peony Drive."

I want to ask how he knows my address, but there's a clog in my throat the size of an apple. If I open my mouth, I'll cry.

Most girls love bad boys: their charm, the aura of danger, their controlled arrogance... Aisha's books are full of guys like that and they sell out like warm cakes.

But bad boys are only great in books.

Nico holds his jacket over his knee as we pull away from the curb. The expensive silver watch adorning his wrist contrasts the black tattoos marking both of his hands and arms.

He's worth a fortune, but money isn't what I'm attracted

to. Or *was* attracted to before he made assumptions, not letting me explain.

It's his confidence I adored. The way he knew exactly how to handle me and watched me like I was something important that should be cared for.

Disappointment floods my system, settling deep in my gut. For a moment, I thought he could be interested in me, but that ship sailed. Even if he didn't mind the ten-year age gap, I'm not the type he goes for. He likes short skirts, big boobs, and glamorous makeup.

I don't fit him. Not in the slightest.

He's a predator. Tall, broad, strong. Everything about him screams *testosterone*: from his smell, style, and stance right down to his voice. He's rough around the edges, his chin peppered with two-day stubble, eyes framed by thick eyebrows. Tattoos mark every inch of his upper body... and I'm like that girl from *A Walk to Remember* Aisha compares me to. Small, spineless.

I wish I could be more like my sister—outgoing and un-afraid to act on my desires—because I've never felt so over-whelmed in a man's presence.

Maybe if I had the guts to seize the opportunity, he wouldn't be watching me like he can't wait for the ride to be over.

"Do me a favor and stay away from my brothers," he clips, pushing a long calming breath down his nose. "They don't need problems, and that's all you'll bring."

I stare at the back of the driver's seat, my chest constricting again. He's not wrong. The triplets get into pointless fights on my behalf, no matter how much I beg them not to. It takes as little as some guys calling me *weird* to set them off.

"You won't talk to me now?" Nico asks, his voice dripping with annoyance. "Very fucking mature."

My nails bite into the palms of my hands. "Why are you acting like this? I didn't do anything wrong. I—"

"You let the guy touch you! You didn't stop him, but you *did* look at me for help. I've dealt with girls like you before. I lived through this shit. It doesn't end well."

"I didn't mean to look at you. I didn't need help," I force the words past my lips, though all I want to do is tuck and roll out of the moving cab. "I was looking for Aisha so she'd wait with me outside, and... I didn't let him touch me, Nico," I whisper the last part, not trusting my voice anymore. "I pushed him away. I just needed a moment to—"

"To *what?* Get enough attention on you? Maybe you didn't let him, but you sure didn't fucking stop him."

God, why is defending myself so difficult? It shouldn't be. I did nothing wrong, but thanks to Nico's attitude, guilt sprouts in my stomach, making me feel so, *so* small. I should react faster. I know I should... it's just that if I make one false move, I lose.

"It gets very noisy and overwhelming inside my head when I'm touched by someone I don't want touching me," I say.

The need to change his mind about me burns a hole in my chest. Or maybe the need to retaliate spurs me on.

It's an odd, disturbing feeling. I've never gone down the eye-for-an-eye route before, always the one to give up, but Nico's attitude awakens part of my character I didn't know existed.

"Things resurface," I continue, even though he probably already karate-chopped me dead in his mind and doesn't give a damn about my excuses. "I get nauseous, panicky... I need a minute to get a hold of myself. A moment to push the panic down, assess my position, and find a way out."

"It's not rocket science, kid. You shove the fucker away, and you tell him not to touch you."

I swallow hard, chancing a glance his way. "Stop calling me that. What did you say when you taught me self-defense? That I should stay calm because fear will choke me, correct?"

His jaw ticks, but he bobs his head once.

"That's what I do." I glance out the window, watching as we exit the town center. "Do you know how I met your brothers?"

Nico huffs quietly, either losing his patience or growing bored. "What does that have to do with anything?"

"More than you'll ever understand. We may have been at the same schools since kindergarten, but we never talked until last year at *Q*. That night, I did what you said I should've done today. I pushed a guy away." I adjust myself in the seat, toying with the hem of my skirt. "And then I kicked, screamed, and tried to fight him, even though I couldn't hold my weight properly because of whatever he slipped in my drink."

Nico doesn't say a word, his unease betrayed by a nervous clenching and unclenching of both fists. I've got his undivided attention, and by the look of him, he knows where I'm going. He knows this story doesn't end pretty. He probably heard about it from the triplets, Shawn, or maybe even the guy who owned *Q* at the time.

"The harder I fought, the worse it got. I couldn't think. I couldn't see a way out because I panicked. For some reason, your brothers kept an eye on me that night. And it was only thanks to them that Asher didn't get what he wanted. When Conor pulled him off me, he already had his hands under my skirt."

I pinch my lips, tasting the salty tears silently escaping my eyes. I hate reliving that night. I hate the scar Asher left on my thigh when he caught his signet ring in my flesh, ripping it open. I still feel his hands on me sometimes, and wake up drenched in sweat at all hours of the night. I'm not ashamed of what happened, but it doesn't mean I enjoy talking about it.

"So, yes," I admit, wiping my face. "I didn't push Justin away immediately. I took a moment to assess our position and check where I could hit if saying *no* wouldn't work." The car halts outside my house, the driver as silent as Nico. "It's not what you'd expect me to do, but I won't apologize for keeping myself safe the only way I know how. It's been a year, and so far, no one's trapped me the way Asher did." I unzip my bag, pulling my wallet out, but Nico covers my trembling hand with his.

"Look at me," he rasps, his guilt swirling in the air like fine dust. "Please, baby... *look*. At. Me."

I wipe my eyes once more, suppressing the agonizing need to let the tears run free. Faint heart never won the battle, and this is what it feels like. A battle to see who'll come out on top. I might be weaker than a frail stem holding the weight of a sunflower blossom, but I *am* holding it. I won't let Nico reduce me to a pathetic, whimpering mess.

"You're sorry, aren't you? Sorry about what you said, how you acted, and sorry that Asher almost raped me." I bite the inside of my cheek, meeting his haunted stare. "That's nice, but I don't need your *sorry*. I don't need your pity. It's done. I could let it define me or use it to toughen up." I take a fifty out of my wallet, passing it to the driver. "Can you wait a moment, please? I'll be right back."

He nods, glancing in the rearview mirror, his face a picture of embarrassment. "Sure thing."

I exit the car, cross a narrow pathway, unlock the door, and click-clack down the hallway into my bedroom. The gift

I chose for Nico's birthday waits on my nightstand. He doesn't deserve it after how he acted, but getting it took time, effort, and many favors. Despite how big of a jerk he's been, I want him to have it.

When the triplets invited me to his party, I pulled all the strings to get Nico Aerosmith's first LP in mint condition, signed by the band. You can get one online for a few hundred dollars, and I'm sure he already has one in his collection but working in the industry comes with its perks.

The LP on my nightstand, wrapped in pink paper, came straight from the band with a personalized dedication.

Moments later, I'm back standing by the car, holding the door open. Nico's eyes meet mine, his face full of contradictions. He's angry, worried, and... I'm not sure what I see there, but it wraps itself around me like a thick, fluffy blanket.

"I'm sorry I couldn't make your party last night." I hold the gift out for him. "Happy birthday."

"You got me a gift?"

"It would be rude to turn up empty-handed." I wipe the last tears from my eyelashes, waiting for him to take it. "Almost as rude as you not accepting it."

He grabs it immediately, frowning like he doesn't know what to say. "Thank you."

"Goodnight, Nico."

The cab stays on the driveway as I kick my heels off in the hallway and sit in front of the piano, playing every song that soothes me until late into the night.

Ten

Nico

I HACK THE BACK OF THE PASSENGER SEAT with my fist when Mia disappears inside the house. Her tear-stained face lingers at the forefront of my mind. I'm so uncomfortable in my own fucking head I wish I could rip it off.

Knowing that my twisted personality: the jumping-to-conclusions way too fast, and the gas-light temper are why she's upset drives me insane.

I never want to see that girl cry again. I never want to see her chin quiver and those big eyes fill with tears.

"Are you gonna go after her or...?" the driver asks.

The headrest on the passenger seat has split in two under my fist, and the concerned, frightened look on the guy peeking in the rearview mirror tells me he'd be more than thrilled if I got the hell out of his car. He can't be older than me, but he's half my size. I doubt he'll try his luck at forcing me out.

I pull a wad of cash from my wallet to cover the fare and damages. "Nineteen-oh-six Port Ramsey Way."

"That's too much, man." He taps the meter, where the fare isn't even twenty bucks yet. "Besides, she already paid."

"Then you're getting paid twice. The rest is for damages. I don't have the energy to argue. Take it and get me home, alright?"

"Yeah, alright," he hums, turning the radio up loud enough that I make out "Scrubs" by TLC but not loud enough to stop him talking. "You want to break a window or two? Slash a tire? You know... get your money's worth and unwind."

I leave it without comment, ripping the pink wrapping paper off the gift. My head hits the back of the seat when I pull out the LP Mia got me. I've got this album at home, but I sure don't have it signed by the band with *Dream on, Nico* written across the front.

I've no idea how she made this happen. It must've cost a small fortune and a lot of favors unless she's friends with the band.

Even trashing the whole car wouldn't put a dent in my foul mood now. I'm sure Mia didn't mean it that way, but this gift, the thought behind it... fuck. It feels like she purposely extracted every last ounce of humiliation from this situation, trying to put me in my place.

A job well done.

I thought I had her all figured out. *Twice.* But I was wrong both times. She's nothing like Kaya, and she sure isn't as spineless as I pegged her for since she managed to put this dent in my confidence.

I grab my phone, letting Toby know I won't join them in *Q*. Then I text Cody.

Better he finds out from me than Mia.

Me: I made your girl cry.

And I've never felt so raw.

Kaya bawled her eyes out a hundred times, but her tears never hit me like Mia's. A kick to the balls is a walk in the park in comparison.

Instead of a text, an incoming call flashes up, my brother too impatient to shoot messages back and forth.

I inhale a deep breath before answering.

"What did you do?" Cody clips. "Why were you even with her? She's with her sister!"

"Not anymore. Aisha prefers Toby. She ditched Mia and I... I jumped to conclusions. Why didn't you tell me she's the girl Asher almost raped last year?"

"Because it's none of your business and not my story to tell. *What* did you do?!"

I push my flaring temper back down. Cody has the right to be pissed off. "Justin Montgomery was all over her in *Tortugo*. She didn't push him away but shot me that look Kaya always did when she let assholes touch her—"

"And you thought she's just like your ex. Fuck! She's not. She's a little awkward and barely holds her own, Nico."

She can hold her own just fucking fine if you ask me.

"She timid and useless at confrontation," he continues, his tone bordering on a scream. "She's *nothing* like Kaya."

"Yeah, I gathered that much when she explained why she didn't push Justin away. Then she told me about Asher." I pinch the bridge of my nose. "Listen, just check up on her, okay? I brought her home."

"Did you apologize?"

"I tried. She didn't let me."

"You're unbelievable! I knew you'd find a way to hurt her. I just assumed you'd fuck her when you said she's gorgeous."

He's hundreds of miles away, but his words fly all the way here, hitting me right in the gut. Cody's changed a lot over the past few years. From a careless, stupid kid to a man who not only has principles but acts on them, too.

He's more like me than any other Hayes in that department. Less of a short-tempered prick, though. That's Colt.

"She's yours, Cody. You're my brother. I wouldn't go after her, regardless of how pretty she is. I'm sorry I upset her, okay? I didn't want you to find out from her first."

Cody scoffs. "She won't tell me shit. She'll be too scared we'll argue."

"Too late for that."

"Damn right. Just stay away from her. She doesn't need your bullshit. She's got enough to deal with."

He cuts the call, not letting me get another word in. And once again, I'm uncomfortable in my own head. I never argue with my brothers. We disagree, sure, but I've never pissed any of them off the way I did Cody tonight.

It only goes to show how much he cares about Mia. He might be taking his sweet time, but he's serious about her. And I need to let that thought finally sink.

"We're here," the driver says, pulling me out of my head. "That your house, man?"

"Yeah."

He bobs his head, glancing out at the three-story villa I call home. "I don't feel bad about taking your cash anymore." He turns in his seat, handing me his card. "Call me if you ever need a ride."

I grab the card, ready to leave, but something on the seat

catches my eye. The peacock feather lies there crumpled, the stem broken in two places.

A moment later, I'm in my house, the feather in my hand and a questionable idea in my head.

Eleven

Mia

AISHA'S MOANS, TOBY'S GROWLS, and the bed slamming against the wall wake me up a few minutes past midnight.

Again.

Toby spent the weekend here, and judging by the size of the bag he brought yesterday, he won't leave anytime soon.

Aisha's not known to keep her men around longer than a night or two, so Toby might be a keeper. In her book, more than one night is grounds for a happily ever after. All the more that Toby already was in her bed.

And *he* was the one to call it quits last year.

I stuff two earphones in my ears, starting Nico's playlist to drown them out and get some sleep. I'm not mad at him anymore. I dissected what happened, taking the evening apart on a molecular level. I overanalyzed every second and realized not only was his reaction normal and justified, but his anger meant he was disappointed.

Maybe he likes me.

The *real* me.

I'm catching at straws, but I can't stop thinking about him, no matter how hard I try.

"Go" by Delilah plays in my ears, hitting all the right nerves and lulling me back to sleep. Nico has great taste in music— nothing rowdy, loud, or heavy.

The next time I wake up, it's bang-on six in the morning, the house perfectly silent.

Half an hour later, showered and dressed, I enter the kitchen, where Toby's making himself at home, brewing coffee in nothing but a pair of gray slacks hanging low on his hips. His colorful tattoos dance across his muscular back with every move.

"Morning," he says, smiling like the cat that got the birdy as he pushes a cup my way. "I love Mondays, don't you?"

"If I had three orgasms, I'd probably love Mondays, too."

He swallows a large gulp of his steaming coffee. It must hit the wrong pipe, and he breaks into a coughing fit. "You heard, huh?" he wheezes, coughing some more. "Sorry, we thought you were asleep."

"I was, but my sister would wake the dead. Don't look so mortified. I've had years to get used to this. Aisha's always been a screamer." I take an apple from a fruit bowl on the counter, snapping off the stalk before biting in. "And you're not the quietest, either."

An expression of bemused horror spreads across his face, and he parts his lips, but Aisha's voice cuts him off.

"That's why I bought you those cool headphones." She appears in a short silk robe, rising on her toes to kiss Toby's lips, the scene R-rated when she slides her hand to his groin, making him jump back. "So you won't eavesdrop." She looks over at me. "While we're on the subject of noise pollution, we're inviting a few friends over on Friday for board games. Either make yourself scarce or get a playlist ready."

"Since when do you play board games?"

Aisha shrugs, stealing Toby's coffee. "Since I'm dating a nerd. Toby here is a D&D king."

"It goes to show how much you know about D&D," he says. "They're called masters, not kings, and I've never played that. I hear it's fun, though."

Aisha shrugs again, utterly disinterested. "Whatever you want to play, as long as there are shots and a tiny chance we'll get bored and hit the club, I'm game." She shoots me a stern look. "I'd ask you to join us, but I know it's not your thing. You'd be bored."

I wouldn't. I'd probably have a better time than she would, but what's the point in arguing?

My good mood sinks like a stone flung in a river. "I'll stay out of your way."

Aisha never wanted me to spend time with her friends, fighting Dad to the bone whenever he said she had to take me to the movies with her. Any other day, her blatant '*I don't want you around*' would fly over my head, but today I'm disappointed. Nico will probably be here on Friday, having fun one room away while I'm locked in my bedroom.

"Alright, good," Aisha chirps, shoving a travel mug Toby filled with coffee into my hand to silently send me on my way.

***

"Time's up, kitten," Brandon hollers, entering the auditorium. "Deal or no deal?" He strolls closer, smiling at Blair, who sits a few rows down.

"No deal," I reply, leaning back to increase the distance between us after he stops a mere foot from my desk. "Should I expect you not to ask permission next time?"

"Alright, alright," Mr. Finch says, entering the room, wearing his signature no-nonsense expression. "Settle down, everyone. Brandon, unless you want to repeat freshman year, I suggest you get out of my class."

Brandon's jaw tightens as he leans over the desk. "I'm not an animal, kitten. I won't touch you unless—"

"Out, Mr. Price," Mr. Finch clips. "I won't ask again."

"This conversation is *not* over," he seethes, staring me down before he turns around and marches out the room.

As soon as he leaves the auditorium, Blair's attention is on me. My stomach churns, the first tendrils of a headache settling in. This won't be a good day. I know the reason behind her ugly scowl. She's jealous...

God knows why. Brandon's no prize, and I'm far from interested. He's vile, using Blair whenever he wants a break from sleeping around with half the girls on campus. She's the only one he comes back to for more, but the relationship Blair dreams about won't happen.

She cocks an eyebrow, her eyes shooting daggers my way before she nonchalantly turns away, focusing on Mr. Finch. Not even five minutes later, she excuses herself and doesn't return for the rest of the lecture.

Mr. Finch bores everyone in the auditorium, his voice sending half the students to sleep. Instead of making notes, I spend the hour writing lyrics.

I'm the first one out of there once class is dismissed but I stop dead when I glance at the opposite wall of the corridor, wallpapered with pictures of *me*.

Well, my face, not my body. Not a single picture of me naked exists, so these must've been photoshopped. They look like stills from a porn movie.

The woman uses toys, palms her breasts, sits on someone's face, or holds someone's dick. So many pictures of her on all fours pushing big dildos up her ass or being taken from behind in the shower. There's one in the backseat of a car where she spreads her legs wide, jamming two fingers inside her pussy...

Cheers erupt around me as students leave their classes, stopping to admire Blair's collage. I know it was her idea. She did this before, back in high school, but the pictures she tampered with back then were just lingerie models.

The football players howl, sauntering down the corridor, sleazy eyes jumping between me and the wall of pictures.

I can't unglue myself from the spot.

I can't utter a single word, and I can't peel my gaze away.

Brandon stops beside me, draping one arm over my shoulders. "Nice rack, kitten."

"It's not me," I whisper, tugging my rings. "They aren't real."

"Your tits aren't real?" he cackles, pulling me in.

"What did Jake always say?" Jessie Longman, Jake's best friend yells, exiting the auditorium. He elbows his way to the exhibition, snatching a picture of the woman sucking someone's dick. "Blow Job Lips. Fucking perfect!"

"What's this gathe—" Mr. Finch halts beside me, glaring at the wall, his face redder than Santa's hat.

"Those aren't real," I mutter again, pressing my hand to my lips, feeling sick and dizzy.

"Calm down, kitten. Nothing to be embarrassed about. You've got the sexiest body I've ever seen."

"Mia!" Cody booms somewhere close by.

Within seconds, he's right next to me, shoving Brandon away, and Colt's there, blocking my line of sight. In a confused daze, my legs move on their own accord as they usher me out and across the parking lot.

"Are you okay, Bug? Do you need to puke?" Conor jogs up, opening the back door to Cody's Mustang.

"What happened to your face?" I ask, pointing at a trickle of blood from his split lip.

"I couldn't hit Blair. She's a girl, but I could and did hit Brandon." He beams, demonstrating the right hook he sent Brandon's way. "Felt good."

"Please don't do that. It's pointless. He won't give up, and all you're doing is proving Nico right. I'm trouble, and—"

"You're trouble? You did nothing wrong," Cody growls, securing my seatbelt. "It's them that need to grow the fuck up. And Nico's an idiot. Who cares what he thinks?!"

"I do," I mumble, hiding my face in my hands. "Ugh, this is why he doesn't like college girls, isn't it? All that drama... I can't even blame him. I mean, this is ridiculous!"

"Um... Mia?" Conor summons my attention, turning around. Confusion flickers across his face as he stares from the passenger seat, his eyebrows pulled together, barely visible under the curls kissing his forehead. "Are you..." He shakes his head softly, dismissing that, and tries again. "Do you like Nico? Like, *like* like him?"

"Like like like him?" Colt repeats, hopping in beside me. "You should go back to high school, bro. And you only *now* realized she likes him?"

"I don't *like* like him," I blurt out, a whole level too defensive. "I mean, he's nice and caring and hot—" I slap a hand over my mouth, then hide behind a veil of hair, my skin warming under the blush spreading like a flame over my cheeks. I'm sure the triplets need no more. "Ugh, okay, fine. I do like him. I'm sorry..."

Cody forces a short, pained chuckle, readjusting the rearview mirror. "Hot, huh? I'll give you that, but *nice*? Come on! That's overkill. We're nice, Mia. Don't let his looks fool you. Nico's not an easy guy to deal with. He's a short-tempered, arrogant, foul-mouthed control freak, and you can't stand up for yourself. He'd swallow you whole."

"He's not that bad," I mutter, glancing between Conor and Colt only to find the former digging through my bag for snacks and the latter glaring at Cody. "What's wrong?"

"Nothing," Colt says, marshaling his expression into what I think he believes is relaxed but looks more like he's trying to smile while chewing a lemon. "All good. How about we take you out for coffee and ice cream?"

I lean to the side, nuzzling my cheek against him. "Sounds nice."

***

"Ah, just who I wanted to see." Finn Ash, the football team's cornerback, steps in my way.

Whatever he wants, I don't have time or energy to deal with another football player who's undoubtedly here to *do me a favor*. Considering the plan Justin mentioned without divulging information, it's safe to assume Finn's in on it, too.

I'm almost jogging down the corridor toward the recording studio where Six is waiting, overly excited about a track he's working on. He called while I was having lunch with the triplets and asked if I could write the lyrics.

Reluctantly, I stop, adjusting the strap of my bag to grip it so I can use it as a weapon if need be. It's not every day I'm approached by someone from the football team, if not counting the quarterback himself.

I glance around, checking if there's anyone else nearby, but no. We're alone. The thought makes my heart beat a little faster.

"Why did you want to see me?" I ask, inconspicuously unzipping my bag to easily access the pepper spray.

"What are you doing tonight? Wanna grab dinner?"

My eyes widen, and my mind reels. I check the corridor again before a light bulb lights up over my head. "Those pictures weren't real, Finn. It wasn't me. My face was photoshopped in."

"I know. I'm doing graphic design, and that was a lousy job. I'm not asking you out because of the pictures."

"Then why are you asking?"

He shrugs, shoving his hands in his pockets. "You're cute. I like that you don't let Brandon get his way. You're intriguing, and I want to get to know you."

"Oh, um... thank you," I mutter, believing none of it.

"So? Can I pick you up tonight?"

"No, sorry."

"Come on, one date. I'm not trying to put a ring on you. What's the harm in grabbing dinner? You'll leave if it's not fun and no harm done. We're not all idiots, you know?"

"I'm sure you're not, but—"

"Mia, you alright here?" Six rounds the corner, emerging from a side corridor. "Come on, we're on a tight schedule."

I send Finn an apologetic smile. "I have to go."

"Yeah, okay, but think about it. I'll find you later." He winks before strutting away.

"What did he want?" Six asks as we fall into step toward the recording studio.

"He asked me out."

"Shut up!" he yells, pushing me away playfully. "No way, you little liar. You're not his type."

I'm a bit taken aback by his disbelief. He knows I've been out on a few dates, but he's acting like I just grew a second head. "How would you know what his type is?"

"I see him at the frat parties. You're not the type any of the football guys go for, Mia. You're too... *soft*."

Don't you just love when people judge you by your style? I love pretty dresses, but that doesn't mean I'm soft. I've always taken care of myself, growing up without a mom, because Faith Harlow wasn't cut out to be a parent. She was overwhelmed by the responsibility, too young to appreciate kids.

She was only sixteen when Aisha was born. She tried to suck it up for a few years, but just when she started to regain her independence, I happened. An unplanned accident that destroyed all her plans.

She bailed, craving the life she never had because she got pregnant at fifteen.

Dad did his best to juggle his career and raise two daughters, but he wasn't around much, traveling the world with his F1 team. The person who was supposed to be responsible for me and Aisha—our grandad—battled alcoholism until he died four years ago. I've endured years of bullying, ridicule, and humiliation, but I never let any of that define me.

Am I socially awkward? Sure. It's hard being the life of the party when I'm excluded at every turn. I'm an introvert by necessity, not choice. I'm quiet, wary, and *weird*, but I'm *not* soft.

"So? What did he want?" Six inquires when I come in the recording booth, dropping my bag.

"I told you. He asked me out."

"Fine, let's say he did. You know there's some hidden agenda there, don't you? Don't be stupid, Mia."

"Of course, because no one could possibly be interested in me otherwise," I clip, putting the headphones on.

"Hey, don't get upset. I didn't mean it that way, you know? I'm sorry, it's just that—"

"Put the music on."

He shuts up, the words wiped off his lips. A second later, the beat starts in my ears, and words flood my mind.

Twelve

Nico

TOBY MADE HIMSELF COMFORTABLE at Aisha's place, which she shares with her little sister. They invited a few friends over for board games tonight...

Maybe it'd be wiser to stay home, away from Mia, but I'm not fooling myself. I want to see her again.

I *need* to see her again.

The triplets are attending yet another frat party, so I've got a range of solid excuses at the ready. I should keep an eye on Mia for Cody. Yeah, that's cool. It's nice of me, right?

Wrong. Bullshit is what it is.

I just can't shake this girl. The more I get to know her, the deeper I sink. Her mindset, personality, cleverness, and talent draw me in more than her body ever could. I hop in my car around seven in the evening, and ten minutes later, I ring the doorbell. Anticipation tingles in my neck—yet another reason

I should've stayed home.

Mia's getting under my skin.

Fuck that. She's already deep under my skin. I need to stop seeking her out to save us both the misery.

After all, I'm not blind. I see how she reacts to me, and the fact my brother wants her makes everything about this situation fucked up.

Shit, even if Cody was still just her big brother by choice, Mia's not what I need. She's gullible and trusting. Innocent... oblivious to the monstrosities of the world.

I'd bend her to my will without an effort. She'd let me. She'd dance to every tune I'd play, and that's a big *no*. I need a woman who won't let me get away with shit I can't control.

"Hello there, baby boy," Aisha chirps, letting me in. "Glad you made it."

She leads me across the hallway into the open-plan living area. An off-white grand piano partially hides floor-to-ceiling windows. A Yamaha, just as Mia said.

How fucked up is it that I want to order a bright yellow model C for her? I overheard Cody say it's Mia's favorite color, and a Steinway would fit perfectly in this space.

Toby sits in one of the two identical navy wing chairs, and Adrian's sprawled on the five-seat leather sofa with some woman, but no sign of Mia.

I shake their hands, accepting a drink from Aisha, then scan the room more, taking in the immaculate mid-century modern interior, rows of books on floating shelves, and huge pictures of both Harlow girls dotting the southern wall.

In one of them, Mia plays the piano in a white, flowy dress, her blonde locks cascading down her back, fingers on the keys. The other picture is a portrait. She gazes into the camera, resting her arm on an electric keyboard propped against the wall. Her hair is curly, her lips parted, eyes bright.

"You see something you like?" Toby pats my back, walking past to help Aisha. "She's not here."

Aisha zeroes in on me, cocking one eyebrow. "She's out. She's got a hot date."

A surge of possessiveness spills under my skin like a contusion, and this time, I swear, it's not just for me but Cody, too. I'd much rather see Mia with my brother than some random guy. At least that way, I could keep an eye on her; make sure Cody behaves himself.

"A date?" I grind out. "Who with?"

"Some guy from college."

I pull out my phone and text Cody.

Me: You know your girl's on a date right now?

"About time she gets herself out there instead of sitting at the piano all day," Aisha muses. "Maybe once she finds a guy she likes, she'll stop being so odd."

My phone vibrates in my hand.

Cody: Fuck. Who with?

Me: Some guy from college.

"Isn't *date* just a euphemism for *sex?*" Adrian asks, scratching his beard. "Girls can have fun too. She's a teen. It's what they do, isn't it?"

Aisha bursts out laughing. "Way to put everyone in the same bag, asshat. Sure, some teenagers sleep around, but others don't. Mia's in the latter group. She almost burst into flames when she saw Toby in his boxers. Just because we're sisters doesn't mean we're alike. Far from it, actually. I had my cherry popped at homecoming my sophomore year of high school, and Mia's still a virgin at nineteen, so no, she's not hooking up with guys she eats dinner with."

I can't say I'm surprised Mia's not had sex yet, but the confirmation still almost knocks me off my damn feet.

It's a good thing I'm sitting.

My head fills with images of her on my bed, hair sprawled across the pillow, lips parted as I push into her in an unrushed rhythm. Mia on all fours, boobs crushed against the sheets, fingers digging into the side of the bed while I plunge as deep as I can get to make her tremble.

Mia on her back, my face buried between her legs...

Sex is physical. It's primal. It's *natural*. While men are more or less born understanding this, women learn in the process.

The first time is important not because it's a magical threshold but because it starts a lifetime of pleasure. The more comfortable the girl feels, the higher the chance she'll demand what she wants and take what she needs later.

Men experience sex differently. A shitty first time probably won't ruin it for a guy for years to come, but it might for a woman. Girls need to feel safe and comfortable in their skin. If the guy is an egotistical asshole, it might take a long time before she learns to enjoy sex instead of overthinking how she looks or sounds.

People don't talk about sex enough. It's still a hush-hush topic in many families, and that shielding hides it away on a taboo pedestal where it doesn't belong. Sex is one of the most basic human needs.

We breathe, eat, sleep, and fuck.

"Hello!" is yelled from the hallway.

Alex, one of Adrian's soccer buddies, walks in with a blonde teen on his arm and another right behind. One glance at the unnatural movement of his eyebrows proves he brought her for me. He still didn't get the memo: I don't touch teens.

But I'd touch Mia.

God, I'd touch her *everywhere.*

Alex wraps his arms around Aisha, kisses her cheek, and hands over a bottle of tequila.

"Shots?" she asks, eyeing the girls. "You sure?"

"Yeah, I'm sure."

It takes two hours of playing *Hot Seat* before Mia comes back. The quiet click of the front door has my head turning in the direction of the hallway, but instead of joining us, her soft footsteps retreat, and another door closes behind her.

"She won't even say *hey?*" Adrian asks, his eyebrows pulled together. "That's rude."

"She's doing what she's told," Toby clarifies with a scowl. "Aisha doesn't want her here."

"Because she's such a buzzkill!"

She's been riling me up for months but never this fast. "She's your sister."

"Doesn't change facts, does it? I invited her to spend time with my friends once, and Mia got so uncomfortable with jokes she puked her guts out."

"Nico's right. She's your sister, babe," Toby drawls, wrapping his arm around her shoulders. "Ask her to come out here. She doesn't have to play. She can just have a drink."

With a huff and an eyeroll, Aisha stumbles down the hallway. We hear the knock but not their conversation, and a moment later, she's back alone. "She's busy."

"Which door?" I ask, not buying that.

"Second on the right."

I head down there, tap my knuckles against the frame, and enter. My mind goes quiet at the sound of "Graceland" by Allan Rayman. Since I heard him on Mia's playlist, I've listened to everything he recorded.

Mia jumps, startled, and my brain fucking freezes.

She stands by the bed. Her blonde waves dance around her face, kissing her arms before falling lower.

My attention is not on her hair for long, stolen by her body dressed in nothing but a pair of low panties cut out to accentuate the curve of her hips. She covers her boobs with her hands but isn't doing a good job. Pale pink areolas peek between her fingers.

I think I'm having a stroke.

My heart rams in my chest so hard every beat pulsates in my fingertips. My cock hardens faster than I can blink.

I'm aware that I'm staring... silent, *speechless*, taking her in over again, skimming down from blonde hair, rosy cheeks, and barely parted lips to protruding collarbones and the delicate skin of her cleavage. The hourglass dent of her waist, deep navel, and round hips. Smooth legs, gold anklet, then up again, drinking in the sight.

Committing it to memory.

My chest tightens so hard it's enough to fucking choke me.

"Jesus..." I whisper on an exhale, then fill my lungs again, looking into Mia's green eyes. "You're beautiful, baby."

Her body taunts me, draws me in, and tortures me in ways I never thought could cause pain.

Her cheeks blush like a well-trained sunrise, and she shudders, fighting to hold my gaze. "I didn't say *come in.*"

"Fuck," I pinch the bridge of my nose, turning away from the girl I want so much I question my sanity. "I should... I should apologize for walking in, Mia, but..." Why? Why is she so gorgeous? Why is she Cody's? "...I can't. I'm *not* sorry. I'll let you get dressed, but not in that night dress you've got ready on your bed. I expect you to join us for a drink."

"Um... okay," she says quietly.

And I leave, bursting out of there like I'm being chased by cops. The image of her, almost naked, is burned into my hippocampus for-fucking-ever. I'm not getting it out of there even if I open my head and pour a bucket of bleach in.

I down my drink in one go, taking a seat on the piano stool. I'm mentally pep-talking myself, keeping it together until Mia comes over a minute later.

"How was the date?" Aisha asks.

"It was fine."

Her tone is far from fine. I don't like the insecurity radiating off her or the fact she hasn't looked at me once. Either she's embarrassed or still annoyed about my stunt last week.

"So? Second date material?"

Mia cringes as if the mere idea of seeing the guy again makes her nauseous. "Unfortunately, no."

Thank fuck for small favors.

She sips the wine, then makes her way across. I think she'll take the empty wingchair to my left, but she sits arm-in-arm with me on the piano stool.

I'm relieved.

Maybe she's not that mad.

"Okay, what happened?" Toby demands after he introduces Mia to Alex. "What did I tell you before you left? Tell me what he did."

"He kissed me."

I'm starting to really hate my mood swings. From aroused and calm to fuming in a flash. Violence quivers within me like a loose wire at the thought of anyone's hands or lips on Mia's delicate body.

"Okay, you'll have to explain this a bit more," Toby says, scratching his chin. "You shot him down because he kissed you on a date?"

"No. I shot him down because he *can't* kiss."

Alex bursts out laughing. "I had no idea there's a wrong way. I mean sex, sure, either you're good at it, or you're not, but kissing?"

Mia crosses her legs, the movement nowhere near the iconic scene in *Naked Instinct* but five times more titillating. My eyes are drawn to her ankle bracelet, or rather the tattoo just above. I've noticed it before but couldn't make out what it was: a word in a foreign language. Greek, I think.

"You can definitely do it wrong," she admits. "Take Finn. His kiss was a five out of ten."

"This is actually interesting," Toby says, leaning back in the wing chair to make room on his lap for Aisha. "Come to think of it, I've had my fair share of lousy kisses, but never rated them. Do you kiss every guy at the end of the first date?"

"No. They kiss me. I let them because what's the point in taking things further if they can't kiss well? I like it too much to date a guy who can't."

My phone vibrates in my pocket, stealing my attention. Good. I'm barely keeping my hands to myself right now.

Cody: Is she back yet?

Me: Yeah. You can relax. Finn can't kiss, so no second date. What the hell are you waiting for? Act before someone steals her from you.

If he forces my hand, it will be me.

"Alright, let's check." Alex gets up, pulling one of the teens with him, and shoves his tongue down her throat while his hands grope her butt.

Cody: I'm working on it. I see she told you about her rating system. You two are getting close, bro. Back off.

The fucking nerve of him. Who the hell does he think he is to see right through my bullshit?

Me: Whatever your strategy is, it's failing.

"Rate that from one to ten, babe," Alex purrs, pulling away.

"About... six and a half?"

"*Six*?!" he exclaims, disbelieving, then all-out embarrassed when we burst out laughing. "Seriously?! So you all have a rating system? Where has this information been all my life?"

"I'll give you a few pointers," Toby smirks, but Aisha chooses that moment to shoot him down.

"You're barely a nine yourself."

"Nine? No way. I'm a ten."

"You're a ten when you kiss my other lips. Those..." She pats her mouth, "...you need to work on."

And he does, determined to up his score.

I turn to Mia, leaning closer for no reason. My body drifts toward her whenever we're in the same room. Now she sits inches away, the sweet scent of her wafting around us...

My bones have been broken, my knuckles bled a hundred times, yet not being able to touch Mia is the cruelest torture.

"What does it mean?" I ask, pointing at her tattoo.

"*Soteria*. In Greek mythology, she was the goddess of safety and preservation from harm."

That's an odd choice, but I bet there's a story behind it. "You got any more?"

"We've got sister tattoos." Aisha pulls away from Toby, jumping to her feet and rolling her blouse up, showing me a small dandelion under her bra line. "Mia's got it in the same place."

"I guess it's not without meaning."

"It symbolizes joy and youth," Mia admits.

"What else do you have?"

She turns her back to me. "Just under my hairline."

I watch goosebumps appear in the wake of my fingers brushing her skin. My chest tightens. The urge to kiss the tender spot below her ear hits me like a snake in tall grass. I keep the desire on a leash, touching the little musical note on Mia's nape. The meaning of this one doesn't need explaining.

I let her hair fall freely before she tugs the fabric of her skirt higher. My pulse speeds up with every inch of her bare skin. She's trying to fucking kill me.

Another tattoo comes into view. One word: *strength*, curled around a pale scar. Maybe I would've noticed it just now when I saw her almost naked if I weren't so dumbstruck.

"That's all of them," she says, pulling the dress back down. "For now."

"Right, we had fun. Now we're going out," Aisha chirps, pecking Toby's head. "I'll get changed," she adds, then speaks through clenched teeth. "Do you want to come, Mia?"

141

"Um... no, thank you."

"Maybe we could stay?" Toby asks, treading lightly not to upset Aisha. "Mia's had a lousy date. Let's play more games. Monopoly?"

Aisha frowns, a flat sheen of murder glowing in her eyes for a second before she realizes Toby's watching. "Oh, sure." A pained smile crosses her lips, but she's trying hard not to come across as a bitch who doesn't give a crap about her sister. "Yeah, why not. Monopoly sounds super fun."

"I'm fine," Mia says, coming to Aisha's rescue. "Go have fun."

"Only if you're sure!" Aisha sing-songs, already halfway down the hallway.

She's back in a heartbeat, still zipping up a tiny black dress. Panting and wheezing, she turns her back to Toby, urging him to deal with the stuck zipper.

If Mia were mine and decided to go out dressed like that, she'd be an accessory to fucking murder. I'd never forbid her wearing whatever she wanted, but I'd throw my fists at anyone who'd dare to look longer than appropriate.

Soon enough, the cab arrives, and Aisha almost breaks a leg, rushing to the door with the other girls. "I'll clean the mess up when I'm back, sis."

Everyone's out the door two minutes later while I'm casually strolling toward the kitchen to place my glass in the sink.

I don't want to go. Not without Mia.

"Have fun!" she shouts, grabbing a handful of shot glasses off the table.

"Can I apologize for last weekend without being interrupted?" I ask when she joins me in the kitchen.

"No need. I wasn't mad, just hurt, but you had a point—"

"No, I didn't. I let my own experience cloud my judgment.

Don't change how you deal with guys like Justin if it keeps you safe." I spin her around, hooking my index finger under her chin, and tilt her head back. "I'm sorry."

"I know. It's okay."

"It's not okay, Mia. Don't let me off the hook that easily. I don't like seeing you sad, and I hate I made you cry," I insist, letting my guard slip as I drop my gaze to her lips.

I've never wanted to kiss a girl so much.

Whenever she's this close, I forget about whatever feelings Cody has for her. I should talk to him because this... this is wrong on every single level. I'm a pendulum around her.

I want her, and I don't want her.

I want her, and I can't have her.

I want her, and she doesn't need my crazy.

From what I've learned so far, Mia wants her man to take care of her, but I'm sure she wouldn't want the unhealthy overprotectiveness I picked up three years ago.

The jealousy.

The rage.

She wouldn't want me keeping tabs on her to ensure she's safe; deciding whom she could be friends with so she wouldn't waste time with people who are bad influences or those who can't be trusted. As much as I'd like to keep that part of my character in check, I know it was why Kaya cheated on me with Jared. She couldn't stand the control.

No sane person would, but knowing I'm overreacting and ridding myself of the compulsive habits are two different things.

It's a disease like alcoholism.

I'm an addict, but my poison isn't lethal, no matter the dose. My poison affects those around me more than me, but it's as hard to quit as heroin or vodka.

"You're forgiven," she says, her voice a loaded whisper.

"Come with us, Mia. One drink. I'll take you home if you don't enjoy yourself."

"Thank you, but no." She leans her back against the cabinets. "You've got the other girl to take care of. Why do you want me to come?"

I grip the marble countertop on both sides of her waist, the gesture uncontrollable. The moment I see her resting against something, I want to box her in, act on the intense need to keep her close, sheltered, *safe*.

"I don't want her. One drink," I repeat quieter.

"One drink," she agrees with a shy smile. "You make me self-conscious when you look at me like that."

"Like what?"

"Like I'm a warm triple chocolate brownie with a side of vanilla ice cream, and you're on a strict no-sugar diet."

The electric stress between us rears its full power, and I snap. So fucking fast I don't see it coming. I grip her waist, hauling her onto the kitchen island, and immediately move my hands to her thighs.

She's soft and warm and smells so sweet. "I've been on a no-sugar diet for a while."

I slide my hands up, up, *up* her thighs, the tips of my fingers disappearing under her skirt. She trembles. Softly, but it sends heat surging across my nerve endings.

God... I need her lips more than my next breath. We're both softly panting with need. Sparks fly between us, and I almost fucking lose it when she parts those plump lips, her eyes darting to meet mine as she pulls down a shaky breath.

"Is... um, is the other girl a brownie, too?"

"She's a peanut M&M at best."

My phone vibrates in my pocket. Two short vibrations mean it's a text message. Instantly, without checking, I know it's Cody.

My insides freeze. Lust morphs to shame, but I can't unglue my hands from Mia's warm skin. "Push me away," I tell her, the words like razorblades slicing my tongue. "Now. You need to push me away."

Her eyes lose their glow, and her smile slips. Disappointment clouds her pretty face, but like a good girl, she braces both hands against my chest, barely putting any pressure.

"I'm sorry, Mia, but this... *we*... we won't fucking happen."

Thirteen

Mia

"I KNOW YOU DON'T LIKE FLYING, but maybe you could come watch?" Conor asks, shielding his eyes from the spring sun.

It's almost the end of April. The temperature outside finally holds in the low seventies, and coats and cardigans are no longer required.

"If you promise you won't try and convince me to jump, I'll watch."

The Hayes clan is skydiving on Friday, raising money for Monica's Charity. This time, she chose to help a women's shelter in Newport. Nico immediately pledged ten thousand for every Hayes and plus one who jumps.

Cody hands me a small tube of cookie dough ice cream he bought at the cafeteria. "It'd end with you puking all over the plane. Don't worry. We won't push. Just come and watch. I'm pretty sure Shawn will cry. You don't want to miss that."

"Why is he jumping if he's scared?"

"Ego," Conor says, stuffing his mouth with a spoonful of my ice cream. "We've got bets going on who'll bail. You want in?"

"I bet *you'll* be the first one out of that plane, and you..." I point at Cody, "...will land somewhere you shouldn't."

"Nico will be the first one out of the plane," Colt predicts, then scowls at something behind my back.

I turn to see Justin Montgomery making his way across the field, eyes on me.

"Not again," Cody mutters, ripping the label off his coke bottle. "I don't fucking like this, Mia. Don't you think it's odd they all suddenly want to take you out?"

"I don't like it, either," Colt huffs. "I could understand Finn, but you've been hit on by three different guys today alone. Something's off, Bug."

"You're overreacting," Conor drawls, laying back on the bleachers. "I overheard Finn talking to Ryan this morning. He sounded pretty bummed you shot him down."

"And suddenly, every guy wants to date her?" Cody hisses quietly, glaring at Justin, who's making his way up the bleachers like he's climbing the stairs. "They didn't know she existed before our Spring Break party."

"Exactly." Conor throws his arm over his eyes. Unaware that Justin is now within earshot. "Now they do. She's polite, smart, and really pretty, don't you agree? Why wouldn't they want to date her?"

"I agree," Justin says, bro-shaking hands with the triplets. "Come on, Mia, we need to talk."

I pull my eyebrows together. "Why? Is something wrong?"

"You can talk here," Colt adds, folding his arms.

"No, we can't. Come on, sweetheart. Five minutes."

Cody clamps his jaw, grinding his teeth when I get up, following Justin down the steps and around the corner, where he stops at the mouth of the tunnel leading to the changing rooms.

He bends his knee, propping his foot against the wall, gaze locked on me as he rubs his neck before pushing a sharp breath down his nose. "I'm risking my head here, so you gotta promise this stays between us."

I don't like the sound of that, but I nod, waiting for whatever he has to say.

"You've been marked, Mia."

"Marked? What does that mean?"

"It means you've got a big red X painted on your back courtesy of Brandon. Remember when I told you he's getting really creative? Well, the game's afoot. The guys who asked you out? Sorry to be the bearer of bad news, but they don't want to date you. They want to fuck you. The first one who does wins the money."

"Money?" I choke, feeling as if he smacked something hard against my temple. "What money?"

"You didn't take Brandon's deal, so he put five grand up for the first guy who gets you in bed."

Shame mixes with disappointment. Tears immediately prickle my eyes. "This makes no sense... he wanted me for himself, why would he—"

"My guess is he hopes you'll give up once the guys start getting too forward. The prize is internal, limited to the guys on the team, but you know shit spreads like wildfire here. It won't be long before this gets out, and then who knows how many guys you'll have to deal with." He rakes his hand through his hair, pushing away from the wall. "I told you I was trying to do you a solid. My offer stands. Brandon will find a way to break you sooner or later, so just think about getting ahead of him."

I scoff, swatting the first tears away. "You think offering to punch my V card to spite Brandon is doing me a solid? If you want to help, *lie*. Tell him I caved. Tell him we had sex."

Justin lets his eyes rove my body. "I wish we did. I won't play the game. I don't care about the money, but I won't lie." He lifts his hand, pushing a wayward lock of my hair behind my ear, then wipes my cheeks with his thumbs. "It's just sex, Mia. Think about it. And maybe don't tell the triplets about the prize. I have a feeling they'll go throwing punches, and that'll only rile Brandon up."

He drops his hand, walking away, leaving me alone and shaking. I take a few deep breaths to calm down, ignoring the hot ball of hurt burning my stomach.

"What did he want?" Cody clips when I sit down beside him, gathering my things. "He asked you out?"

"Yes, but don't worry, I said no."

"Where are you going?" Conor asks, hauling himself around to sit up.

"Library. Don't wait for me. I'll take a cab home."

***

I peer up from the music sheet at the sound of rain pattering against the windows. It's dark outside. I didn't notice it get dark. After the chat with Justin, I left the triplets and went home, ditching my last lectures to play piano at home.

"There's a storm rolling in," Toby says, and I damn near jump out of my skin.

I turn around, finding him on the couch with a sketchpad in hand and an empty cup of coffee on the table.

"You sure get in the zone when you play. I've been here for an hour now. I even asked if you were hungry."

"Sorry, it's been a long day."

"It's cool. Turns out, listening to you play fuels my creativity." He turns the sketchpad, showing me a tattoo design. A typewriter with strings of words rising like smoke and different flowers complementing the picture. "What do you think?"

"Is that for Aisha?"

"Yeah, she wants a whole sleeve. This is just the start."

"I think you're very talented."

He smiles humbly, and we both look out the window when a flash of lightning clips outside like a camera flash.

"That's my cue," I say, a jolt of excitement heating the blood in my veins.

Toby shouts something behind me as I bolt to my room, but the bang of my door closing cuts him off. I pull a hoodie from the wardrobe, throwing it over my dress. It's gray, five sizes too big, and not even mine.

I got it from James, a driver on my dad's team, when I went to see the race in Austin last year. We sat outside until the early morning hours in front of a dying fire, toasting marshmallows and drinking champagne with a few other drivers. The air was chilly, so James pulled his hoodie off and forced it on me despite my weak protests. I never gave it back.

"I'm going out!" I yell into the kitchen not a minute later, pulling the hair on top of my head into a ponytail. Then I slip on a pair of white sneakers, grab the keys, and close the door behind me.

I breathe in the fresh, crisp air, feeling giddy like I'm floating out of my body. I pull the hoodie up, heading down the driveway, turning right at the bottom, toward the beach. The rain drenches my clothes within minutes, but it doesn't bother me. It's refreshing. Purifying, somehow.

A low rumble comes from the seaside, and seconds later, another bolt of lightning cuts across the sky, illuminating the black canvas above with stark bluish whiteness.

The beauty of the spectacle forces my legs to work harder. I don't want to miss another second of the show. I break into a jog, trying to avoid the puddles initially, but a few hundred yards later I no longer care. I sprint, hearing another low rumble.

Halfway across the street the piercing sound of a horn makes me jump. Too impatient to stop, I wave my hand in apology and keep going.

Darkness settles around me when I reach the sandy beach a few minutes later. I made it in time. A bright, long burst of lightning tears through the sky, hitting the ocean far away, jolting zestful energy through my bones.

I kick my shoes off, enjoying the wet sand under my bare feet, then climb the lifeguard station and sit on the floor under a narrow overhanging roof.

The wind grows in strength, screaming in my ears as the rain slams against the foaming, angry sea. White-crested waves claw at the shore, reaching further inland where the sand dances under the attack of heavy raindrops.

It's reassuring to watch something so sinister and dangerous and not feel an ounce of fear... funny because my heart almost bursts at the sound of *his* voice.

Fourteen

Nico

I ALMOST KILLED HER.

She jumped onto the street out of nowhere, running mere inches from the hood of my car. I stopped, stamping the brake and simultaneously slamming my hand on the horn, making her jump.

Her hood fell off, revealing a mass of wet, blonde hair and the side of a pretty face that made me realize *who* this careless girl was.

She didn't stop, just waved her hand and ran into the darkness. Into the pouring rain, cutting across lawns and between buildings. I followed, driving around until I found her at the beach, kicking off her shoes.

"What the hell are you up to?" I mutter, watching her run toward a lifeguard tower. "Fucking reckless," I groan, killing the engine.

The rain hammers the windscreen hard enough that the wipers can't keep up. According to the weather forecast, it's supposed to get worse. A red weather warning has been issued in OC with projected winds reaching eighty miles an hour. And she's out on the beach like it's an eighty-five-degree sunny day.

I slam the door shut, shuddering under the pouring rain. I'm drenched within a minute as I cross the pavement onto the sand, jogging toward the tower.

"What the hell are you doing?" I boom, rounding the corner. "It's pouring it down, Mia."

She watches me climb the ramp. "You know, once every now and then, you could start a conversation with *hey* instead of yelling. How did you know where I was?"

"*Hey.* You jumped out in front of my car. I almost hit you. Why are you here?"

She gestures to the angry ocean. "I'm enjoying the show."

"Get up. I'm taking you home."

"Thank you, but—"

"I said *get up.* You'll catch pneumonia if you stay here any longer. You're soaking wet, and this will get worse fast."

"I'll be fine. I always sit here when it rains."

I crouch before her, growing more annoyed when I realize the hoodie she's wearing is a men's size large at least. "Whose hoodie is this?"

She glances down like she has to check which fucker's hoodie she put on today before she answers.

"Um, it's James's. Why?"

"And who's James? Your boyfriend?"

Lighting crashes into one of the lamps on the pier, and we watch the rest flicker out one by one.

"No, he's a friend. The best driver my dad ever had in his

team if you want to believe his word."

I clench my teeth, reining the urge to tear that hoodie off and give her mine. "I'll fling you over my shoulder if I have to. Don't fucking test me, Mia. Be a good girl and get up."

"I know this is uncomfortable, wet, and cold... Please don't feel you have to stay. I know my way home." An adorable frown twists her pretty face before she quietly adds, "You can't tell me what to do."

"Watch me." I lunge forward, grip her waist and—as promised—haul her up, then over my shoulder, not breaking a sweat. She weighs a quarter of what I bench at the gym. I wrap my hand around her thighs so she doesn't slide down my back and face-plant the ground. "We're leaving."

"Let me go!" she squeals, bombarding my back with tiny fists. "Oh God! What are you doing?! Put me down!"

She's soaked through and so cold. "If you end up sick, we'll have a problem."

"Nico!" Mia whacks my back again, the blow barely noticeable against the raindrops. "Put me down! This isn't funny."

"Am I laughing? You're not staying here in the rain."

She wiggles a little bit, arching further down my back as her hip butts against my head, and then—

"Fuck!" My grip tightens around her legs. "You did *not* just do that. Open your mouth."

She clamps her teeth harder into the flesh around my ribs, then eases off enough to speak. "You lied! You said hands go where it hurts! Put me down!"

"No." I quicken my pace, stepping onto the pavement. My back straightens like a metal rod when she bites again. "Stop it, Mia." I open the passenger door, nudging her butt. "Let go." She shakes her head, still buried in my flesh like a vampire, her teeth digging deeper. Without thinking twice, I lift her skirt and slap her ass. The sound of my palm connecting with her damp, cold skin makes my cock twitch. "I said *let go.*"

That does it. She gasps, twisting back enough to hold herself straight and brace against me, her cheeks scarlet, a tiny river of rain trickling down her chin.

"You spanked me," she mutters, doll-like shock painting her gorgeous face.

"Only once. You bit me twice." I arrange her arms and legs until she's safely tucked in the passenger seat.

"You *spanked* me," she says again when I take the wheel.

A gleam of puzzled delight shines through her surprise, and my cock stirs hell.

Jesus, baby... you liked that?

"Next time you pull a stunt like this, I'll put you over my knee. You won't sit for days." I'm not sure if it's a promise or a threat at this point.

"You're insane..."

I readjust myself in the seat, filling my mind with toads, cauliflower, and rats to counteract the anxious prickling of desire coursing through my veins.

It works. My cock settles, and I shift into reverse but don't release the brake. "Put your seatbelt on, Mia."

She stares me down, all adorable defiance, but folds quickly, buckling up.

"Good girl. You better hope you didn't catch a cold out there." I reverse onto the road, taking the shortest way to her house so she can take a hot bath.

"I've got Tylenol and a huge backlist of books to get through. I won't mind a few days in bed."

"You also have a Ball to attend this weekend."

***

Forty minutes later, I slam the door to my house, stomp up the stairs, and get straight under the showerhead, stripping off the wet clothes as a stream of hot water patters my back. You wouldn't think my dick could be hard again while my teeth clatter, but it is.

Painfully hard.

Fuck...

Mia all wet, angry, and turned on by the slap. I have that aroused, surprised gleam of her eyes saved in my memory bank, the *delete* button grayed out, unavailable.

I palm the base of my cock, squeezing hard, and let my mind off the short leash. I need to live out the fantasy. I've imagined fucking her, but those clips were short, second-long bursts of me thrusting into Mia... I can't live on scraps anymore. I need the whole thing, or I won't move forward.

Once.

Just this once, I'll give in...

I've not done this since the night I met her, refusing to jerk off to the thought of my brother's girl, but it's either that or popping pills.

The door to my bedroom closes with a click, and my head snaps in that direction. She's there. Soaking wet, trembling from the cold rain saturating her dress and that hoodie she better never wear again, or I won't be held accountable for my actions.

She steps forward, holding my gaze. "I'm so cold," she utters softly, chin trembling as she stops by the pane of glass separating the bedroom from the showcase shower.

Gorgeous. So fucking gorgeous.

Every tense, knotted muscle in my body relaxes. The buzz littering my head fades; nothing but soul-soothing quiet blanketing my thoughts. That's what she does. She cages my demons, introducing a kind of stuffed-inside, tranquil feeling.

"Come here." I hold my hand out, waiting for her to take it. Waiting for her to trust me. To lose herself, obey, and submit to the pull between us.

Instead of a step forward, she steps back, pulling the gray hoodie off before reaching behind her to unzip the dress. It falls down her smooth thighs, every inch of her petite body as perfect as I'd memorized.

I stroke myself. Slowly. So fucking *slowly*, savoring every second, prolonging the moment.

Mia steps out of her dress, nothing but lacey, beige lingerie covering her body. Lord, you created perfection. Shy, cute, unreasonably titillating. She steps forward, one small foot after the other, and takes my hand, giving up control.

I yank her to me, the urgency of my touch like the kickback of a gun. She's close. As close as I've wanted for weeks. Her back to my chest, my arms around her, one under her ribs, the other clasped over her collarbones.

I hold her, soothe her... *protect* her.

"You're trembling." I drop my head, pressing an open-mouthed kiss to the dip in her shoulder. "Your pretty butt will sting for days if you ever do that again."

She sighs, leaning into me. "I like the rain."

"And I like knowing you're safe, warm, and comfortable."

She spins around, tracing the muscles on my arms with the tips of her fingers as she looks into my eyes. "I'm here now. You've got me, Nico. What will you do with me?"

I tilt my head back, letting the hot water patter my face,

and squeeze my cock at the base, stroking faster.

"I'll take care of you, baby." I haul her up. She wraps her legs around my waist. "Warmer?" I ask, standing in a spot where the water cascades down Mia's back.

"Not yet. Hold me closer."

My lips are level with hers. The feverish need to taste her spreads through my veins, giving me second-degree burns.

"You have me where you want me," she reminds me, resting her forehead against mine, her small hands cupping my face. "Why aren't you taking? Take, Nico."

I bury my face in her neck, breathing her in. Honeysuckle. Sweet... so fucking sweet. I peck her skin lightly, *slowly*... letting her feel the heat of my breath.

The pace of my hand pumping the length of my cock turns unforgiving.

I look up, our lips, our *kiss* a whisper away...

And I still just as the release detonates at the base of my spine, and the load splatters the tiles. A low, pained growl flies past my lips.

"I can't have you, baby," I grunt into the empty room, my eyes closed, the orgasm stripping me of the firewall. "You're not mine to take, no matter how much I want you."

This is messed up. I can't even fuck her inside my head because my brain is a cockblocker.

Fifteen

Nico

THE WHOLE FAMILY gathers at the Country Club on Friday morning, where a luxury bus waits to take us to an old military airfield outside of town.

Mom's events used to be more low-key, but since I bought the club and she started organizing the Balls here, her Charity became a hot topic in OC.

With an abundance of important guests came a change in how she hosts. The quarterly events now span two days. A sophisticated dinner party for the biggest donors on Friday and the main invitation-only event on Saturday.

My brothers and I are invited to Friday dinners regardless of how much we donate. We all help Mom with press releases, admin, and accounting throughout the year.

"Time to party!" Cody booms, entering the building.

We're greeted with a glass of champagne, the spacious lobby

full of our parents, grandparents, and older brothers. Save for Thalia, who's pregnant, Mia, who's afraid of flying, and my grandparents, everyone is sky diving today.

Thirteen people.

I pledged ten grand per head to convince them to get off their asses, but in reality, Mom gets seven figures out of me every year, so a check for a quarter of it—two hundred and fifty thousand dollars—is already in her pocket.

"Oh, I'm so happy to see you!" My grandmother charges past me and the triplets as if we're invisible. Her chiffon throw, cardigan, or whatever it is, shimmers as she wraps her arms around Mia. "How have you been? You're pale, honey. Were you unwell?" She glances at Grandad on the other side of the entryway. "William! Look who's here!"

I know they play Bridge every week, but I've not realized how close Mia is to my grandparents. And they must be *very* close if my grandmother picked Mia over her three favorite grandsons standing to my left with their dates.

I know the girl on Colt's arm. I don't remember her name, but she sneaks out of my house enough that she must be his regular lay. It's hard to forget her head of bright-red hair, freckled face, or thick British accent.

Conor's date has that girl-next-door vibe he's so into. Her makeup isn't overdone, she's in funky jeans and a t-shirt, and her hair's up in a messy bun.

"I'm fine, thank you," Mia says, hugging my grandmother before she wraps her arms around my grandfather, who sauntered over here as if he's thirty years younger.

He's been complaining about arthritis in his knees since he retired a few months ago, but it must've magically gone away.

Once grandma's happy that Mia's had breakfast, isn't hungry, thirsty, tired, or unwell, she pecks her cheek and finally notices her grandsons.

I can't make out Mia's quiet conversation with my grand-father but notice the fondness painting his face as they talk. I don't remember the last time I saw him wear a full smile.

"Right, since we're all here now, I say we get going," Logan yells over the chatter, either impatient or nervous, as he bounces on the soles of his feet.

Forty minutes later, we arrive at an old military airfield, where three small planes sit on a short runway. Instructors, inside a huge hangar, are waiting for us to disembark the bus so they can start the safety briefing.

Mia spent the ride at the back with my grandparents while I gawked over my shoulder too often.

Doomed is what I am.

Fucking *doomed*.

One of the instructors comes closer when we gather in a large group on the tarmac.

"Right," he says, frowning as he quickly counts the heads. "I've got a note that fourteen are jumping."

"Yes, some are just here to watch," Cassidy supplies, handing the buggy with Noah to grandma.

"Actually, it'll be thirteen," Cody says. "Mia's not good with flying."

"Make it twelve. I'll skip the fun today." I regret saying it before the words fully roll off my tongue.

The only reason I want to stay on the ground is to spend half an hour alone with Mia.

"Why? It was your idea." Theo's eyebrows draw together, utterly confused since I'm always the first one geared up, ready to go.

"He's done it so many times it's not much fun anymore,

right?" Colt says, his piercing stare searing right through me before his eyes quickly jump to Mia and back, a silent *I know what you're doing* in that look.

Shit... busted.

I glance at Cody, wondering if he connected the dots, but he's chatting with Logan, paying me no heed.

"Okay, twelve it is," the instructor says, impatient to get things started. "Everyone jumping, follow me."

I'm sure Colt will bust my ass at the earliest convenience, and my mind blanks on how to save my face. Nothing justifies me spending time with Mia while Cody's crushing on her. *Nothing.* I've got no line of defense.

Everyone follows the instructor into the hangar, and I'm struck that Cody didn't say one word to Mia. He just walked right off. He needs a lesson on how to properly take care of a girl like her. But... I won't be doing him any favors. It's not Cody she wants. It's *me.*

My grandad sits on one of the plastic chairs lining the hangar wall, and my grandma takes advantage of the portable coffee machine nearby while Noah's asleep.

"Why aren't you jumping?" Mia asks, following slowly in their steps. She's in sneakers, her white, fitted tee tucked into a pair of high-waist jeans.

I love that she's so tiny. I could fucking hide her in my arms without an issue. "I'll jump if you'll jump."

"I wish I could." She smiles small when we reach the table. "I really do, but you've not seen me on a plane. I'll break down halfway up."

"You only live once," Grandad says. "Look at me! I'm eighty-two. I'm too old to do a lot of things I was afraid to do when I was your age, and I regret them all."

"He's right," Grandma adds. "I think you should at least try. For us, the old farts who *can't.*"

"One day..." she muses, watching my family as they strap up.

Grandad doesn't push further, and neither do I, even though I want to strap her in the harness and take her eighteen thousand feet above the ground to help her overcome the fear.

The skydiving party leaves the warehouse thirty minutes later. The jumpers split into three groups, board the planes, and soon enough, they're in the air, one after the other.

"Where will they land?" Mia asks, glancing around as if expecting a big X spray-painted on the tarmac.

"Wherever they can. They should aim for the field." I point ahead. "But I'm sure we'll see at least one person land in the trees. My money's on Cody."

"I'd expect Conor to do something like that just for laughs."

The planes rise steadily, circling above us for ten minutes before they reach the correct altitude, and everyone starts jumping out. Mia scrambles to her feet, shielding her eyes from the sun with her hand.

There's awe on her face as she watches my family join in one big circle, free-falling from eighteen thousand feet. I take my shades off, covering her eyes.

"Why aren't they opening their parachutes?" she asks after thirty more seconds, her voice higher than usual.

"It takes one minute twenty to get to five thousand feet, baby." I glance at my watch, catching a surprised, tight-lipped smile on my grandmother, who looks between Mia and me. Shit. I forgot they're here. I also forgot Mia's not mine, and I can't call her *baby*, no matter how good it feels. "Thirty more seconds before they can open the parachutes," I add, doing my best to act casual.

No biggie.

Mia mouths numbers, counting down, neck craned to watch the sky. "They're still falling!" she cries, ripping my shades off and gunning me down with those big eyes as if she wants me to get off my ass and... I don't know... catch them?

"Look up," I tell her, seeing the first parachute unfold and more follow in quick succession.

Mia lifts her hand, counting white dots in the sky. "That's amazing!" She beams, bouncing on her feet.

I can't suppress my smile when I watch how excited she is, stepping from one foot to another. She spins around, pumping her little fists, her excitement palpable.

"You want to jump, don't you?"

"Um... I'm not sure. It seems like so much fun, but—"

I grab her hand, pulling her toward the hangar where two instructors stand at the door, watching the sky. "Don't think. One step at a time. Harness first. That's not scary, right?"

She shakes her head, tightening her grip around my fingers. "Don't let me back down."

"You need a safe word, Mia." I turn to the instructors. "Get us ready." I show them my skydiving license. "She's tandem jumping with me."

"As in, I'll be strapped to you?"

"Yes," the instructor supplies. "You're certified, but company policy is that we always send at least one instructor out with you."

"As long as she's with me, I don't care how many of you want to jump."

He bobs his head, and we get a condensed safety briefing while I'm gearing Mia up, triple-checking every strap before I get my gear on.

I'm buzzing, and it has nothing to do with skydiving. I've completed my fair share of jumps, but now that I have Mia with me, it'll be something else.

"I'm scared," she says when the first plane lands. "My heart is going so fast."

I take her chin between my thumb and forefinger, tipping her head back. "Don't think ahead. All you have to do is trust me that I'll get you back down safely. I've done this plenty of times. I've got you."

The instructor runs to the cockpit, waving us over.

"Red," I say, clutching Mia's hand. "That's your safe word. Unless you say *red*, we're taking the fast way down. I don't care if you hit me, puke, or cry. I don't care if you scream or beg. I'll slap your pretty butt if you bite, but I won't listen until you say *red*, understood?"

"Keep talking, okay? Anything, just talk."

I halt, catch her jaw, and turn her head my way. "What did I just tell you?"

"That you'll spank me," she utters, cheeks rosy.

"You make it damn near impossible not to when you blush like that. What's your safe word?"

"Um..." She looks around, biting her lip. "Red."

"Good girl. Use it if you have to."

Half a minute later, we're on the plane. I sit Mia between my legs for take-off, my arms around her even before the instructor straps the pretty little blonde to my harness.

Nothing ever felt as natural as holding her close.

"Talk," she pleads, wiggling her fingers like she's typing a long essay. "Please, just talk."

And so I do.

I talk all the time.

I tell her I expect she'll play one song for me at the Ball

and that I want a dance. I tell her I know her dad, and that he sent me VIP tickets for the Austin GP in September. It's a given Mia will be attending, so I promise to drive her there since she's afraid of flying. I'd fucking carry her there on my back just to spend time with her.

Her pulse accelerates along with the plane, reaching its limit when we start ascending. I knot our fingers, wrapping our arms around her tiny frame.

"The first time I jumped, I was twenty-four. Nothing compares to the first jump, so take in the views."

"Sixty seconds!" the pilot shouts.

"I'm scared," Mia wails, clutching my fingers hard enough to cut off circulation. "I changed my mind. I want to go back! Please, I don't want to do this anymore! I feel sick. Oh *God*! Yellow! Orange! Please, I'll do anything you want, just—"

"The word is *red*, and you're doing great. Don't think." I haul us up, gripping the handle. "Close your eyes, Mia. Breathe in for me."

I can't see if she followed the first instruction, but she's definitely breathing.

She's fucking hyperventilating.

"Please, we don't have to do this! It's so far down. What if the parachute doesn't open? What if we crash? What if..." She chokes on the words.

My arm curves around her middle. "We won't crash. The parachute will open, and you'll love this. I promise."

"Thirty seconds!" The instructor opens the door, and Mia starts trembling so hard I wonder if she's crying.

Still, no *red*.

"You're such a good girl," I say in her ear, leaving a kiss there. "Breathe. Don't think. You're safe with me."

171

"Fifteen seconds!"

"Oh, no, no, no, *no!*" Mia shakes her head, leaving angry, half-moon marks in my arm with her nails. "No, please! I don't want to do this! Let me go!"

"*Red*, baby. Say *red*, and we stop."

But instead of the safe word, she chants *no* on repeat like it's a coping mechanism.

The instructor gives me a hand signal as if he knows it's better not to yell *jump*, or Mia will freak out. Not that she isn't already... I fucking love that about her. She's not pretending, not hiding her feelings. She's fighting the fear.

I grip both of her hands, knotting our fingers, and step toward the edge of the plane, nothing but open space as far as the eye can see.

"No, please, please, I can't do this, I can't..."

I stamp a kiss on the crown of her head and outstretch our hands to the sides, tilting us forward. We're out of the plane the next second, and Mia's screaming.

The high-pitched wail cuts through the air like a scalpel. I'm pretty sure it's supposed to be a very long *e* in *red*, but too late.

"Open your eyes," I yell over the sound of air going by us at a hundred and twenty miles per hour, even though I shouldn't talk in freefall. "Look around!"

The screaming ceases instantly, and Mia's fingers tighten their hold around mine. She's excited. I can tell. I fucking *know* her so well by now that I read her reactions with ease.

I remember my first jump, the sensory overload, and I'm so glad Mia's experiencing this in my arms—the earth from an angle she's never seen before, the feeling of weightlessness as we fall, the smell of the freshest air you can get.

This is my six-hundred and thirteenth jump, but except for

the first, none compare to this one. I hold Mia's hands in mine and steer, bending her elbows and forcing my body into an arch until we do a three-sixty flip in the air.

"Again!" she cries, the word barely reaching my ears.

This time she arches with me, making the flip easier. We're getting closer to five thousand feet, so I let go of her hand, showing her the signal for *pull*.

I glance around, checking the position of the two instructors behind us before I pull the line. We're jerked in the air when the white canvas takes the strain.

Mia lets out an ecstatic cheer that makes me feel weightless. There's no fear left in her petite body: just adrenaline and happiness.

"We jumped!"

I steer the parachute toward the field far below, where my family is, nothing more than a few dots scattered around the grass and tarmac.

"That wasn't so scary, was it?"

"We jumped out of a plane!" She bounces in the harness, swinging us from side to side.

"I know you're excited, but you need to stay still, or we'll land in the river."

She stills, but her fingers pump around my wrists like she'll explode if she doesn't let the emotions out somehow.

"Thank you! I'm glad you didn't let me back down!"

I dip my head and press my lips to her hair, only realizing what I did once the honeysuckle scent invades my nose.

"You did great. Long-haul to Europe will be a breeze."

The parachute jerks about, swinging us back to front when she starts bouncing again. I take a long way down, circling longer than necessary.

Mia's turning her head left and right, taking in the views. I want to prolong that for her as much as possible.

"Legs out," I instruct when we're about to land.

She gets in position, surprising me that despite all her fear she managed to focus on what the instructors were saying during the safety briefing.

When I land alone, I end up on my own two feet, but landing with Mia isn't graceful. It's a mess, if I'm honest. I'm trying to hit the ground first, so she doesn't bruise that perfect ass.

It works. I bruise mine instead.

We're on the ground on an uphill part of the field, quite the distance from the tarmac. I lay on my back in the longish grass, Mia on top of me, her back flush against my chest. I unbuckle the harness that straps us together when the parachute settles over us like a huge blanket.

"That was—" *fun*, I want to say, but she rolls onto her stomach, and those perfect, plump lips cover mine.

The kiss is short, sweet... nothing more than a peck. I'm sure the emotions she has no idea how to unleash are to blame, but I'm done.

I'm *done* the second her lips touch mine.

My fingers disappear in her hair when she tries to move away, and I pull her back, seizing the moment as I sweep my tongue along the seam of her mouth, begging for more.

She opens for me on cue, making me groan. She tastes like candy. Sweet. *Too sweet.*

Fucking addictive.

My heart threatens with a coronary, pounding so hard it resonates in all directions. And I swear the world stops spinning on its axis when I bite her lower lip, sucking it into my mouth the way I imagined for weeks.

Mia's fingertips gently press into my cheekbones. The featherlight touch annihilates the noise that's layered my thoughts for years.

It's never been this quiet in my head.

There's nothing there save for Mia. Save for the softness of her hair under my fingertips, the plumpness of her lips working with mine, and the weight of her warm body.

She ghosts one hand lower, tracing the column of my throat until she grabs a handful of my t-shirt. I grip her jaw, steering her gorgeous face, devouring that sweet mouth over again, but I can't get enough. I'll *never* get enough of her.

This is more than I imagined.

More than I ever hoped for.

I drape one hand around her back and grip her waist, ready to flip us over, so I'm on top, dictating the pace, but Theo's amused voice booms somewhere on my right.

"Shit, are you okay there? That looked like a hard landing."

Fuck.

Fuck, fuck, fuck!

His words bring a reality check that hurts more than if he hit me square in the jaw. The world beyond the parachute canvas didn't exist for a moment.

Now, it seeps back in, unwanted.

My eyes fly open, my head far from quiet. In fact, there's so much going on I feel the tendrils of a badass headache setting in. Mia's still on me, her cheeks deliciously pink, the green of her irises almost wiped out by blown pupils.

Shame washes over me like some biblical hurricane when reality settles in.

What have I done?

What have *we* done?

What the fuck has *she* done?!

I still hold her face with one hand, my thumb sweeping her bottom lip. My stomach wrenches with a mixture of nerves, longing, and shame. God, I want her.

Mine.

My girl...

Cody's.

"We're okay," I say, swallowing hard.

Theo tugs the parachute, trying to pull it off as more footsteps approach. I move Mia to my side, my mind all over the place. Even though I'm the biggest asshole, I want that sweet mouth of hers back on mine so much it feels like I'm walking against the strongest blizzard, fighting not to kiss her.

I'm shaking, but that might be because I'm mad at Mia, myself, Cody, and karma.

"I'm sorry," she whispers, her cheeks deliciously pink, lips even plumper—swollen from *my* kisses.

She doesn't sound like she means it. I should apologize too, but I definitely wouldn't mean it, so I don't.

Besides, it's Cody who deserves an apology, not her.

Theo pulls the parachute away, and the first person I see is the one with a metaphorical knife in his back. He's smiling. And it feels like he's kicking me when I'm already down.

"You jumped!" Cody cheers, dragging Mia to her feet. "I'm so proud of you! Did you like it? Was it fun?"

"The scariest and happiest moment of my life." Mia beams and then turns to me. "Thank you. That was amazing."

I can't even be mad at her for not feeling guilty about kissing me. She and Cody aren't together. I'm the one to blame. I'm the asshole here.

She's innocent. Oblivious to Cody's feelings.

Theo grips my arm, hauling me up while Conor and Colt help Mia out of her harness. She moves her attention to me, and the piercing gaze of those emerald greens peels all the layers protecting my mind. Skin, soft tissue, and bone. And she's there... where I don't want her. In my head. Holding every thought hostage at gunpoint.

I storm past them all to get the hell away from her before I knock Cody unconscious, fling the little girl over my shoulder, and make a fucking run for it.

Sixteen

Mia

THE MINUTE CODY DROPS ME OFF HOME, I lock myself in my bedroom.

Nico hasn't said a word to me since Theo pulled the parachute off, and I have no idea what to make of it. He's hot and cold, pulling like he wants me, then pushing like he doesn't want to want me. It feels like a game, but I don't know what we're playing. I don't know the rules or if I'm winning.

My thighs quiver whenever I recall the kiss. The lacy fabric between my legs is so wet it's uncomfortable.

He kissed me back.

He *kissed* me.

Another anxious prickle of lust elevates the need for release. I can't keep doing this. I can't keep playing with my body while thinking about Nico. It's wrong... but it feels so right when the itch gets scratched.

I rise from the floor, stripping off my clothes to get in the shower because the family dinner is starting soon, but instead of entering the bathroom, I crawl onto my bed.

Just one last time.

My body hums with the primitive, primal thrill, my breaths coming out in shallow puffs. Just thinking about Nico's lips urgently working with mine has me on the brink of release. The way his fingers tugged my hair and how he bit my lip, deepening the kiss... it's as if he had a first-row seat to my deepest desires, knowing exactly what I want, what I enjoy.

I skim my hand down my stomach, jerking on the bed as I brush a ticklish spot, then sink into the pillows as I circle my clit. I'm close, poised on edge, ready to fall. God, I was coming apart at the seams when Nico was kissing me.

Is that even possible?

My mind conjures an image of him, hovering above me; his hooded, hungry eyes and tattooed chest as he drives into me, pumping in and out. I imagine him whispering in my ear, his tone low, husky, and demanding.

You're almost there, aren't you? Come for me, baby. Let loose.

That's all it takes for the orgasm to hit, pressing in on me from all sides. My back arches off the bed, and my loaded moan ricochets off the walls. I picture Nico dipping his head, drinking in that moan while he prolongs my orgasm, wringing out every last bit of please until I'm deliriously overstimulated.

I don't open my eyes, holding onto the visual for a little while. I took care of the ache, but I've learned that the satisfied feeling doesn't last long. I'll be back needing Nico's touch in a few hours at most.

***

The VIP party starts at six in the afternoon. Cody picked me up, dressed in a black tux, his hair sleeked back and in a bun.

"Can we stop at a shop, please?" I ask when he finishes telling me what's on the menu tonight.

If Nico wants to play games, so can I.

"Why? What do you need?"

"Oh, um... it's just something I want to give Nico later."

He flips the indicator, pulling up outside a gas station. "What kind of something, Bug?"

"You'll see, it's a little inside joke."

I run inside, scouting the shelves. Overly proud of my clever idea, I pay the cashier, tuck my purchase in my bag, then get back in the car.

We're the last ones to arrive at the Country Club. Well, almost. Nico's nowhere around, and I've not spotted his car, although he does have three, and I only know two, so maybe he's here.

The foyer acts as the meet-and-greet area, where we spend half an hour mingling with the sophisticated crowd.

I'm struck by how mature and eloquent the triplets are, discussing politics with the upper class.

They don't show that side every day.

Logan comes over to complain that my sister's been blowing up his phone, asking him to pose for another cover: a sequel to *Sweet Truths*. Before we can get into the conversation, Cassidy waves him over, and he excuses himself. I watch as he wraps his arm around her middle, kissing her temple before he pays the man Cass is talking to any attention.

Theo takes his place, the only Hayes I've not been properly introduced to before today. He's got a sense of humor a lot like Conor's, and he's a bit like Colt with those bright, assessing eyes. I don't think any detail slips past him.

"Mia!" Monica Hayes cheers, rushing toward us. A dazzling smile stretches her pink lips before she air-kisses my cheeks. "That's a lovely dress, honey." She takes my hand, twirling me around. "Are you ready to play tomorrow?"

"Yes, I've been practicing all week."

"Perfect!" She squeezes my hand softly. "I can't wait. My mother's been singing your praises for months."

"Exaggeration," I say with a smile. "All of it."

"No need to be so modest." Her eyes cut across the room, where little Noah's just started crying in the nanny's arms. "I better go and see if I can help." She rushes away, intercepting her grandson from the nanny's hands like she doesn't trust the woman to do her job.

"Did you call your dad to tell him you jumped?" Cody asks.

"Not yet. They're racing in Azerbaijan this weekend, and it's late there now. I'll call him tomorrow. I doubt he'll believe me, though."

"You'll have proof," Conor says, approaching with his date. "One of the instructors who jumped with you and Nico took pictures. We'll have them next week."

"That pirouette you did in the air was cool." Shawn stops beside us with his husband, Jack. "Cody said you're terrified of heights. Why did you jump?"

"Why did you?" I counter, biting back a smile. "I don't mind heights. It's flying I can't stomach, but you all looked like you were having so much fun up there..." I trail off, catching a glimpse of Nico as he enters the building.

Our eyes lock, and he slowly takes me in the way he always does, inch by inch, like he's savoring every second. My chaotic feelings force my heart into a faster rhythm when he approaches our little gathering.

I'm silently, openly staring, and at least five seconds have passed since I stopped talking. "Once we got on the plane, I begged Nico to take me back down."

"You didn't want to go back down on a plane," Nico says. "You would've said *red* instead of *yellow* and *orange*."

"Red?" Cody questions.

"She told me not to let her back down but muttered *no*, and *I don't want to do this* non-stop during the safety briefing, so I picked a safe word she could use if she really wanted to stop."

"I used it. Just a little too late."

Nico squares his shoulders when I smile at him, his posture tense, jaw clamped tight. The smile slips from my face as if falling off a cliff.

They talk about me screaming on the way down and the flips we did, but I'm not involved.

Was I naïve to think Nico was interested after he kissed me back? I didn't plan to kiss him. It just happened. Pumped up on adrenaline, I reached for the one thing I ever wanted this badly.

Someone taps a fork on a crystal glass, a signal for everyone to find their seats. Cody ushers me over there while Monica stands on the stage, thanking people for their lucrative donations. I've never been a guest at one of Monica's Balls, but I heard plenty from the triplets. They rarely attend the uptight Friday evening dinner, so I know more about what happens tomorrow.

The room isn't even half-full tonight, but an aura of importance surrounds every person here. I'm thankful to whoever created the seating plan when I sit across from Nico. Ten seconds later, I'm not so thankful. His face curdles into an expression of distaste, and his jaw works when he catches me staring.

He kissed me back. Why is he so annoyed?

The dinner is served by an army of overdressed waitresses in black and white outfits. One of them, a tall, dark-haired girl, steals Cody's attention as she places a plate before him.

"I think she's a little too young for you," I say as his eyes walk her back toward the kitchen. "She looks about sixteen, Cody. Behave."

He chuckles, moving the sauteed mushrooms I don't like from my plate to his. "You look about twelve, Bug. Relax, I'm just enjoying the view."

"I'm not tense, but... I don't know. Maybe ask for ID? I don't want you to get in trouble."

He laughs again, drapes his hand across my shoulders, and pulls me closer, whispering in my ear. "I think Nico's too old for you, but it doesn't stop you looking, does it?"

"I'm... I'm sorry," I stutter quietly, doing my best not to glance at Nico even though I feel his gaze. "I, um..."

"I know," he whispers before I glue together a coherent sentence. "He's *hot*, right?" He grins, moving away. "Eat. It's getting cold."

I poke the meat, my eyes drawn to Nico's burning gaze on their own. He looks between Cody and me, the small frown pulling his eyebrows hard to decipher. I focus on my plate, forcing a few pieces of meat down my throat, and flushing them with my spritzer.

Irritation leaks like battery acid into my mind, and the idea I had in the car changes. Nico's still getting what I bought him, but the execution will be different.

The dessert is served: chocolate brownies with a scoop of vanilla ice cream. The waitress places a plate before Nico, and he drops his fork, making a lot of unnecessary noise.

I pinch my lips together, feeling smaller and meaner than

a bee when I open my clutch bag, then reach for Nico's plate. In its place, I leave a pouch of peanut M&Ms.

"You'd rather have this, wouldn't you?"

He pins me with a pointed stare, his fingers balling into a tight fist on the table. For the first time, I don't look away first. My heart triphammers in my chest, my knees quiver under the table, but I don't look away.

He does. He pushes himself back with the chair that scrapes loudly against the parquet floor and storms out of the room, grasping the yellow packet of M&Ms.

Mission failed. He was supposed to say *no, I'll take a brownie every day* or something along those lines.

Urgh, I really suck at this game.

Everyone at our table watches me, and a raging glow heats my cheeks. "It was a joke," I mutter when Conor cocks a questioning eyebrow. "You had to be there to understand."

"I was here, and I don't get it."

"Not now. We had a chat about brownies the other day." I wave him off. "Never mind." I push my dessert his way. "You want it? I don't feel like sweets."

He grins, digging into the brownie. He's got a black hole instead of a stomach, I'm sure.

"Come on." Cody takes my hand when the music changes from jazz to modern, signaling that the dancing can begin. "We'll get this party started."

He pulls me to my feet, twirling me around his finger like a rag doll until we're in the middle of the dancefloor. I give into the music, focused on Cody.

Dancing with him comes naturally. I know what he'll do next, how to position myself, and I can't contain the smile when he gently pushes me away, then twirls me around his arm into his chest and swings from left to right.

I'm spinning again, singing the lyrics while Cody makes the dancefloor into his stage.

Colt, Conor, and their dates join in when the next song starts. In a step that seems almost rehearsed, the triplets swing us around, and I end up in Colt's arms, adjusting my moves to his. Halfway through the next song, I'm with Conor, then back to Cody before the music changes again.

More people are dancing now, gliding across the makeshift dancefloor, each to their own pace and style.

Theo takes my hand two songs later, twirls me away, then yanks me back, and I bounce off his chest. "Shit, sorry. You're a tiny thing," he laughs, gripping my waist to lift me up. "Featherweight. Alright," he mutters, setting me down. "Let's try again." His hold loosens as we fall into step.

"I can follow your lead just fine," I say when he yanks me too hard again. "Use your hands to tell me where you want me. Twist left, and I turn left." I twitch his wrist, showing him what I mean. "Twist right and I turn right, push, and I'll back away."

A tight-lipped smile is his only answer, but soon enough, it no longer feels like he'll rip my arm out the socket. Britney blasts from the speakers when he leans me back so far I'm sure my hair sweeps the floor.

"You need a drink," he says two songs later, leading me to the table. "But I'm not done with you. You're fun!"

I chuckle, plopping down in my seat. Nico's back there, no trace of the loaded-gun attitude. What's more, a fresh glass of spritzer and a tall glass of lemonade wait by my clean plate.

"Thank you," I say, hoping he won't glare at me again.

He smiles a barely-there smile, warming me inside. I want his lips on mine, his hands in my hair, and his strong muscles under my fingertips.

Seconds later, his mother approaches, asking him to dance, leaving just Theo and me at the table. He's not getting up unless the music changes to something less demanding so I leave him alone, walking down the long table to stop by William.

"May I steal a dance?"

I love how he readjusts his smart jacket and tie as he gets up, then kisses my hand softly like the undeniable gentleman he is. "Take it easy on me, young lady. I'm a little rusty."

"You lead; I adjust."

We squeeze through the crowd of dancing bodies, stopping in the middle, and William slides his hand to my waist. I'm swept off my feet when we start dancing, gliding across the dancefloor, his moves aristocratic in their measured perfection. I expect him to run out of steam by the end of the song, but we dance another one before he bows, kissing my hand again and leading me back to my seat.

"I'll take it from here." Nico steps in our way, pulling my hand out of his grandfather's grasp. "May I?" he double-checks with me, but it's William who says, *of course.*

He steps away, and Nico pulls me in, almost flush to his chest, his touch urgent. One of his hands is on the small of my back, the other holds mine, and only then do I hear what's playing: "Senorita" by Shawn Mendes.

We dance, but it's nothing like any other dance tonight. This is slow. It's intense, flawless, but a struggle. I tremble when he twirls me into his arms, dark eyes not veering from my face, the lyrics as if written for the two of us. As if whoever watches from above plays this game, too, toying with my emotions.

"Are we okay?" I ask, breaking the loaded silence. "I'm sorry about the dessert and the kiss, too. I—"

"Do you regret it?"

"I get the feeling I should."

"That doesn't answer my question."

"You don't answer any of mine, so call it even."

The song fades, changing to "One More Night" by Maroon 5, and I try to step away, but Nico doesn't let me, drawing me back to his chest.

Every time he pulls me in so desperately, it's touchdown in my belly, and eighty thousand fans cheer wildly.

"One more," he says. "And yes, we're okay."

The urge to kiss him comes back ten times stronger when he makes the same move Theo did, and my hair sweeps the floor before he pulls me up.

"I don't regret it. You're a solid eight," I reply.

"Then don't apologize." He twirls me around his finger, before wrapping his arm around my middle. My back is suddenly flush with his chest, his warm breath in my ear contrasting his icy tone. "Eight? I'm an *eight* in your book?"

"Don't sound so upset. It's good. I've never had an eight."

"Eight?" he echoes again, downright baffled. His step falters for a brief moment before he recovers, lowering his voice to a throaty whisper. "What the fuck is wrong with my kisses, baby?"

I spin around, meeting the heated gaze of his dark eyes. "They're too short."

Seventeen

Nico

THAT GIRL SURE KNOWS how to keep me on my toes. First, she shows me a confident, cheeky side she's been hiding God-knows-where, stealing my dessert and replacing it with fucking M&Ms, then she rates my skills at eight.

Here I was, replaying our kiss all evening, thinking it was the *best* kiss in my life, and she rates it *eight*?

Way to drive me nuts.

I want to prove her wrong, up my score, and kiss her until our lips are numb, but... *I can't*. She's not mine to kiss.

She's Cody's.

The back of my head hits the wall. I can still taste her sweet mouth. One kiss and I'm fucking addicted. How the hell do I stop this? The neurotic thoughts; the growing, burning need; the—

Who am I kidding?

I can't stop or step aside.

I'm too far gone to give up without a fight.

I never thought I'd consider going against my brother, but I've reached a point of no return. Not one thought today has been unrelated to Mia.

She's all I've thought of for weeks.

She's too young, still in college. She should have fun, party, and enjoy her youth before mundane life begins. I'm not the guy for her. Too obsessive, too fucking possessive, but...

I'll make it work.

I've been learning how to handle, touch, and talk to her for almost two months now.

She's not as soft as I initially thought. Every time I see her, I discover a new part of her character. She argues: shows me my place, and stands up to me when she feels strongly.

She's two parts gasoline and one part match. She's got a spark, too, and once all that fuses together, she'll burn bright.

I toss the cigarette to the ground and enter the building, taking no time to rethink what's already decided. There's no turning back now.

Win or lose, I'm done pretending I can't stand on the sidelines, watching my brother attempt to woo the girl I want.

Everyone save for the triplets, and Theo, is gone. The room emptied half an hour ago, but Mia's been home much longer. She was exhausted, barely keeping herself awake at the table. Since Cody was nowhere to be found, I called the cab driver who took us home a couple weeks ago and slipped him a hundred so he'd wait until Mia got inside.

Better safe than sorry.

I push the door to the Ballroom open with both hands, letting the wings bang against the wall. "Where's Cody?" I ask, not spotting him by our table.

"He's here somewhere," Conor says, rolling a bottle of vodka across the table. "Sit down. We're having shots."

"Not until I talk to Cody."

"Why?" Theo narrows his eyes at me. Either he's frowning, or he's drunk and seeing double. "Come on, bro. Spill your guts." He pats the chair next to him, slurring his words. "You've been on edge all day today."

"He's always on edge," Conor muses, launching a grape in the air and catching it with his mouth.

"Not like this," Theo continues. "You're a different kind of tense today, and you're freaking me out because I *know* that tension. I've seen you like this before."

"I'm good," I clip, not in the mood to divulge the subject. Whatever Theo thinks he knows, he's wrong. "Where the fuck did Cody go?"

"It's Kaya, isn't it?" Theo sighs, pouring a round of shots. "Your *ex*. That's what's riling you up, right?" He grabs my shoulder, squeezing hard as he leans in closer. "Last time you acted so odd was when you were with her. You're mad she didn't make it tonight?"

"I didn't know she was invited."

"Adrian said he saw you two talking at *Rave* a few weeks ago..." He pushes a defeated breath down his nose. "Listen, I love you. I've *got* you, alright? If she's what you want—"

"You think I'd let her crawl back to me? We're not together, Theo. And before you ask, we're not fucking. She was drunk off her ass, begging for another chance at *Rave*, but that's not happening."

"Thank God." He falls back in his chair, theatrically wiping his forehead. "I'd be here for you, but I'm glad you don't want her."

"He didn't go home, did he?" I ask, my leg twitching against the floor.

"Who?"

"Cody."

"No, he's here," Colt chips in, lifting a shot glass and gesturing for us to follow. We all throw our heads back, swallowing the disgusting liquid that burns down my esophagus. "You being tense today isn't about Kaya." He points his finger at me, eyes glassy, too much alcohol in his bloodstream. "Can't fool me, bro. You're into Mia."

I knew he'd throw that at me at the first opportunity. I've had two drinks tonight, but my ears ring, and shame washes over me once more.

I open my mouth, but he bangs his hand on the table before I get a word out.

"Don't lie. Don't lie to me, Nico. I see how you watch her, how you fucking hold her and worry when she's one bit uncomfortable."

"Mia?" Theo pours us another shot, chuckling under his breath. "The blonde with Cody? You're drunk, bro. No more for you. Isn't she like in high school?"

"College," I correct. "I'd love to entertain you, Colt, but Cody's the one I need to talk to."

"Oh, he knows," Conor chuckles, launching another grape. "He's not blind. None of us are."

Fuck. My hands grow cold, coated with sweat, and an airless mounting sense of unease settles in my lungs.

I should've talked to him sooner.

"*You* convinced Mia to jump out of the plane with you, and *you* glare at Cody whenever he's not attentive enough," Colt says, leaning back in his chair. "You fucking kissed her, Nico.

You *kissed* her."

"She told you?"

Or maybe something less incriminating...

Theo gasps, hiccups, and gasps again. "You kissed Cody's girlfriend? Bro!" His eyes widen, bigger than silver dollars. "That's... nooo, that's just *nooo*. What were you thinking?!"

"Mia's not Cody's," I growl, squeezing the back of my neck. "He wants her, but she's not his. Not yet." I lift my gaze to Colt. "I can't believe she told you."

"She didn't, but I saw how she touched her lips the whole bus ride back here earlier."

She did? I wouldn't know because—pissed off—I took the front seat, shoved both earphones in, and blasted Guns N' Roses on full volume.

"*She* kissed *me*," I explain with a deep, defeated groan. "We just landed. I think she needed to let the adrenaline out somehow and used me. It was *nothing*, Colt. A peck at best, but..." I rest my elbows on the table, massaging my temples. "...I lost it. I pulled her back because I couldn't *not* kiss her. I've been fighting this for weeks."

Maybe it's good they know. Maybe they'll help. I need them to tell me I can get over this crush. That I can forget about Mia. That it's not a big deal.

"Believe me, I don't want to feel this way, but she's on my mind the second I wake up, the last second before I fall asleep, and every fucking second in between." I down the shot, slump my elbows back on the table, and hide my face in my hands while my brothers keep quiet. "So, yeah... I kissed her. I like her, and I *hate* that I do, but I can't stop."

"You like her?" Theo echoes on my right, his tone hovering between skepticism and surprise. "But... she's small. Like, really,

really small, and you're not." He nudges me, so I'd lift my head. "You look like you could fucking eat her, Nico."

Conor bursts out laughing. "I bet that's all he wants to do."

"She's young!" Theo continues. His hands flap, missing my face by an inch. "Shy, and... did I mention small?!"

"I get it. She's short."

"Short? She'd need a stool to kiss you." He slams his hand on my back. "I hate to break it to you, but you fucked up. You deserve whatever Cody throws your way when he finds out. Liking her is one thing but kissing her was way out of line. Even if she's not Cody's yet, you had no right to go after her."

"I know," I grind out. "Don't forget that *never touch your brother's girl* was my addition to our rules."

"Okay, just for a moment, imagine Cody's not interested in Mia," Colt says, twirling an empty shot glass on the table. "What do you do?"

"Don't make me think about it."

"Entertain me," he insists, and Conor elbows his ribs, hissing something I can't hear. "What do you do? You fuck her and leave her hanging like the rest of them?"

"No." The word shoots from my lips. "This isn't about sex, Colt. I don't know if I want her because I can't have her or because I'm—"

"Falling in love?" Theo cuts in, horror greasing his voice. "Shit, this is fucked up. You can't do this to Cody!"

"I think you've had enough for tonight." I snatch the bottle from his hand and take his shot glass. "You're drunk. I'm not falling in love with her."

"I think you are," Conor hums, wagging his eyebrows. "It doesn't matter, though. You wouldn't last. She's not adventurous or forward enough for you. She's a good girl. Mellow. As innocent as they come. In *every* sense of the word."

"She's a virgin?!" Theo exclaims, his drunken theatrics in high gear. His face will get stuck in a permanent state of deep shock if he's not careful. "How old is she?"

"Nineteen." Colt hands the bottle of vodka back to Theo, gesturing for him to pour a round. "You're our brother, Nico, but Mia's our lil' sis, and we *will* break you if you hurt her."

I narrow my eyes, wondering which of us is drunker because he's talking nonsense, and I'm thinking nonsense, rehearsing my next sentence.

I won't ever hurt her.

I throw the disgusting liquid at the back of my throat, enjoying the burning sensation as it warms my insides.

"Mia and Cody?" he scoffs, irritation evident by a shake of his head as he stares Conor down when he elbows him again. "They won't happen. We all love her. We all keep her safe, but Cody's the most big-brotherly." He leans over the table like he wants to make sure I'm listening. "He's not into her. He just didn't want her to be your toy."

"Why did you tell him?!" Conor whines, throwing his hands in the air. The drunken bliss on his face morphs into a confused mess. "Cody will kick your ass!"

"A toy?" I repeat, my voice barely a whisper. My mind races at the speed of light, connecting the dots, and suddenly, everything comes to a grinding halt. "You made me *think* Cody's in love with her, so I'd stay away? Why did you even think I'd be interested? She's—"

"Not what you usually go for? That's what I told Cody, but then I saw you with her when you taught her self-defense, and I understood why Cody did what he did."

"He fucking *lied*."

"Yeah, he did. To you and to us." He points between him and Conor. "He made us think he's in love with her, too. Took us two weeks to get the truth out of him. He panicked when he saw you eyeing her up at the party and did the first thing that came to mind."

Jesus... I'm not an asshole, after all.

I wasn't fantasizing about my brother's girl.

"You're absolute jerks," Theo booms, sporting a supersized grin. "But I got to say, I'm glad you care about someone so much you took drastic measures to keep her from getting hurt. I sure as shit wasn't as considerate at your age."

Cody enters the room, two shirt buttons undone, empty bottle of wine in hand, and a satisfied gleam in his brown eyes. I know that look on him... it means he got lucky.

"Where the fuck were you?".

"Probably fucking the waitress," Colt supplies. "Someone's got a confession to make," he adds, pointing his chin at me, and Cody meets my gaze.

"I want her," I say, cutting right to the chase. "And she wants me, so I'm taking her."

"I know," he sighs, plopping down on the seat across from me. "I knew I couldn't keep this up much longer. I know you like her, Nico, but—"

"They kissed," Colt cuts in, beaming. I've no idea what's so amusing. "*Mia* started it."

Cody's face pales. "You kissed my girl?"

"She's *not* your girl."

"Calm down." Theo pats his shoulder, handing him a shot glass, and proceeds to fill all five. "He felt adequately bad before Colt told us you're not into Mia. Give him a break."

Cody downs his shot before we grab ours. "Hurt her, and

I'll make you bleed, bro."

"You should bleed. All three of you should. We're brothers. We *talk*. You should've told me you don't want me around Mia instead of playing stupid games."

The four of them scoff in sync.

"Sure, we talk, but be real. You kissed her thinking Cody wants her," Theo says. "You'd get your dick wet and flee like always."

He might be right. If Mia was available right off the bat, I wouldn't have stopped to get to know her.

"She likes you," Cody says, sounding like he can't comprehend why. "And I know you care, which is why I won't tell you to stay away from her, but you better think your next move through *very* carefully."

"Time to stop thinking every woman's like Kaya," Theo adds. "Mia's seems like a pleasant change. I like her. I approve this match." He laughs, pouring another round.

Colt rakes his hand through his dark brown hair, forcing it back. "Mia's a great girl. Out of control at times, but lovely. She keeps us in check, and we keep her safe."

"I know she's nothing like Kaya. I also know she's ten years younger and way out of my league."

"That won't stop you," Conor mumbles, his mouth stuffed with grapes since that's the only thing left on the table. "It *shouldn't* stop you, bro. You're already way over your head. Now that you know you're in the clear, don't fuck it up."

Two bottles of vodka later, we stumble out the building. It's close to four in the morning, and we're all trashed as we get into a cab. I can't remember when I was this drunk.

I also can't remember when I talked to my brothers like this. We've been chasing our lives lately, forgetting to take time for ourselves.

Sure, we go out drinking every couple of months, but we've not had a heart-to-heart in ages. Theo spent half an hour gushing about his blissful life with Thalia and how excited he is about becoming a dad, and the triplets told us about their after-graduation plans.

Cody had his career path figured out years ago. He wants to work for *Stone and Oak* with Logan, but in a more hands-on way: leading the construction teams. Conor's diving deeper into becoming a production sound mixer, and Colt's all about business management.

When they were younger, I thought they'd choose the path of least resistance and open a business together, delegating tasks among themselves, but despite being identical on the outside, they're completely different inside.

Mia

Summer holidays before middle school

"NO WONDER NOBODY LIKED YOU, MIA. *Look at yourself!" my mother huffs, shoving me in front of a mirror, touching my hair like it's rotten and disgusting. "You're ugly. God, why do you wear glasses?!"*

She takes them off, and my vision blurs too much to move around the house unassisted.

"I can't see," I say, twirling the hem of my sweater. "I need them."

"Nonsense. You need laser eye surgery. Why do you think kids call you four eyes? *Because you've got four eyes, Mia. Those glasses are thicker than the bottom of those Nutella jars you stuff yourself with."*

I pretend I don't hear her. I pretend the insults don't hurt. After all, I should be used to this by now. I've been bullied, ridiculed, and harassed by kids at school for five years, but coming from Mom, it hurts more.

She wasn't around when I cried for two years because everyone called me Cootie Mia. *She wasn't around when Grandad chopped my hair*

off *after Blair stuck three sticks of gum in it. She didn't see my bruised knees and scraped elbows whenever kids tripped or shoved me to the ground.*

She left Dad when I was four and moved to London. Today marks the first time I've seen her in person since. We only spoke a handful of times. She was never interested in me. She's only proud of her first-born.

Aisha's her mirror image: pretty, popular, a cheerleader with a line of boys waiting to fall at her feet.

I've always been Daddy's girl. He's not been around for much of this either, traveling the world for work, but at least he knows. He calls and talks to me. Never calls me ugly.

"Stop feeling sorry for yourself and show them what they're missing. You're a Harlow. That name always means the world. I'll get you booked for surgery, and you need to go on a strict diet. You're getting fat, Mia. That won't help you make friends in middle school."

Eighteen

Mia

"PLEASE, *STOP*," Aisha whines from the sofa. "You've been practicing those songs for days. You know them, sis. Go get ready. Take a bath or something. Relax a bit."

"I'm not tense," I lie, turning in my seat. The truth is, I'm a ball of nerves, going back and forth over the idea that popped in my head this morning. "Do you think you could help me get ready for the Ball?"

Aisha cocks an eyebrow, straightening in her seat. "What, like... do your hair?"

"Um, yes. And makeup. And maybe I could borrow one of your dresses?"

"Makeup? You've not had makeup on since that one time in high school. Why do you want makeup? You know my dresses are way sexier than you're used to."

I nod, picking my nails. "I know. I'm thinking of mixing

it up a bit. I want to be sexy tonight."

Her lips spread into a knowing smile. "Aww, you're trying to impress a guy! Who is it?!" She jumps to her feet, clapping once. "Nico. Am I right, or am I right?! I've got the perfect dress!" She grabs my hand and drags me into her room, pushing me down at her dressing table. "I've seen the women he goes for. I'll make you look ten times better, promise."

I glance at her in the mirror while she pulls makeup supplies from a vanity box. "Do you think it's a good idea? I think he likes me, but—"

"But you dress like a schoolgirl. Men aren't into that. Especially men like Nico. I mean, you're pretty, so sure, he likes you, but he doesn't *want* you." She turns the chair, so I face her, then grabs a bottle of foundation. "He'll kneel on hot coals to fuck you once I'm done."

It won't hurt to try. I want him to see a woman when he looks at me, not a dainty little girl.

An hour later, my lips are blood-red, the color making them even bigger than normal, and winged eyeliner completes the smokey-eye Aisha swears by. Blush, highlighter, concealer, bronzer, mascara. I've got cheekbones. My face isn't so round anymore. It's amazing what contouring can do.

My hair is arrow straight in a sleek ponytail, and I wear a dress to match my lips: floor-length, fitted so tight I'm afraid to breathe. Backless with a deep neckline and a slit running from my hip.

It starts so high I can't wear underwear.

I look older, sophisticated... *sexy*, but my heart rams against my ribs, my idea idiotic now that I look in the mirror and see an impostor. This isn't me.

I might look beautiful, but I feel awful.

If this is what Nico expects, to keep his attention I'd have to spend every day pretending I'm someone else.

I want him, but flushing who I am down the drain is too high a price. I want him to like me for who I am, not who I can morph into with a splash of makeup and a revealing dress.

I sit on the bed, gathering my things into a clutch bag when the doorbell rings.

Cody's early.

It's only five o'clock. There's still time to wash my face and pick a different dress. Pink with frills or a chiffon skirt.

You won't know if this is what he wants if you get changed.

True. At least if I go to the Ball dressed like this, I'll see Nico's reaction. I'll judge if he pays me more attention while I'm done up to perfection.

If he does, I'll wave a white flag.

I slip my feet into black heels, standing up. There's a knock on the door, but it opens before I say *come in*. Instead of the Hayes I expected, a different one takes the width—and height—of the doorway.

Nico halts mid-step, looking me over slowly, taking in the provocative dress—my thigh peeking through the slit. His eyes eventually come back to meet mine. He does a double take, two lines marking his forehead.

"What are you doing here?" I ask, clutching my bag with both hands. "Where's Cody?"

"What the fuck are you wearing?" he shoots back, striding across to where I stand. His chest rises and falls faster as he turns my head, inspecting Aisha's artwork. "I've never seen you wearing makeup."

"I never did... do you like it?"

"You did this for me?"

I stare at his chest, pinching the sequins on my bag between my fingers. "You didn't answer my question."

"Do you want me to be nice or honest?"

"Honest, please."

He tilts my head back, dark eyes boring into mine. "I know you're blushing right now, but I can't see it under all that concealer, Mia. I fucking hate it." He brushes his thumb along my lower lip. "How am I supposed to kiss you with all that lipstick?"

I hold my breath, my tummy knotting itself tightly. "I'm sure you've kissed women wearing lipstick before."

"A simple peck won't up my score." He smirks, grazing his thumb along my jawline. "You're blushing again, aren't you? I want to see, Mia. Is this how you think I want you to look?" He gestures up and down my body.

"You didn't want me in pink dresses."

His features pinch, and he hauls me into his arms, marching me into the bathroom. He stands me under the shower, turning the hot water on. "Wash your face."

I'm soaking wet, makeup, hair, and dress ruined. I shouldn't feel relieved, right? I should be upset. Aisha spent an hour drawing lines on my face, straightening my hair, and helping zip me into this tight dress.

I should be upset... but I'm far from it.

Nico leaves, closing the door behind him with a quiet click. Ten minutes later, wrapped in a towel, I tiptoe back into my bedroom, where he sits on the bed, one of my dresses beside him. It's dirty pink, the tulle skirt embossed with silver crystals.

My heart flutters like the wings of a caged bird when he gets up. Anticipation courses through my veins and my lips start tingling, but Nico doesn't kiss me.

"Get dressed," he says, on his way out.

I do as I'm told, confused but curious. I slip into the dress he chose and find a box with silver heels under the bed before I dry my hair, braiding a crown. Once ready, I find Nico leaning against the opposite wall in the hallway.

"How's that?" I ask.

He closes the distance between us in one stride, grips me by the waist, and hauls me into his arms, pushing me back into the room.

The door slams shut.

And everything falls into place when his lips catch mine for a short peck like the one I gave him yesterday. "Show me I'm the one you want," he says, pinning me to the wall.

I brace against his shoulders, my mind in tumult. I don't understand his attitude, but I take what I crave now that he's close. I kiss his upper lip, then lower, and slide my tongue between, kissing him gently, savoring the feelings he evokes.

I brush my fingers along his jawline and turn his head to the side, nuzzling my nose in his cheek as I deepen the kiss at an unrushed pace.

"Jesus... how can you taste so sweet?" he whispers a second before he reclaims control, dominating the moment.

I'm still wrapping my head around the fact that *this* is happening. That his tongue sweeps the silk of my mouth, his lips hot and demanding, his massive body pressing into me, triggering a wave of desire.

It's intense, greedy, and everything I ever hoped for.

The second I shudder, Nico deepens the kiss, and a burst of endorphins rushes through my bloodstream. The thunder of my pulse mixes with the sound of our hastened breaths and our lips working in sync. A soft moan escapes me when he bites my lower lip, pulling gently.

"What's my score today?" He lifts one hand, tracing my swollen bottom lip. "Still eight?"

"And a half. I guess you're not mad about yesterday?"

He sits on the bed, maneuvering my legs until I'm comfortably straddling him. "I wasn't mad you kissed me. I was mad I couldn't have you. And it had nothing to do with your pink dresses. I thought you were Cody's."

"You thought I was dating Cody? Why? I mean, I—"

"It's a long story. Let's just say my brothers are very protective of you." His hands move on my thighs. "Now that I know you're not his..." He grips my neck, pulling me in for another kiss, "...eight and a half won't cut it. I want to be a ten. Any pointers?"

I ghost my index finger along his lips, and he opens, catching it between his teeth. "I intend to give you plenty more lessons now that you made the short list of men qualifying for a second date." White-hot lust ignites my senses, and I circle my hips on reflex, grinding into him.

"How many dates before you're mine?" he grinds through clenched teeth, holding me still.

"Yours?"

"Mine," he confirms, caressing my thigh, his fingers traveling north to cup my butt.

Oh... *his*. Right, of course. My cheeks heat, but I push the embarrassment aside. "Whenever you want." I've been waking up soaking wet, dreaming about him for weeks. I want all he can give me, and I'll give him anything he'll ask for. "Just a heads up, I might not be much fun the first time. I've never had sex, so you'll have to show me—" I bite my tongue when his lips pinch into a thin line, barely holding off a smile.

"You're fucking adorable, you know that? I don't mean sex. I mean *mine*. My girl. How many dates?"

My girl. God, I'm so giddy I might burst.

"You think you can tell me something about you I don't already know? I don't need dates, Nico. We're past dates by now, don't you think?"

"Good girl. Say it, Mia. Tell me you're mine."

I dip my head, stealing a quick kiss, but Nico doesn't let me pull away. He sinks deeper and tastes me all over again, his tongue skimming mine, our bodies flush together.

"You really like being kissed, don't you?"

"I might be a little insufferable until I get my fix."

"Good. You need to teach me how to be a ten." He moves his lips to my neck, nipping my ear. "Use your words, Mia. Tell me you're mine."

I arch back a little, my hands shaking with uncontainable glee. "I'm yours, and you're mine, but I'm still Cody's date tonight. I can't ditch him."

"That won't work. You're coming with me. Cody already found someone else."

"Really? Who? And what about your date? She bought a dress and probably went to the hairdressers, and—"

"And I booked her a Spa weekend with her girl. Believe me, she's not losing out." He hands me a small box from the inside pocket of his jacket. "Happy Birthday. I couldn't get it any sooner."

I eye a square, light-green box with a white satin ribbon. "Um, it's nice of you to—"

"Open it."

Biting my cheek, I pinch the ribbon, pulling until it sighs to the floor, then open the lid. A gold chain and a two-inch long, gold peacock feather encrusted with diamonds, tiny emeralds, and a large sapphire sits inside.

"You left the real one in the cab, but it was crumpled and

broken. I thought you could use a sturdier replacement."

"It's beautiful... thank you, but it won't serve the same purpose. I'm done trying to get into Aisha's good graces."

"It will serve the same purpose, only with a different person." He clasps the necklace around my neck. "The first wish is yours."

"You think you can handle my wish? You have no idea what you're getting into."

"Whatever it is, I'll do it. Do we have a deal?"

"Yes."

"Good girl. Don't make me wait long."

Nineteen

Nico

Mine.

Fucking *mine*.

Mine to hold, kiss, and take care of.

Finally.

As soon as we arrive at the Country Club, Mia rushes off to find my mother and get ready for her performance, and I'm intercepted by a concerned Theo.

"You doing okay? You need a drink, bro?" He grabs my arm, steering me toward the garden. "Some Xanax? Or better yet, how about a joint?"

"I see you had one." I frown when he shoves me through the door. "What the hell is going on?"

He takes a deep breath, pulling out a pack of cigarettes. "I know you won't smoke a joint, so at least take this. I'll get you all the vodka you'll need."

"You do remember I know Kaya's here, right?"

The patio slides left, and the triplets pour out wearing matching scowls that look dangerously similar to the one Theo had on a moment ago. They're a breed of their own with curly hair, long noses, and bushy eyebrows, but it's scary how one facial expression almost morphs them into Theo, Logan, me, or Shawn.

Cody shoves a glass of neat bourbon into my hand, patting my back. "You good? You gonna be the bigger man here?"

"I'm fine."

Just as I say it, I realize, again, that the triplets just walked through the door, and everyone I trust stands around me, waiting to see what I'll do next.

And Mia's not here.

She's in the venue, unattended.

I flick the cigarette to the floor, my muscles bunched when I turn to get inside. Both Colt and Conor grab my arms, halting me in place.

"Whoa, hold your horses, bro," Conor chirps. "Relax. Calm down. Don't go throwing a big-boy tantrum in there. It won't do you any good. Fuck that bitch. And fuck that asshole too. It's in the past. Big breaths, come on."

He sure gets his theatrics from Theo.

"I won't make a scene if they stay away from Mia," I say, shaking them off.

The last thing I expect is a supersized grin splitting Cody's face. "I never thought I'd be happy my brother stole my girlfriend."

"She wasn't yours," I snap, but I'm calmer knowing he doesn't mind. What's more, he seems pleased.

"Yeah, I know. She's *yours* now. Just remember. Don't mess her about. She's a good girl."

Yeah, she is. Too good for me.

I shake off that thought before it takes root, forcing me to question this entire thing. Mia would probably be better off with someone without my baggage, someone who doesn't go batshit crazy with jealousy, someone who doesn't have to fight his instincts daily to keep his protectiveness in check.

That guy? Whoever he is, is a better fit for Mia, but the only way he'll get anywhere near her is if he risks a one-on-one with me. The track record of fights I won versus fights I lost in my life is not in that guy's favor.

I can't remember exactly how many fights I won, but those I lost are easy to count. There were none. Whoever tries to steal Mia from me doesn't stand a chance.

Jesus, this is *insane*.

It seems all I've done the past two months is bottle my ever-growing feelings, and an hour ago, when Mia said she's mine, the corks went flying.

No way I can bottle them again. Cap whatever's left to stop it all spilling? Maybe. *Hopefully*, or she'll run away screaming before the evening ends.

"We'll keep an eye on Mia," Colt assures. He motions for Cody to get going, then turns to Theo. "You're babysitting Nico tonight. Make sure he doesn't kill Jared, alright?"

I scoff. "You'll end the night with a few hundred bucks in your pocket if you bet the right number of teeth I knock out of Jared's mouth. My money's on two with one blast."

Theo barks a burst of nervous laughter. "Two? I was at the club when you knocked out three and dislocated that guy's jaw when he spilled a drink on Kaya. Have you lost the steam, bro?" He squeezes my bicep. "I think you can do better. Three. And I bet a grand."

It's stupid, fucking childish, but it helps reduce the tension, so neither of us stops. Colt's the brightest of the triplets, so it's not surprising he catches onto the idiotic idea of betting against Jared's teeth and bones to distract me.

"Fifteen hundred on a broken nose."

"I'll take that," Conor says. "No way he can break Jared's nose in one hit. He always aims for the jaw first."

Challenge fucking accepted.

They keep placing bets, bickering about my punch-throwing skills. I've no idea who's keeping track, but someone should, or they'll be sorely disappointed when they can't remember who bet what if shit hits the fan.

We get back inside, and I scan the Ballroom, searching for a pink dress and a head of blond hair. *There she is.*

Right where she belongs, getting comfortable on the stool in front of the 1904 Steinway, little fists pumping while my mother bends down beside her, talking through a smile.

A moment later, Mia turns in her seat, looking around the room, determination lighting up her pretty face when her eyes find me. She bends her index finger in a *come here* motion.

Either she wants a drink, or she's nervous and wants me to talk my mother out of making her play. Whatever she needs, she doesn't need to ask twice.

I cross the room with Theo hot on my tail until he realizes where I'm going and backs off. Mom raises a curious eyebrow, stopping mid-sentence when I reach the stage and bend over Mia's shoulder, my ear to her mouth, expecting a whisper.

Instead, she unclasps her necklace, dangling the feather between us. "You can say no."

Like hell I will. There's not one thing I wouldn't do for her. I grab the necklace, fasten it behind my neck, and tuck the feather under my shirt. "What's the wish?"

"Play with me." She pats the stool, scooting to the edge to make more room. "Please."

I did not expect *that*.

My mother's gaze burns the back of my head when I cave. "I can't promise I'll keep up with you." I take a seat beside her. "Ten years' worth of rust on these fingers."

"It's like riding a bike. You don't forget. I know you play by ear, so hopefully, the nine times you heard this song on our way here is enough."

Now I know why she kept pressing *replay*.

"Clever girl." I lean over, pressing my lips to her temple. She's going to own my ass real soon. "You start. I'll join."

She places her hands on the keys, and the room falls silent with the first note of "Feeling Love" by Kim Ven and Lamalo. Her eyes are glued to my fingers when I join in. It's an unusual combination—tattoos and something as sophisticated as a grand piano, but I've caught Mia staring at my ink enough times to know she's in awe of it.

Ten seconds later, I'm the one not looking at the keys when she starts singing, her delicate voice sending my mind into that calm, trance-like state.

Maybe it's wishful thinking, but I hope she chose this song because it fits *us* so fucking perfectly.

My fingers skim the keys in sync with Mia until the room erupts with applause over the last lingering note.

"Thank you," she says as I wrap my arm around her, pulling her in. "Your mom will love me now."

"You're trying to get into her good graces now that you're dating her favorite son?"

"You're hardly her favorite, but with my help... who knows?"

The clapping dies down as we get up, and my mother is right there, blocking our way. "You're amazing, sweetheart," she chirps, pulling my girl into a hug. "And you..." She wipes her teary eyes, beaming at me. "I'm so glad I got to hear you play. Thank you. You must have magic powers, Mia. I've been begging him to play for ten years."

"I can be quite convincing."

"Oh, I'm sure." Mom hooks their elbows together, leading Mia away.

Before I take one step after them, Theo appears on my left, using his body as a shield that blocks my view of Jared and Kaya sitting at a table nearby.

"We'll end up slow dancing until the morning if you don't give me room to breathe," I say. "Relax. I won't go throwing punches for no reason. We both know I should thank the fucker for taking Kaya off my hands."

"True that." He motions his chin at Mom and Mia, chatting by our table. "You've been dating this chick for five minutes, and she's already Mom's favorite. Fucking figures."

"They've known each other for a while," I say, crossing the room. "Mia being mine isn't a factor."

"Bullshit," he mutters quietly as he takes his seat. "You've always had it easy."

I grip the back of Mia's chair and lean down to kiss her head. "You want wine or a spritzer?" I bite my cheek, trying not to laugh at my mother's gleeful expression.

She's basically swooning.

"Spritzer, please."

That's all the conversation we have for the next hour and a half while the guests take turns on the stage, boasting about their contributions.

Theo breathes down my neck when Kaya gets up there, pretending to care about the abused, battered women her donation will help.

It's a tax write-off for her, nothing else.

She hasn't changed much. Same dark brown hair, perfect makeup, and bright-red lips that used to summon my attention. Same thin figure, her tight dress hugging a clearly defined ribcage, and the same vile, toxic interior.

I glance between her and Mia, wondering what I saw in that woman. Although it'd be better to wonder what I see in Mia. She's the odd one out in the long line-up of women I looked at twice. Yet in some twisted way, seeing her earlier dressed and done up like every woman I ever fucked had my insides wringing with disappointment.

Kaya raises the champagne flute higher, zeroing in on me. She stumbles over her words when I purposely kiss Mia's head but recovers quickly, reciting the rest of her cheap speech.

All the while, I'm willing the time away so I can take Mia home. We're both seemingly listening to the speeches, but I catch her watching me as often as she does me.

I'm itching. Impatient. I want to be alone with her.

Thirty more minutes and the waitresses clear the tables. Cody's back to his usual flirty self now that he's not pretending he's into the girl he considers his little sister.

One of the waitresses leans over the table to grab my plate. Cody grazes his fingers over the back of her knee, making her squirm, the plates clattering in her hands. She sends him a warning glare. He ignores it, yanking her arm and pulling her closer to whisper in her ear.

Not even ten minutes later, he excuses himself from the table with a self-indulgent smirk.

Twenty

Nico

"I WANT TO STAY WITH YOU TONIGHT," I tell Mia when the cab driver pulls up outside her house just after two in the morning.

Her cheeks heat, but a small smile makes an appearance. "I want you to stay, too."

"Stop blushing, baby." I give the driver fifty bucks and help Mia out of the cab. "I've had three whiskeys, and you had two glasses of wine." I dip my head, kissing her neck while she rummages through her bag, searching for keys. "I'm here to sleep. Nothing else." As soon as the door opens, I haul her up, cross the threshold, and carry her into her bedroom. It's easier to kiss her when she's not craning her neck. "We will have sex," I whisper, laying her on her bed. "There are so many things I want to teach you... but not tonight. I want you comfortable around me first."

"Don't make me wait long. I am comfortable."

"Oh yeah?" She wouldn't be blushing every goddamn minute if she were. I sit up, pulling her with me. "Strip."

"Strip? As in...?"

"Get naked, Mia."

It's a dare. One I know she won't take when that alluring pinkness spreads like a flame all over her face and neck. She opens the nightstand, pulls out a brand-new toothbrush, then hands me a towel. "I need a shower. There's another bathroom at the end of the hall. Toby's been using it, so I'm sure you'll find whatever you need in there," she says, locking herself in the en suite.

The shower starts running, and I smirk, falling back into a mass of fluffy pillows, surprised that Mia's shyness doesn't annoy me. I'm not used to this. The women I've surrounded myself with all my life are her polar opposite, but instead of the eyeroll moment I'd expect, I find Mia entirely too adorable.

I'm twenty-nine. Sex is natural. Definitely not something to fuss over, but Mia's untouched. That makes sex a big deal.

Now that she's mine, I don't mind the wait. It doesn't matter how long it'll take before she's ready for me. And it's bizarre because this thing between us started with a dirty thought. I wanted her body from day one.

Now I'm all about her heart and mind.

I take a quick shower, not thrilled about wearing the same pair of boxer shorts once I'm done, but it's either that or sleeping naked, which might not be the best idea the first night I fall asleep with my girl.

She's still in the en suite when I sit on the bed to answer a few work-related texts. I instructed all my employees and business partners not to call me today. I guess I should've told them not to text either.

"Nico," Mia utters, her voice soft, almost a whisper.

I peer up from the screen, my phone slips from my grasp, landing on the floor. She stands in the doorway, cheeks red, and damp hair over one shoulder as she toys with her rings, nervously twisting and turning.

And she's *naked.*

My gaze dips to her perky breasts. They're not big. A handful at most. Pale pink areolas almost melt into her complexion. A small beauty mark in the valley between her breasts begs me to kiss it. I glance lower, her waistline as perfect as my seared-in memory. Clean-shaved pussy, round hips, smooth legs.

"You have no idea how beautiful you are," I say.

She really doesn't. I can tell. It's in her stance—the self-consciousness and insecurity. She knows she's pretty when wrapped in a cute dress, but she has no idea how fucking beautiful she is dressed like Eve.

I get up, take her face in my hands, and kiss those unbe-fucking-lievable lips. I'll never get over how full they are. How soft. I scoot her off the floor, aware I seem to do this every time I kiss her. She's tiny. She weighs close to nothing, and having her legs wrapped around my waist is too enticing to pass on. I can't fucking help myself, and I'm sure I'll be carrying her around *a lot.*

"Comfortable?" I ask, laying her on the bed.

"As comfortable as I can be, I guess." She pushes her damp hair back. "This is new. A little scary."

I trace my fingers from her neck across her collarbone and lower, touching the side of her breast. She tenses immediately, her breathing shallow. Instead of retreating, I set camp in that spot, caressing her skin until she starts to relax.

"Getting naked when you're in the heat of the moment, working your way up to sex, is easier than what you're doing for me now. What's the scary part?" I move my hand lower, making her squirm when I ghost the line of her waist and hip, then slowly up again.

"I'm not sure. Not knowing whether this..." She motions to her body, "...will live up to your expectations—"

"You exceed my expectations on every corner. Your body's not an exception, Mia."

God, I want to suck those pink nipples. I want to trace my lips down her stomach, dive between her thighs, and lick her until she comes, moaning my name and tugging my hair. I want to know how she tastes. Sweet, I bet. Everything about her is sweet.

"Okay, I believe you. You're comfortable around me. Now get dressed before I have a fucking aneurysm." I dip my head, kissing her neck. "I want a taste, baby. I want you to come on my lips, but that's not happening tonight."

She squeezes her thighs together, pupils blown.

"You're already soaking wet for me, aren't you?"

"I've been wet for you since we met," she admits quietly. "I wasn't far off volunteering to be your one-night-stand."

"It could never be just one night. You're too deep under my skin." I dip my head even lower, kissing along her collarbones. Her pebbled nipple touches my chin, making Mia squirm beneath me. "Still comfortable?" I drop my nose between her breasts, inhaling deeply.

"Yes," she utters on a sigh.

That does it. My restraint goes to shit.

I veer off to the left and take her puckered nipple between my lips, gently grazing it with my teeth. Mia lets out a quiet, needy whimper, her fingers grasping a thick tangle of my hair.

"Good girl," I whisper, toying with the other nipple between my thumb and forefinger. "Don't ever hide how I make you feel. Don't pretend you're not aroused when I touch you. Own it. Show me. I want to see it." I reluctantly grab a blue night dress from where she's laid it out on the bed, pull it down over her head, then sit up, taking her with me.

She makes herself comfortable in my lap, all the pink blush gone from her cheeks. "Close your eyes," she whispers.

"Why?"

"Please. Just close your eyes for a minute."

I do, curious and unable to refuse. At this pace, she'll have me wrapped around her finger by morning. I feel her fingertips on both sides of my jaw. She slides them lower to meet on my chin, then higher, over my lips and nose, brushing my eyelashes gently like she's committing every inch of me to memory.

She moves her hands to caress the soft spot behind my ears, runs her fingers up the nape of my neck and into my hair, then cups my face, thumbs under my eyes, as she stamps a kiss on my forehead.

I'm gone. Swallowed by the intense feelings. Overpowered.

She won't own me.

She already does when she kisses me slowly, slipping her tongue between my lips. I grip her neck, and my fingers disappear in her hair as I match the rhythm of her lips.

I've touched and kissed a lot of women; had sex with many, too. Wild, breathless sex, but nothing in all my twenty-nine years ever came close to the intimacy of this moment. It's not what I imagined I wanted. Nothing like any of my deepest fantasies.

Mia's more. So much more.

My whole life was a lie. An illusion crafted from a social

definition of beauty and fulfillment—tall, confident, career-driven brunette. That's what I thought I craved.

A petite, sweet, helpless little blonde is what makes me tick. She's all I think about. I want her safe, happy, and mine.

I flip her back, laying her flat on the bed, never breaking the kiss. I don't want more than this. Her lips, her touch, the cautious tenderness... it's enough.

It's fucking *everything*.

"I'll take care of you, baby," I whisper, my mouth grazing her cheek until I nibble her ear, my hand under her sky-blue nightdress setting another camp, caressing her hip. "I bet I won't want to leave once I'm in there."

Her cheeks heat again, but she fights embarrassment, toying with a thick tangle of hair at the back of my head. "I bet I won't want you to leave. I waited a long time for you."

So am I. She's a blank canvas. The first time I claim her body will lay the grounds for our sex life. I want her to be comfortable in her own skin, focused on her pleasure, and courageous enough to ask for what she needs.

Happy, at ease, confident.

That's the goal.

"I've wanted you since I met you," she says quietly.

"You have me, baby. You had me before I saw your face." I scuff my thumb across her lower lip. "I don't want to scare you, but I'm already fucking crazy about you."

"I don't want to scare you, but so am I."

I peck her head, pull the comforter aside, and pat the mattress. "Hop in. It's late."

We get under the sheets, and Mia starts busying her hands by pinching the comforter, a nervous ritual. "Um... will it be a problem if I put a nightlamp on? I'm—" She trips over the words, inhaling deeply. "I don't like darkness."

It takes me two heartbeats to understand what she said. My only response is, "Why?"

"It won't be bright, I promise. It's not really a night lamp, it's a projector, and I can dim—"

"You're evading, Mia. If you don't want to tell me, say so. Don't pretend you didn't hear me. Put the light on."

She leans out, turns on the projector, then flips the overhead lights off. It feels like I've stepped out of the space station. The ceilings and walls are covered in constellations, stars, and planets.

"I was bullied in school," she admits, curving into my side. "Kids used to lock me in the janitorial closet for hours after school, gagged and tied. It was pitch dark in there."

"Bullied? Why were you bullied?"

"Why is anyone bullied?" She kisses the underside of my chin. "This isn't a conversation I want to have the first night I get to fall asleep next to you. Let's save it for a rainy day, okay?"

I let out all air from my lungs. "Yeah, okay, but we're not spending that rainy day soaking wet on the beach."

Twenty-one

Nico

"SO..." Toby starts when I stumble into the kitchen early Sunday morning after the restaurant manager woke me up.

It's for the best. Theo, Logan, and Shawn decided we should start golfing again now that we own the Country Club and Logan's no longer tending to his pregnant, bedridden wife-to-be.

"You and Mia, huh? Just so you know, I called it when she was getting her tattoo done."

"Based on what?"

He shrugs, grinning behind a cup of coffee. "You didn't take your eyes off her for a second, man. And you acted out of character, cautious... like you were afraid she'd disappear if you made one false move."

I was. Mia makes a baby-deer first impression. Tiny little thing that needs tiptoeing around. It's not really the case, though. Now that I got to know her, I realized that, despite her unapologetic femininity, she doesn't need to be handled like a China doll.

Not that it'll stop me.

Mia's delicacy is what draws me in most. She's not a princess waiting for the prince to rescue her from the tower. She wants him to lock her in there and never let anyone touch her.

"My mother used to say people who are meant to be together are like two halves of the same apple, but..." Toby muses, blowing steam off his cup. "Mia's half a ripe raspberry, and you're—"

"I'm a blackberry."

A derisive snort flies past his lips. "If it's rotting, then sure, you're a blackberry."

I'd flip him off if I weren't holding two coffees and walking toward Mia's bedroom. She's not in bed anymore. The comforter is kicked aside, and the en suite opens seconds later.

"Morning," she says, crossing the room barefoot and smelling like peppermint. "When did you get up?"

She hasn't changed out of her night dress or brushed her hair, and I fucking love she feels comfortable enough around me to let me see her like this. She's effortlessly gorgeous, and the *I-woke-up-like-this* look doesn't diminish it in any way.

"About ten minutes ago." I grip her waist, lay her on the bed, and sink into her minty mouth for a kiss. "I hope you weren't about to come looking for me wearing this." I tug the frilly hem, covering her ass as much as the short fabric allows. "Tell me you don't parade the house dressed like this when Toby's here."

"Um... I do, but I also wear my swimsuit when he's here. I'd say this covers more."

I rest my forehead against hers, taking a few deep breaths

to rein in my flaring temper. Just thinking about anyone seeing her in this has my psyche sputtering like a defective neon.

It's toxic. I know it is. I've been trying to suffocate that flaw for years with little success.

"It upsets you to think he sees me like this..." she whispers, speaking her mind out loud, then wiggles out from under me, getting to her feet to tie a matching sky-blue silk robe around her middle. "Better?" She twirls around.

"Much better," I agree, pulling her back on the bed. "Don't let me get away with things like that, Mia. I'll get it under control."

"It's okay, I don't mind. Now, kiss me, and go. I believe you're golfing with your brothers today."

"Yeah, but I'll pick you up later. Pack a bag. You'll stay in my bed tonight."

***

My brothers wait by the first hole when I arrive. I don't mind golfing, but I can think of ten better ways to spend my Sunday morning. I do, however, enjoy catching up with my brothers. Before I caught Kaya cheating, we golfed every week.

Now that Logan and Shawn have kids and Theo's about to become a dad, we decided twice a month is a safer option, but with their busy lives, we'll drop it down to once a month soon.

"I'm telling you it's serious!" Theo's outraged voice cuts through the morning air. Narrowed eyes, gnashing teeth, and arms crossed over his chest: he's pissed. Cornered by the other two about something. "You want me to prove it?" he snaps, pointing between them. "Fine. You'll fucking see."

"No way it's serious, Theo, don't embarrass yourself," Shawn says, startling when I drop my bag to the ground behind his back. "Hey, bro," he drawls, his expression morphing into a cheeky grin. "Someone's unusually cheerful this morning. Could a certain awfully young blonde you couldn't keep your hands off last night have anything to do with it?"

"Are you still drunk?" I'm far from cheerful. In fact, a deep eleven marks my forehead because I don't want to be here. I also know what's coming, which isn't helping the situation. "Go on," I encourage them. "Get the digs out of your system. She doesn't fit me, right?"

Theo scoffs. "Who cares? It's not like you're marrying her, right? Have fun, bro. She's young, pretty, tight, and—"

A split-second rage consumes me in a blast comparable to an H-bomb. My fist whooshes back, then forth, connecting with Theo's jaw so fast he can't see it coming.

Even *I* didn't see it coming.

He clutches his face, but I'm not done. I'm a fucking bull at a Spanish corrida, pawing the dirt, getting ready to charge, but I don't get in his face like I want. Logan and Shawn grab my arms to hold me in place.

"What the fuck is wrong with you?" Shawn yells, yanking me back a step. "What was that for?"

"He knows exactly what it was for."

Theo lifts his hand, cringing when he touches his split lip, annoyed, amused, and apologetic as he looks me over. He was the one putting me back together after Kaya cheated. The one getting drunk with me until I stopped feeling betrayed and realized I should be thankful she was gone from my life.

By the look of him, he might have some sort of understanding of my paranoia.

He wipes the trickle of blood, glancing between Logan and Shawn with a smile. "Told you he's fucking serious about her."

Fuck. He's absolutely mental. "You were trying to prove a point?" I ask, my jaw tight. "I could've knocked your teeth out!"

"You'd pay for new ones. You know I didn't mean it, right? I just wanted to see if you'd snap."

I shouldn't snap. It's not normal that I lose my temper faster than I can form a coherent thought.

Theo comes over, patting my back. "We good?"

"Yeah, we're good. Next time you want to know something, *ask* the question." I trail off, calming down slowly. There's nothing new or extraordinary in my reaction. I was far worse when I was with Kaya, but... "Fuck, I need to get myself sorted. I can't lose my temper like that around Mia."

"True that." Theo hands me a driver. "I don't think she'll handle your outbursts. We need to get to the root of this and fix the problem ASAP."

"You want to psychoanalyze me?" I ask, looking over my shoulder at the sound of an approaching cart. "I'll make it work, Theo. I'm fine."

"Fucking peachy. My face proves that." He points to his swollen lip. "You still got a decent shot. It hurts like a motherfucker."

"Don't say shit about my girl, and you won't be in pain."

236

Twenty-two

Nico

LATER THAT EVENING, Mia sits on the breakfast bar when I enter the kitchen, my hair damp from the shower. She sips her wine, another glass waiting for me by the bottle.

"We're going out," I say, making room for myself between her legs. "Dinner. What do you feel like? Italian, Greek, Spanish?"

She hooks her index finger in the collar of my t-shirt, tugging until I get the hint and kiss her.

"Don't do that." I bite her lip when she sighs softly. "I know you love it when I kiss you, but you need to keep those sweet little sounds in for me."

She peers up, her eyes glossy, velvet with desire. "Why?"

"I don't have nearly enough restraint when you sigh and moan in my mouth."

Her lips form a small *o*, and she sighs again, making my dick twitch. "I'm not hungry, Nico." She tiptoes her fingers up my chest. "Not for food, anyway. I want to have sex."

A ball of blazing heat detonates behind my ribs, the images those words summon redirecting the blood in my veins straight to my cock. "So do I, baby, but no rushing. I won't fuck this up. We'll get there when we get there."

"We're there." She squeezes her thighs around mine, her ache like a separate living organism inside her trying to claw its way out. "You want me to beg?" She grips my hand, steering my fingers under her dress, over the inside of her thigh, until I touch the lacy fabric of her panties, and my brain turns to mush.

She's soaked. Warm. So fucking *mine*.

"Do you think I'm ready?" Her breathing hitches when I stroke her, barely putting any pressure. Her lips graze my ear, her words reduced to a whisper and softer with each one. "Do you have any idea how frustrating it is to take care of myself when all I want is to have you touch me?"

I close her lips, my pulse speeding up. Lust takes over. The need to bury myself inside her, take care of her ache, and find release after weeks of imagining her naked body in my arms is so intense it feels like my bones are shaking.

"Now you've done it. I'm taking that first. Now."

She sighs again, on fucking purpose. I lift her up, my hands knotted under her bum for support as I cross the hallway.

"You need to trust me. You need to understand that I know what I'm doing," I say, making her tremble, and I want to tear her clothes off right here on the staircase. "I'll make you feel good, baby. I've got you. I'll take care of you."

"I'm yours, Nico. Do as you please."

I put her down to stand in my bedroom, spin her to face the wall, and kiss her neck while I unzip her dress. It falls to the floor in a heap of white, pink, and gray. Her bra follows.

I spin her back, my fingers weaving through her dirty-blonde waves, my mouth covering hers. I hook my thumbs over the elastic of her panties, pulling until they fall around her ankles, and Mia steps out, lips still on mine.

"You've got one chance to run," I say, lifting her up again. She wraps her legs around me, hot pussy pressing against my stomach, my t-shirt wet with her ache.

"I'm not going anywhere."

"I don't think I'd let you run." I lay her down, scrutinizing every inch of her. She's perfect. Every beauty mark and blemish, every curve, even the scar on her thigh. *Perfect.* "Tell me you trust me to take care of you."

"I trust you. I'm not afraid."

I yank the t-shirt over my head, and before it hits the floor, my mouth closes on her breast.

She arches back with a quiet hiss.

I waited weeks for this to happen. I imagined her in my bed a thousand times, so I know exactly how I want this to go.

"First," I say, kissing up the column of her neck as I slide my hand down her body. "You'll come on my fingers."

Her lips part, eyes flutter closed, and a barely audible sigh finds a way out when I circle her clit.

"Good girl," I whisper, my cock straining against the zipper of my jeans. "Focus on how you feel and nothing else." My fingers slide left and right, then in small circles, her wetness aiding my work, bringing her closer. "Chase that high, baby. You want to scream? Scream. You want to keep it in? Do it. Don't think."

With each stroke, her moans lose their softness, and her petite body shudders with waves of pleasure. I love how she pulls me in, rediscovering my lips over and over.

"I'm so close," she utters minutes later.

"That's good, focus. Let it happen." I tease her entrance, rubbing her clit with my thumb. "You're beautiful. You're mine. Every sound, every spasm, every—" A low growl bubbles in my chest, cutting off words when her orgasm hits. "There it is, good girl. Ride it, baby."

Her breathing hiccups, and she's coming. Hard. So hard her legs shake, and toes curl, and her lips part. She gouges her nails down my back, scraping long lines as I watch.

I *stare*.

She throws her head back, throat exposed, and moans in a soft staccato. I brush my lips along her collarbones. She squeezes her thighs together, still shuddering.

"Best view in the city," I say. "You're perfect, you know that? Now you'll come on my lips."

"I... I—"

"You've never made yourself come twice in a row?"

"No, I didn't think I could."

I take my jeans off and move to the foot of the bed, hooking my arms under her knees. "You can. Relax, and focus on you." I nose a line down her abdomen before licking her slowly.

She tastes like fucking candy. Sweet... so sweet.

Her thighs quiver around my head as a needy whimper hits my ears, and my cock twitches to spring free.

Mia grips my hair, her boobs pressed in her arms as her back bends from the bed with every lick of my tongue. I could spend hours between her legs, using my best tricks to make her squirm.

She moans, the sounds louder, as if she can't hold her inhibitions, and I feel I might burst any minute.

I flick her clit with my tongue, using my thumb to tease her entrance, and Mia pushes me down harder, lifting her hips off the bed a little, begging for more.

And more I give her, sucking her into my mouth once, twice, and she's coming again, clutching my head in place and grinding into me for a few intense seconds before her legs open enough to let me out. I mark a line of open-mouthed kisses between her breasts before we're at eye level.

Flushed face, full lips even plumper, swollen from my kisses, and long eyelashes casting shadows on her cheeks.

"Look at me, Mia," I say, hanging over her, my fingers ghosting the side of her warm body. "The way you come... I can't get enough of seeing you like that."

She smiles a blissful, satisfied smile, eyes still closed.

"Suddenly speechless, are you?" I trace my nose across her cheek. "Let's see if I can get you audible again. Now, you'll come while I'm inside you."

I get up, pulling my boxer shorts off, and Mia lets out a quiet gasp, eyeing my cock. "Um, it's so—"

"Big?" I supply, my ego pleasantly stroked.

"No. I mean, yes, it's big, but I wanted to say soft."

I blink twice before a burst of laughter rips from my chest. "Soft? *That's* what you're going for? It's as far from soft as it gets. We'll have to work on your dirty talk."

"I didn't mean it like that." She blushes, scooting to the edge of the bed. Reaching her small hand out, she stops, glancing up at me. "Can I touch it?"

"That's the first and last time you ask permission. If you want to touch me, do it."

Her gaze drops again. She trails the veins, her touch light but arousing when she smears a bead of precum over the head with her thumb. "So soft," she murmurs.

I grip her hand, wrapping it around the hilt. "That's how you do this, Mia." I clamp my hand over hers, stroking it over myself a few times. "We'll save that lesson for a different day."

She moves back, nodding when I pull a condom from the nightstand drawer and rip it open.

"I've got a contraceptive implant," she says before I roll it on. "It helps with my periods, so we don't need this unless—"

"We're not ditching condoms, Mia. It's just latex. It doesn't change how my body works. Hormones do, so I'll be the one using protection, baby." I climb back on the bed, hovering above her. "I won't tell you to take the implant out. It's your body and your decision, but I will tell you I don't want you to have it."

"Can we talk about this another time?"

"Sure." I kiss her head, push a pillow under her head, and slide another under her butt, positioning myself between her legs. "Relax. I'll take care of you."

I've imagined this moment for two months. Two fucking months, and now that she's finally here, it's *nothing* like my fantasies. I always skipped this part, going straight into picturing myself already inside her...

But I need to get there first without hurting her, and despite hiding it well, I've never been so nervous before sex. I've never taken a girl's virginity, but every cell in my body is wound up tight, ready and determined.

"You're more worried than I am. Relax." She lifts her head off the pillow, imitating my tone. "You've done this before."

I watch her face, waiting for any signs of pain as I move my hips forward slowly. I don't get far...

She tenses when the head of my cock finds resistance. Not

every girl has a hymen, I know that much, but Mia does, which means I need to be even more careful.

"Just rip the band-aid," she utters, tensing more with each passing second, the anticipation of pain worse than the pain itself.

"Look at me." I retreat, then slide back in, barely making contact with the barrier.

Her eyes pop open. Big, round, filled with unease that has me on edge, almost ready to pull out and try another day.

Fuck.

This girl...

This little, sweet, innocent beauty has been my focus point since I laid eyes on her.

"You trust me, Mia. This isn't a band-aid. I won't hurt you."

She nods, smiling small, and I wipe that smile off with a kiss. She's like playdough around me, adjusting to my rhythm and melting in my arms.

I tease her with shallow, slow thrusts, her body adjusting to take me inch by inch. The more she relaxes, the further I sink. The barrier stretches slowly, letting me in deeper. It takes at least five minutes of cautious movements and my lips working every inch of her skin in reach before I'm as deep as the position allows.

"How's that, baby? Does it hurt?"

"No, it's..." She pinches her lips together, frowning a little, "...nice. It's nice."

I graze my nose up her cheek, leaving a kiss on her temple. "You're a lousy liar, Mia. Say what you want to say."

"You're so big!" she complains, holding onto my shoulders.

"You sure you don't mean *soft?*"

She whacks my back. "Don't joke! This is serious."

"No. Sex is supposed to be fun, not serious."

"God, there's no space there. How did you fit it in? I'm really stretched... it's... it's..." She circles her hips like she's checking something. "Not bad, just odd."

I rise on my elbows, looking her over. I don't know why, but her babbling makes me fall for her that much harder. "Believe me, there's absolutely no room. I barely fit in, but that'll work in our favor, you'll see."

"Well...?" she muses, raising an eyebrow. "What now? What are you waiting for? Move."

I retreat my hips slowly and slide back in, loving how she bites my lip, her nails digging into my biceps.

"Okay, *now* it's nice. Do it again. It doesn't hurt."

"I told you I won't fucking hurt you." I cover her mouth with mine, teasing her tongue while I pull out and push back in. "You have no idea what you do to me."

Being with her, being inside her, is surreal. I never want to be anywhere but this close to her. Ever.

My moves remain cautious for a while before I'm confident enough to up the tempo. She moans, arching off the bed, kissing my neck, face, and lips while her nails glide up and down my back, drawing faint lines.

I've never been so aroused. Every thrust is fucking sacred. Every sound she makes blows my mind. She's a drug, and I'm addicted to the point of madness, my chest heavy with over-powering emotions. I'll make this work.

For her, I'll be the best version of myself.

"I need to be deeper," I say, sitting back on my calves. "You need to feel me deeper. Turn around and kneel."

"My legs are too weak."

It's been a while since her last orgasm, but her knees still buckle when she tries to get in position.

"I'll hold you." I pull her up, wrapping my arm over her stomach and turning her around. "Grab the headrest. Don't let go until I tell you."

I cuff her wrists in one hand and hold her hip with the other as I slip inside, pressing my face into her hair.

"Oh God," Mia breathes, her legs buckling again.

"There it is." The angle lets me sink balls-deep, her tight pussy like a gloved fist around my shaft. I have to summon all my restraint not to come. "Don't move your hands," I grunt in her ear when she starts wriggling them out of my grasp. "You're already almost there, aren't you? Chase it, Mia. Focus on how good it is when you're with me."

Another satisfied, loaded moan ricochets off the walls, fueling my arousal. Sweat coats my back, my orgasm building at the base of my spine. I spread my fingers over her throat, pulling her back until she rests against my chest, and I tilt her chin up, watching pure ecstasy paint her face.

I'd love nothing more than to squeeze a bit and control how much air she takes in, but I'll bruise her if I use my fingers as a necklace, and that's not happening. Instead of elevating the high that way, I settle for upping the pace, driving into her faster.

"I don't think—" she chokes, her breathing hiccuping when my fingers toy with her nipples. "I can't handle another one."

"You can." I kiss her shoulder, holding my primal instincts at bay. I'll lose it if I'm not careful, and she's not ready for me when my brakes give out. I can't fuck her hard and fast yet. Not while she's learning how to take me. "Don't think, Mia." A few more deep thrusts, and I'm literally shaking, trying to hold off so we'll come in sync. "Now, baby. Let me feel you."

The second she spasms around me is the second I come

too. Mia moans and shakes, clawing my arm as I grip her chin, turning her head to drink those moans straight from her lips.

I thrust a few more times, riding the orgasm until it's too intense, and I stop, holding her upright while she trembles all over, her petite body limp.

"I think I like sex more than kissing," she admits when we fall back, my arms around her hot frame. "I'm giddy." She presses the back of her trembling hand to her forehead.

"Not what I was going for, but I'll take it."

She opens her eyes, beaming at me. Her post-sex face is just like her: adorable. "What were you going for?"

"Satisfied and exhausted."

"Mission accomplished. I know I need to go grab a shower, but I'm afraid my legs won't hold me." She flips onto her tummy. "I knew you'd make this amazing."

My legs are weak too, but it doesn't stop me scooping her off the bed. I can't recall ever coming so fucking hard. I stand Mia under the shower and turn it on, one arm wrapped around her middle while she holds onto my neck.

"I've never been so weak, no matter how hard I pushed myself at the gym," she says, smiling up at me.

"You've been working out all wrong."

"I feel like I've run eight hours straight. Why did you let me have three orgasms?"

"Let you? You make it sound like I get to decide whether you can have an orgasm." I grab a bottle of shower gel and lather it all over her body, taking extra care with her perfect, perky boobs and swollen pussy. "Making you come is my job, Mia. I'm not here to hand out permissions." She turns around, pressing her soapy boobs to my chest and making me groan. "Keep doing that, and you'll get three more."

Twenty-three

Mia

THE BITTER SMELL OF COFFEE pulls me out of sleep when the mattress dips behind me. Warm fingers brush the hair off my nape while I lay motionless on my stomach, one knee bent, one arm under the pillow.

Nico kisses the spot where my spine starts, then moves lower, pressing his lips to every vertebra. He stops between my shoulder blades, nosing a line back up to kiss my temple, his warm breath fanning my skin.

"Morning."

My back arches, and I stretch my arms, then flip onto my back, rubbing sleep from my eyes. "What time is it?"

He gets up, grabbing his coffee from the nightstand. Another one is there, waiting for me. Gray tracksuit bottoms hang loosely over his hips, his tattooed chest in my face, reminding me of the desire burning in his eyes last night. Black hair falling carelessly to his forehead, and muscles on his arms shifting beautifully with every move he made.

That's a visual that'll always get me all worked up.

"Ten past six. I've been talking myself out of waking you up for an hour."

I roll over to reach for my coffee, and a low growl fills the room, making me realize that the black fabric of Nico's t-shirt has rolled up while I slept in it, and my bottom is on display.

"You like what you see?"

He's back by the bed, and the mattress dips again under his elbows resting on both sides of my knees, his hands on my hips. I squirm when his warm lips touch the back of my thighs, drawing a vertical line until he nips my butt.

"You've no idea how sexy you are."

I take a few small sips of the steaming vanilla coffee, setting the cup back on the nightstand as Nico climbs further up the bed. The moment I release the handle, he flips me onto my back, pushing the hem of his t-shirt over my breasts before palming them gently and kissing between them.

I wrap my arms and legs around him to gain leverage, and three moves later, he's on his back while I straddle him, feeling his erection press against my pussy.

He's big and heavy. I know he helped me a little, rolling onto his back, but I still grin down at him, grinding into him.

"Someone's excited this morning."

"He's always excited when you're around," he admits, tugging my hands until I lay flat on his chest.

I jerk back when he tries to kiss me and wince as I get to my feet. "I need to wash up. No kissing till I brush my teeth."

"You're sore," he clips, rising on his elbows. "How bad?"

"I'm fine. You made sure it didn't hurt last night, but you

couldn't expect me not to feel anything down there this morning. It'll pass. It's not that bad." I stand by the sink, furiously brushing my teeth, my feet cold on the tiles.

Nico grabs me as soon as I'm done and within his reach. "I want to see."

"You're going to examine me?" I ask when he pushes my tee up, then spreads my legs.

"I want back in, baby, so yeah, I'll examine my sore pussy."

All air ejects from my lungs when he kisses the tender flesh. I relax, focusing on how amazing the delicate licks of his tongue feel. "Your minty breath helps."

He looks up, a focused expression on his rested face. "Don't leave the room." He kisses my stomach before getting out of bed. "I'll be back in twenty minutes."

"Where are you going?"

"Twenty minutes, Mia. Don't move."

I sit up as he rushes out of the room, his heavy footsteps thumping down the stairs. The door at the bottom closes with a bang, and I fall back onto the pillow, squeezing my thighs together, aching for his touch.

Never did I expect sex to feel this good.

Orgasms are great, but I've never given myself one as intense as those from Nico's hands and lips. I want more. I want him to watch me the way he did last night. Like nothing matters more than us moving together.

The door downstairs opens again not even fifteen minutes later. Nico's rushed footsteps echo up the stairs before he comes in with a small, brown paper bag.

"Where were you?"

"Pharmacy," he says, moving to the foot of the bed. He pulls a blue tube out of the bag, then squeezes a pea-sized amount of clear gel onto his index finger.

"What's that?"

He rubs the gel over my pussy, eyes not veering from mine. "Cooling lubricant. How's that? Better?"

"Yes," I mutter, enjoying the tingling sensation. "So... *oh,*" I moan when Nico pushes two fingers inside me.

"I've got you, Mia," he says, voice thick with emotions. "I'll always make you feel good." He dips his head, licking me slowly.

"Is it edible?"

"Shush, baby, focus."

I do. My eyes close, and I drown out everything other than the feelings he evokes, the pleasure coursing through me, and the orgasm that's oh so close when he skillfully strokes my G spot.

I fist thick tangles of his hair, letting my body do what it wants before my brain can intervene. My hips meet his strokes, almost riding his face.

My moans fill the room until the desire peaks, exploding like a firework. Everything tightens and releases, spasming every muscle inside me as I tremble, submitting to the bone-melting pleasure.

Nico's on his knees when my thighs release his head. He squeezes more lubricant onto his hand and then palms his cock, spreading the gel in long strokes.

"My turn," I say, hauling myself up. "I want to be on top."

His eyes skim over me, darkening when he rests his back against the headboard, pulling me closer until my knees dig into the bed on both sides of his hips.

He holds the base of his shaft, guiding himself, helping me sink down, taking him in with a quiet hiss.

"Does it hurt?" he asks when I still.

"No, I'm just so full... I'm okay."

"You make me crazy." He grips my hips, caressing my skin with his thumbs. "Fucking *crazy*. You frown, and I'm tense." He slides me back, aiding my moves, then drags me forward, burying himself to the hilt. "You might be on top, but I'm in control, Mia. My girl does as she's told. Can you handle that?"

I nod, a genuine thrill sweeping me from head to toe. Giving up control is easy when that's all I ever craved.

"Good girl. Hands behind your back."

I don't hesitate, lacing my fingers behind me as Nico lifts my hips, impaling me over again. I've never felt more beautiful than I do as his eyes flare, roving my body. Our hastened breathing mixes with my moans, our moves gain pace, the promise of another release humming up the backs of my thighs.

"Easy, baby," he says, pressing me down hard, and sliding me back and forth instead of up and down. "Don't rush. You need to get used to me first."

He curves one hand around my back, forcing me closer, then wraps my braid around his wrist, tugging hard enough to tilt my head back. I brace against his shoulders, feeling the heat of his open-mouth kisses on my neck, and a low growl builds in his chest, throwing me back into that hastened rhythm.

"Hands. Behind. Your. Back," he emphasizes each word.

I press myself against him, wanting to crawl under his skin, only half aware he's talking. I'm delirious, so close to the edge, grinding against him, taking care of my needs first.

Nico stops me in place. "That's not how sex will work for us. You do as I say, understood?" He sucks my bottom lip before lifting me off him. "On your hands and knees."

He huffs when I hesitate and spins me around, maneuvering me until I'm where he wants: on all fours, hips in the air.

The room's suddenly perfectly silent.

He's not touching me.

I can't see him, and an awkward feeling fills my chest.

I'm exposed. Naked in a compromising position. My heart rams harder as irrational thoughts take over my mind.

Why isn't he touching me? Why isn't he moving? Why is he so silent?

It's only been three seconds, but something is wrong.

"Grab the edge of the bed," Nico instructs, putting pressure between my shoulder blades like he wants to push me down.

I outstretch my hands until I grip the edge, my boobs flat on the sheets, hips in the air. I swallow hard, taking a deep, calming breath. We're okay. He was just looking at me...

The touch of his hands and the warmth radiating from him as he leans over help me relax further.

"Remember your safe word?"

"Um, yes. Red."

"Use it if I'm pushing your limits too fast." He jerks his hips forward, filling me in one urgent stroke. All my unease disappears instantly. "Because I will push, Mia..." he says, and a powerful slap lands on my ass.

The sound of his hand connecting with my flesh makes the muscles in my abdomen contract. I'm wet, my body reacting to the slap with a pleasant shiver.

"I'll push until nothing we do in bed makes you blush." He slaps me again. "Until you learn to demand what you want and give me what I want." He grips my wrists in one hand, the pace of his thrusts gaining speed.

A loaded moan leaves my lips when he hits the perfect spot deep inside. I drown in the moment, hungry for everything he can give me.

"Straighten your legs and cross your ankles," he orders, desire coating his voice.

I do as I'm told, enjoying the weight of his body over mine.

"Oh God," I whimper.

"You're close, aren't you? Chase it, Mia."

I can't think when my body shudders with every thrust. I lift my head, resting it against his shoulder, eyes closed, and I squeeze his fingers till mine turn numb.

The tempo of his hips rocking into me turns unforgiving, scooting me further up the bed. Every gasp filling the air seems to double his efforts. My orgasm builds, the sensation so close I feel I can reach out and grab it.

"That's it," he says, pressing his forehead to the back of my head. "You're doing so well, baby. So fucking good. Come for me. Don't hold it. Let it happen."

And I do. I let go. The pleasure stacks up, up, *up*, and then... it topples over, the orgasm so sharply intense it's almost a pain. A delirious, delicious pain.

Nico grunts, the sound low, loaded, and so hot it's enough to prolong the orgasm lashing through me like a hot silk whip. He slams into me again and again before he stills, gently biting my neck as his cock swells inside me.

We're panting, our bodies slick from sweat. Even though I woke up less than an hour ago, I'm spent; sleepy.

"I think I know why Aisha's addicted to sex," I say when Nico lies beside me, fingers brushing the line of my spine.

"Tell me why you were uncomfortable on your hands and knees." There's no annoyance in his voice, but my cheeks heat on their own accord.

"Um... I don't know."

"I want you to feel good about your body, Mia. You said you're comfortable with me, but you tensed."

I press my lips together, fighting the urge to hide under the pillow so he can't see me blush. "You were quiet, you weren't touching me, and I couldn't see you..."

"I was taking in the view. You're beautiful from every angle." He flips me onto my back, spreading his fingers on my stomach. "Does it bother you that I tell you what to do?"

"No, of course not. That's a turn-on. I like that you're in control. I just..." I swallow hard, aware of how silly this sounds. "I need to see you or feel your hands on me, so I know we're okay, so I know you enjoy me, us, and sex."

"I enjoy *us*, Mia. I enjoy you and..." He kisses my nose, "...sex is off the charts. Talk to me, okay? We won't learn what we like if we don't talk. Always tell me if I'm doing something wrong or you don't enjoy any part of sex. And if you want to stroke my ego, tell me when I'm doing things right, too."

He gets up only to come back half a minute later in a pair of boxer shorts, washcloth in hand. He spreads my legs, pressing the warm, damp cloth to my pussy.

"It works both ways, Nico. Whatever you want, you have to tell me. I'm new to this."

"I know. You're doing great, baby." He wipes between my legs, raising on his elbow to look me over. Two tendons on his tattooed neck pulse in the rhythm of his jaw working in tight circles. "My girl is adventurous," he says, dipping his head to kiss my collarbone. "Confident..." His hot breath warms my skin before he takes my nipple between his teeth, and my breathing hitches all over again. "Demanding... courageous..." He kisses a vertical line up the column of my throat. "Willing..." he whispers, his lips hovering over mine.

I'm not breathing. My blood boils with lust, but every word pierces me like a bullet. I'm nothing like *his girl*. Not a single quality he listed resides in my character. My throat constricts so hard I'm afraid I'll choke on disappointment, but I push it aside, pulling him down for a kiss.

I can be all those things... I think.

I hope.

He's only been mine for a day, but I never want to lose him.

"I want back in, baby," he says with a small smile, pulling away. "Told you I won't want to leave once I was in."

"I don't want you to leave, but I should get ready for college. I'm sure you need to be in the office soon."

"Two things, one: don't mention college unless you absolutely have to, baby. I hate that you're so young. And two: fuck work. We'll stay here and have sex all day."

Another low blow to my stomach. I knew the age difference was an issue, but I didn't expect I'd have to hide a whole part of my life.

"I can't do anything about my age," I say, toying with my bracelets. "As tempting as a day in bed sounds, the—" I bite my tongue before I tell him the finals are approaching. "I need to get ready."

"Fine. Stop by your house later. Pack more clothes and grab that book we've been reading."

When he stayed over on Saturday, I was so excited about having him in my bed I couldn't fall asleep, so he tucked me in and quietly read *Alice in Wonderland*.

"You enjoyed it? I thought you were just helping me fall asleep."

"It's not a book I'd choose, but it wasn't boring." He gets up, throwing a pair of sweatpants on. "Come on. Get moving. Let's get this day over and done with, so I can have you naked again."

Twenty-four

Mia

I TRY NOT TO WINCE as I get up to leave the auditorium, but Nico sure didn't help when he put me on all fours earlier. Sex this morning was an entirely different experience from last night, and if I'm being honest, I liked it better today.

He was more himself, no longer worried about hurting me. He dominated every second, barking orders and manhandling me into the positions he wanted. I hope he won't stop controlling our sex life because I love his possessive, demanding tone. He knows what he wants, what I want, and how to make it happen.

"Not so fast, kitten." Brandon blocks my way when I step into the corridor. He backs me into a corner, a scowl twisting his face. "We gotta talk."

"I have nothing to tell you."

"You sure about that? I hear you're not liking the attention you're getting. My boys say you're avoiding them, shooting them down."

I fold my arms, hoping it'll be enough to stop him pressing into me. "Your boys are correct."

"Who told you about the prize?" He glides his finger along the line of fabric on my chest and tilts my chin when I don't answer. "It was Justin, wasn't it? Cheeky fucker. I'll deal with him later, and you..." He sweeps his thumb along my jaw. "You have one last chance to play ball. I want that first, Mia."

"And yet you let your friends try and score with me. That's an odd way of saying *I want you*."

"I don't want *you*. I want your pussy. There's a difference."

I grit my teeth, pushing down nausea threatening to eject the contents of my stomach into his face. Maybe I should just roll with it. Projectile-vomiting all over the star quarterback would be the highlight of my college career.

"You're too late," I say, swallowing hard. "Both I and my pussy are taken."

He cocks an eyebrow, looking me over, surprise fading from his snobbish face quickly. "Nice try, kitten. I'm not falling for that. My boys played nice until now, but you just had to ruin the fun, didn't you? Imagine that instead of asking you out, they'll get handsy."

"That's sexual assault. Even you're not stupid enough to order that."

He traces one hand down my side, making me shudder with disgust. "You think anyone will prosecute them for slapping your curvy ass? I doubt it. Let's see how long it'll take before you come crawling, *begging* me to fuck you." He pats my butt, and on reflex, I slam my knee into his groin.

"You won't like what follows if you ever put your hands on me again."

He holds his breath and his balls, doing a surprisingly decent job of not doubling over. "Twenty grand," he grumbles, his face changing colors like a kaleidoscope. "And I'm opening the game to *every* guy on campus."

That does it.

The thought of being harassed by the entire male population of this nightmarish ecosystem has my stomach twisting into tight knots. I'm flooded with images of obnoxious, hungry-for-cash guys cornering me in empty corridors, forcing me to use the self-defense moves the triplets taught me.

Brandon's friends aren't short for cash, but there's plenty of students here whose parents don't own yachts and ocean-view mansions.

"You wouldn't dare..." I suck in harsh breaths, shepherding my raging nerves. "Brandon, this isn't funny."

He doesn't reply, walking away with a triumphant smile while I try to sever the tendrils of an onrushing panic attack. It proves useless when, in the thinning crowd, I spot Blair surrounded by a tight circle of friends. She silently simmers, clenching and unclenching her fists, jealousy painting her face red.

She made my life miserable since kindergarten. I know what she's capable of... she can bring more hurt than the twenty grand prize. The cruelty she threw my way over the years flashes before my eyes, turning my stomach further.

That's it. Not even mint can help now.

I faintly register that the triplets entered the building, but I don't wait for them to come closer. I run toward the bath-room, one hand clasped over my mouth as I burst into the first cubicle, and lean over the toilet, dropping to my knees.

The door opens again, probably Cody, Colt, or Conor hot on my tail while my breakfast and coffee pour into the toilet.

I've no idea why the triplets are still in my corner, but they've had my back for a year now, and the thought of losing them has my heart breaking clean in two.

Wave after wave of powerful shudders shake my body dotted with goosebumps. My throat burns. My eyes water. There's nothing left to throw up, but dry heaves aren't easing.

Whoever's in here comes closer, looming behind me, not saying a word. I feel them gather my hair, holding it out the way.

I can't get a word out, still spitting down the toilet and gasping for air between pathetic whimpers.

My hair fans down my back.

Footsteps beat a fast retreat.

The door bangs closed, and a stench of something burning hits my nose.

My mind stops spinning around Brandon, focusing on what's burning. The smell is so strong that I—

A pained cry tears from my mouth when intense heat blazes up my back.

No, no, no, no, *no*...

I jump to my feet, spin around, and catch my reflection in the mirrors above the sinks. Flames consume my blonde locks faster than fire runs in dry grass.

Adrenaline kicks in, my senses razor sharp. I turn the faucet and dip my head, shoving it under the water.

That's when the fire alarm starts, drowning out my distressed cries. A second later, the sprinklers douse my hair, face, and clothes. Water patters down my bare back, but... I have a blouse on... I reach behind me, feeling big holes burned through the fabric, my skin hot and tender.

Slowly, I look up, the initial frenzy wearing off, replaced by a sense of impending doom.

My hair is half its length now. The locks that fell to my butt seconds ago barely reach my shoulder blades.

Tears spill, disguised by the sprinklers drenching the bathroom. I slide to the floor, hugging my knees.

"Mia?" Colt shoves his head between the door. His eyes land on me, and he rushes in, letting the door bang against the wall. "What the fuck happened?! Cody! Get in here!" He kneels on the wet floor, gripping my shoulders.

"Don't touch me," I choke, swallowing tears. "It hurts..."

"Jesus, sweetie, your hair..." He trails off, combing his fingers through my damaged locks. "Who did this? Was it—"

"Blair," Cody clips from the doorway, nodding toward the mirrors. "*Stay away from him, bitch*," he reads what's been written in red lipstick.

The sprinklers turn off, and the building is suddenly blanketed by gloomy, tragic silence. Conor shoves Cody aside, making room for Mr. Finch, who stops two steps in, his assessing eyes taking in the scene.

"Miss Harlow, do you require medical attention?"

I shake my head, gritting my teeth as Colt cuffs my wrists, helping me off the floor. He tucks me under his chin but stops short of wrapping his arms around me.

"Mia, your back... you need to see the first aider."

"I'm okay. I've got burn cream at home." I swat my tears away, inhaling a calming breath, but tiny rivers trail my cheeks, despite my efforts to keep the pathetic whimpers in. "Can you take me home?"

"I must insist—"

"You heard her," Cody cuts off Mr. Finch. "She wants to go home, so she's going home. And you better make sure Blair's not here on Monday."

"Blair Fitzpatrick? Was she the one who..." He gestures at me, twirling his finger in the air, "...did this?"

"I don't know. I didn't see anyone."

"You know it was her," Cody says, his voice one level off yelling. "She's a psycho. Don't let her get away with it."

"It's my word against hers. There's no witnesses. Do you want to guess how many people will vouch she was with them on the other side of campus?" I rest my forehead against his chest. "Just please take me home."

***

"You think Thalia or Cass could fix her hair a bit?" Conor asks his brothers when Cody parks on my driveway.

"I'll do it myself." I lift my head from Colt's lap. "Thank you for bringing me home."

This isn't the first time Blair destroyed my hair. She stuck gum in it all the time in elementary school and chased me with scissors in kindergarten, nipping whatever she caught between the blades. She clipped my skin, too. That's when the teacher walked in, finding me hiding in the corner, bleeding and crying, locks of my hair littering the floor.

"I hope you don't think we'll leave you here alone," Colt says, squeezing my hand. "We're staying."

"No, you're not because I'm not staying. I promised Nico I'll grab a few things and stay with him tonight."

"Wait till he hears that bitch burned your hair," Cody says, getting out of the car to open the back. "He'll lose his fucking shit." He takes my hand, helping me out.

"He won't find out. Promise you won't tell him," I plead as we enter my house.

"Why the hell not?" Conor asks, jogging to the fridge. "You think he won't notice your hair's half the length?" He pulls out a pack of string cheese, hauling himself onto the kitchen counter.

"I'll make something up."

"Why?" Cody demands, leaning against the cupboards beside Conor. "Is he being an asshole? Are you afraid of him?"

"What? No, of course not, but he... he..." I trail off, remembering what Nico said this morning. *Don't mention college unless you absolutely have to.* "He won't stick around if I start bringing pointless trouble."

This is too juvenile for him, and I'm determined to keep my school problems away from his ears.

"He should know, Mia."

"And how will it help? My hair won't grow back if I tell him. Blair won't stop being jealous, Brandon won't quit thinking of ways to get me in his bed, but Nico *will* question whether the ten-year age gap is too much. I just got him, Cody," I mutter, standing there like an orphan. Hayes brothers are loyal to a fault, and lying, or rather withholding information on my behalf, is not something the triplets will take on lightly. "Please," I whisper. "I don't want to lose him two days in."

Three pairs of eyes study me in silence.

Cody rubs his face, exhaling a heavy breath, and they exchange *the look*. "We'll go with whatever story you fabricate under one condition," he says, pushing himself away from the countertop to hug me. "Slow down, okay?" He pecks my head. "You're falling in love with him too fast, Bug."

My mouth opens to protest, but the contradiction gets stuck on its way out. I am falling in love with Nico. I have been, slowly but surely, since the Spring Break party almost two months ago, and I've not stopped since.

"I'll try," I say, but I don't mean it.

Nico makes me whole. Happy. Why would I suppress that? Because it's too fast? Because we just started dating? We did, but we've been spending time together for weeks. I know more about him than I know about my own sister.

"I'll take a shower, and we'll see what I can do with this." I point at my hair. "Feel at home. I won't be long."

The coffee maker starts going before I lock myself in the bathroom. I cry again when my damaged hair snaps in my fingers. I wash it three times to rid the burned smell, and once I'm done, the drain is blocked. It takes two handfuls to gather up the hair littering the shower floor.

My back is red where my blouse burned through, but thankfully no blisters. Nothing a few coats of cream won't fix. I slip into a pair of shorts and hold a towel close to my chest, my cheeks hot when I tiptoe in the living room.

"I can't reach," I say, glancing between the triplets. They're all drinking coffee, looking comfortable in my living room. I hold out the burn cream. "Could you—"

"Come here." Cody holds his hand out. "You can't let Blair get away with this, Bug. Fuck..." he whispers, voice thick with emotions as he smoothes the cream on. "How the hell will you explain this to Nico?"

"I'll lie, but only a little."

Twenty-five

Mia

IT'S HALF PAST SEVEN when Nico comes home with a tall stack of takeout food. I sit at his piano, playing everything that springs to mind, tears gone from my cheeks. It's just hair, and not the first time I lost it.

As bad as it sounds, I got used to the bullying. It hurts, but after years of suffering, I know what to expect. I cry and move on because what else am I supposed to do? Standing up for myself ends with hugging the toilet and more hurt coming my way, so it's easier to rinse and repeat.

"Hey," I say when Nico leans over me, pressing his hot lips to the crown of my head. "Do you always work so late?"

"Why did you cut your hair?" he counters, forcing me to scoot forward as he sits behind me, legs boxing my thighs, one hand around my middle.

"Stop starting conversations with *why* and *what*."

"Hey, baby. Why did you cut your hair?"

I lean back, pressing myself closer to his warm body. "You can't ignore my questions and expect I'll answer yours."

His muscles bunch, his chest suddenly brittle. "You're asking for trouble, Mia. Don't think I won't put you over my knee for acting out." He places his hand on the keys, adding a few notes to the melody I'm playing. "I never leave the office before six. Once I'm done there, I stop by the restaurant, *Q*, and all the cocktail bars I own. I'm usually home around nine."

"Short day today?"

"I couldn't get home fast enough. Your turn. Why did you cut your hair?"

"It caught fire," I admit, adamant about keeping the lies to a minimum. "Candles," I add quietly so he doesn't hear my voice breaking. "I wanted to take a candlelit bath... I lit the candles, leaned over the tub, and *puff*... my hair went up in flames. You have no idea how fast it burns. It's a miracle I saved as much as I did."

He moves my hair to the front, looking down my blouse. "Fuck... you burned your back. Did you go to the hospital? Why are you wearing a bra? You're making it worse."

The song ends abruptly when I straddle him. "I'm fine. It's just surface burn. It's tender but doesn't hurt, and the cream helps." I press my finger to his lips when he goes to speak. "I'm fine, okay? It's just hair. It'll grow back."

"I know, but you should've called me."

Closing my eyes, I rest my forehead against his, basking in the comfort of his undivided attention. I've never felt this safe.

"I missed you."

He grips the nape of my neck, catching my lips with his. He's a ten already. No need for pointers, but I'm not about to tell him. I wouldn't mind if he kept practicing until the end of time. His tongue teases mine, tasting, tangling, and rekindling the ache he extinguished this morning.

Pushing his big hands under my skirt, he sinks his fingers in my hips, hard enough that an aroused thrill tingles my thighs but not hard enough to bruise. I grind into him, my panties soaked, desire like hot honey coursing through my veins.

"Good girl," he growls in my ear, nipping the soft skin. "Do that again. Use me. Make yourself feel good."

I circle my hips, loving the friction his zipper offers. "I want you in," I whisper, tilting my head back as he kisses my neck.

"Cough, cough... is that what we should expect to walk into all the time?" Cody snaps us out of our lustful haze. "Get a room."

"Get a house," Nico fires back, but he sounds amused as he drags his hands down my thighs, looking over his shoulder. "Food's here. Thalia sent your favorite."

"Hell yes!" Conor cheers, rubbing his hands together. "I'm fucking starving."

"When aren't you?" Colt mutters, opening the boxes.

"Before we eat..." I say, and making sure the triplets aren't watching, I discreetly grind into Nico again. "How would you feel about going away with me?"

"Do that a few more times, and I'll let you take me wherever you want."

"Europe," I supply, circling my hips a little more. "My dad called earlier. Now that I jumped out of a plane, he's bugging me to fly to Monaco. I always wanted to see the Grand Prix there, and I have a better chance of surviving the flight if you're with me. I know you can't leave work for long, but..." I press into him harder, his eyes hooding over. "Maybe a week?"

He grips my thighs, holding me in place. "I'll see if I can

find someone to keep an eye on everything while we're gone." He kisses my head, patting my hip so I'll get off him, then disappears into the kitchen to fetch plates.

A sudden headrush hits me when I cross the room to sit on the sofa. "Figures..." I sigh, watching the first drop of blood plip into my hand.

I pinch the soft part of my nose with two fingers, making a small bowl with the other hand to catch the blood before it stains Nico's white rug. After the eventful, stress-filled day, the nosebleed doesn't come as a surprise. I half expected it to happen when the triplets brought me home.

Cody glances up, his brows meeting in the middle. "Shit. Another one? Hold on, I'll grab a towel."

Nico comes back, his step faltering when he looks at me. "What happened?" The plates clatter as he drops them on the table, rips his white t-shirt off his back, and wipes my hands. "What did you do?"

"Nothing, I'm okay," I mumble through the fabric he presses to my nose.

"Tilt your head back, baby."

I look at Colt, hoping he'll explain because right now, I need to breathe through my mouth, not talk, or blood will trickle down my throat.

"It's actually the wrong way to do it. Trust me, bro. She's doing this right. She gets nosebleeds a lot."

"Two, sometimes three times a month," Cody adds, returning with a roll of paper towels. "Time it," he tells Conor.

"Way ahead of you." He taps his watch, stuffing his mouth with chicken skewers.

"Why are you timing it?" Nico asks, stroking my thighs repetitively. "Are the nosebleeds because of the disease she has? I can't remember the name of it."

"Von Willebrand. We'll have to take her to the emergency room if it doesn't stop in half an hour."

"Half an hour?!"

I want to weave my fingers through his hair, soothe him somehow because he's clearly worried, but my hands are occupied. "It hardly ever happens," I say on an exhale. "If you plan on spending more time with me, get used to nosebleeds."

***

My eyes pop open, my body shuddering softly under the influence of the dream. My cheeks burn as hot as the unfulfilled ache swelling within me. Muscles contract in my abdomen, my thighs tingle, the orgasm right there, so close, but so far away at the same time. I bite the pillow, unsatisfied desire driving me livid.

"What's wrong?" Nico asks, reminding me I'm in his house and in his bed. "Bad dream?" He sets aside the laptop he's apparently been working on while I slept. "No... good dream, wasn't it?" He pushes his hand further under the comforter, gripping my hip to pull me under him. "You better tell me I was in it."

I hide my face in the crook of his neck and catch his wrist to stop him touching me because every stroke of his fingers sends a new wave of desire rippling through my body.

"I woke up too soon, so not that good," I breathe against his warm skin. "And yes, you were in it."

I'm turning into my sister.

We had sex right before I fell asleep to Nico quietly reading *Alice in Wonderland*. According to the clock on the nightstand, not even an hour has passed since, but here I am, soaking wet and needing him again.

He frees his hand from my grip, moving higher, his thumb toying with my nipple. "No way I'm letting my girl fall asleep so needy. Was that the first dream about me you had?"

"No. I've been waking up like this for weeks."

He smiles against me, and the embarrassment fades away, kicked to the background by overwhelming need and the words he spoke not long ago.

Don't ever hide how I make you feel. Don't pretend you're not aroused when I touch you. Own it. Show me. I want to see it.

He yanks my night dress off, leaning back on his calves. I love how he looks at me. As if he can't get enough.

He traces his hands up my thighs, his touch gentle but confident. "Touch yourself," he says, smirking when my eyes grow wider. "I told you I'll push you out of your comfort zone, Mia. Show me how you made yourself come thinking about me when you woke up wet."

"It's nothing special," I mutter, toying with my rings. "I'd rather have you touch me."

"I decide if it's special." He guides my hand until my fingers brush my clit. "You can close your eyes this once. Next time, I'll expect those emeralds on me. Start slow, baby." He dips his head, nosing a line between my breasts before settling back beside me, head propped on his elbow. "Don't make me take over. Touch yourself."

I close my eyes, circling the bundle of nerves. I'm wet, ready, and not far off an orgasm, but knowing Nico's watching makes the road to release that much longer.

"There you go," he says in my ear, kneading my breast. "That's it, don't stop. Remember the dream." He skims his hand lower, spreading his fingers on my stomach, just high enough not to interrupt me. "Good girl. Faster."

I up the tempo, fueled by his possessive tone. By the urgent touch of his hands. A soft moan slips past my lips, but my cheeks don't warm. I feel powerful, beautiful—

"My girl," Nico grunts. "Tell me when you're close." He nips the skin on my neck right above my pulse. "I want to feel you come around my fingers."

"Mm-hmm," is all I manage while my mind and body plunge faster toward a release.

The shame fades. There's just the need to come and please him. Even though I'm the one on the brink of orgasm, he's getting a bigger kick out of this. He wanted nothing more since day one than to have me give in to his dominance. I may have surrendered control in every aspect of our life, but touching myself while he watches is a different ball game.

"Now," I pant, and within half a second, Nico slips two fingers inside, stroking my G spot and tipping me over as if he can't help himself.

"Ride it," he growls when the orgasm blooms. "Let loose, Mia. I've got you."

I spasm, bucking on the bed, the orgasm hitting faster than an arrow from a bow. I don't see stars. I see entire constellations flicker on the backs of my eyelids.

"In," I moan, reaching for him. "Please, I want you in."

He smiles against my neck, sucking a bit of flesh to leave a hickey. "Mine. *Marked.*"

Twenty-six

Nico

MIA'S NOT READY WHEN I ARRIVE at her house twenty
minutes before seven, having finished work early so I could
take her to *The Olive Tree* for a proper date.

We've not had much time together since she woke up in
my arms on Tuesday, but now it's Friday, she'll stay with me
all weekend.

"What happened to *baby boy*?" I ask Aisha when she greets
me with a simple *hey*.

She purposely rolls her eyes before leading me into the
kitchen. I shake Toby's hand, taking a seat by the breakfast bar,
where he's flipping through a stack of takeout menus.

"You're with my sister now," Aisha says, opening the fridge.
"As much as I enjoy pissing you off, I think I should stop before
I take it too far. You want a beer?"

"No, I'm driving." The more time we spend together, the

more I enjoy our banter. It's like having a younger sister. "Who's going to take your place if you stop getting on my nerves?"

"I'll throw something your way every now and then if you insist." She winks, pulling out two bottles of Corona. "I just don't want to get in your bad books."

"Too late for that. You're not there for pissing me off, Aisha. You're there because of how you treat Mia."

Who knew? Aisha can blush too. Her cheeks pink up, shame spilling down her neck. It's not as adorable as it is on Mia, though.

"She's growing on me," she admits quietly, stealing a quick glance at her boyfriend. "I even invited her to come out to *Rave* with me for a girls' night out."

My back straightens immediately, a jab of anger flaring my nostrils. "She's not going out with you."

"Excuse me?" Aisha grips her waist, snapping into defensive mode. Her pink cheeks have turned red, and not due to shame. I think she's about to bite my head off. "What kind of caveman bullshit are you trying to pull off? You won't dictate her life. She's going."

Jesus Christ. The world these days is madness. One sentence, and I'm immediately labeled a caveman. Fucking sue me for doing what I think is right for my girl.

"Save the righteous lines for your books, alright? You want to spend time with her?"

"Of course I do! She's my sister. She's *family*." She glances at Toby, checking he's paying attention to her sudden change of heart. It's all for show. Toby's as family-oriented as I am, and I'm sure Aisha's dismissive attitude toward Mia doesn't sit well with him. "Why else would I invite her out?"

"Why does it have to be out?" I snap, grinding my teeth. "If you really want to spend time with Mia and not just score points with Toby, organize a girls' night *in*. Show me you care about *her*. That you give a crap about what's happening in her life."

"What's the fun in that? We sit home all the time!"

"You need to be waited on, right? Fine. Take her out for drinks somewhere you can talk. Show me you won't ditch her at the first opportunity. Show me she can fucking count on you. Then we can talk about *Rave*."

Aisha scoffs, pointing her long, manicured nail at me. "Why would I ditch her?! I'm with Toby now. I'm not looking for guys. Clubbing is fun, Nico. Mia doesn't have fun and—"

"She's not going out with you!" I bang my hand on the breakfast bar, my patience hanging by a thread. "Either a girls' night in, or if you want to be waited on, I'll get you a private room at *The Olive Tree*. I'll even cover the fucking bill, but you're *not* taking Mia dancing unless I'm there."

"Don't argue," Toby cuts in when Aisha opens her mouth again. "You won't win with him on this one."

"Like hell! She's not his property! What if she says she wants to go, huh?!" She comes closer, little torches swimming in her eyes. "What then? You'll forbid her? You can't control her!"

Toby rubs his face, looking between us, the calm mediator. "He's not trying to control her, babe. He just doesn't trust *you*. This conversation would be different if you were one of the triplets or if I were joining you."

Aisha folds her arms over her chest, visibly hurt. "So what? You think I'll let something happen to her?" she asks, lifting her chin to challenge me. "I have her back. I'd never let anything happen to her."

I saw Aisha in *Q* and *Rave* a few times during the past few years. Three drinks in, she only pays attention to the guys ogling her from the bar. Maybe she changed now she's with Toby but *maybe* isn't enough to risk Mia's safety.

It's been years since I took care of someone. The need to watch over Kaya wasn't half as intense as with Mia. Kaya was more like Aisha, not letting me do my thing.

Mia gives me room to breathe. Every little thing she lets me do gives an outlet to my protectiveness. I don't need to suppress my reflexes around her. She doesn't mind that I buckle her up in the car or tuck her in at night.

I still need to tone down my paranoia, so I don't get carried away. It wouldn't take much inattention to cross a line, considering I want Mia on my lap, curved into my chest *non-stop*, but I can't smother her like that. I'm here to watch over her while she spreads her wings, not pluck them off.

But that doesn't mean I'll risk her safety.

Aisha has to prove she'll be there for Mia if things go south. A few weeks ago, she didn't want her little sister playing board games with us, so nothing speaks in her favor.

"You don't even have your back, Aisha," I say, massaging my temples. "I don't know your friends, and I sure as fuck don't trust you with Mia."

"Please stop arguing," Mia says, and we all look to her standing where the kitchen morphs seamlessly into an open-plan corridor. "I don't want to go."

"That's not what you said last night," Aisha clips. "Don't let him control you! This is wrong, sis. You're going."

Mia shakes her head softly. "It's okay. I don't feel like dancing, anyway." She's wearing a gray, fitted sweater with long sleeves that partially hide her hands, and a dirty pink pinafore dress. "Do I look okay?" she asks me, twirling around on her ankle boot. "Or not fancy enough?"

"Perfect, baby. Come here."

Now that I'm sitting on the barstool, we're almost eye level. I grip her chin between my forefinger and thumb, sinking into her mouth, searching for that addictive low. Nothing calms me down the way having her close does.

She's an antidote to all the rage coursing through me.

The static and clutter clear enough that I can think clearly. Mia's young. She should have fun. I know she misses her sister and that it means the world to her that Aisha invited her out.

"Did you say you want to go?" I ask her.

Her face blanches, not a trace of a blush. "Yes."

I turn her around, pressing her back to my chest, and look over her shoulder to Aisha. "Compromise. *Q*, not *Rave*. I book the booth. One of the bouncers will watch Mia all evening, and she only drinks what *he* gives her."

"A *bouncer*?!" she fumes, growing redder. "So he can report her every move to you? Nah-ah. Not gonna happen, *baby boy*. You need to trust her!"

"It's you I don't trust. If you ditch her, at least I'll know someone's looking after her. Take it or leave it, Aisha."

"I don't mind the bouncer, sis," Mia says quietly. "Even if he tells Nico what I'm doing, that's okay. It's not like I plan to do anything he won't approve of."

God, she fits me so fucking right.

Aisha's pout slips, morphing into a wide, self-assured grin. "So, if there was someone with us you trust, there'd be no need for the bouncer, right?"

I nod, grinding my teeth. She's got a plan in place, I can tell. She'll fight me on this to the bone.

Well, she met her match.

"Okay, fine. This is *not* over. You sure you don't want one?" she chirps, waving a bottle of Corona.

"I'm sure. How about you come with us to *The Olive Tree* instead of drinking beer and eating pizza in front of the TV?"

Her mouth falls open a little. "What? Like a double date?" She glances at Toby and beams wider, slamming her beer on the counter. "I'll be ready in ten minutes!" She rushes out of the room.

Toby smacks the back of my head as soon as the bedroom door closes behind Aisha. "Thanks, man. We were gonna fuck once you took Mia out."

"I bet you already did today. Mia's staying with me all weekend. You'll have the house to yourselves until Monday. When was the last time you took Aisha out to eat?"

Toby shrugs, shoving menus into a drawer. "My girl's not like yours. She doesn't need wooing."

"Won't hurt, though, will it?"

"Oh, don't look so sour," Mia chuckles. "Sex can wait. Aisha won't tell you this, but she'd like to be more than a booty call."

"She is! Don't give me that shit. You know I love her."

I spin in my chair, one eyebrow raised. "You lost my number, man? Why am I not in the loop?"

Instead of explaining why he didn't call me, he shrugs like it's not a big deal. Maybe it wouldn't be if this wasn't the first time since I've known him that he proudly admitted to being in love.

"Fine, dinner it is," he mumbles. "Let me get changed."

I wrap my hands around Mia, my chin on her shoulder. "Tell me you know I trust you."

"I do," she admits quietly, toying with my fingers. "I like it when you do that." She tilts her head back a little, whispering in my ear. "When you hold me like I'm so precious."

"Most of the time, that's all I want to do, baby. I know you need to have fun, but you're mine now, and I need to know you're always safe."

She spins on her heel, her fingers back on my cheekbones, and the softest, sweetest kiss on my lips. "I am yours. Your girl. And your girl does as she's told."

"In bed, Mia. That applies in bed."

"Everywhere," she insists. "If you do something I won't feel comfortable with, I'll tell you, but until I do, you can be sure I don't mind how controlling you are."

She shouldn't have said that.

Managing my paranoia is mission impossible on a good day. Knowing Mia will submit to my will makes it much harder to rein in my overbearing personality.

Aisha's ready within ten minutes as promised, and no more than half an hour later, Mia sits across from me at my favorite table, tucked by the window overlooking the ocean. She tied her hair back on our ride here, leaving a few blonde locks dancing around her face that taunt me as she studies the menu, her lips swollen from my kisses, eyes glassy, happy, relaxed.

She's gorgeous. So fucking gorgeous.

I catch her hand, brushing my fingers across her knuckles.

"What are you having?" she asks.

"You choose. I want to know what you like."

Another smile, another tight squeeze in my chest. It's surreal that I want to lock her up in my bedroom so no one can touch or look at her. We've been officially dating for a week, but tonight's the first time I took her out. It's the first step of millions I have to take to avoid getting carried away.

The waiter stops by the table, his eyes lingering on Mia one second too long as they sweep between the four of us. That's enough to make my spine straighten like a metal rod.

"Are you ready to order?" he asks.

"Yes." Aisha beams, setting the menu down.

She and Toby get their orders in while I focus on Mia's pretty face to drown out everything else.

"We'll have the grilled prawns and halloumi for starters," she says as her turn comes around. "And I heard the souvlakis here are the best, so we'll take that twice with a side of Greek salad. A glass of Chablis, and..." She peers at me over the menu.

"Water," I supply.

"So? What's new?" Aisha asks once we all have drinks. "I, for one, am writing a new book, and you two..." She points between Mia and me, "...are my inspiration."

Mia's cheeks instantly burn bright. "Please don't. Your books are full of sex. I don't want you imagining us..."

Aisha squeals, bouncing in her seat. "You *had* sex?!" she whisper-shouts. "Oh my God! When?! Why didn't you tell me?" She playfully shoves Mia away. "Was it good? Did it hurt?"

"We are *not* talking about that," Mia mutters, kneading the tablecloth. "Tell me more about the book."

"God, you're such a prude. Come on, give me something! *Anything!* Was he good to you? Did he make you come?" She shoots me a pointed stare over the table. "You better—"

"You better stop getting on my nerves."

She rolls her eyes but changes the subject, complaining about a model she hired for a photo shoot.

"He was hitting on Cass the entire time," she says, rinsing a bite of food with wine. "You should've seen Logan when he walked in with Noah and found the guy leaning over the counter, shirtless, making eyes at her."

"I can imagine. Logan loses his cool almost as fast as I do."

"Well, he didn't hit him, but he took him outside for a chat, and when they came back, the guy didn't even look at Cass again."

"He probably threatened to feed him his dick," Toby laughs.

"Maybe." She shrugs, and her eyes light up. "And oh my God, how freaking cute is your godson? He's the first baby I actually like. They're all whiny, but Noah's just a cutie pie."

Looking at her now, at how happy she is with Toby, touching him whenever she has a chance, and watching his every move with awe, I have a feeling this thing between them will escalate quickly. Wedding by the end of the year, and a kid a few months later.

We spend two hours eating and talking before we part ways and I've got Mia in my house all alone. Toby and Aisha hopped in a cab outside the restaurant, heading to *Tortugo* for drinks, and the triplets are out partying as always.

I pour us two glasses of wine, listening to a very distressed voicemail message from one of my ex-clients, then call my assistant as Mia enters the kitchen.

"One minute, baby," I say, kissing her head and handing her a glass of wine when Jasmine answers. "Jas, I need you in the office tomorrow. Arnold Grey pulled out all his money last week and just called to say he lost everything."

"Surprise, surprise," she sing-songs in my ear. "You told him not to do it. Why are you helping him? Should I remind you what kind of shit he said before he banged the door?"

I follow Mia into the living room, where she sits by the piano, wiggling her fingers like she's been itching for this all day.

"Karma got him back, don't you think?" I tell Jasmine, taking a seat behind Mia. "He's coming over at nine with whatever he's got left. I'll send you the trades I want set up for him."

"Yeah, alright. I'll be there. Send me the trades."

"In an hour," I confirm, cutting the call and trailing my lips up Mia's neck. "Next time you play here, I want you to wear that tulle skirt from the Spring Break party."

"Why?" Her delicate fingers flit up and down the keyboard, playing "Lucy The Tease" by Allan Rayman.

"I imagined my head under that skirt when I first saw you here. It's time we turn that into reality."

She squirms, her breathing hitching, the images my words paint enough to make her wet. Ready for me.

"Sing, baby," I whisper in the shell of her ear, my hand tracing along her thigh from knee to hip.

She does, leaning back as she sings, every word heavy with emotions. I fucking hope she's not just singing.

I hope she means every word.

Twenty-seven

Nico

WORK, WORK, WORK.

It never bothered me that I work twenty-four-seven. If I'm not at the office, I visit my other businesses, deal with emergencies, or answer one call after the other.

Mia's been mine for less than a month, but I'm already sick of work. I hadn't realized I was filling a void buying cocktail bars and clubs and spending late evenings at the office. I never had a reason to rush home, but since Mia, that's all I do.

Or try, at least, but as fate would have it, the past month has been a nightmare. Not an hour goes by without a phone call. Not a day without issues. Not one evening without something going down that requires my attention.

We were supposed to head to the movies tonight with Theo and Thalia, but a pipe burst in one of my cocktail bars half an hour before I picked Mia up. Instead of an evening with my girl, I spent four hours getting the mayhem under control.

"She's asleep on the couch," Aisha says when I arrive at half past nine. "She wasn't feeling well."

"Why? What's wrong?" I cross the hallway, heading straight to the living room.

"Chill out," she mutters, trailing behind me. "She's on her period. Are you staying the night?"

I was going to take her back to my place, but Mia's curled on the sofa, cuddling a pillow. "Looks like I am. Why?" I grab a blanket from the back of the couch, cover her up, and gently pull her into me, my chest replacing the pillow.

"No reason," Aisha says, biting back a smile. I can tell there's a solid reason she doesn't want to share. "I'm heading out, that's all. I'll stay the night at Toby's, so don't expect me back."

"Won't miss you."

"I have a feeling you might," she chuckles, flinging a bag over her shoulder. "Have fun. Oh, and don't think I forgot about the night out. We postponed it, but it's happening in a couple of weeks."

"As I said. *Q*, a bouncer, and I take Mia there and back."

"We'll see about that," she chirps, already halfway down the hallway. "I have a plan."

I bet she does.

Mia stirs, cuddling into me harder as if she feels my presence even asleep. She holds a hand across my chest, fisting the t-shirt, one leg bent at her knee and resting on my thighs.

I settle for a movie, ghosting my fingers up and down her arm and growing concerned over my mental health.

It can't be normal that every muscle in my body tenses painfully whenever Mia's not well. The fucked-up part of my character, the controlling, overprotective part, is harder to tame as the days go by... as my feelings morph from infatuation to something dangerously close to love.

Half the time, I fight my paranoia, assuring myself Mia doesn't require constant supervision. That she won't pull stupid stunts for attention, won't encourage men to touch her.

My jaw clenches, and my temper flares. I derail that train of thought, focusing back on the movie.

Halfway through *The Wolf of Wall Street*, someone enters the house. Aisha left in heels, and whoever just entered isn't click-clacking toward the living room.

My hold on Mia tightens while I listen to the footsteps and what sounds like something being dragged across the tiled floor. I'm ready to flip Mia over and beat the living shit out of whoever walked in, but five seconds later, I'm tense for a whole different reason.

Mia's father stops at the mouth of the corridor, eyes on me, eyebrow raised, small suitcase in hand.

"Hey, Jimmy," I say quietly.

He scans the room, tilting his head like a curious dog. "Hey to you, too." Two deep wrinkles mark his forehead when he spots Tylenol on the coffee table. He walks in further, leaving his suitcase by the wall. "Is she unwell?"

"You could say that."

His frown deepens before his face flashes with recognition. "PMS, right? It's the VWD that makes it worse. She told you about that, didn't she?"

I conducted comprehensive research on the topic after Mia's twenty-four-minute-long nosebleed. I stayed up for hours after she fell asleep, reading every study about Von Willebrand available online, then asked Mia a hundred questions over breakfast. Now, I'm prepared for any situation.

While reading up about the disease, I found an article that mentioned PMS, so I know Mia's contraceptive implant lessens the severity of her periods. Needless to say, I'm no longer opposed to her having that thing.

"She did," I say, trying not to wake Mia as I untangle myself from her hold and cover her with a blanket.

"So *you're* the boyfriend..." Jimmy muses when I approach to shake his hand. "I gotta tell you, I wouldn't have guessed if I had a million tries."

"I didn't realize she told you about me."

"She didn't. She said she's bringing her boyfriend over for the Grand Prix next month but wouldn't tell me who he is." He moves to the living room, taking care not to make much noise as he grabs two crystal glasses and a bottle of bourbon out of the drinks cabinet.

Looks like we're drinking.

"I expected a Hayes... just not you," he continues. "I assumed it was one of the triplets, and I prayed it's not Cody. No offense, but that kid gets on my nerves like nobody's business." He pulls a bag of ice from the freezer.

I move one barstool to the side of the island where I've got a better view of Mia. "Cody's very talented when it comes to getting on people's nerves. Why do you think she didn't tell you who I am?"

"She knows we're friends. I guess she wanted to surprise me," he chuckles, pouring bourbon over ice, before sliding a glass across the counter toward me. "And boy, am I fucking surprised. I never pegged you for the type."

"Neither did I," I admit, my guards safely in place.

He might act cool but let's face the facts. I've been friends with the guy for three years. We went out together more than once. I saw a few women stick their tongues down his throat or grip his dick through his pants, and he sure saw a few chicks dry hump me at the club.

This now is the first time I've ever felt awkward...

"I didn't plan on coming home," he adds. "But I got curious when Mia said she was bringing a boyfriend to Monaco. I wanted to grab a drink with the guy." He lifts his glass up, eyes boring into mine. "So let's have a drink, Nico."

"I sense a few heavy questions."

He waves his hand. "I know my daughter. I might not see her often, but I know everything there is to know. At least I did before you happened. She called me every time she had a date. I knew which guy she liked and which kissed like a puppy."

"A puppy?"

"Yeah, apparently, he licked her face."

"Remind me to ask her how he ranked on her scale."

"A two, if I remember correctly." He finishes his drink, and urges me to do the same, pouring another two fingers of bourbon into his glass, then mine. "How do you rank?"

Argh... I walked right into that one, didn't I?

"A nine."

Jimmy tsks, amusement flickering in his eyes. "Keep working." He twirls the glass around, lost in thought.

"Ask away," I encourage. "I'm sure you've got questions."

"Oh, I do. Not for you, though. You'll tell me what I want to hear." He casts a glance at his daughter, still asleep on the couch. "She'll tell me the truth."

"I've never lied to you. And I won't start now."

He lifts the glass to his lips, taking a long, measured sip. "Alright, let's check that theory. How long have you two been seeing each other?"

"A few weeks."

"You had sex yet?"

I choke on the bourbon, inhaling a sip instead of drinking it. "What the fuck, Jimmy?"

He pats my back, chuckling quietly. "You know why I'm asking. You've got quite the *hit it and quit it* reputation. If you've not had sex yet—"

"You'll assume that's all I'm waiting for before I cut her loose," I finish for him.

"You met Aisha by now, right? She's a nymphomaniac. I walked in on her having sex more times than I'm willing to admit. You get immune after a while. The topic of my daughters' sex life doesn't bother me like it does most fathers. You said you won't lie, so don't fucking lie and don't evade."

"The answer is *yes*, and if we break up, you can be fucking sure it'll be her who leaves me, not the other way around," I seethe, squeezing my glass harder. "Next question."

He chuckles, patting my shoulder. "Relax. I don't want the details. Mia's always been a loner. Always quiet, but for the past few weeks, she's been unusually cheerful. You make her happy."

I sure hope so. Navigating our relationship is a challenge like no other. Instead of getting easier, it's getting harder because she's easily influenced. She hardly ever stands up to me. I'm flying blind, but I think I'm doing okay.

"She makes me happier," I admit, looking over to where she's still asleep, holding the blanket to her cheek. "I guess it might bother you that I'm ten years older—"

"Don't assume, Nico. Mia only went out with two guys her age, everyone else was at least five years older, so I expected this." He gets up, opening a cupboard to pull out a bag of peanuts. "Listen, you've not been dating long. It's all fresh, so we'll save the heavy for later, alright?"

I bob my head, spinning the glass on the breakfast counter. For over an hour, we talk about work before he asks about the skydive. Mia flips onto her side halfway through my story. I'm surprised she hasn't woken up yet. We're not exactly keeping our voices down.

"She did very well. She screamed for ten seconds after we jumped out but stopped when she looked around."

"I've seen the pictures," Jimmy says, slurring his words a little. The long-haul and time difference must've taken a toll on him. "I assume you're staying the night?"

"If that's not a problem. I'd rather not wake Mia every couple hours to check on her."

"It's fine." He crosses the room, pulling another bottle from the drinks cabinet. "You need to try this. Just one drink."

"I should get Mia to bed before we start another bottle."

He waves me off. "Yeah, do that and come back."

I get the bed ready before moving Mia. Thankfully she's already in her pj's. Jimmy and I don't stop at the one drink. When I finally crawl into bed around two in the morning, I know I'll wake up with a banging headache.

Mia
First day of high school

"HOLY SHIT!" *Jake yells when I stop by the lockers.* "*Someone did some growing up over the summer. You're not fat! You need a new nickname.*"

I don't look his way. It never ends well. I open the locker, shove my bag inside and take the books I need for my first class—Chemistry.

"*Are those...*" *he says, feigning surprise.* "*Are those* real *boobs you've got there, or have you stuffed your bra?*"

Students laugh, the sound like thousands of tiny needles pricking my nerve endings.

"*You won't talk to me, huh?*"

I close the locker and grab the earphones, putting them in my ears and hating Aisha for putting makeup on me. I feel like I'm wearing a mask. Like I'm trying to fit in when I stopped hoping to long ago.

If the likes of Jake are the people I'm supposed to fit in with, then I'd rather be a loner.

I crank up the volume and make my way to class, eyes on the floor,

steps small. I don't even make it to the end when the music stops playing, and I see Jake from the corner of my eye, scissors in hand and a wide grin.

He cut the cords.

I grit my teeth, adamant not to show him how much it hurts me to be robbed of the one thing I find comfort in.

"What is that*?" he cackles, smearing the raspberry lip gloss across my lips and face with his thumb. "That pouty mouth of yours would look great wrapped around my dick," he states. "Yes! Fucking EPIC! That's your new nickname. Blow Job Lips!" He scans the crowd of onlookers and starts chanting* BJ *over and over until not a single person within earshot isn't chanting with him.*

There's no stopping the tears that pool in my eyes. There's no stopping my instincts when I turn on my heel and run out of the building, bailing on my first day as a freshman.

Twenty-eight

Mia

A SLAP LANDS ON MY ASS while I'm on my way out of the college building. Laughter erupts behind me, and without thinking, I spin on my heel to find a guy I don't know, wagging his eyebrows.

My mind flares, my pulse soars, and a feeling I've only felt a few times whips across my nerve endings: courage.

Before I can think through my next move, my hand sails through the air, landing on the guy's face. I don't have enough strength to make his head turn, but the slap must sting because he holds his cheek, eyes growing wide.

"Don't ever touch me again," I say, pushing down the panic threatening to diminish my courage when I recognize the two guys cackling nearby.

Jessie and Michael. Jake Grey's best friends. They used to make my life a living hell in high school, and just seeing them laughing brings back memories I tried hard to bury.

The guy who slapped me lunges forward, pushing me against the wall hard enough that my head bounces off the concrete, and he's right there, towering above me, madness and embarrassment flickering in his eyes.

"You stupid bitch, you think—" The breath is knocked out of his chest by my knee connecting with his groin.

I shove him away, my heart ramming against my ribs. Adrenaline jolts me into action, and I *run*. A few students turn to watch as I bolt down the corridor, but no one stops me to check if I'm okay, even though they saw what happened.

Other than ostentatious, inappropriate comments, no one touched me against my will until today. A few guys asked me out, and some left suggestive notes for me to find, but overall, Brandon's plan was failing.

He must've thought everyone is as childish as him...

Looks like some are. Childish and deranged. This guy wasn't even trying to hide. He cornered me while other people watched like he didn't give a damn about the consequences.

"Where to?" Dad asks when I slide into the passenger seat two minutes later, my hands still shaking. He's been picking me up from college and taking me out for food every afternoon since he landed four days ago. "Can we go back to *The Olive Tree?*"

"Sure, I don't mind."

"Good, call Nico, maybe he'll—" He cuts himself off when my ringtone pours out of the speakers, the phone connected to the hands-free system.

"Talk of the devil." I smile, showing Dad the screen. "Hey, I was about to call you."

"And I'm about ready to put you over my knee," he clips, making my cheeks heat. "Baby, I'm glad you're spending time with your dad, but you need to find two hours for me tonight."

"Nico—"

"Two hours." His tone brooks no argument. "Make it happen. I've not felt you in four days, and I miss you like it's been an entire goddamn century. Unless you want me to cuff you to the bed while your dad sits in the next room, I suggest you do as you're told."

I sink into my seat, melting into the leather when Dad clears his throat. "Hey, Nico. That shouldn't be a problem. I'm meeting a friend for a few drinks later, so you two will have the evening to yourself."

"Oh God." I'm sure I'm the color of a ripe tomato. "Why? Why are you so *casual* about this?!"

My dad chuckles, shaking his head like he's dealing with a clueless child. "It's just sex, Mia. Why are you blushing? Don't act like it's such a novelty."

"It is!" I cry, horrified that he thought I slept with one of the dates I told him about. "It's very much a novelty."

"You mean to tell me Nico's your first?"

"Right, I'll leave you to it," Nico cuts in, sounding amused. "I'll see you tonight, Mia."

"Don't you dare hang up!"

"What did I tell you? Sex is natural. It's normal."

"Agreed," Dad says, nodding vigorously. "I'm still very much shocked you only *now* had your first time, but I can't say I'm not glad. Some of those dates you told me about—"

"Jimmy," Nico warns, jealousy clear in his voice. "Leave the past where it belongs."

My father cocks an eyebrow, shooting me an amused look. "My bad. I hope you've got nothing planned for tomorrow morning because I've got a bottle of the best bourbon money can buy, and once I'm home, we're drinking."

"Sure. I'm off tomorrow."

"Good. I'll see you around eight?"

"I'll see you then," Nico confirms. "Mia? Be good, baby."

"Always."

***

Nico bursts inside my house at quarter to six in the afternoon, drops his keys on the counter, and sweeps me off my feet stopping me halfway through making sandwiches.

His lips catch mine, the kiss greedier than usual. He's radiating that restless energy like he's about ready to explode. Every muscle on his body is harder than stone, a kind of unruly anger shining in his eyes.

"Um... hey." I weave my fingers through his hair. "Is everything okay?"

"It's been a long day and an even longer week," he says, entering my bedroom.

The door slams shut behind us, and he pins me to the wall, one hand under my butt, the other steering my jaw, his heart thudding against his ribs and resonating through me.

"What's wrong?" I whisper between his urgent kisses. "You're angry. What happened?" I don't get an answer. He shuts me up with another kiss. He's riled up, and I think he needs me to calm him down. "Tell me what to do," I whisper against him. "Tell me what you need me to do."

He bites my lip, pulling back before he sets me on my feet and dips his head to look in my eyes. "I have nothing but respect for you, you know that, don't you?"

"Yes."

"Good girl. I need you to take the edge off, or I'm going to fucking lose it when I get inside you." He yanks at the zipper of my dress until it falls to the floor. "I'll teach you how to take care of me. You're beautiful, Mia. Mine. So fucking sweet," he chants quietly like he's in a delusional trance as his fingers skim my neck and collarbones. "You won't be able to say *red*. Tap out if it gets too much." He unbuckles his belt, pulling it through the hoops. A gesture that hints at what's about to happen. "On your knees for me."

I sink. Not a moment's hesitation. My cheeks heat, but it's not embarrassment for once. It's excitement. I've wanted to do this since I first touched him.

Nico frees his cock from his boxer shorts and wraps my hand around the hilt, squeezing harder than I'd dare if I were in charge.

"Open," he rasps, his eyes flaring as he watches my lips part. "Good girl. Make me come, baby."

I keep my fingers where he placed them, squeezing him just as hard, and guide him into my mouth. His eyes immediately roll back, pure, unrestrained pleasure twisting his handsome face.

Twirling my tongue around the head, I taste the first salty drop of precum. A low grunt building in his chest tells me I'm doing something right, so I keep going, stroking his length, and licking the tip as my lips pump back and forth.

He grips my hair into a tight fist, his cock swelling even more. The veins on his neck bulge before he looks down, grips my jaw, and pins my head to the wall.

"Keep your mouth open for me and breathe—" he grunts when I suck him in deeper. He pushes his hips forward, eyes on mine when he hits the wall of my throat, pulling back just before my gag reflex sets in. "Good, relax. You're doing so fucking good, baby. Breathe through your nose."

This might be the most primal, shamefully arousing thing he's ever done to me. The feral, lustful energy radiating off his movement quadruples my desire as he falls into a rhythm, sliding in and out faster, chasing his release.

I hold onto his hard thighs, my nails gouging into his flesh, leaving half-moon marks. My eyes water with every deep stroke. He grips my hair tighter, pumping in and out faster before he yanks his hips back.

"Out," he growls when I move with him. "I'll come in your mouth if you don't let go."

A pleasant thrill zaps my thighs. I might as well check if that's something I'll enjoy, so I suck harder, holding his hips to keep him in place. With a low groan, he pins my head to the wall, resuming his pace, using me to get off. And then he stills.

Warm trickles of seed fill my mouth.

His knees buckle.

Tendons on his neck pulse as he comes, bracing against the wall for support.

"Swallow, Mia."

I do. It's not easy, but I think he enjoys my throat constricting around his shaft, wringing the last drops. He pulls out slowly, adjusting his jeans before he crouches before me, his chest rising and falling faster.

"Was that okay?" I ask. "Was that nice?"

"Perfect." He lifts me up only to lay me on the bed. "You can be shy any time of the day, but when you're with me, when I touch you, focus on how good I make you feel and nothing else. I want to push you further out of your comfort zone."

"You just did."

"Even further. You're doing so fucking good." His teeth nip my neck right above my pulse, then he kisses the spot, soothing the mild sting. "I want more."

I bite my lip, unease already battling with the tingling sensation bubbling in the pit of my stomach. "Will it hurt?"

"No. I told you I'll never hurt you, but if anything's too much, use the safe word, okay?"

"Red. Okay."

"Good girl." He pecks my temple. "You don't get to touch me now. And you don't get to see or hear me." He gets up and grabs three silk scarves from my wardrobe. "Face down, baby."

"But—"

"Do as you're told. Face. *Down*. Now."

I let out a shaky breath, flipping onto my stomach. I hate not seeing him, but I focus on his touch, ignoring the swish of scarves as he ties my ankles and wrists.

He flips me onto my back, looking me over inch by inch, his pupils blown, arousal on display when he climbs onto the bed, bending down to kiss me.

"You need to relax so you can enjoy this."

I nod, words piling up on the tip of my tongue when he blindfolds me, and I'm left at his mercy... exposed.

"You're beautiful, Mia," he coos, skimming his lips down my stomach. "You're mine, and I want to play with what's mine, so you'll be my little toy tonight."

Music, slow, dark, and sensual, starts in my ears when he pushes two earphones in.

He grips my legs, resting my tied ankles on his back before he closes his lips on my clit, eagerly sucking it into his mouth.

I can't touch him. I can't see him, but it heightens the pleasure his urgent licks inflict. I can't hear him growl, but the vibrations of his voice resonate on me, bringing me closer faster than before.

He doesn't let me come. He stops when I'm seconds away and scrapes his teeth on the inside of my thigh before moving off.

My heart immediately thumps faster.

I can't see him. I can't hear him, and now I can't feel him.

My pulse grows louder in my ears, but I lay still even though I want to rip off the blindfold to check he's there.

The mattress dips by the headboard and Nico flips me over again, manhandling my body until I'm right where he wants me... face down, butt in his lap, legs bent and spread wide.

I can't focus on what he's doing. I'm squirming in place, thinking how exposed and vulnerable I am.

Nico gathers my hair in a fist, then wraps it around his wrist while the other hand reaches its mark. He circles his thumb around my entrance, making the muscles in my abdomen spasm.

The pleasant sensation dies quickly at the reminder of my position. I'm bent over his lap, and I have no control. The blindfold isn't necessary. Shame burns my cheeks. I'm squeezing my eyes shut, trying to even out my breathing.

Nico tugs harder, making me arch, and I feel his lips on my temple as he slowly pushes his finger in. He releases my hair, grips my throat, and squeezes gently, massaging my neck while his finger plays with my G spot in a slow, torturous rhythm.

The music changes to something darker, more sensual. I'm starting to relax, the heightened sense of touch lets me feel Nico's efforts three times more intensely.

The orgasm builds, stacking slowly, but the shame is gone once it's within reach. There's just the need to come... the fire that needs extinguishing.

I arch my hips, focused on the high that's oh so close.

He slips a second finger in, pumping faster. My moans grow loud enough that I hear them over the music, but I'm too far gone to control myself. And I know Nico wants me to take what I need, only caring about myself.

I fist the sheets, and with the first circular motion of his thumb on my clit I'm coming, writhing on his lap while he prolongs a wave of orgasms. One, two—

The earphones are snatched out of my ears.

"One more," he says, his tone urgent, his strokes faster. "I know it's there, Mia... you need to come again for me. You've got *one more* in you, and I want it," he chants. My walls spasm around his fingers. "That's it, baby. That's it. Chase that high."

It comes like a tsunami... one, two, three. The pleasure resonates along every nerve ending in my body, and Nico's aroused, satisfied voice intensifies the pleasure tenfold.

"There it is..." He bends down, pressing a hot, open-mouthed kiss to my nape. "Good girl. Ride it out. Let it happen."

White spots flash before my eyes. I squirm in his lap, the orgasms long, torturous, and exhausting.

I bite the pillow, the sensation overwhelming when he eases his fingers out, gently rubbing my sensitive clit before he flips me over, covering my lips with his.

He lifts the blindfold, grazing his nose across my cheek. "Look at me," he utters, voice full of greedy desire. He hangs over me, one hand cupping my face. "I've been trying to trigger your back-to-back orgasms since day one. It's not easy." He smiles, ghosting his fingers down the line of my waist. "Now that I know how, I want to know how many you can have so close together."

"I didn't know it was possible. Three are enough. That last

one was so intense."

He smiles again. "Yeah, I saw that... I felt that, baby. You like it when I talk. You like my voice."

"I love your voice."

"Next time, we'll forget about the music."

Twenty-nine

Nico

"WHERE'S MIA?" Jimmy asks, walking into the house ten minutes past eight, his step bouncy.

"Asleep."

I didn't think I'd be ready for more after she took care of me with her lips, but seeing her come four times in a row skyrocketed my desire to uncontrollable levels. I had to have her. She couldn't hold her weight, and after two more orgasms on my cock, she fell asleep while I took a quick shower, recalling the image of her beautiful lips wrapped around my length.

She'll be on her knees for me a lot going forward.

Seeing her plump lips open for me almost tipped me over right then. Her pace was off, she only worked the head of my cock, but that delicacy and uncertainty painting her face were *everything*. I never came so fast from an oral. It usually takes much longer, and nine out of ten times, it doesn't happen at all, but that was a different level of perfection. The orgasm rattled through me like an earthquake, powerful enough to cramp my thighs.

Jimmy shimmies out of his jacket, smirking as he rounds the breakfast bar to pull a bag of ice from the freezer. "Tired, is she?"

It's odd... his nonchalance toward my sex life with his youngest daughter. My father's the same, but I bet it's different when you're raising seven sons.

Jimmy's casualness seems unnatural, and I can't decide if the fact we're friends makes it less or more odd.

"She's not been sleeping well the past few nights," I lie, hoping to cut the subject, but he only grins wider.

"Yeah, I bet the two hours you needed had nothing to do with her falling asleep at eight in the evening."

Way to piss me off.

If any other girl was concerned, this conversation wouldn't be a problem, but I'm falling in love with Mia. She's mine. My girl. What we do in bed is off-limits to anyone's ears.

"There are many things we can talk about," I clip, folding my arms. "But what I do in bed with your daughter isn't on the list. I respect her, I care about her, and that's all you need to know."

He holds his hands up in defeat, already slightly tipsy. "My apologies. You're right. I just wish she'd stop blushing whenever sex comes up. She's nineteen."

"She's only like that around you. I know Aisha has no filter, but Mia's embarrassment shouldn't surprise you. You said you know her, so you should know that talking about sex with her father isn't something Mia will take lightly. It's probably worse because you and I get along."

He pours us two glasses, nodding along. "We've touched on a lot of different topics the last few days, but no matter what, whenever Mia's mentioned, you get awfully territorial."

I sip my drink, propping my ankle on my knee. "I don't think you understand how much I care about her. I know you don't mean anything bad, so I'm not reacting. You can get away with many things being her father. Most people would bleed if they asked the things you did about our relationship. Territorial, overprotective, possessive... I heard it all before, and believe me, it doesn't begin to cover it."

He beams wider with every one of my words. What the fuck is so amusing?

"I'd be pretty pissed off at that silent threat, Nico, if I hadn't seen you with her. She's at the heart of everything you do."

"She's Daddy's girl, Jimmy, and that won't change, but she's mine now. Mine to care for. Mine to keep safe."

He reaches out to clank his glass to mine, leaving my hasty confession without comment. We spend the rest of the evening booking flights and hotels for Mia and me; it'll be my first vacation in years. Two weeks with my girl in Monaco and Italy, watching F1 races, dining in the fanciest restaurants, and sightseeing.

I can almost smell the authentic Italian cuisine already, almost hear the F1 cars lining up on the grid and imagine the bliss painting Mia's face as she inconspicuously cheers Ferrari on when her dad isn't looking.

Life doesn't get much better.

***

Jimmy boards the plane early on Friday morning.

We'll see him soon enough. The Monaco GP is in three weeks. Despite the anxiety of leaving my businesses in my brother's hands, I can't wait to get away from work.

"You're allowed to call with emergencies only," I tell Jasmine, briefing her on the plan of action on Friday afternoon. "Moody clients are your responsibility. I don't want to hear about Mr. X's idea to diversify his portfolio or any other shit like that."

Jasmine nods, pushing her glasses up the bridge of her slim nose. "Unless the market crashes, you're unavailable," she mumbles, making notes. "Got it. I won't bother you."

"No, you won't. Every time you think about calling me, call Colt. Any messages you want to give me go through him."

Her head snaps to meet my gaze so fast I swear her neck cracks. "Colt? Your younger brother? I can do this myself, Nico. I don't need anyone's supervision."

"That's not negotiable. Whenever you feel the need to call me, call Colt. He'll decide if it's emergency enough to interrupt my first vacation since college."

Colt's the one I've been bouncing ideas off for the past couple years. He's bright, quick, well-organized, and a problem-solver, making him the ideal business partner. I've been pondering the idea of bringing him into my business for a while. Now, I'll have the perfect opportunity to check if he can handle the pressure.

A text pings in the group chat while I'm gathering my things to leave the office.

Theo: GET ME OUT OF HERE! Thalia's driving me fucking insane. I've been in the shop three times today for pickles and licorice. I puked twice, too, watching her eat that. I need a beer. Who has time?

Logan: Sure, I could use a beer or five. Where and what time?

Cody: No can do. We're busy tonight.

Theo: Yeah, no shit. I'll send Thalia your way, Logan. She'll keep Cass company. Nico? Shawn?

Shawn: Working.

Mia's recording with Six, getting new songs ready for another party the triplets want to throw at the start of summer.

I can't wait to hear the outcome. She doesn't realize the potential stirring within her. That voice? It's mighty. A hidden gem, and she writes songs: music and lyrics. You'd expect her to tour the world and line her shelves with Grammys, but Mia's not interested in fame.

To be perfectly honest? I'm glad. I can't imagine thousands of men swooning over my girl. I can't imagine not seeing her whenever I felt like it because the Atlantic Ocean was in the way.

I'd make it work if she decided it was something she wanted to do, but I'm not about to force her. She's perfectly content recording for fun and selling lyrics to the biggest names in the industry.

Me: Alright. Country Club in an hour?

A wave of thumbs up follows. I leave the office, call my girl to let her know, and exactly one hour later, I enter the building. My brothers are already there. Theo leans against the bar while Logan shows him something on his phone.

"Stop wearing matching outfits," Theo says. "Don't force

your questionable sense of style on the kid."

"I have the *best* sense of style out of all the Hayes. You're all boring... predictable."

I tap the bill of his cap that he wears backward as usual. "Says the guy with eighty baseball caps and a hundred Los Angeles Dodgers jerseys."

"At least the color scheme of my wardrobe isn't limited to shades of gray," he bites back, waving the bartender over.

Within three minutes, with beers in hand, we find a tall table by the window overlooking the golf course and go through a whole beer before Theo's done listing all the weird cravings his wife's been having.

"I'm sure she does this just to screw with me," he huffs.

"You put a kid in there," I say, calling out a waitress clearing a nearby table. "Get us another round," I tell her, turning back to Theo. "Quit whining and feed your wife."

"I've not had a full night's sleep in forever, and the kid isn't even here yet. She's either sending me shopping, asking for massages, or waking me up because she can't sleep. Was Cass like that?"

Logan shakes his head. "I can't relate. The only thing Cass craved were lemons. Easy enough to find."

"Lucky bastard. At least tell me you weren't getting any. I'm riding solo almost since the start. No way we'll have any more kids if this is what every pregnancy is like."

"Can't help here, either, bro." Logan pinches his lips, clearly amused. "Thalia wakes you up for licorice and pickles, right? Cass woke me up for sex. Almost every night. Sometimes twice." He smirks, then all-out laughs when Theo folds his arms over his chest like a moody kid. "Stop pouting. It was fucking awesome, but not easy to keep up with her needs."

Theo shoves him away, feigning annoyance. "Boohoo. Cass didn't eat weird shit, and you had sex all the time. That sure sounds like torture." His eyes dart to me, and he automatically straightens his spine. "What did she do to you?"

I cock an eyebrow, looking at the waitress who just set another round of beers on the table. "She didn't do anything. Why?"

"Not the waitress. Mia. What did she do to you?"

"I know you think you're making sense, but you're not."

"You're not wearing your AirPod," he explains, explaining absolutely nothing. "You're not barking or glaring, and... shit, man, you're *smiling*."

"Which you shouldn't do," Logan chips in, eyebrows pulled together. "Honestly, quit it. You look weird."

"She didn't do anything."

"Yeah, she did," Theo insists, emphasizing every word. "Spill it, bro. Is it the sex? That good, huh?"

I punch his shoulder harder than intended. "You want me to split your lip again? Mia's just..." I trail off, searching for the right words. "I don't know. I've been in the highest gear for years, working, chasing money, searching for *something*."

"You mean a woman?"

I shrug, chugging a mouthful of beer. "Isn't that what we all want? Life revolves around love in one way or another. Family, friends, that one person you come home to. I wanted that someone, but I was looking at the wrong women. I thought I needed a female version of myself... high-maintenance, career-driven. I was high—"

"High?" Theo mouths, exchanging a concerned look with Logan. "You mean drugs? You were on *drugs*?"

"I think you'd know if I were using, don't you? I meant the

chaos in my head. I was always on the go, never stopping, but since Mia came along, I'm low. My head is quieter. Not silent, but the chaos is manageable. She's not exceeding my pace. She doesn't have a pace. She rolls around in neutral, going with the flow, and I'm learning to do the same. I switched my phone off the other night for the first time in years."

"Considering that thing is glued to your hand most of—" Logan huffs, waving me off when I pull my cell out, feeling a short vibration. "Baby steps, I guess."

Mia: Hey, while you're with your older brothers, could I go out with the younger three?

No.

No, baby, stay home. I'll be there in twenty minutes, is what I want to reply.

There goes my mellow composure...

Images of Mia dancing at the club fill my head. Her delicate moves, hips swaying while her fingers run up and down her sides, lipsyncing every song. Bliss on that pretty face. How oblivious she is to the men staring, craving what's *mine*.

Looks like Toby was wrong. Not even the triplets can take Mia out without my mind going into fucking overdrive. I want to leave the bar, drive to her house and spend the night making her moan in my ear, then strangle my brothers in the morning for even thinking that taking my girl out is a good idea.

I toss the phone on the table. "Fuck."

"What's wrong?" Theo asks, his eyebrows pulled together.

"Mia wants to go out with the triplets." I get up, the screaming in my mind not letting me sit still. I grip the back of the chair with both hands like it can anchor me in place. "Cheeky fuckers waited until I made plans and swooped in."

"Very tiny baby steps," Logan mutters, resting his elbows on the table. "You have a long way to go. She's going out for a drink. You know the triplets will keep her safe. What's the problem? You're acting crazy... and I'm more comfortable with that than you smiling, so hit me. What's going through your head?"

I know I'm acting crazy. He doesn't have to tell me. I'm in low gear with Mia, but my protectiveness never hit as high.

She's young. She should have fun, enjoy life, and get the parties out of her system. I fucking know all this. That line is a mantra I recite ten times a day to keep myself in check.

I don't want Mia to miss out. She's been slowly opening up about the bullying, telling me gory stories about the harassment and humiliation she suffered for years. She never had real friends, always alone, always verbally and mentally abused. It's a fucking miracle she's still trying to find her place. That she's capable of trusting the triplets not to act like everyone else and that my temper didn't scare her off at the start.

She never went to prom; missed every homecoming dance, every football game, every high school, and college party. Years of fun lost, years of experiences and memories never made.

I don't want her to look back in ten years thinking she should've partied instead of being with me. *But...* if I could, I'd lock her in a padded room on a deserted island.

Mia shouldn't *ask* for permission.

I have a love-hate relationship with her insecurity. I love when she's timid around strangers, but I hate when she's like that with me. And she is more and more often the longer we're together, like she's afraid that one day I'll up and fucking leave.

That text shouldn't be a question. It should be a statement.

I'm going out with the triplets. I'll call you when I'm home. That's what she should've said.

But she didn't.

"Nico," Theo urges. "They've been friends long before you two met. She'll be fine."

I hate when he's right. I can't smother her. She already lets me get away with a lot of shit.

"I know she should go out and that I can't be with her all the time." I bang my fists on the table, inhaling a deep breath. "I can't keep her safe if she's out alone."

"She won't be alone," Logan points out. "Of all people, the triplets won't let a hair fall off her head, so what's this really about? You're jealous? You need to trust her. She's a good kid."

It has nothing to do with trust. I trust Mia more than I trust myself. She doesn't look at other men, she doesn't encourage anyone, and she keeps herself safe.

Jesus, she broke Brandon's nose, for fuck's sake. She's not helpless. She just looks it, and that's messing with my head.

I take another deep breath, sit down, and grab my phone. Mia's pretty face smiles from the screen, muting the incessant buzzing blanketing my thoughts as I dial.

"Hey," she answers. I can tell from the tone of her voice she's uncertain. That she's questioning texting me in the first place. "I don't mind staying home."

A tight rope ties itself around my chest. "You're not staying home. Go, Mia. Have fun, but I want to know sooner next time so I can drive you."

She's silent for a whole ten seconds. "Are you sure? I wasn't allowed to go out with Aisha—"

"That's different. And I never said you're not allowed. You're mine, baby, but I don't own you. I don't make your decisions,

321

I keep you safe, and I don't trust Aisha to do that."

"Do you trust your brothers? I don't want you to worry."

Like that's a possibility.

Honest to God, I never stop thinking about Mia.

I never stop worrying, and I'm pretty sure I need professional help to fix whatever the fuck is wrong with my head
because it can't be normal that I want to have her wrapped in
my arms all the time.

"I do. Have fun but call me if you need me. And call me
when you've had enough. I'll come and get you."

"Okay, I will. I promise, but if you change your mind—"

"I won't. Be good, baby."

"Always."

I'm definitely falling in love with her. So fucking fast.

She cuts the call, and I immediately down the rest of my
beer, sending a message to the group chat.

Me: Well played, boys.

Colt: Check, mate, bro. You can't monopolize Mia like that.

Conor: We demand joint custody. You can't keep her from us.

*Me: I'm not her owner. If she wants to go, she goes. All I ask is
that you keep her safe. You won't like what follows if anything happens
to her while she's with you.*

*Conor: Shit. I expected more resistance. I had a whole game plan
ready. You always ruin the fun.*

I shouldn't. I know I fucking shouldn't, but I'll turn gray

overnight if I don't, so I call the head of security at Q and instruct him to delegate one bouncer to keep an eye on Mia.

It's just this once. After all, it's the first time she's going out since we're together, and I just need a bit of reassurance. It'll be different next time.

I'm a bit better knowing she'll be looked after.

I'm a bit worse knowing I'm fucking insane.

"They'll hate you for that," Logan says, chugging the rest of his beer. "They kept her safe for a year, Nico."

"I know. I'm working on this, okay? Really, I am, but it's not easy rearranging my entire personality so fast." I rub my face, closing my eyes briefly. "The triplets will keep her safe if they see something happen, but what if they don't? What if they're in line at the bar, and she's alone?"

"You're paranoid, bro. I mean, nothing new there, you've always been a bit looney, but I really don't get it this time. You weren't going overboard like that with Kaya."

Theo folds his arms over his chest, a self-assured smirk curving his mouth. "He wasn't in love with Kaya."

I guess that's one way of putting it.

Thirty

Mia

THE BOUNCER STOPS ME and the triplets at the entrance to Q, looking me over with a dumbstruck expression and a deep frown. "Are you Mia Harlow?" he asks, shaking hands with the triplets.

"I am. Why? Is there a problem?"

I left my fake ID at home, so if that's what he wants—

"Not at all, I just..." He trails off, shaking his head as if dismissing whatever he wants to say, then presses a finger to his earpiece. "Mia's here."

Cody grunts beside me, good mood slipping off his face. "He's got to be fucking kidding." He pulls out his phone and taps the screen, jaw locked tight.

"He?" I mutter. "Who?"

"Nico," Colt supplies, resting his long arm over my shoulders. "Looks like he called security to keep an eye on you."

"He sure did," the bouncer admits. "You've got the VIP booth upstairs, and Johnny here..." He points at the guy exiting the club, "...will be your shadow all evening."

"That's unnecessary—"

"Boss's order," Johnny cuts me off. "Don't worry, you won't notice I'm around. I blend in very well, and I'm only supposed to ensure you're not left alone."

He's taller than Nico, so no way he can blend in.

"It's cool, man. I'm not that surprised he called," Conor tells him, swaying me left to right. "At least he let you come out with us, Bug. That's big considering he's like a fucking rottweiler around you. Come on, I'll make your head spin."

"Next time, we won't tell you where we're taking her," Cody snaps into the phone, his tone dripping with irritation. "We've been taking her out for months, and nothing ever happened!"

Conor pushes me gently, urging me to move. "Six is playing in an hour," he says in my ear, ushering me through the crowd, up the stairs to our booth.

Colt heads for the bar, and once he's back with a tray of drinks, Cody joins us.

"You need to stand up to him, Mia. He'll end up controlling every part of your life if you let him get away with this."

"You're making a big deal out of nothing," Conor chips in. "He let her come out with us, right?"

"*Let* her?" Cody seethes. "Do you hear yourself? He doesn't get to *let* her do anything. She's not a fucking child."

It's like Aisha versus Nico all over again. Only this time, it's his brothers arguing on my behalf.

"Dance with me," I blurt out before this escalates.

The truth is, I don't mind Nico calling security. I wouldn't even mind if he said I should stay home. I've never been a party girl. Much as I enjoy spending time with the triplets, I'd happily do it elsewhere. The arcades, the beach, at home watching movies, or playing piano while Cody plays guitar.

If Nico feels better knowing there's a bouncer looking out for me, then so be it. It's not like I plan to do anything he wouldn't approve of.

"Yeah, alright. Come on." Cody grabs my hand, taking me downstairs. Johnny follows suit, not blending in. "He'll dictate everything you do if you let him, Mia," Cody says, pulling me into his side. "And I mean *everything*. From where you can go and who you can be friends with to what you can wear. He's a good guy, but he gets carried away easily. You need to stand up to him."

We step onto the dancefloor, giving me the perfect opportunity to nip the topic in the bud. I doubt Cody would understand if I told him I find Nico's controlling personality ridiculously appealing. It draws me in because letting him take the lead makes me feel safe.

I'm *his*. And he's *mine*.

I've never felt like I belonged anywhere before. Not at home with my absent parents, or my sister, not at school where no one would utter a word in my direction, scared to end up on the wrong side of Jake Grey. The first glimpse of *belonging* came with the triplets.

And now?

Now I really feel I belong. That being with Nico is where I was supposed to land. That all the years of loneliness finally paid off because they brought me to him.

"My turn," Colt shouts twenty minutes later, snatching me from Cody's arms.

There are at least a dozen people in the booth when we go

back upstairs after another five songs. The triplets are popular, so whenever we're out, it's never just the four of us for long. People flock to them, expecting good times and great friends.

"There, drink that," Johnny says, placing a lemonade on the table.

"He told you to keep her hydrated, too?" Cody huffs. "Is she allowed to pee unattended, or will you hold the door?"

"Your fight's with your brother, man. I just work here." He walks away, taking a stance nearby in case he's needed.

"Just ignore him," I tell Cody, running my fingers down his arm. "I don't mind."

"You should. I bet you're not allowed to dance with anyone other than us, Mia. He doesn't fucking trust you."

"When have you ever seen me dance with anyone but you?"

"That's beside the point."

I slam my glass on the table. "Your annoyance is beside the point. I get you think it's wrong, but *I* don't. That should be enough for you to drop this. I'm not naïve, Cody. I know this isn't how most boyfriends act, but I also know Nico's working hard to tone it down."

He really is. I see the small adjustments he makes, how he checks in when he thinks he's going overboard.

"And he does trust me," I continue. "He's just worried. Whatever your problem with him is, it's *your* problem." I stand up, pointing at the guy sitting beside Colt. I think his name's Grayson. "Dance with me."

He cocks an eyebrow, glancing between the triplets like he's checking it's okay.

Oh, look at that. I'm not allowed to dance with anyone else without their permission, either.

Seeing no disapproval, Grayson gets to his feet, adjusting

his t-shirt in one tug. "Yeah, sure."

Johnny moves from his post to stand beside me, but doesn't intervene.

"See? I'm allowed," I tell Cody, and before he can say anything else I follow Grayson downstairs.

The one thing I overlooked while proving my point is that I now have to dance with a guy I barely know. We squeeze through the crowd on the dancefloor, finding space by the stage where Six is setting up to play his set. For now, "Jungle" by Fred Again blasts through the speakers, and Grayson starts jumping, carried away by the beat.

He takes my hand, spinning me around, then pulls my back flush to his chest. Not even thirty seconds later, there's a shift in the air, and different hands slide around my middle, holding me firmly so I can't spin on my heel to check who's there.

"Here, kitty, kitty," Brandon purrs in my ear, his voice raising the hairs on my neck. "How's my *pussy...* cat?"

"Not yours." I tilt my head so he can hear me. "Aren't you bored of getting shot down? Let me go before I get security."

"I like this game we play." He slowly moves side to side, disregarding the upbeat rhythm pumping around us. "Ready to give up?"

Johnny's watching, one eyebrow raised in silent question. I could wave him over, but I'm sure he'd tell Nico I needed help and I am not involving him. He's overlooking my age but avoids talking about college to the point that he immediately changes the subject whenever the triplets ask me about finals. While Brandon's game remains nothing but an inconvenience, I'm not telling Nico.

"It'll be a cold day in hell before I give up. Save your face. Your plan isn't working."

"Not working? So you're saying you're not even a little bit scared of what the guys might do?" He spins me around, his warm breath fanning my face. "I find that hard to believe since you kneed Dennis in the balls the other day."

"He slapped my ass, and only my boyfriend gets to do that. I told you I'm no longer available."

Brandon trails his fingers down my back, stopping an inch above my ass. "Your boyfriend, huh? How come I've never seen you with this guy? He's imaginary, right?"

"God, no." I spin around. "He's very much real."

Brandon smirks, looking me up and down. "I've not fucked you yet, kitten. You can call me God when you're coming on my dick." He stares at something over my shoulder. "I'll bite. Who's the lucky guy? It sure isn't Conor unless you don't mind that he's currently sticking his tongue down Ann-Marie's throat. That leaves Cody and Colt. Which one's getting the money?" He leans closer, both hands on my waist as he sways to the music. "Or is it, Justin?"

"Justin?" I scoff. "He might be a decent guy, but he's still your friend, Brandon, and anyone who sticks by you can't have much common sense. Let me go, or—"

"Or what? You'll knee my balls? I dare you, kitten." A lick of malice flares his eyes as he grabs my wrist, yanking me closer. "Hit me again, and I'll stop being so fucking nice."

His grip tightens, bordering on painful, way past bruising point. This will take some explaining when Nico spots the bruises tomorrow.

The music fades, drowned out by blood whooshing in my ears, panic settling into my gut. This feels too familiar... *Q*, a guy touching me against my will...

Memories blur reality, diminishing my composure. Brandon's

face morphs into Asher's and back, over and over, the tighter he holds me.

I can feel myself shaking, but I can't stay grounded. My head's too loud. Too chaotic to think straight, to weigh the consequences when I look to the side for help. Johnny's still there, apparently blending in if Brandon hasn't noticed him by now.

Our eyes lock, and that's all he needs.

My pulse soars immediately. Not because of Brandon. Not because Johnny grips his neck, gouging his fingers into his flesh so hard his nails whiten. Not even because Conor is suddenly beside me, shoving me back and nailing Brandon's face.

It's because Johnny will report this to Nico, and I'll have to lie again. If he finds out about the prize, he'll leave me.

I'm not losing the best thing that happened in my life over Brandon Price's misogynistic worldview.

"What the fuck?" Brandon booms, thrashing against Johnny's hold. "Let me go, man! What's your problem?!"

Two of his buddies jump in to help. One sends a clenched fist to Conor's stomach, and the other jumps on Johnny's back, climbing him like a tree.

All hell breaks loose.

Someone shoves me back again, and I slam into a hard chest. The last thing I see before Cody spins me to face him is a glimpse of an enraged Colt charging Brandon. All fire and brimstone as he steers out a punch.

"He put twenty-five grand up for you?!" Cody yells over the surrounding noise. "Why the fuck didn't you tell us?!"

"I-I... I'm sorry, I—"

"Save it for later," he snaps, tucking me against his side as more bouncers and more football players arrive.

Colt hammers his fists into Brandon in a deranged frenzy,

paying no attention to his bleeding nose and split eyebrow. Random partygoers jump in, lashing out at everyone in their path, and the brawl gets out of hand within seconds.

"Get her outside!" Johnny yells, pointing to the exit.

Cody grips my wrist, forging a path through the crowd of onlookers. No one in sight is dancing anymore. Everyone stopped to watch twenty men throwing fists.

I double over as soon as we're outside, pumping crisp evening air into my lungs.

"You gonna puke? Fuck, your bag's upstairs."

"I'm okay," I mutter, leaning against the wall. "Please don't tell Nico about the prize. Please, promise you—"

"No way! Don't ask me to keep that a secret." He steps back, tearing his hair out of his head. "Why didn't you tell us?! How long has this been going on?!"

"Since the Spring Break party," I mutter, staring at the ground beneath my feet. I should've stayed home... nothing would've happened if I'd just stayed home tonight.

Argh, who am I kidding?

The triplets would've found out soon enough, and I'd be right where I am now—about to lose the man I love.

Once Nico realizes that on top of all my flaws, I bring a heap of trouble and drama, he'll question our relationship.

He'll move on.

I might excite him now, but long term, not much speaks in my favor. In this day of feminism, strong personalities, and confident women who know what they want and how to get it, I'm a freak. An anomaly. Someone to pick on and laugh at. I'm cautious, weak, and shy. I'm afraid of the dark and nervous around strangers. I'm awkward, insecure, and inexperienced.

Nico deserves a woman who'll own every room she walks

into. Let me in that room, and the only thing I'll own is the best corner to hide in.

He deserves someone who'll be his equal and challenge him every step of the way.

A woman who'll make his life exciting but *easier*. He's got a lot going on without me adding stupid college drama to the mix.

"Who told you?" I ask, disappointment clutching my heart.

Even if Nico doesn't point blank cut me loose the moment he finds out, our relationship will expire soon enough.

"Grayson," Cody snaps. "But it should've been *you*! Jesus, Mia!" He grips my shoulders, pulling me into his arms. "You have any idea what could've happened, Bug? You should've told us. You should've told Nico."

I shake my head, my breathing shallow as tears threaten to spill. "He's the last person I want to know about this."

"Why?" He pushes me away. "He'll take care of it."

I step back, tucking loose strands of hair behind my ears. "He'll also realize I bring nothing but problems. He gives me everything I ever wanted, and I... I'm just a phase."

"You're not a fucking phase, Mia, he—"

"It's okay," I say, my chin quivering. "He was worth the wait, and he's worth the tears." I pinch my lips together, forcing a smile. "I'll get my bag. I'm sure Johnny called him by now, and he's on his way."

"Stay here. I'll get your bag."

"No, you won't," the bouncer manning the door says. "You're not allowed back in."

"I wasn't fighting," Cody seethes. "She's not going in there alone, man."

The bouncer shrugs, stepping aside when Johnny exits the club, holding Brandon and Colt by their collars, and shoves them outside.

Cody shoots forward like a spring, gripping Brandon by his neck. "You'll call it off. *Tonight*, you got that?!"

Using a second of their inattention, I get back inside. Johnny's hauling two more guys out, and another bouncer trails behind Conor, nudging him toward the exit.

The party's back on track, fight under control. I climb the stairs to find Grayson in the booth with a few friends, my bag safely tucked behind his back. Once I have it, I make a stop in the restroom, needing a moment to gather my thoughts.

Passing two girls in the doorway, I find the restroom empty and a little quieter than the rest of the club. The music never stopped while twenty-odd guys threw punches. It's still pumping as Six plays his favorite set.

I grip the sink with both hands, looking into my glassy, teary eyes in the mirror.

One day at a time.

That's what I've been telling myself since I kissed Nico. I knew this was too good to last, and I fought not to get too comfortable, not to let my romantic side take the reins and imagine a future I'd never have.

I wipe my cheeks when the door swings inward, flooding the restroom with Six's take on "I Got 5 on It" which drowns the tornado of thoughts brewing in my head.

For a second, I fail to realize this isn't a unisex restroom.

I fail to realize these three guys shouldn't be in here...

It all clicks when my eyes lock with *his*.

He's changed a bit since high school: lost weight he never had much of to spare. His skin is ashen, eyes dull, but disdain shines clearly, and a giant cold fist clutches my stomach.

The air shifts immediately. An unrelenting aura of impending doom fills the space when his best friend, Michael, slaps a makeshift *Out of order* sign on the door before yanking it closed. He stands his ground, barricading the exit with his big body and greeting me with a sly smirk.

I don't care much about him or Jessie, who scrutinizes me with a hard edge to his narrowed eyes. My focus is on Jake Grey, his steel-gray irises almost completely swallowed by blown pupils, the way he grinds his teeth back and forth, the tremble of his hands...

"Missed me, BJ?" he asks, cracking his neck as he casually leans his hip against the sink.

Cold fear slithers in my gut, the space between us less than five feet. I've got no chance, but I snatch my bag off the sink, tugging the zipper.

"Grab her!" Jake booms.

I almost close my hand around the pepper spray. So close, but Jessie rips the bag out of my grasp, tossing it aside, and ties my hands behind my back, his bony fingers hurting my wrists.

Panic kicks in. An unreasoning, nerve-shaking, blood-to-water-turning sort of horror courses through my veins, rendering me momentarily useless.

"Calm down, BJ," Jake chuckles. "I'm here to help."

"Help?" I choke, glancing right and left, up and down, assessing my position, the distance to the pepper spray that rolled out of my bag, stopping not far from where Michael's barricading the door. "Help with *what?*"

He pulls his phone out, tapping the screen. "I hear Brandon Price is playing games with you. He put a prize up for the first guy who fucks you, correct?" He looks up from the screen, his nostrils flaring. "*Correct?!*"

I nod, struggling against Jessie's hold. "Let me go."

"Not so fast," Jake tuts, taking a few wobbly steps from the sinks, pointing at the ground before him. "Get her on her knees."

"N-no," I stutter. "Please, just—"

"*Please, just stop,*" Jake mocks, imitating my voice. "Relax, BJ. It'll be fun. I've wanted that pouty mouth of yours wrapped around my dick since I nicknamed you Blow Job Lips back in fucking high school," he muses, unbuckling his belt.

The realization of what's about to happen grips my throat like cold, dead hands squeezing hard enough to cut off my air supply. Every self-defense technique the triplets taught me evaporates from my mind.

I've got nothing. My mind blanks. Panic grows swiftly, annihilating rational thought.

I thrash about, losing the battle before it begins. Jessie manhandles me to where Jake stands. He bumps the back of my knees with his, and I hit the ground, wincing when a sharp jab of pain shoots up my legs.

"You hated me for years," I choke, grasping the only rational thought: play for time. The triplets are outside. They'll start looking for me soon. I've been here too long already. I just need to stall. "You didn't want me to touch you all through kindergarten, and now you want me to blow you?"

He grips a fistful of my hair, yanking me back so hard I yelp. "I don't have to like you. I think the fact I *don't* like you makes this even more exciting."

Tears drip down my nose.

My stomach curls into a hard, hot ball, and I tremble all over while Jessie holds my hands behind my back.

"What happened?" I pant through the sting of my hair getting almost ripped out of my skull. "You bragged about how girls fall over themselves to get a taste of you every day back in high school. No one wants to blow you willingly anymore?"

Jake scoffs, outstretching his hand that holds the phone, grinning like a maniac. "Strap in, Price." He turns the phone, tilting it down, so I'm visible on the screen. A red dot at the bottom tells me he's recording. "The show's about to begin." He lets go of my hair, slides the zipper of his jeans, and frees his hard dick, proudly showing it off to the camera. "Come on, BJ. Don't make this awkward. People are watching." He looks in the camera again, shoving his dick closer to my lips. "Grab a pen, Price. I'll be collecting that check soon."

Money? He wants the money? Confusion knocks the breath out of my chest. Jake's loaded. His father...

Oh, God.

Nico's conversation with his assistant a few weeks ago comes back like the aftershock from an earthquake.

Arnold Grey pulled out all his money last week and just called to say he lost everything.

I didn't think much of it back then, but now it makes perfect sense. Arnold *Grey*. Jake's father.

They're broke...

I look up at Jake, my teeth clenched tight as the head of his cock hangs less than an inch from my lips.

Fifteen years ago, he wouldn't go anywhere near me, afraid he'd contract *cooties.*

Ten years ago, I was too chubby for him to consider me anything other than disgusting.

Five years ago, he called me four eyes and destroyed my glasses whenever he had the chance, laughing when I held onto the wall because I couldn't see.

And now, he stands before the girl he wouldn't touch with a stick, his eyes ablaze, pants down, buzzing erection twitching with precum, and one goal in mind: to win twenty-five grand.

"Don't be like that, BJ," he coos, artificially friendly for a second before his words turn thick with hatred. "It'll be more pleasant if you don't fucking resist."

I grit my teeth tighter. My pulse hammers in my neck like a bird in a box, and tears come on stronger. High, hysterical sobs reverberate off the tiles like the wail of a violin.

Jake has no idea what he's getting into. I'm no longer the outcast or a loner. I have people in my life who care about me. People who will do anything to protect me.

A boyfriend who'll tear him apart when he finds out Jake's trying to hurt me. I want to scream, tell him whose girl he's about to touch, but if I part my lips, I lose.

"Open her mouth," Jake snaps at Jessie, who immediately digs his thumb and index finger into the hinge joints of my jaw.

Pain zaps my nerve endings. The harder I clench my teeth, the worse it becomes.

Jake angles his phone, recording as he strokes his stiff cock, smearing small beads of what's dripping from the end around his Prince Albert piercing. He was absurdly proud when he got it done. A picture of this exact cock with this exact piercing was glued to my locker daily for weeks before graduation.

Tears drip down my nose and chin, gaining momentum as Jessie increases the pressure. It feels like my face is being squeezed by metal clamps and my bones will fracture any second.

I can't take it anymore.

I whimper, and more tears follow when my mouth opens despite my best attempts.

God, where's Cody? Where's Colt?

"Good," Jake huffs, hooking his thumb over my lower teeth. "Pretty, pretty, pretty," he chants. "Relax, BJ. I know it's big, but if you keep your mouth wide open, I'll fit in there just fine."

I'm thrashing about, trying to break free, but Jessie's grip on my wrists tightens, and he's pressing on the backs of my ankles with his whole tibia to keep me in place.

I'm powerless. I can't stop him when he jerks forward, guiding himself into my mouth. His piercing touches my tongue, and he unhooks his thumb from my teeth to lower his pants.

His balls spring from their confinement, hanging low, dangerously close to my chin. The musky, sweaty smell makes my intestines crawl up my throat, and fifteen years of bullying flicker before my eyes in a maddening clip of cruelty, my mind like an intersection with too much traffic.

Every time Jake tripped, pushed, and shoved me comes back like a recoil of a fired gun. Every foul word, everything he ever threw at me, every time he made me cry, it all resurfaces. All the sandwiches I ate in the bathroom, too afraid to enter the cafeteria. All the things he destroyed...

I'm a pot of boiling milk. There's no more room left in me. I can't take any more, and for the first time, I'm struck with a burning need to fight.

He trapped me in a corner.

My fight or flight response kicks into its highest gear. One rational thought, like a stark-white bolt of lightning, ignites my senses, and I do the only thing I can, not thinking twice... I brace my teeth behind his piercing and clamp down with all my might.

I rip it out.

Warm, metallic blood floods my mouth a second before excruciating pain registers with Jake.

"Fuck!" he roars, jumping back. His phone lands on the floor. "Fucking whore!" He balls his hand into a fist, landing a powerful blast on the side of my face. "You filthy bitch!"

I'm dizzy... my head spins... I feel stupefied when Jake jerks away, holding his cock sputtering blood in crimson ejaculation.

I spit his piercing out, shaking like a newborn puppy sniffing for food. In most other high-stress situations, I'd be puking my guts out by now, but nausea doesn't register yet. Survival instinct sharpens my senses, clears my head, and spurs me on.

Michael pales, still manning the door, his resolve wearing thin. A blizzard of uncertainty twists his face as he watches Jake. Two heartbeats later, he bails, scrambling out so fast he almost trips over his legs.

Jessie still holds my hands, but he's back on his feet, muttering Jake's name. Blood squirts onto my face, neck, and dress as if it's being sprayed from a water gun.

I don't take a second to consider my position. I act, converting adrenaline into courage as I dip forward, then wing myself back, ramming the back of my head into Jessie's groin.

It hurts *me,* so I can only imagine how much pain I caused him. He lets go of my wrists, hissing profanities under his breath while Jake's still two feet away, crying real tears. He drops to his knees, frantically trying to stop the bleeding, teeth clattering from pain, shock, or both.

I jump to my weak legs, wobbling on stiletto heels. I need a weapon. I'm too small to cause much damage with my fists, so I need something to hit with. I'm not thinking clearly, not weighing the consequences when I burst into the first cubicle and grip the ceramic water tank cover on the toilet.

I tear it off, stumbling back a step, then spin around, raising it over my shoulder like a baseball bat. It's heavy. Under normal circumstances, I'd lack the strength to lift it with such ease, but nothing's impossible when you're cranked up on adrenaline.

"You're fucking insane, bitch!" Jessie roars, jostling to his feet, arms outstretched like he wants to catch me.

He won't touch me.

I won't let either of them touch me.

I swing on my heel, the heavy cover almost tipping me over. I use the momentum to my advantage, ramming Jessie across the side of his head, my muscles stinging with the effort.

The cover shatters against his head, and Jessie's unconscious body folds to the blood-stained tiles. His head thuds on the floor as the restroom door swings open, hitting the wall with a bang.

Johnny fills the height of the frame, his face glowing red. "What the—" He pauses, taking a quick look around, his complexion blanching. "Shit... fuck!" He walks in slowly, hands up like he wants to show me he has no bad intentions, but I stumble back, twisting my ankle, and barely manage to keep my balance. "Easy, there, it's okay," he mutters softly. "It's okay, Mia, you're okay. I won't—" He cuts himself off again and stops mid-step, the white of his cheeks turning ashen.

I'm not sure why.

All I know is I'm backing away from him. Everything blends together. Sounds distort. The music fades, masked by the thunderous pulse drumming in my ears...

The rage seizing every cell in my body disintegrates, leaving me defenseless.

Nausea wrings my stomach when I follow Johnny's line of sight. *That's* why he stopped talking. Jake's piercing glistens on the floor with bits of flesh attached. I thought I only ripped the piercing, but Jake's missing a mouthful of dick.

I catch a glimpse of my reflection in the mirrors above the sinks and take an involuntary step back. Blood mixes with tears on my face, neck, and dress, the sight like a still from a cheap horror movie.

Jake's still crying, ripping his t-shirt off, probably trying to stop the bleeding, unaware of what's happening around him. I don't think he even noticed Johnny arrive.

My legs give in.

I collapse to my knees, adrenaline long gone, body limp, cold, and exhausted. I crawl into the cubicle, shaking all over when I grip the toilet with both hands and finally throw up.

"Fuck!" Johnny booms. "Mia! Mia... shit! Hold on, I need to..." His voice trails off when everything I ate today comes back.

"Nico..." I rasp, coughing, gagging, and gasping for air. Cold sweat coats my back, inducing a shivering fit. I grip the toilet harder, holding on for dear life as I beg, "...please get Nico."

Thirty-one

Nico

MY PHONE RINGS IN MY POCKET as Theo sets another round of beers on the table. I pull it out, my hands growing clammy when *Johnny Q* flashes on the screen.

"Is she okay?" I ask.

His voice fills my ear before the words fully roll off my tongue. "You need to get over here right now!" he booms. "How fast can you—" He pauses, then his voice drops in volume even though he's still screaming. "Hey! Stay there, you piece of shit, or I'll break your fucking neck!"

Fear clutches my throat first, closely followed by worry erupting inside my chest like a fucking volcano, filling my veins with hot lava. I never stop worrying about Mia, but it's a controlled kind of unease. One I can cap to an extent.

At least I like thinking I can.

Now? Now it's a mixture of unrelenting fear and fury

jolting me upright in a split second.

"What the fuck happened?" I snap halfway out the building without one word to Logan or Theo. They read the tone of my voice perfectly, following suit, their chairs scraping along the floor as they scramble to their feet.

"I've got two guys here," Johnny says, breathing heavily as if he ran ten flights of stairs. "One's unconscious, one has a mouthful of his *dick* missing, and your girl is hysterical."

My blood turns to cherry slurpy, and my stomach bottoms out like a runaway elevator. "Where are you?"

My brothers catch up with me when the engine of my G Wagon springs to life, disturbing the otherwise quiet evening. They hop in, both as tense as I am, both silent when the hands-free system activates, and Johnny's voice seeps from the speakers.

"Restroom upstairs. This doesn't look good. I'm so fucking sorry! I had her, I watched her all the time, but your brothers started a fight downstairs. Thirty assholes joined in! We were kicking them out and..." He pushes a shaky breath down his nose. "Mia went back in to grab her bag—" A loud thud sounds in the background, and someone cries out in pain. "What did I say?! Stay there! Don't fucking move!"

"Johnny!" I snap, gripping the wheel tighter as I back out of the parking space, wheels squealing. "Where's Mia?"

"She's throwing up. Fuck, it's a bloodbath here. I don't know what went down but from what I can make out, this is too much to handle. She was gone five minutes tops before we started looking!" Another thud, quieter this time. More of a thump, really, as if he hit the wall with his fist. "Goddamnit! Where are you?!"

"On my way. Ten minutes. Pull yourself together." I press my foot down, imagining the scene from the little information

I have. Blood. Mia—scared enough to puke. Two men. I grind my teeth, praying those fuckers didn't *touch* her. "Is she hurt?" I rasp, my throat tight, words struggling to come.

"I don't think so. She's not said anything. Just told me to get you. I think... oh, man..." he whines, clearly distraught. "There's blood everywhere." He takes a few steps; the sound of his heavy boots beats out of the speakers. Another thud—a kick to someone's stomach judging by the cough and whimper. "What did you do to her?!"

"Johnny!" I boom again, hands shaking like I'm coming down from a week-long drinking session. "Tell Mia I'm on my way. Did you call the cops? Are the triplets there?"

"Yeah, they're here. I've not called the cops, not yet."

I don't have to tell my brothers to get it done. Theo pulls his phone out immediately.

"Clear the club and don't let those motherfuckers get away."

"On it," he says quickly. "I'm on it, boss."

I hack the wheel again when he cuts the call. My pulse is going so fast the drumming in my ears borders on painful.

"Shawn's on his way," Theo says, weighing every word.

He knows I can barely hold my composure as I redial Johnny.

"Stay on the fucking line!" I snap when he answers. "Shawn will be there soon. How's Mia?"

"She stopped puking. She's okay, not hurt."

I should be there with her. I should hold her. Calm her down. Calm *myself* down. Instead, I'm veering around traffic on Main Street, breaking too many laws and willing the miles away. "Are those fuckers still there?"

"Yeah, both unconscious now." He lowers his voice to a whisper. "One isn't breathing, Nico."

My foot falters on the gas pedal.

Not breathing? Fuck. Gruesome scenarios flood my brain, but I push them away.

Mia's safe.

She fought them off.

She's okay.

Not hurt.

I turn left, then right, and left again, speeding down the street before I slam the brakes, stopping by the curb. I'm out the car in two seconds flat.

There's a small crowd outside Q. Most guys are bleeding, and a few try arguing their way inside with the bouncers. Half the college football team watches me shove guys out of my way.

"Clear the fucking club," I tell the head of security. "Right now. Everyone out!"

"We're getting it done, boss. Ten minutes tops."

I break into a sprint the moment I'm inside, my brothers hot on my tail. Every second stretches like bubble gum. I feel like I've been running for hours when I push the restroom door open, and stop, taking in the scene.

One guy lies on his side in the middle of the room, unconscious. Blood seeps from a large gash on his skull. His mouth hangs open, eyes shut, his back arched in an unnatural position.

The other guy's half-sitting, half-laying under the sink, pale like a ghost. What looks like a scrap of t-shirt is tied around his limp, purple, injured dick. His hands and clothes are smeared with blood. There's more all over the place, including the fucking walls. Red splashes here and there as if someone flicked paint all across the off-white tiles.

The floor is littered with broken pieces of what must've been a ceramic cover from a toilet's water tank.

Images of Mia swinging the heavy cover fill my head. How

scared—how pumped up on adrenaline—was she to rip that thing off in the first place?

I'm jolted back into motion when my eyes come across the triplets. Colt and Conor stand by the cubicle, and Cody crouches by Mia, gently stroking her back, his eyes on me, face twisted in disbelief. All three of them look as scared as I feel.

"Move," I say, elbowing my way to her.

She's on the floor, her shoulder against the left wall of the cubicle, hair, face, neck, and dress stained by blood. She looks like *Carrie*. Pale, tearful, covered in red, scared, and so fucking helpless it makes my heart break clean in two.

I cuff her wrist, lifting her off the tiles and into my arms in two moves, cradling her fragile frame into my chest, one hand under her thighs, the other around her shoulder blades.

"I'm here," I say, pressing my lips to her temple when she shudders, nuzzling herself as close to me as physically possible. "I've got you, baby. You're safe."

I'm both relieved she doesn't flinch at my closeness and on the verge of letting my rage take the scene. She's so cold, trembling all over.

Knotting her fingers on my nape, she nuzzles her face under my chin. "I'm okay," she whispers, sounding seconds from bursting into tears, but trying her hardest not to cry. "I'm not hurt. It's not my blood."

"I know. You're okay." I turn around, looking at Logan and Theo standing in the doorway. "Come on, I need you."

I carry Mia out of the restroom, her tears trickling down my skin into my t-shirt. She's not making a sound, though. I hate that she's so vulnerable, but I also love that she trusts me enough not to pretend or hide how she feels.

"Shh..." I tut quietly and slide to the floor, readjusting my hold on her. "Shh, baby, you're safe. I'm here. I take care of you, remember? I won't let anyone hurt you."

She nestles her face harder into the crook of my neck, inhaling me in short, ragged breaths. "I'm okay," she utters again.

I pull out the keys to my car, tossing them to Logan. "There's a hoodie in the boot and a pack of baby wipes in the glove box. Grab that for me."

A single nod and barely audible, *yeah, sure,* is all I get before he jogs away.

Mia's motionless, silently choking on her tears. All I can do is whisper in her ear and stroke her back as she processes whatever the fuck went down.

Not even two minutes go by before Shawn arrives, followed by four police officers and Logan.

"She said anything yet?" Shawn asks.

"Not yet. Deal with the motherfuckers first. You can interrogate Mia at home."

He bobs his head, too smart to argue while I'm *this* close to turning into the goddamn Hulk. On the outside, I'm composed. I'm everything Mia needs: calm, focused, determined.

Everything happening inside is an entirely different matter.

I take the hoodie from Logan and pull it over Mia's head, not bothering with the sleeves. I tug the fabric until it covers her butt, then press her to me, caging her in my arms.

She's not talking, and I'm not pushing. Not yet. She needs to calm down first. She's too stiff. Her muscles have no give. It's fucking unnatural because she's always like playdough around me: adjusting to my rhythm, submitting to my dominance. Right now, she's numb. Detached.

My brothers move away a few extra steps when more cops arrive while I'm wiping blood off Mia's face.

It's not easy. Cleaning dried blood off her skin using wet wipes is like cleaning red wine off a carpet with paper towels. I'm not making much progress, but she's calming down the longer I do this, so I don't stop.

"You're so fucking brave," I whisper, one arm draped across her middle. "You want something to drink?"

She nods softly, and Cody walks away before I can ask anyone to fetch a bottle of water from the bar.

Shawn comes out the restroom, a phone to his ear for a moment before he tucks it away, scratching the back of his head. By the look of him, he's not seen anything like this before. "Does Mia need medical attention?"

"No," she whispers. "I'm not hurt."

He looks her over as if making sure she's not lying. "Alright, take her home, Nico. Get her cleaned up, and we'll take her statement later. I'll need your statements, too," he tells the triplets.

"We'll do it at my place," I say before Shawn pulls Johnny to one side.

Mia grips my shirt tighter, panic etched into her expression when I try to get us off the floor.

"We're going home. I'm not letting you go, baby."

I want to.

I want to pass her over to Cody and get my revenge on the two unconscious motherfuckers just behind the wall. I'd risk being detained if it meant punishing the ones who hurt my girl, but regardless of how much pain I could inflict, it wouldn't help Mia.

She'd spiral deeper into her fear.

There are women walking this earth who'd judge her lack of self-sufficiency. They'd point fingers, try to toughen her up, and teach her what feminism is all about.

The thing is... Mia can take care of herself just fine if she has no choice. She almost raised herself, dogging her mother's lack of interest, Jimmy's career, and Aisha's love of guys and partying.

But she doesn't want to be independent. She doesn't want to count only on herself.

And that's probably why I fell in love with her so fast... because she fits me so well. She's all I ever wanted without realizing. I *needed* a girl like her. One who'd consider my protectiveness a good thing, not a leash.

She wants, needs, and expects to be cared for. I want, need, and expect her to let me do that.

We're a match made in fucking heaven.

Thirty-two

Nico

EIGHT.

That's how many times Mia brushed her teeth before she let me kiss her. It was far from what I wanted. A tight-lip peck.

I've not let her out of my arms for one fucking second of the half hour we've been home. I bathed her, washed her hair, and almost doubled over when I noticed a shadow of a bruise forming on her face.

I dressed her, too, even despite her protests. She's wearing my hoodie. The same one I wore last night when we sat in the garden, eating pizza. My heart squeezed tightly when she said she wanted it because it smells like me and calms her down.

She sits between my legs on the bed while I do a lousy job braiding her wet hair.

"He called me *Cootie Mia* in kindergarten," she says, her voice detached, emotionless. "And *four eyes* in middle school because I wore very thick glasses."

"He?" I part her hair in the middle for the third time, dividing it in three sections. "The guy who hurt you tonight?"

"His name's Jake. He nicknamed me *Blow Job Lips* in high school. Pushed me, slingshot spitballs at me, tied me up, and locked me in the janitorial closet for hours." She sighs softly, no longer shaking but still too tense. "Blair was his right-hand man. She cut up my clothes or stole them when I showered after Phys Ed. She stuck gum in my hair, threw food at me in the cafeteria, shoved me to my knees... It stopped at college. Jake's father shipped him off to Brown, and Blair got busy with boys, but everything started again when I broke Brandon's nose."

"You're being bullied?" I ask, the muscles in my back tensing painfully. "Why didn't you tell me?"

"It's not how you imagine," she admits, her voice breaking like eggshells. "I'm sorry, I—" She gets up, taking a few steps away, and the braid I've been working on falls apart. "Don't be mad at the triplets, okay? They didn't know."

"About *what?* Baby, I don't want to push if you're not ready to talk, but I need to know what happened. Johnny said the triplets started a fight."

She bobs her head, toying with her bracelets. She hasn't done that for a while, growing more confident as the weeks go by, but she's afraid again, uncertain...

I hate seeing her like this. All the more because she's been avoiding my gaze since I brought her home.

She drapes her damp hair over one shoulder, sinking her teeth in her bottom lip. "Conor hit Brandon, and soon enough, everyone was fighting. I think Grayson told them what Brandon did after the Spring Break party..."

"What did he do?"

She sits beside me. Her chin trembles and fresh tears pool in her eyes. "I'm sorry. I didn't think it would get out of hand like this. It was just a stupid game. I tried to deal with it myself. I didn't want you to know." She bites her lip, gouging her nails into my hand. "When college resumed, Brandon said I had to pay for the parties he missed because of his broken nose. He said I had to spend two weeks in his bed." She's pinching her rings, clearly afraid to look at me. "I said no, but he wasn't getting the message, then Blair's jealousy started getting out of hand."

"What does Blair have to do with this?"

"She loves Brandon. Whenever he gets too close to me, she makes me pay. Coffee in my face, the pictures, my—" She halts, leaving the sentence unfinished. "The point is—"

"Not so fast," I cut in. "Finish what you were going to say. What else did Blair do?"

Another tear rolls down her cheek, and she swats it away, inhaling deeply. "Brandon stopped by one of my classes, and Blair got jealous. She wallpapered the wall outside the auditorium with pictures of me naked in pornstar poses. They weren't real, just my face photoshopped onto actual porn, but everyone laughed and..." She pushes a long, calming breath down her nose. "I got nauseous, ran into the bathroom, and the next thing I knew, my hair was on fire."

"*She* burned your hair?" My pulse throbs in my fingertips, a biblical kind of fury sweeping me from head to toe. "You said it was candles! Why did you lie?"

Seeing her so scared and vulnerable guts me like a fucking fish, and knowing she's afraid of my reaction makes it ten times worse. She's shaking, quiet defeat painting her face.

"Mia... there's more, right? What else are you hiding?"

"He offered money," she blurts out, pinching her lips and

wiping more tears off her nose. "Brandon. Five grand for the first one of his teammates who gets me in bed."

A few long, silent seconds pass while I make sense of what she said. Once it sinks, I can't fucking sit still.

"Shit," I huff, jumping to my feet, feeling like a loaded gun that's unsure where to aim. I'm fighting not to let my colors shine, but my temper is uncontainable. I see red. Literally red. Anger has always been my primary addiction. Now, it spreads like the vibration of a church bell as the next sentence gets pushed past my clenched teeth. "Did anyone try to win?"

She nods, tearing her cuticles off. "Brandon kept it clean for a while. Five grand, just the football team... I think they had to have consent, but all bets are off now. It's *twenty-five* grand, and the whole campus knows."

"Is this why the triplets were teaching you self-defense? They know about this?"

"No! Of course, not. They only found out tonight. The lessons were because of Brandon. He's been trying to get me in bed for a long time. They did come in handy, though. Only twice. Most guys are decent. It's not about the money for them. They just want to stick it in Brandon's face."

"It sure was about money to that fucker tonight," I snap, then ball my fists, shepherding my temper. "Jesus, Mia! You should've fucking told me! Why didn't you say anything?!"

"I didn't want you to think you were right."

"*Right?* Right about what?"

"About not dating college girls," she whispers, wiping her face. "I didn't want you to wonder if you made a mistake."

Now I'm sick to my stomach, ready to double over and throw up. The defeat tainting Mia's pretty face, how she mind-lessly toys with her rings, the tears, how she trembles... it has nothing to do with what happened tonight.

She's afraid she'll lose me.

I crouch before her, curling my fingers under her chin. "You think you're on a probation period?"

She wipes her cheeks, sniffling pathetically. "You told me what your girl is supposed to be like." She meets my eyes, no longer trying to keep the tears in. "I tried to be her."

"Her?" The veins on my neck pulse, and my jaw works tight circles. "What are you talking about?"

"Courageous, adventurous, confident..." she lists quietly. "That's what you want, but that's not me. I'm none of those things."

"Mia—"

"I tried, Nico," she continues, not letting me cut in. "I tried to be the woman you want, but I'm not her."

"You *are*. Your only problem is your self-esteem's so fucking low. You don't believe in yourself."

"I'm none of the things you want. I'm not brave or—"

"You are. You just don't see it. Mia, you jumped out of a plane with me. That takes a hell of a lot of courage, especially for someone afraid of flying."

I grab her waist, haul her into my arms and sit back on the bed, maneuvering her until she straddles me.

"You're confident, baby. You don't shout, you're not aggressive or rude, but you've put me in my place more times than I can count. And you're the most adventurous person I know. I push you out of your comfort zone in bed, and you enjoy it." I take her teary face in my hands, wiping her cheeks with my thumbs. "You're all I ever wanted."

She sighs, resigned to whatever lie she fed herself. "You were right that day in the cab. All I bring is trouble, Nico. Trouble and drama, and everything you don't need. I don't have anything good to offer. I don't complete you the way you complete me."

She has no fucking clue...

I had no idea I was living in a box until she came along, full of everything I didn't know I needed, and let me out.

"You make me a better man, Mia. You calm me down, tame my fucked-up personality, and show me that life's not just about work." I pull her into my chest, wrapping my arms around her. "You're not self-sufficient, baby, but that's why we work so well. You want your man to be a man. You want me to take care of you, and that's exactly what I want to do." I stroke her hair, kissing the side of her head. "I'm sorry I made you feel you had to change. You don't. You're perfect."

"I'm too young. Don't deny it, Nico. You said I can't talk about college, like you're trying to forget I'm ten years younger."

I push her away enough to see her face. "You're right. I hate that you're so young, but only because I need to take things slow. You're nineteen, Mia. I have to stop myself making plans you're not ready for yet. You need to finish college. You need to have fun so you won't have any regrets."

There's something disturbing about our relationship. We've not been dating long, but I feel it in my bones that she's *it*. I love everything about her. Despite spending seven months with Kaya, the feelings can't compare.

I can easily picture Mia in my future in a beautiful white dress with a ring on her finger. I never thought about the future with Kaya, but Mia's so deep under my skin I can't shake her. I can't cap my feelings, and I don't fucking want to. I'm twenty-nine. I've met enough women to know Mia's the one.

She sniffles softly, her green eyes dull. "What Jake did... I can't take that back, Nico. Once I tell you—"

"Nothing will change. You're mine," I emphasize, holding her face so she can't look away. "Do you understand? I love you, baby. I'll always want you." I close the distance between our lips, slipping my tongue inside her warm, sweet mouth.

She stills but doesn't push me away. Her trembling fingers weave into my hair, and in a heartbeat, she melts against me the way she always does, like she's feeding off my dominance to calm down.

"I love you more." She breaks the kiss long enough to say it, then resumes the slow tempo of our lips working together, every tease of her tongue and touch of her fingers designed to show how much she cares.

I flip her over, covering her frail body. She's locked between my arms, her moves limited the way she loves most. She told me she never felt safer than that day I held her immobile while teaching her self-defense.

"Mine," I say in her mouth. "Always mine, baby. Say it."

Another one of my favorite barely-a-suggestion kind of smiles blooms across her lips. Tears no longer well in her eyes and the tightness clutching my chest ebbs away.

She'll be okay.

She can't see it, but Cody was right last year. She *is* a tough one. Regardless how much hurt is thrown her way, she's still smiling. Still trying to find happiness.

"Use your words, Mia. Tell me you're mine."

"Always yours."

"Good girl. Never doubt me. Never lie to me, and never hide things from me again. Promise."

She lifts her hand to caress my face: a move I've grown fucking addicted to. The cautious tenderness she radiates drugs my entire structure.

"I promise."

We both damn near jump out of our skin when someone knocks on the door at the bottom of the staircase.

Shouting *come in* would be useless since the space is sound-proof, so I peck Mia's nose and get up, jogging down to check who wants in.

Logan's there, arms crossed over his chest, eyes betraying he's on edge. "Shawn's here."

And I'm suddenly on edge, too. Mia hasn't told me what Jake did, but while I cleaned and dressed her, I had time to think it through ten times over. There's really only one explanation. One I desperately don't want Shawn to confirm.

"Yeah, okay. Tell him we'll be down in a minute. Are the triplets back?"

"Nah, not yet. We tried calling, but their phones are off. How's Mia doing?"

"Better than you'd expect." I step down the last step, closing the door behind me, so she won't hear me. "I'll need you and Theo tonight."

He bobs his head, the unspoken promise of a fight jolting him with restless energy I know too well. "Anything. You know we've got you, but the guy's detained. We can't fuck him up."

"It's not Jake we'll be visiting. There's a twenty-five grand prize for Mia at college. First guy to fuck her wins."

A look of menacing bewilderment crosses his face, two vertical lines creasing his forehead. "Shit, what the hell is wrong with people? You know who set the prize?"

"Brandon Price. I need you to come with me and keep me from killing the kid."

"Yeah, okay, I'll tell Theo." He grips my arm, keeping me in place as I turn to get Mia. "There's something you should know..." He steps from one foot to the other, squeezing the bridge of his nose. "That fucker recorded everything he did in that restroom. Shawn has the video, but from what he said, I don't think you should watch it."

I definitely shouldn't.

The mouthful of flesh on the floor and Jake's purple, bleeding cock paint the picture, but I don't have a choice.

If I can, I have to see it.

Mia's more concerned about us than what went down tonight, but the trauma's there. It'll hit her when she least expects it. If I have any hope of helping her, I need to know exactly what happened.

"I'll get Mia," I tell Logan, leaving him as I jog up the stairs.

But when I look at the bed, she's asleep, curled into a ball on the California-King bed, wrapped tightly in my hoodie.

No way I'll wake her up. Adrenaline must've worn off, and her system came crashing if she fell asleep so fast without my arms around her. I was only gone three minutes. She needs to rest, recharge, and then start processing this nightmare.

Shawn has the clip. He knows what happened, and if he still needs Mia's statement, he'll have to wait. For just one short minute, I think about asking him to come back tomorrow, so I can crawl beside Mia, but I need to know what went down.

Putting it off won't do me any good.

I kiss Mia's head, pull the comforter up to her chin, and switch on the galaxy projector I bought after the first night she spent here.

Thirty-three

Nico

I PEER UP FROM SHAWN'S PHONE when the clip ends. My hands shake, and my mind is alive, in constant, jittery motion like a nest of snakes. I'm practically fucking glowing with all-consuming wrath.

If I had Jake here, I'd tear the fucker apart.

Mia's cries resonate inside my head on repeat, adding a brand-new layer of evil to my messed-up mind, but everything comes to a screeching halt when I spot the triplets in the doorway, faces pale.

I've not heard them come in.

Once Mia bit a chunk of Jake's dick off, he dropped his cell, and nothing more than the ceiling was visible, but her face and blond hair flashed up on the screen a few times as she rammed the toilet cover across Jessie's head. There's a second where you see him fall, and then it's just the sound of Mia puking, Johnny on the phone with me, and my brothers bursting in, their voices raised before they tend to Mia.

They look worse now than two hours ago as they stare at me, waiting for my move. Cody wasn't bleeding in *Q*, but he is now, his lip split, knuckles bruised.

It's nothing compared to what Brandon Price looks like, standing between Colt and Conor, face swollen, nose broken. Large blood-mixed tears slide down his cheeks, creating a Halloween-worthy mess.

He's not looking at me, his gaze glued to the floor, both arms held by my brothers, though I doubt he'd run.

He wouldn't get far.

Anger barges into my battered mind like a Soviet icebreaker, diminishing the composure I've assembled thus far. It's overwhelming without Mia by my side. Without her magical ability to pacify the worst kind of fury.

But she's not here. She's upstairs, asleep after suffering what no woman should ever suffer, because of this fucker who stands in my living room, crying.

I don't give a damn about his remorse.

A soul-burning, primal madness buzzes in my head, burrowing into every muscle. "Shawn," I grind out, teeth gnashing between my lips, eyes searing into the fucker responsible for Mia's hurt.

In my peripheral vision, I catch Shawn leaning forward, either to see me better or get ready to do as I say. "Yeah, bro?"

"Get out."

He's off the clock now, no longer in uniform, but he *is* a cop. I don't want him watching what's about to go down and turning a blind eye. He would. He did in the past when I took my anger out on Jared and when Logan battered Asher a few years ago. If any one of us asked, he'd fucking do it, but jeopardizing his career isn't my intention.

A distressed whimper builds in Brandon's throat.

His hands ball at his sides, and he has the fucking audacity to open his mouth.

"Say *one* fucking word, and I'll make sure it'll be your last," I snap. "Get out of my house, Shawn. Now."

I can tell by how his knee nervously bounces that he's torn. On the one hand, he has Jack, Josh, and his job to think about; on the other, he wants to have my back and maybe stop me going overboard.

Neither Logan nor Theo will get in my way unless things get out of control, and their definition of *out of control* is different from Shawn's.

"I'll stay," he says, leaning against the couch. "I've got a shitload to deal with, Nico. I don't want to be back here in an hour, detaining your ass, and we both know your brakes will give out without me."

Cody and Colt shove Brandon forward. He stumbles over his legs—a sight to fucking see... the almighty quarterback almost falling to his knees. Not so cocky today.

His attitude betrays he knows I'm unpredictable. At least, I used to be while I was with Kaya. No one could stand toe to toe with me and say he won.

I broke too many bones back then.

And I'm about to up the number. Mia broke his nose, but I intend to snap his fucking spine.

"Man, I'm sorry. It was just a prank, alright? Just for laughs, you know? How—"

"Just for laughs... Was Mia laughing when you forced her into your lap at the Spring Break party? Was she laughing when you told her she had to fuck you for the broken nose?"

My restraint dies a sad death two sentences in. I spring to my feet, and my older brothers do the same, ready to either grab me or help me. Two will help for sure. The verdict's out on Shawn. He might be the mellowest of the Hayes, but he has an unpredictable side.

Neither one reacts when I grip Brandon's collar, shoving him against the wall. The sound of his head bouncing off the brickwork flips my stomach. It's dangerously close to the sound of the ceramic water tank cover connecting with Jessie's head.

"Was she laughing when she was harassed? When she had to knee some fucker in the balls, so he'd let her go?" I ask, getting in his entitled face. "Was. She. *Laughing?*"

"No." He clears the clog of fear lodged in his throat. "No, she wasn't. No one was supposed to touch her unless she allowed it."

I shove him back again. It's fucking unnatural that I've not knocked him unconscious, that I'm controlling myself even though Mia's calming magic is two floors up.

But the thought of her works, too. To an extent.

My elbow falls back, and my fist connects with Brandon's already broken nose.

I wouldn't be myself if I didn't land at least *one* punch.

His head cracks off the wall again, and I step away before his blood stains my t-shirt.

"You'll call it off." I pause, cracking my neck. "You'll call off the hunt, scrap the prize and inform everyone not to lay a finger on her. You'll apologize on your fucking knees, and you'll swear on your dick that you'll deal with everyone who says one foul word to her. That includes your psychotic girl-friend. Got it?"

He nods repeatedly, up and down like a bobblehead. Yeah. You got it. I'll call it all off, but... I don't know what girlfriend you're talking about, man. I don't have a girlfriend."

"Better you never get one," Theo mutters, settling back on the couch beside Logan.

"Blair," I supply. "Deal with her. And if I ever find out you're playing games, gambling on another girl's safety, you'll choke on your dick."

"Never, I swear. Now I know what can happen..." He trails off, his eyes pooling with fresh tears. "Shit, man. I'm sorry. I didn't think it'd end like this. It was just a game."

"Girls get raped for much less than twenty-five grand," Shawn says, still on his feet, still ready to intervene.

He's right not to trust me. I'm not sure I'm done.

"They get raped for fucking free, kid," he continues. "You're loaded and apparently clueless if you can't put yourself in the shoes of anyone without money. You'd puke your fucking guts if you saw some of the shit I did over the years. You have no idea what people do for money."

"I'm sorry. Really, I am," Brandon chokes, meeting my gaze as he wipes his face on his sleeve. "You know I'd never do anything so stupid if I knew Mia's yours."

"What difference does it make whose she is?!" I snap. "Grow the fuck up. You have a *sister*! Put her in Mia's place for a second. Would it still be a game if it was Kathy in that restroom tonight?"

"No, of course not. Fuck, man... this is so surreal. That clip you played will haunt me in my sleep."

"I hope it eats you alive. What Mia went through is *your* fault. Make no mistake, kid. Anyone touches her again, there'll be fucking hell to pay. Now get out of my house."

"I'll take care of it. I promise. I'll call it all off."

Colt grips his shoulder, ushering him toward the door. As soon as it bangs closed behind him, the Holy Trinity unites, standing arm-in-arm and blocking the doorway.

"Listen, we're sorry, Nico," Cody says, sounding like he's barely holding it together. "We had her, we always have her, but when Grayson told us about the prize, we jumped Brandon, and—"

"I know," I huff, massaging my temples.

"No, you don't. We fucked up. We should've paid more attention; we should've..." Colt cuts himself off. "We won't ask you to let us take her out again."

"No, you won't. I'm not her fucking owner, so you don't ask me. You ask Mia. And you better do. She needs those nights, Colt. I need her to go out and party so she doesn't regret not doing it later." I plop down on the couch, accepting a glass of whiskey from Theo. "I don't blame you for what happened tonight. You were looking out for her when you jumped Brandon, weren't you?"

They all nod, each taking a glass from Theo, who's playing bartender, fixing drinks in silence.

"I didn't ask Johnny to keep an eye on Mia because I don't trust you to do it right," I say, taking a big sip. "I just... I'm working through my shit, trying to tame that controlling side. It takes time."

Cody lets all air out of his lungs, then grits his teeth like he's trying to get a hold of himself. "She's in love with you, you know? And she's scared you'll leave her."

"I know," I say, setting the glass aside. "I've made a few mistakes along the way, but I'm learning how to navigate this. She's not what I'm used to, and I've fucked up a few times, but don't worry. I promised I won't hurt her, and I won't."

He stares me down, in a mixture of apology and relief.

"How is she? You need us to do anything?"

"No. She's asleep. I don't think it hit her yet, but we'll all be here for her when it does."

"She's tougher than she looks," Colt admits, taking a seat on the piano stool.

"Yeah..." Conor drawls on a long exhale. "Too tough for her own fucking good sometimes."

***

Mia didn't wake up screaming.

Not once. She didn't move much all night.

And she's still asleep, lips pursed, one hand across my ribs, the other under the pillow.

So fucking gorgeous.

I ghost my fingers up and down her arm under the comforter, getting ready for whatever comes when she wakes up.

Her hair is sprawled on her pillow, which she hardly ever uses, nestling her face in the crook of my neck or my chest, and I fucking love when she's so close.

It's not the most comfortable position, lying on my back most of the night, but if it means having Mia curve into me, I'll gladly suffer the lower back pain.

She only sleeps in my arms on the weekends. It's starting not to be enough. Every night without her warm body beside me, it gets harder to fall asleep.

My wristwatch tells me it's nine-thirty when she starts stirring, changing positions every few seconds like she's trying to find one that'll let her sleep a little longer.

I've been awake almost two hours but didn't dare untangle myself from her hold.

"Morning," I whisper, kissing her head.

"Morning," she breathes, pulling the comforter so high nothing south of her nose is visible. "Did Shawn come over last night?"

"Yeah. He's coming back today around eleven to talk to you." I tug the comforter and nudge her until she lies on her back. A nasty bruise on the side of her pretty face kick-starts the bright-white freeze of anger worming my mind.

The bruise is larger than my fucking hand. Red and purple from her cheek to her jaw.

"That bad?" she asks, combing her blonde locks over one shoulder. "I wouldn't have this if not for the clotting factor deficiency. It'll be gone in about a week." She pinches her lips together, and a hot glow of pink spills over her cheeks. "Did you see the clip?"

I grip her waist, pulling her under me. "I did, baby, and before you ask, it changes nothing. I'm sorry you went through that." I kiss her forehead, moving my elbows flush against her ribs. "I'm sorry you didn't feel you could trust me. I won't let you down again."

"It's not your fault. Please—" she whispers, biting the inside of her cheek. "Don't do this. Don't blame yourself, the triplets, or anyone else, okay? It doesn't help anyone. It happened. It's done. We can't turn back ti—"

"Don't act like it didn't happen. You need time to process it," I cut in, anticipating where this is going. She's invalidating the whole thing, lessening its severity and consequences. "Don't rush. I'm here, and I'm not going anywhere."

"I'm not rushing, Nico, but I've been through this before. After Asher, I kept everything in. I didn't talk to anyone for weeks. Ask your brothers. I spoke in monosyllables, replaying that night over and over. It took me a long time to heal. I don't want to make that mistake again."

"You can talk to me. I saw what happened, but I'll listen if you want to let it out. I'll find you a therapist if that's what you need."

"I was in therapy last year. I know how to deal with this. I don't want to keep thinking about what Jake did or wonder what would've happened if I had done one thing differently. I don't want to look back because if I do that I can't go forward. I'll talk to Shawn and tell you everything you want to know, but then I want to move on, okay?"

"Can I help somehow?"

"You can start by repeating what you said last night."

A small smile curves my lips when she beams, eyes sparkling. She's so fucking strong...

"What did I say?"

She huffs, bracing both hands against my chest, trying to wriggle out from under me. "I won't tell you."

I take her hands in mine and box her in again, looking into those green eyes that hold my soul hostage. "I love you, baby." I dip my head to kiss her, but she slaps one hand over her mouth, shaking her head.

"I love you, but I won't kiss you until we brush our teeth."

Thirty-four

Mia

"MIA!"

I immediately tense at the sound of his voice. Taking a deep breath for courage, I spin on my heel, standing face-to-face with Brandon.

Over a week went by since the incident at *Q*. I stayed with Nico since then, skipping a week of college for his sake as much as mine. He asked me to wait until my bruise healed before going back, but with finals only days away, I can't afford to skip any more classes.

The bruise is almost gone. Nothing but a yellow-green shadow over my jaw. It makes students and professors stop mid-step, openly staring at me with pitiful expressions.

No one has said one word to me since I walked through the door two hours ago, even though *everyone* knows what happened. The clip Jake recorded wasn't just saved on his phone. It uploaded into the cloud...

Someone hacked Jake's account, downloaded the video, and sent it flying around campus. I almost doubled over and threw up when the triplets told me, but I realized something while I stayed locked in Nico's house.

I'm *not* ashamed of what happened. I'd rather not have the entire college ecosystem watch Jake Grey shove his dick inside my mouth, but if the clip proves a wake-up call for people like Brandon, that's one good thing to come out of it.

Getting my sister back is the other.

She cried for hours on Sunday, apologizing for not being there for me throughout the years. We cleared the air, worked out the differences, and she's been stopping by every day to keep me company while Nico's at work.

I didn't have time to be bored. Every member of the Hayes family came over at some point. Theo brought me food from *The Olive Tree* when Nico couldn't take time off during lunch, and Rita practically lived with us, arriving early every morning and not leaving until Nico came home at five o'clock.

Shawn came over twice, once for the statement and once with an update I didn't care much about. Jake's father couldn't afford to post bail, so he's locked up, awaiting trial, and Jessie's still recovering at the hospital. He's getting better. The whack he took to his head won't leave any lasting damage, but it didn't look promising at first.

"Mia," Brandon repeats, his tone measured like he's afraid to startle me. He stands at a safe distance wearing his signature look: a letterman jacket and blue jeans.

His blond hair is combed to the side and styled the way rich, entitled boys style it... too much product. His cold, bluish-gray eyes skim over me, but there's no cocky grin twisting his battered face. I don't think I've ever seen him without it.

"Listen, I'm sorry," he says, swallowing hard. "Truly. I know it doesn't mean shit, but I really am sorry. I called it all off, I swear. You know news spreads like wildfire around here, so it shouldn't take long before everyone knows not to touch you, but if any of those idiots are suicidal enough to say one fucking word to you, come straight to me, alright?"

I stare at him blankly. Nico mentioned he talked to him that night. While I expected Brandon to call off the prize, I didn't expect an apology.

"Mia," he urges. "Did you hear what I said?"

"I'm not deaf. Please just leave me alone, okay?"

He clenches his fists, but instead of annoyed, he comes across defeated. "I will. I promise, but if anyone bothers you, let me know. I'll take care of it."

"You're the last person I'd ever come to for help."

He runs his fingers through the perfectly styled hair, but it does nothing to mess it up. "I know you've got no reason to trust me. I get it, but I meant what I said. I'm here if you ever need anything."

"Just stay away from me. That's all I ask." I turn on my heel to leave and find another person I don't want to see in the middle of the corridor.

I veer to the left, getting out of Blair's way, but she steps into my path, holding one manicured finger up.

"Give me a minute," she says. "I owe you an apology."

"Save it for someone who cares," Cody's voice booms behind me, and a shudder of relief rattles down my spine.

I'm still absolutely useless at confrontation.

"I'm trying to apologize," Blair insists, glaring as his hand snakes around my middle.

"Bullshit. You're trying to make yourself look good."

She sinks her teeth into her bottom lip, eyes locked on Cody, tears welling. "I've seen the video... I didn't hurt her, but—"

"You've been hurting her for years."

She swallows hard, lifting her chin. "You're right. And I'm sorry about that, and about..." She lets out a defeated breath. "I feel responsible. Maybe if I said something... I'm a girl, too, you know? What Jake did... I feel for Mia."

"You're not a girl, Blair. You're a bitch, and you don't *feel*. Save the theatricals for someone who gives a fuck."

He ushers me down the corridor, away from Brandon and Blair, away from the curious eyes of other students who stopped nearby, pretending to talk with friends while listening to the exchange.

"You didn't have to be so rude," I say when we emerge from the building. "People change, Cody."

He scoffs. "She hasn't changed. She's just aware everyone's looking out for you now, and if she keeps acting like a bitch, it'll come back to bite her ass. Don't forget all the shit she put you through, Mia."

I wish I could forget. What's the point in dwelling on the past? All it does is bring me down. Nico was right when he said I don't believe in myself.

What happened, happened.

I dealt with Asher.

I dealt with Jake.

It's time I deal with the bullying and ridicule I suffered for years so my self-esteem stops taking a nose-dive. Maybe forgiving people who hurt me is the first step to healing?

Thirty-five

Mia

I ZIP UP THE SUITCASE, all packed and ready for the morning flight to Monaco. Nico sits on the bed, talking on the phone when I straddle him, running my fingers down from his chin to his zipper and back.

He's been tiptoeing around me for two weeks, giving me time and space to process what Jake did. While I was glad at first, I'm not anymore.

Every day the invisible line he drew introduces more doubts. He kisses me like there'll be no tomorrow. He holds me close whenever I'm within reach. He acts the same, but he hasn't touched me the way I need him to.

And I really do need him *in*. Not just to reassure myself that we're fine. That the clip he saw hasn't changed anything, but also because every touch of his hands on me nearly tips me over. I miss him. I miss seeing his hooded eyes, feeling the heat radiating off his big body, and watching him come undone.

"I'll call you back," he tells whoever's on the other side of the line and cuts the call. "What's wrong, baby?"

"Nothing." I lean in for a kiss, sweeping my tongue along the seam of his mouth, then in, tasting, teasing.

He weaves his fingers in my hair, matching my rhythm but not taking control like he did many times before.

"You've been a ten for a long time, but you're losing points," I whisper, knotting my fingers on the nape of his neck. "Kiss me like you mean it."

He grips me hard, stopping me in place when I circle my hips, grinding into him. "Not yet."

"Why?"

"It's too soon. Don't rush this."

"I'm not rushing. I want you to treat me the way you did before. I need to know you still want me."

"I do." He flips me over, hanging over me as he rests his weight on his elbows. "Of course, I want you, baby. Nothing changed, but—"

"Prove it. Show me you still want me. I don't need time. I had enough, Nico. I need *you*. In. Please... I want you *in*."

He leans over me, staring so intently it feels like he's trying to read my mind like he can pull my thoughts out of my head if he tries hard enough.

"I want a taste first," he finally says, pushing me further up the bed. "Stop me if—"

"I won't. Please... I need you to take me the way you always do. Don't change anything."

He stops pulling my panties down my legs and looks up, studying me for another long, tense moment like he's looking for something he lost. Whatever he finds seems to satisfy him because he slides my panties off, throws the white scrap of lace over his shoulder, and dips his head, spreading me with his thumbs.

The first slow, thorough lick of his tongue has me fisting the sheets with a soft moan. It's been too long.

"Good girl," he whispers, gripping my ass, and licks again, bottom to top like he's trying to drive me wild with need. "Fuck... you're so sweet, baby. I missed this."

I missed this, too. The cramps in my abdomen, the sinking feeling, the closeness, and bursts of endorphins. My hips arch off the bed, and I clamp my thighs around his head, keeping him in place. Nico slips a finger inside, hitting my G spot a few times before the orgasm hits, zapping my nerve endings like a tiny earthquake.

"One," he utters against me. "I want at least five, Mia. There's nothing I like more than seeing you come."

He crawls over me, pulls a condom out of the bedside cabinet, and gets in position, looking down, searching my face again before the first urgent thrust scoots me up the bed.

"I missed you." He hovers above me, resting his weight on one elbow while his other hand holds my neck.

"I missed you too," I utter, the words a breathless staccato when his thrusts gain pace and I wrap my legs around his waist. "Oh, God..."

The chant repeats through my lips for half an hour.

Nico's relentless. He's changing positions every few minutes like he wants to make up for all the lost time in one sitting. He's trying to be his usual controlling self, but his touch is more tender. His tone is softer when he orders me around.

Still, he reads my body perfectly and doesn't hold back.

"Again," he demands, after four orgasms, maneuvering me

onto my tummy. "One more, Mia." He cuffs my wrists behind my back, driving deep inside me, every thrust hitting the right spot with measured precision. "Focus, baby. Give me one more."

I don't have to focus. The orgasm is right there within my grasp, but I'm fighting it because I'm sure I'll pass out if I come again. I'm already seeing double and feel like I'm floating ten inches above the bed.

"I don't think I can."

Nico grips my jaw, turning my head to the side. "Had enough?" he asks, but he's not slowing down, burying himself in me over and over again.

"Um..."

"Don't *um* me. Big girl words." He digs his fingers into my waist, using my body as leverage, and plunges even deeper. The unforgiving pace of his hips rocking back and forth doesn't falter. "Say the *word.*" I feel his forehead rest on the back of my head, his chest heaving, his body on fire against mine. "What's your safe word, baby? Say it, and I'll let you rest."

Instead of *red*, a moan flies past my lips.

I stop fighting. I'm exhausted but nowhere near ready to use the safe word. I'm not in pain. Far from it, and I love that he's not acting like I'm fragile.

I love the possessiveness radiating off his every touch.

"I didn't think so," he breathes, laying my cheek on the pillow. "Again, Mia. One more."

And when I give in to the orgasm pressing in on me from all sides, my senses stop working, and there's just the overpowering pleasure coursing through me. My eyes flash with white spots, my body spasms, and my lips part, but I can't hear the sounds I'm making while everything tightens and releases inside me.

"Good girl," Nico says in the shell of my ear, his cock swelling as he comes with me. A few long, delirious seconds pass before I faintly register he's slowly pulling out. "That was beautiful, baby. Tired?" He flips me over, pressing a kiss to my forehead.

"I can't move," I whisper, my eyes closed. "I'm so weak..."

He kisses me again, getting out of bed. How does he have the energy to move? I'm pretty sure I won't get out of bed in time to catch the flight tomorrow.

"Open those pretty emeralds," he says, spreading my legs and pressing a warm washcloth to my pussy.

"You wore a condom," I remind him. "Why—?"

"Does it feel nice?"

I peek a little and then a little more when I see the smile on his lips. I don't think I'll ever get over how mesmerizing he looks when he smiles.

"Yes."

"*That's* why." He pulls me under the sheets, tucking me against his side, my head in the crook of his neck, one leg sprawled across his thighs, washcloth still in place. "Comfortable?" he asks, grabbing my book from the nightstand.

He just made me come five times.

My butt is sore from the spanking, and my legs won't hold my weight for a while, but here he is, flipping the pages until he lands on chapter seven.

"There was a table set out under a tree in front of the house, and the March Hare and the Hatter were having tea at it: a Dormouse was sitting between them, fast asleep, and the other two were using it as a cushion, resting their elbows on it, and talking over its head," he reads quietly, holding the book in one hand while the other ghosts the line of my spine.

"I'll never let you go," I whisper, kissing his neck. "Never.

I love you so much."

He stamps a kiss on the top of my head. "I love you more. Now, quiet. It's about to get interesting."

"How would you know? You said you never read this."

"I haven't, but you're pumping your hand around my bicep, so I know you're excited." He pulls me in closer, resting his cheek on my hair. "The table was a large one, but the three were all crowded together at one corner of it: 'No room! No room!' they cried out when they saw Alice coming. 'There's plenty of room!' said Alice indignantly, and she sat down in a large armchair at one end of the table."

Epilogue

Nico

A LOUD THUD JOLTS ME UPWARDS. The clock on the nightstand shows seven on a Sunday morning, but a quick pat on the right side of the bed tells me Mia's no longer here.

The mattress is cold, so she's been up for a while. I can't remember the last time she got up before me.

I rub the sleep from my eyes, flinging my legs over the edge when another thud fills the silent morning air.

"What the hell is that?" I mutter, throwing a pair of tracksuit bottoms on to leave Mia's bedroom at the exact same time Jimmy emerges from his across the hallway.

He's back in Newport for a week ahead of the Austin Grand Prix next weekend. Once again, he decided to make it a surprise visit, so Mia and I had to pack a few things and move here for a few days.

She's been unofficially living with me since the start of

summer. Unofficially, because not all her stuff is in my house yet, but once college broke up for the summer, I stopped taking her home for the night.

Unless Jimmy flies in for a few days.

Sleeping here while he visits isn't usually problematic, but this weekend we're babysitting Noah. Logan took Cassidy away to finally pop down on one knee. Took him long enough.

"Was that you?" Jimmy asks.

"I was going to ask you the same thing."

"It's me," Mia sing-songs from the living room and *thud* again. "Sorry, I didn't want to wake you."

"You'd wake the dead," Aisha grumbles, exiting her bedroom. "It's the middle of the night! What the hell are you doing?"

Toby stumbles out behind her, wearing nothing but boxer shorts, and we all move to the living room, where Mia sits on the floor with Noah. Another *thud* when she drops a big flat thing on the floor. It pops open at impact, turning into a ball.

"It makes him laugh," she explains, smashing the ball to flatten it out again. "It's seven in the morning, don't look so grumpy. We've been up since five."

"Five?" Aisha gasps, plopping down beside her sister. Her five-month-old bump makes the task less gracious, but it doesn't stop her shooting Toby a dirty look. "I am *not* getting up at five with your kid. Forget it."

"You find a way to detach your milk-making boobs, and I'll get up at whatever o'clock," he assures, pulling out cups. "Who wants coffee?"

Everyone save for Aisha, who has to tame her moody morning self with a healthy shake Toby's making.

Noah flips onto all fours, crawling across the floor toward Jimmy. He spent last evening in his lap, playing with his car keys and whatever else Jimmy gave him that wasn't a toy.

"Who are you going to be for Halloween?" he asks, scooting the seven-month-old boy off the floor. Two seconds later, he wrinkles his nose. "Never mind. You're all set, Poopy Monster."

"It's your turn," Mia tells me, beaming from ear to ear.

"We had a deal. I take care of feeding and putting him to bed. You deal with diapers and baths."

"Fine," she mutters, taking Noah from Jimmy's outstretched arms. He's holding the kid like he's a ticking bomb. "But we'll renegotiate this deal when it's our kid."

A surge of pleasant warmness fills my chest. She has no idea what she does to me. One sentence and I'm fucking floating.

I pull her into my side, my thoughts swirling around her words. "Give me a baby, and I'll change every diaper, Mia."

She props Noah on her hip, wiggling her ring finger in my face. "You're not getting a baby until this finger is dressed."

Little does she know I already have a ring. Grandma gave it to me a couple of months ago when I picked Mia up from the weekly Bridge session.

It's in the safe, waiting for... fuck knows what for.

For Mia to finish college, I guess.

My grandmother pulls me aside while Mia's helping Kenneth and my grandad clear the table.

"I have something for you," she says, squeezing my hand as she glances over her shoulder at Mia. "I'm glad you found her. She's a good person, kind with a big heart."

"I got lucky."

She pinches her mouth like she wants to agree, but not aloud.

I get it. Now that my head is clear of the clutter, I realize I've been all over the place the past ten years, slowly losing sight of what's important and paying too much attention to work.

Mia evened out the field. She helped me find balance, tamed my chaotic personality, and helped me forge one clear path through life instead of eight at a time.

Grandma slides her engagement ring off her finger, glancing around to make sure no one saw as she pushes it into my hand.

My pulse soars, kicking into a disorganized thrum, a sense of panic seizing my muscles. "That... it's—" I stutter, closing my fist around the emerald. "Why?" I finally ask although that's not close enough to the what the fuck, Grandma? *dancing at the tip of my tongue.*

"This ring is supposed to stay in the family, Nico. I wanted to give it to Shawn because he's the oldest, but it wouldn't suit Jack."

I step from one foot to another, my hand still between us, as I open my fingers, taking a closer look. It's a simple ring, nothing fancy. Not a diamond like I'd choose if I thought of proposing, but the emerald means more than any diamond I'd ever find.

Still, I shouldn't be the one getting Grandma's ring. I've got two older brothers already engaged or married, and Logan's planning to propose soon. Why isn't he getting the family heirloom? Why didn't Theo?

"What about Theo or Logan? Why are you giving this to me? Why not them? Why not one of the triplets?"

She smiles fondly. "I love Mia like she's my own, honey. I love Cassidy, and Thalia, too, but Mia has a special place in my heart." She glances over her shoulder, looking at Grandad and Mia talking by the piano. "It's thanks to her that Grandad agreed to retire, and I'm sure you've noticed it made a difference. He's happy, Nico. He's enjoying life for the first time in years." She wraps her arms around me, curving herself into my chest for a quick hug. "Whenever you're ready."

My chest squeezes tightly. I'm grateful. I don't think I've ever felt this grateful, but it's too fucking soon. We've only been dating a few months.

"Thank you. You'll be the first to know when the time comes."

"Don't rush, but don't wait too long." She points at herself with a cheeky grin. *"You'll be old sooner than you think."*

"Dress that finger whenever, but no babies until she finishes college," Jimmy warns, joining Toby in the kitchen.

"It's my life, Daddy," Mia shoots back. "You were sixteen when Aisha was born. If I got pregnant now, I'd be——"

"You'll be pregnant in half an hour if you don't stop talking." I gently push her toward the bedroom. The image of her, round with my baby... *nope.* Not going there again. It's too soon. She's too young. "Deal with the diaper, Mia."

The first time I saw her holding Noah was enough to wake my paternal instinct, stirring brand-new hell inside my head.

We were at my parents' house. Mom played the piano, and everyone was scattered around the living room, chatting.

I sat on the couch, watching Mia on the other side of the room with Noah in her arms. He grasped a thick tangle of her blonde locks, and Cassidy jumped to the rescue, unclasping his little fist before he tore Mia's hair out.

"What's wrong?" Logan asks, plopping down beside me. *"You're looking at Mia like it's the first time you see her."*

"It is the first time I see her like this." I motion my chin toward her, squeezing my glass tighter. *"She's too young."*

He turns to me, eyebrow raised as he quietly says, "No way... you want her pregnant? You want kids? I never pictured you as a dad."

The images of Mia with a bump flicker before my eyes, and even though it's not happening yet, my protectiveness kicks up some more. I'll be fucking unbearable when she'll be carrying my child. It's good that I've

*got enough cash in the bank to last three lifetimes because I'll be breathing
down Mia's neck for nine months straight.*

*"Take him away from her. Now, Logan." I peel my eyes off Mia,
but they snap right back when she laughs, making Noah giggle. "Fuck..."
I breathe, rubbing my face while Logan's barely holding off laughter.
"Take Noah away," I repeat through gritted teeth.*

*"He likes her, and Cass needs a breather. Noah doesn't calm down
even in my arms these days. Sorry, bro, I'm not touching that kid until
your girl hands him back."*

"I'll get her pregnant while you're all eating dessert."

*He bursts out laughing, summoning Mia's attention. She crosses the
room, planting her pretty butt in my lap, her back to my chest, and Noah
in her arms. She holds him over her knee, bouncing him up and down
and singing a nursery rhyme.*

*I wrap my hand across her middle, kissing her neck. "Unless you
want me to put a baby in you tonight, give him back," I whisper in her
ear when Logan walks away to chat with Grandad. "I'm serious, Mia.
I see you with him, and I want you pregnant."*

It was right about then that Aisha got pregnant, and two
months later, Logan knocked up Cassidy again. Now there are
three pregnant women in the family, not helping my case.

Seeing my brothers and Toby so fucking excited when they
touch the life-growing bumps, feeling their kids kick...

I'm happy for them, but I'm also jealous.

Even more when we arrive at my parents' house six hours
later where everyone's congratulating Cass and Logan on their
engagement. He got this backward, if you ask me. Marry the
girl first, then get her pregnant. But whatever, he's engaged,
has a kid, and another on the way. Theo's married and about
to become a dad, and Shawn's thinking about adopting a sec-

ond kid.

Fuck waiting.

I grab Mia's hand, dragging her upstairs while the family's preoccupied with Logan and Cassidy, paying us no heed.

"You're officially the first girl I ever brought up here," I say, letting her into my old bedroom. "You better feel honored."

Not much has changed. Mom hasn't touched a thing in here. The same dark curtains hang around ceiling-tall windows, the same oversized bed stands in the middle, and the same shelves hang on the walls, stacked high with books and CDs.

I prefer my spaces lighter now, less cluttered.

I pin Mia to the wall, devouring her sweet lips the way she loves. This would be better if my pockets weren't empty. Even better if I'd planned this at least a little but aren't the best things in life those that happen spontaneously?

She sure isn't expecting this today.

Even I didn't expect this until three minutes ago.

"First girl I kissed in this room."

She smiles, peering up at me. "Are you throwing me a bone? You took my firsts, so you're finding a few to feed me?"

"First girl I love..." I take her face in my hands, not an ounce of doubt clouding my mind. "First and *last*. Marry me, Mia."

She stills.

Stops breathing, but her heart beats so fast I hear it in the silent room. And then she does what I'll never grow tired of. She melts in my arms, spreading her small hands flat on my chest.

"I'll get you a ring. I *have* a ring. It's in the safe—" I shut up when she scrunches her nose, fighting a smile. "What?"

"I can tell you've never done this before. You're supposed to ask the question, Nico, not bark an order. I can't answer if it's not a question. Try again."

God, I love her so fucking much.

"Will you marry me, baby?"

"You really need to ask?" she chuckles, her eyes shining. "Of course I'll marry you. I told you I'll never let you go."

My fingers weave into her hair, and I cover her mouth with mine, sinking into her bee-stung lips like I've never kissed her before. I have. So many times over the last eight months, but other than that first kiss under the parachute, none compare.

Mine. Always mine.

She smiles against me, inching away, cheeks deliciously pink. "You really haven't brought a girl up here before? Not even back in high school?"

"No. Only three women ever set foot in this room. The maid, my mom, and my wife-to-be."

Her cheeky grin rears its full power, green eyes gleam with mischief. "So... you never had sex in this room."

I grip her waist, lifting her into my arms. The height difference between us, especially when she's not in heels, means my spine gets a kicking whenever I bend to reach her lips. "You're trouble, you know that?"

"So you said," she whispers. "Should we go? I'm sure your family's wondering what's taking us so long."

I cross the room and sit on the bed, cradling her to me, chest to chest. "They'll have to wait." I slide my hands under her skirt, pushing her panties aside. "You like taking my firsts, don't you?" I kiss her neck, working her up, even though the lacy fabric tells me there's no need for that. She's already soaking wet. "I want in. I want my fiancée to ride me."

She arches back, her small hands working my zipper for a moment before she frees my hard cock and impales herself on it without a second thought. "You're a bad influence," she sighs.

"Am I? I like the little devil in you. Focus, Mia. I'm sure one of my brothers will come looking for us soon, and you're not getting off me until you come."

"That..." Her eyes close when she sinks all the way down. "Oh... won't take long."

"Good girl. Faster." I thrust my hips, meeting her moves as she slides back and forth. A soft, barely audible gasp tears out of her. "Shh... fuck, you're so wet, baby."

A few minutes of deep strokes, and she's right there, poised on edge, ready to be tipped over. I lift her skirt, landing a slap on her butt. It works like fucking magic. One slap, and she starts vibrating, hurtling toward the release. "There you go, almost there," I whisper, forcing her forehead against mine when her orgasm hits. "That's my—"

A knock on the door sends Mia into a near-catatonic state. She stops moving, eyes wide, cheeks hot. Her pussy spasms around my cock when the door flies open.

Logan steps in, curiously glancing around the room before his eyes stop on us. Mia hugs into my neck, biting the flesh in the crook, silently coming apart. And all I can think about is how much I want to spank that pretty ass again.

I'm so thankful for her sense of style right now. Her over-the-knee A-line dress disguises that my cock is currently inside her, throbbing, just about ready to explode.

"What's wrong? Is she..." Logan pauses, eyebrows knotting in the middle. "Is she crying?"

I get why he might think that. She holds onto me for dear life, clinging to my chest as she shudders gently.

"No, she's not. Get out."

"You sure? Mia, are you—"

"Out!"

"Forget it," he mutters, walking in further. "Let her go, Nico, before I make you. What the hell happened?"

Mia stirs, bucking against me, and I bite my tongue hard enough to taste blood. I'm so close it's taking everything I have not to spill.

"Logan," I grind out, his name sounding like an insult rolling off my tongue. "She's *fine*. Now get the fuck out of here."

He takes one more step but suddenly halts. His knotted eyebrows meet his hairline as recognition hits. "Oh, shit!" A supersized grin splits his mouth wide open. "Fuck, sorry." He holds his hands up, backing out. "Um, yeah, I'm just gonna—" He slams the door behind him.

Mia's not moving, still as a statue.

"Again," I say, biting her ear. "I missed the look on your face, so you'll have to come again." I push my hips up once, then again, and the third time, she parts her lips against my neck, gasping softly. "Good girl, that's it, relax. We're alone, just you and me, baby. Nothing else matters."

Thank you for reading *Too Sweet.*

Please take a few seconds to leave a rating or a review. It doesn't have to be long, few words is enough.

I hope you enjoyed the story and that you're looking forward to more from the Hayes brothers. Conor's next, and you'll find a sneak-peak of his story when you turn the page.

Love x

I. A. Dice

HAYES BROTHERS SERIES BOOK FOUR

Too
strong

I. A. DICE

One

Conor

"YOU READY YET?" Cody shouts through the closed door, before hammering it with his fist. "Hurry up!"

Impatient as always. The party doesn't even start for another hour, but he's all geared up, ready to go. Always the first to jump on any opportunity to fill Nico's garden with too many people and always the last to clean up after.

The house is set, the decorations in place, but no one's showing up for a while. When we invite people for six, they don't start arriving until at least seven.

"Five minutes!" I shout back, putting my costume on.

Jeans, a t-shirt, my favorite watch from this year's F1 collection, and my brand new, snow-white Jordans. I glance in the mirror, then look around the room. Looks like I over-compensated because what do you know? I'm ready inside half a minute.

Cody's waiting out in the hallway in his low-effort costume. Although considering I bought my *Error 404 Costume not found* t-shirt online, I guess he put in more effort.

He's dressed in white; a red silk ribbon around his ribs—courtesy of Mia, I'm sure—forms a big bow at the front. A large gift tag with *To: All Women; From: God* is pinned to his shoulder, bouncing against his pec.

"No fair," I mutter, annoyed I didn't come up with that. "You're hardly a gift to women, bro. What's Colt dressed as?" I ask, dodging the fake cobwebs hanging from... well, everywhere, as I follow him downstairs.

Having a woman in the house means an upgrade on the decorations. Last year Nico wouldn't have allowed any of this.

Fuck, last year we could only dream about throwing a Halloween party, and now look at him... He spent yesterday morning carving pumpkins, and the afternoon shopping with Mia for decorations. He got up early today to help us put up cobwebs, lanterns, candles, and all the other creepy shit she bought.

"No idea, but I bet he was just as creative as us," Cody says, entering the living room where Mia motions for us to keep the volume down. Cody immediately switches to whispering. "Why aren't you dressed?"

"Five more minutes," she utters, weaving her fingers through Nico's hair. "He needed a power nap."

The emerald engagement ring that belonged to our grandmother has been sparkling on her finger for a week now. It goes well with her tiny hand and even better with her green eyes.

I never thought I'd see the day my brother popped down on one knee. And I was right.

He didn't.

At least not in the traditional, fairytale way. According to Mia, he fucking *told* her to marry him.

Figures. Nico always gets what he wants.

Still, it'll never cease to amaze me how he turned from a robotic, fire-breathing, workaholic, A-grade asshole to this guy asleep with his head on Mia's tummy. He's still all those things, but he's got a softer side now. One exclusively available to Mia.

She's in the corner of the couch, and Nico's on his front, between her legs, arms flush with her sides, face nuzzled into her waistline. It's a common sight these days.

Good thing they're always fully clothed, or I'd have to bleach my eyeballs.

I glance around the room, admiring the final result. Cody, Colt, and I did help decorate, but Mia kept on, putting her own little touch on this place long after we'd gone to take showers. The whole of the downstairs is decorated to evoke a sense of spookiness. Streamers of cobwebs drift from the ceiling like gauzy curtains, and paper bats and spiders flutter on thin strands, wings rustling in the draft wafting through the open windows.

Gargoyles with leering faces, skeletons, and limbless porcelain dolls with wide, painted eyes are scattered throughout the room, adding to the already well and truly eerie atmosphere cemented by the orange glow of candlelight casting shadows across the walls. The air is thick with the smell of pumpkin spice and the finger-food buffet waiting in the kitchen for Nico and Mia's first guests. They have their own separate party, though I'll probably drift between the two to see my older brothers.

Outside, the garden is equally spooky. Gnarled tree branches dressed in cobwebs twist and turn, plastic tombstones poke up from the grass in a miniature graveyard, carved pumpkins are strategically placed around, and more cobwebs cling to the makeshift stage.

It won't be a typical Hayes College banger this time. After everything that happened with Mia, we've been very selective about the guest list. No Jake's friends. No Blair.

Although I won't be surprised if she weasels her way in here somehow. She's been crawling out of her skin lately, trying to befriend Mia, and Cody's losing his shit whenever she's nearby.

He still has that sense of higher purpose wherever Mia's concerned, big-brother mode in full effect. It's probably a good thing we don't have a sister; she'd hate our guts.

"See? That's what happens when you make him do manual labor," I tell Mia, pointing my chin at Nico. "He can't handle it."

"Any excuse to get between her legs," Nico mutters, slowly rising on his elbows before he maneuvers into a seat beside her, pulling her legs into his lap. "I let you throw your first Halloween party, and *this* is what you're wearing?" He points between Cody and me. "Since you're trying to be funny, that gift tag should be on your dick, bro."

"What are you dressing up as?" Cody asks, apparently enjoying the idea as he moves the tag to hang over his groin.

"If you say you're wearing couple costumes, I will not be held accountable for making fun of you all night," Colt says, entering the living room.

"Magic eight-ball?" Mia chuckles, looking at his t-shirt. He's all in black, an eight-ball print on his chest. "Let's see..." she taps her lips. "Oh, I know! Will you fall in love this year?"

Colt huffs an amused puff of air down his nose, turning around to show us a blue triangle on his back with *Google it* written inside.

"This is no fun. You were supposed to take this seriously!"

"Other than you, and maybe Theo, no one will dress up properly," Cody says, propping his hip against the back of the couch. "Girls will come as Harley Quinn, sexy cops, sexy nurses, or sexy... *something*, and guys will either low-effort this like us or go full Joker or Rooster."

"Rooster?" Mia chuckles.

"Yeah, from the new *Top Gun*. I bet we'll see at least a few guys in pilot uniforms and fake mustaches."

"And those will be the guys getting laid tonight," Colt adds.

"Missed opportunity," Nico muses, taking Mia with him as he gets up. "We should get ready."

They disappear upstairs, and Colt grabs us all a beer while we get out to the back garden, checking everything's ready. Six arrives ten minutes later to set up his console, dressed in a glow-in-the-dark skeleton costume. Pretty cool for a DJ.

Bang on seven o'clock, the doorbell rings so I head back inside to let in whichever one of my brothers arrived on time, not expecting Nico and Mia to be ready yet. Whenever they go upstairs together, they're gone for at least an hour and a half.

It's a miracle neither I nor Cody nor Colt walked in on them yet. Mia's been living here since June, so I expected to have a memory bank of unwanted visuals by now, but nope. Nico's uncharacteristically careful about where and when they fuck.

Since we moved here, we've caught him with countless random women. He never took them upstairs into his bedroom though, always got his dick wet in the living room, the kitchen, the garage, even the stairs.

Colt, Cody, and I made it a rule to be extra loud when we come home since he got together with Mia, and take our sweet time in case they need to get dressed, but so far, no life-changing, psyche-scarring encounters.

I saw all my brothers in action at some point in my life, but I never want to see Mia. She's like my little sister, and it's just fucking wrong to even think she's having sex.

"Oh, hey," the girl outside says when I fling the door open. "You must be one of the triplets. Conor, right?"

"Yeah, and you are...?" *Too young to be here.*

We didn't invite the freshmen this time. They're too wild, having just finished high school and getting their first taste of college parties. And this girl is a freshman, for sure.

If that. Maybe she's still in high school. She's dressed for a party, though, so someone invited her. What's more, she's dressed as Wednesday Addams, which is bold, considering it's not a sexy version.

It suits her. Her hair's jet-black, and her eyes almost match. She's not as pale as Wednesday, but the dress, two braids, and a fringe complete the look.

"I'm Rose," she says, rocking on the balls of her feet.

Okay, this doesn't fucking help me whatsoever. I rake my hand through my hair, growing uncomfortable. "I'm not trying to be rude, but I have no idea who you are or what—"

"Mia invited me," she explains quickly. "I guess you'd call me her student. She gives me piano lessons three times a week."

Ah, right. She told us about this girl, but we're never here when she comes over. I step from one foot to the other and open the door further, gesturing for her to come in.

She turns on her boot, waving at the driveway, and I follow her line of sight to find a death trap parked at the bottom of the concrete steps. A battered Mercury Cougar, a relic from another era with at least thirty years under its belt, if not more.

The car's battered and beaten as if it's been rallying through rough terrain, and no one's even tried to fix the dents. The front bumper's only just clinging on by untrimmed zip ties, the side mirror is taped with packing tape, and I have no clue what color is under all that rust. Plus, it's belching out this huge black smoke cloud that could probably kill on the spot.

"I'll pick you up after eleven," a girl in a stripy black and yellow top shouts from the driver's seat. "Don't drink!" The bee antennae on her headband jiggle about.

Rose gives her a thumbs up, and before I have a chance to take a better look at the girl, she puts the car in motion, rolling down the driveway in a toxic cloud.

"Eleven? The party will only just start getting good then," I say when Rose finally steps over the threshold.

"I bet, but I have little choice. She'll pick me up on her way from work."

"Hey, you're here!" Mia cheers, click-clacking down the stairs with Nico trailing behind her.

"No. Fucking. Way," I boom, looking them over.

She's cute as always, wearing a sparkling crown and a black, red, and white tutu dress with a big Q and heart printed on her chest. The soft fabric swishes around her legs as she moves, but it's not her who has my jaw hanging open.

It's Nico. He's all in black, with a K and a heart emblazoned on his muscular pec. A long red cape flows over his broad shoulders, and a matching crown sits atop his big head. He looks like a regal superhero. A deadly King ready to save his Queen from imaginary danger.

"King and Queen of hearts," Rose says, beaming as she closes the door behind her. "So fitting."

"God, you're whipped, bro. Wait till Colt sees you."

"Wait till *he's* whipped," he shoots back with a smirk.

I want to say *no way that will ever happen*, but I said that about Nico, and I couldn't have been more wrong.

Mia pulls Rose into the kitchen, and Nico follows suit, a snarling rottweiler, always at his girl's side.

Nothing here for me, so I join my brothers in the garden, where people are starting to flock through the side gate.

As expected, most girls arrive at the party wearing sexy, barely-anything-to-them costumes. The guys put in minimal effort with theirs, although some are hilarious.

Justin Montgomery has purple cardboard wings on his back and the words *Booze Light Beer* written in fluorescent green marker on his t-shirt. Another guy has gray paint samples stuck to his chest, so I assume he's *50 Shades of Grey* and...

Low and behold, we have a winner.

The only guy in our circle of friends with red hair has five loaves of bread dangling from strings around his neck and a sticker with *Gingerbread Man* on his forehead.

No way anyone can beat that.

Many toilet paper mummies, guys in black shirts with Superman t-shirts underneath, and scary rubber masks later, Brandon Price arrives. The king fallen from grace.

He's been on his best behavior since Nico threw him out of the house the night Mia got hurt.

He's lost his pompous attitude and is trying to earn our forgiveness and prove he's not an incurable dipshit.

The jury's still out on that one.

Mia overheard me, Colt, and Cody debating whether to invite him. The good-hearted little Bug she is, she said we should. We've excluded him from the year-end and homecoming parties, and other than a couple guys from the team, he's basically been abandoned by everyone.

Meanwhile, cred is due where it's due because he's really been walking on water the past few months. I guess we'll see tonight how much he changed.

He enters the garden, the only guy to put effort into his costume: a green onesie covered in hundreds of white plastic thorns. It looks like he cut up a whole box of plastic forks for the spiky effect.

"A cactus?!" Cody exclaims, shaking his hand. "What the hell, man? Why cactus?"

"Dig deeper," Brandon says, patting my back as I stop beside them. "What are those?" He touches one of the thorns.

"You want the technical term? Fuck knows. Spikes?"

"Kind of, yeah, but not what I'm looking for," he admits, shaking his head. "What do they do?"

"They hurt," Cody supplies, brows drawn together. "Is this a game? A rebus? I better win something if I guess."

"They're called prickles," Colt says. "He's a prickly cactus, so you could say he's a..." He looks between our clueless expressions, waiting for it to click. "He's a massive prick, you idiots."

I burst out laughing, but it takes Cody a few more seconds to catch on and join in. "Well, that sure is fitting. At least you know."

Brandon nods, looking up at the living room windows, his features pinched to hide the pain in his eyes. "Is she coming out to sing tonight?"

"Yeah, but only a few songs. They're having their own party

up there. Our brothers are coming over, and our parents too, so you better behave."

He's been pining over Mia since he saw Nico exit *Q* holding her in his arms. It's as if seeing with his own eyes she was no longer available made him realize he didn't just want to fuck her, but keep her for himself.

"Right, I need a beer," Brandon says, squeezing the back of his neck before heading for the table bending under the weight of kegs.

"Could I have one too?" a familiar voice asks.

I turn around to see Rose—aka Wednesday—a few feet away. "I thought that chick told you not to drink."

"That chick is my sister, and what she doesn't see..." She smiles a cheeky smile, leaving the rest unspoken. "So? Would you like me to beg?"

"No need, girl," Brandon says, leaping back to wrap his arm around Rose's shoulders, a slight curve on his lips. "Come on, I'll hook you up."

Oh, hell no.

I don't know where this sudden, intense, aggressive jolt zapping down my spine comes from, but the thought of allowing Brandon's hands anywhere near Rose has me on the brink of bursting into flames.

I'm not the Hayes to lose my shit for no reason (not pointing any fingers), so this is disturbing, to say the least. He might be trying to redeem himself, but he's still a fucking prick, and there's no way I'm leaving Rose under his supervision.

Mia would have my balls for that, I'm sure.

"Not your party, man," I say, breaking Rose free from his

hold. "Grab a beer and have fun, but don't try anything, or you'll be out the door in five seconds."

Brandon holds his hands up in defeat, no longer prone to arguing with my brothers or me. He's gone from a show-worthy Doberman to a lapdog in no time.

"A beer, huh?" I ask, leading Rose across the lawn to the small line at the drink table. "How old are you?"

"It's rude to ask a woman her age."

"When she's fifty." I elbow our way to the Bud Light keg, grabbing a solo cup from the stack. "You're at least eighteen, right?"

"Yes, since last week," Rose admits.

"Fine. You can have one."

She pinches her lips, trying to hold back a smile. "Yes, Dad."

"Call me *Dad* again, and you won't even get a sip. And Wednesday doesn't smile, Rose. Lose the grin."

She snatches the cup from my hand, filling it to the brim, then gulps a third of it down. "Oops. Too late."

"Oops, you're grounded," a voice comes from behind us, and we turn to see the girl with the bee antennae.

Damn... busted.

"Wha-what are you doing here?" Rose wails. "You're supposed to be at work!"

"I lied," she huffs. "I had to know if I could trust you, and guess what? I *can't*. And you!" She grows red in the face, the bee antennae bouncing left to right.

She's got a tight dress to match and even a stinger attached to her butt. She's shorter than Rose and paler in complexion, eyes a striking grayish color, hair like caramel up in a ponytail that swings from side to side over her bare shoulders.

"What the hell is so funny?" she demands, poking me with her finger, her cheeks on fire.

I don't know what's so funny.

I'm not laughing, but it doesn't stop her snatching the cup from Rose and flinging the contents in my face.

"You're enabling a minor!" she snaps.

"Whoa, whoa, whoa," Cody jumps between us. "What the hell do you think you're doing? Who are you?"

"I'm nobody." She shoves Cody aside, then grabs Rose by the wrist, pulling her toward the house, but not even five steps later, she halts, turning back to look at me, eyes suddenly wide in horror like it only just clicked what she did. "I'm sorry."

Now I laugh as I use the hem of my t-shirt to wipe beer off my face. "You ruined my costume, little Bee."

"It's Vee," she says, then rolls her eyes when I cock an eyebrow. "My name. It's Vee. Well, technically, it's Vivienne, but no one calls me that. Just Vee."

"I was referring to your costume."

She looks down like she fucking forgot what she's wearing, and the exasperated red of her cheeks fades when she snatches off her antennae and shimmies out of the stinger, which, I now realize, was on a rubber band around her waist.

She comes closer, a walking contradiction. Every one of her moves is gracious, like she comes from old money, but she sure doesn't act it, throwing beer in my face.

Every look of her silver eyes sears right through me, forcing the rhythm of my heart into a higher gear. She's really pretty. The kind of girl I'd turn to take another look at.

The kind I'd openly stare at all night.

Her light brown hair works perfectly, with freckles peppering her nose and cheeks. There are hundreds of them, an entire freckly constellation.

Her black, laced boots stop an inch from my Jordans, and she peers up, angling her head to meet my eyes. She's not Mia-short but can't be taller than five-three. My eyes are naturally drawn to the perfect, well-defined cupid bow of her lips.

A faint scent of fresh linen and soap fans my face when she lifts her hand, weaving her fingertips through my curls to initiate a wave of tingles over my scalp and down my spine.

I don't even think.

To be perfectly honest, I'm in some alternate dimension right now, blind and deaf to everyone but this girl. I act on impulse, dipping my head to seal her lips.

Don't ask why. There's no rational or even irrational way of explaining why my insides are in knots when she's touching me or why heat detonates in my chest when our lips connect.

A bone-chilling pause settles over us, before the temperature jumps a few degrees, the air growing thicker. A second ticks by. Maybe two at a stretch, the sheer surprise of this moment dawning on both of us, I'm sure, but I don't move away.

Her lips twitch under mine like she's about to kiss me back, but she pulls away. Before I can fucking blink, her open hand connects with my cheek so hard it jerks my head to the side.

Ouch. I don't know what stings more: my cheek or my ego.

"You're unbelievable!" she snaps, arms akimbo, eyebrows drawn together. "I throw a beer in your face, and you think I want a kiss? Read the room." She drops her hands, stepping closer again. "Don't move. I'm fixing your costume."

I'm too stunned to say one word. All jokes evaporate from my head, and I do as told while she pushes the headband into my curly mane, then wraps the elastic around my hips, hooks it back in place, and adjusts the big-ass stinger over my dick.

"Before you say it's not as big as yours," she muses, admiring her handiwork, "at least you've got a proper costume now."

"So I'm a hornet, right?"

"I'd say you're a hoverfly but have it your way."

"Hoverflies can't sting," Colt says, the resident encyclopedia.

I've been so preoccupied with Vee I hadn't noticed him join the gathering. There are more people around than when Rose and I got here, but no one talks or tries to elbow their way to the kegs on the table.

"No, but they follow you around if they like you," Vee admits, flashing a beautiful smile.

She throws beer at me, then tries to fix my costume, slaps my face, and now she's... *flirting*. At least, I think that's flirting.

I'm so fucking confused my head hurts.

"Now's the time to ask me out," she adds impatiently, glancing at her wristwatch: one of those novelty watches you win at the arcades. Hers has Donald Duck on the face.

"Dinner," I blurt out like we're playing *Taboo*, and I'm on the clock. There's no time to think. "Tomorrow."

"*Ruby's Diner*, nine-thirty," she confirms, and with that, she turns around, pulling Rose behind her.

What the hell just happened?

Printed in Great Britain
by Amazon

46335976R00235